EREC REX

THE MONSTERS OF OTHERNESS

EREC REX

THE MONSTERS OF OTHERNESS

KAZA KINGSLEY

Illustrations by Melvyn Grant

Simon & Schuster Books for Young Readers
New York   London   Toronto   Sydney

Check out the other books in the Erec Rex series

The Dragon's Eye

Coming in summer 2009:

The Search for Truth

ÉREC REX

THE MONSTERS OF OTHERNESS

SIMON & SCHUSTER BOOKS FOR YOUNG READERS
An imprint of Simon & Schuster Children's Publishing Division
1230 Avenue of the Americas, New York, New York 10020

First Simon & Schuster Books for Young Readers paperback edition April 2009
Text copyright © 2008 by Kaza Kingsley
Illustrations copyright © 2008 by Melvyn Grant (melgrant.com)
Originally published in 2008 in hardcover by Firelight Press, Inc.
The EREC REX® logo is a registered trademark of Firelight Press, Inc.

SIMON & SCHUSTER BOOKS FOR YOUNG READERS is a trademark of
Simon & Schuster, Inc.
Book design by Jeremy Wortsman
The text for this book is set in Adobe Caslon Pro.
The illustrations for this book are rendered digitally.
Manufactured in the United States of America
2 4 6 8 10 9 7 5 3 1
Library of Congress Cataloging-in-Publication Data
Kingsley, Kaza.
The monsters of Otherness / Kaza Kingsley ; illustrations by Melvyn Grant.
p. cm.—(Erec Rex)
Summary: Twelve-year-old Erec Rex discovers the hard way that doing
what is right is not always easy when he delves into the very Substance
from which our world is woven to save the baby dragons of Alypium,
a magical kingdom he might one day rule.
ISBN: 978-1-4169-7934-0
[1. Dragons—Fiction. 2. Fantasy.] I. Grant, Mel, ill. II. Title.
PZ7.K6153Mo 2009
[Fic]—dc22
2008032025
erecrex.com

To my Aunt Linda, whose support and enthusiasm is limitless

CONTENTS

The Great Secret

KING PLUTO TREMBLED in the shadows. His master had summoned him with a wolflike howl that left him shaking. Something was terribly wrong, he could tell. The howl was tinged with too much excitement. Maybe anger. Did his master think he had turned against him? Told somebody their plans? He would never dream of that.

It was freezing here. Pluto shivered and pulled the layers of fur tighter around his thin frame. He had left his red ermine and crown at home: too eye-catching. People had shot him enough funny looks since he walked through the Port-O-Door into Paris. He hated Upper Earth.

Another howl from his master ripped through his soul, silent to all but him. Pluto winced from its pain. He tried, as usual, to choke it back, but his body responded with a howl of his own. A couple nearby turned to stare at him. He wiped his nose with his sleeve, hoping to play it off as an overblown sneeze.

King Pluto, pulling down his black knit cap, crossed the street into the open arms of La Place des Yeux du Monde. Bright lights glared inside, but a blind man in a dark smock ushered him into a small drawing room lit only by a hearth fire.

The blind servant felt for a chair and pulled it toward the fire. "For your warmth, your highness." He then rushed out of the room, scurrying like a mole through the depths of the complex.

King Pluto sank into the plush chair, his scepter in his hand. Who would think that a king would come to have a master? But Thanatos Argus Baskania offered him more than he could ever have alone. He was always there for Pluto, the father he never had. When Pluto's own father was alive, he was busy with his kingdom in Cyprus. And when he visited he had eyes only for Pluto's brother. It was always Piter this, Piter that . . . and Posey was his darling girl. But the most Pluto would get was a wink. "You don't mind, do you, Pluto? We'll just be gone a bit. Piter promised to show me how he could speak to plants." Speaking to plants! Please! What fascinating thing is a plant going to say? It made him want to throw up.

Pluto rubbed his head. His father never cared about what *he* could do. When he finally learned to create a force field around himself, Pluto had been so excited to show him. At last his father would be proud. Pluto was up all night before that visit—he still remembered it like yesterday, and it was over four hundred years ago—but his father barely noticed him when he arrived.

Pluto had stood there, blue flares of electricity swarming around him like a giant bubble on the grass. His father waved it off and said, "Your brother Piter made a force field around the whole castle. That must've been ten years ago. Try that next time, son. Get Piter to show you how." Then he walked away. Pluto had stood there, frozen in his force field, afraid to let it down because someone might see the tears streaming down his face. He felt like an idiot.

But his master understood. Thanatos Baskania showed up in his room that very morning. Pluto wondered how Baskania knew his feelings. But he helped Pluto realize how his anger could make him stronger. Thanatos believed in Pluto. He showed him a world of magic that Piter could never do, would never try to do. Black magic. Power over power.

And now Pluto waited for his master in front of the warm fire . . . that same angry, lonely boy, waiting to be chastised for a crime he had not committed. In a breath, his master emerged into the room with someone else in his shadow. King Pluto bowed his head and stooped onto one knee.

"Rise, son." The Shadow Prince was tall and broad, with silver-gray hair, a crooked nose, and thin lips that pointed down in a permanent sneer. Today, six eyes peered from his wide, pale face. Just enough to keep surveillance. One of them, a steely blue eye, swept over Pluto's face. "You are worried, Pluto," he said. "But your fears are unfounded. I have called you here to share good news—and prepare you for what you must do." Baskania pulled a silver eye with a coal pupil out of his pocket and absentmindedly stroked it.

King Pluto felt his body relax. The warmth of the fire soaked through the layers of his fur.

Baskania's voice lowered to a purr. "A way has presented itself.

For six hundred years I've tried to attain the Final Magic, but it has evaded me. The closer I get, the more difficult it has been to learn. I have gained more power and mastered more knowledge than anyone on earth, but I cannot rest until the last powers are known to me. Complete control over life and death, the earth, and everyone on it." His six eyes all flashed at the glorious thought.

"There was a secret that for years I could not bear to hear discussed. My dear grandmother Cassandra heard its prophecy right before her death. She had pried it, in a sense, from the hands of the Fates. And then she was murdered. I remember her simple note said the secret was hidden in a miniature—maybe it was a charm or a little statue . . . I never understood."

King Pluto nodded. The Great Secret. The path to the Final Magic.

"Of course you will play a role. It is time to deal with the monsters. That will help me exert my new influence." He smiled. "As will, of course, the dragon eyes."

"And Erec Rex . . ." Pluto threw a glance at the third person in the room, who had yet to say a word.

The Shadow Prince's eyes twinkled. "Ah, yes. I have plans for him. After I pluck his eye out, I will dispose of him quickly."

"But . . . the Great Secret? Is it possible?"

Several of Baskania's eyes curved with silent laughter. "Soon the world will kneel to us. Let's say I will have the help of someone who's passed this way long ago, someone whose very life has been passed into me."

"Your grandmother, Cassandra? But how?"

Baskania pulled a clump of frilly leaves with tiny blue flowers from his pocket. "With these . . ."

CHAPTER ONE
Seeing Green

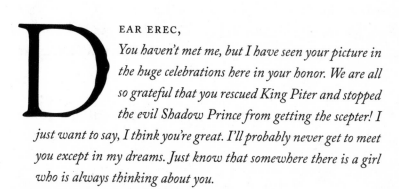

DEAR EREC,

You haven't met me, but I have seen your picture in the huge celebrations here in your honor. We are all so grateful that you rescued King Piter and stopped the evil Shadow Prince from getting the scepter! I just want to say, I think you're great. I'll probably never get to meet you except in my dreams. Just know that somewhere there is a girl who is always thinking about you.

Erec reread the pink frilly letter for the tenth time. It had appeared yesterday in the grass in a shiny hard shell when he was throwing a ball outside with his brother Trevor. One moment he was rolling in the dirt, and the next it was just *there*, gleaming white in the sun, the words "Erec Rex" printed neatly on the side. He picked it up, curious. Trails of slime oozed from the shell, but the pink letter poking out was dry. He almost had it memorized, especially the part about the girl thinking about him, and of course all those *X*s and *O*s.

The sun blazed through twelve-year-old Erec's window, bouncing off the straight dark hair sprouting from the front of his head and getting lost in the tangled curls in back. He stretched in his bed and rubbed his bright blue eyes.

Erec Ulysses Rex was a normal boy, with a few minor exceptions. He had an unusual gift, which he once thought was a curse: his cloudy thoughts. These ideas would overtake him and force him to do whatever they commanded. He used to fight them, but since they had saved his life, he was glad to have them. Also, one of his eyes was attached in the back to a hidden dragon's eye, a gift from the dragon Aoquesth.

But what he found out recently—that his mother knew magic, that he had been born in Alypium, and that he was destined to be king there—took away any feeling of normalcy he'd ever had. Alypium was one of the three Kingdoms of the Keepers, where magic was still known, along with the underground Aorth, and

THE MONSTERS OF OTHERNESS

Ashona, which was under the seas. Not that Erec planned to actually perform the twelve dangerous quests to become king. In fact, there was a big problem he could not ignore. He now knew that becoming king would destroy him completely.

Erec rolled over and read the letter again. For the first time in a long time, his alarm clock had not woken him early. What a relief. Maybe the thing finally realized it was summer . . . now that summer was at an end. The clock usually woke him by throwing things at him. It was one of the strange, lifelike objects that Erec had grown up with, like his juggling coat rack. His mother had gotten them from the Kingdoms of the Keepers.

He glanced at the clock and then sat up, not believing his eyes. It stood in a small pool of water, beeping softly. His mother's magical Seeing Eyeglasses were perched on its round face. Small tearlike droplets dripped down its numbers as it peered through the glasses. The clock was like an annoying pet, always waking him up too early, but now it looked pathetic. When he picked the glasses up, the clock came with them, blinking sadly. Erec pulled, but the glasses stuck firmly to its face.

"Oh, no." Erec smacked his forehead. He had left the glasses out last night, thinking about using them to check on his best friend, Bethany. He had not done it, and now he regretted taking them out at all. They were impossible to take off anybody, maybe even an alarm clock.

He flopped onto his back and gazed at a crack in the ceiling. As he stared, it began to look quite like a minotaur with whom he had once had an unfortunate experience. He closed his eyes and sighed. Part of him wanted to go back to Alypium, where strange things like minotaurs existed and where Bethany was, rather than staying safe and comfortable in New Jersey. Sure, he had never been crushed in a pit under an avalanche of rock at home, nor nearly been killed by a multieyed fiend, or suffered attack fleas, but he also had more fun in Alypium than anywhere else.

But the problem was the scepter. It still haunted him day and night. His dreams were ravaged with thoughts of holding its slick gold, streams of its power flowing through his body. It kept calling for him. From the first moment he had held it, he'd wanted the scepter badly, would do anything to get it. But since he had come home to Upper Earth, his craving for it had grown, and he realized what it had done to him. His mind wandered to it all the time, and not with thoughts of helping people with it or learning about its magic. No. Erec wanted it in his bones. He wanted its power. He wanted to join it . . . lose himself in it . . . use it to complete his will.

His desire for it completely overwhelmed him.

He had used it to too much, too soon, without any training . . . and he knew that if he ever held it again, he would be out of control, lost in its power.

So becoming a king and wielding a scepter was out of the question.

Erec rose from the small cot in the corner of the tiny room he shared with his two brothers. He used to hate being cramped for space, but now he did not care. After everything he had gone through, all that mattered was that his family was alive and safe. He stepped over his sleeping dogs, Tutt and King, and his brother Trevor snoozing in a sleeping bag.

Danny and Sammy, his thirteen-year-old twin brother and sister, stood across the room staring at him and whispering. They looked alike, tall and thin with soft blue eyes. Danny's sandy brown hair stood on end, and Sammy's was smoothed into a ponytail. Ever since he returned from Alypium four weeks ago, they had been acting strangely—following him around, eyes glued on him like they'd never seen him before. It was almost like they were spying on him. His adoptive mother, June, had said they just wanted to keep an eye out for him since he had been missing for so long. But they certainly did not seem like their old selves. Danny had not cracked a single joke, and Sammy was not acting motherly at all. In fact, they seemed serious all the time.

"Excuse me, guys." Erec squeezed between the twins' shoulders into the bathroom. His toothbrush, another lifelike object his mother had bought from the Vulcan store in the Kingdoms of the Keepers, sprang into action. It grabbed an open tube of toothpaste with its arms and legs, rested its bristle head over the opening, and squeezed until a big glob of white popped onto its face. Like a monkey, it swung hand over foot up to Erec's face where, grabbing his mouth, it shook its head dizzyingly across Erec's teeth.

Erec gripped the counter for as long as he could stand it before he ripped the thing out of his mouth. He looked into the mirror and gasped. Two faces were right behind him, staring.

Then he sighed. It was just Danny and Sammy. "You guys scared me. Are you under orders to follow me or something?"

The old Danny would have hit him on the head and told him to shut up, but then again, the old Danny would not have been staring at him to begin with. He shook his head in warning and the twins backed off.

Erec was leaving the bathroom when suddenly a blinding green light flashed through him. In the next second he could see again, but everything looked greenish. White cobwebs hung all around him. Erec watched himself moving, walking—although he was sure he was standing still. He gripped the door frame next to him.

The image before his eyes was so clear, Erec was not sure if it was real. It looked like he was outside, somewhere, running through cobwebs . . . running at his brother Danny.

Danny had a horrified look in his eye as he watched Erec coming for him. Erec sprang at Danny, tackling him, grabbing his neck. No, he thought to himself, what am I doing? But he couldn't stop himself. His own hands were holding his brother down, shaking him hard.

A woman walked by in the eerie green light. She looked down at the two of them in shock. Erec watched his hand reach up, and grab at her belt and . . . yank it from her waist. His heart started pounding. What was he doing? How could he? The woman looked shocked, clutched her skirt to hold it up . . .

And then the image faded.

Erec stood in the doorway of the bathroom, pale and shaking. What had happened? It was like a dream, but he was awake and it felt so real. What was wrong with him? He didn't want to hurt his brother. He looked at Danny across the room and bit his lip in shame.

June, his adoptive mother, had come down the hallway. "Are you okay?" Erec shrugged, not sure if he was all right or not.

"Your eye turned around and the dragon-eye side was showing," she said in awe. "I've never seen anything like it. It glowed like a green light, with a long black slit in the middle. Then it turned back so fast I couldn't believe it." Concerned, she brushed hair from his face. "Did you see something through it?"

Erec rubbed his shoulders, feeling unsettled. "You don't want to know."

"What do you mean?"

"Never mind." Erec did not want to admit he'd had such a horrible thought. He walked back to his cot. What was that all about? This was the first time he had seen through the dragon's eye since he got it . . . and he didn't like what he saw. What made it happen now? And why did the vision have to be so terrible?

He had been glad to have the dragon eye. It was so much better than the glass one he'd had before. Now he could see through both eyes. But what if the dragon eye wasn't so great? What if it was evil? A chill crept through him. What if the dragon eye was going to make him do things like his cloudy thoughts did—only bad things? Was it going to make him really hurt Danny? No. He wouldn't let it.

Erec rubbed his new eye, wishing he could have his glass one back. The last thing he needed was something to make him more out of control. And what if he wanted to get rid of the dragon eye someday? Was he stuck with it?

June went into the kitchen and came back with a letter. "This came yesterday. I forgot to give it to you."

He opened it.

Dear Erec,

I hate to ask you this because I know how you feel about becoming king, and the scepter and all, but it's really urgent. Baskania and President Inkle are going to count your absence from Alypium as a forfeit. If you don't get here within the week to do the first quest, they will hand the throne to Balor, Damon, and Rock, since they "officially" won the contests.

I've been thinking about it a lot, Erec. I know you're afraid of what might happen if you use the scepter again. And sure, being a king sounds a little crazy. But if you really were the king, you wouldn't have to use the scepter, would you? I mean, nobody could make you. Just think about it. I can't imagine what would happen if Balor, Damon, and Rock become rulers

and get the scepters. You know what they would do to everybody
here? Would you consider it, please? Anyway, I wouldn't mind
seeing you again.
Your friend,
Bethany

That settled it. Handing Alypium to the Stain brothers was
not an option. They would turn the place into a wasteland, their
dragon horses breathing fire on everyone, using the scepters for
destruction. Like it or not, Erec was going.

THE MONSTERS OF OTHERNESS

CHAPTER TWO
Police Officerssss

EREC WAS NOT sure what to pack for his trip to Alypium. The last time he had brought nothing at all. He couldn't help feeling like he was making a big mistake. A dream he'd had last night about the scepter was his most vivid one yet. It started the same as usual. He made a command. The scepter's energy started at his fingertips and streamed through his body, building into a roar. Usually he did not remember the command, but this time he was ashamed to remember it only too well. He had told it that he wanted to rule the world. And as the scepter did his bidding—making everybody drop to their knees and bow down to him—he'd heard his enemy, Baskania, laughing wildly.

Maybe Bethany was right. Maybe he could be king and just put the thing in a closet and never look at it again.

Erec swallowed hard. He doubted he could do that. But he pushed the thought from his mind. At least he would get to see Bethany in Alypium, and maybe his secret admirer as well. What would it be like to be surrounded by adoring fans? The thought cheered him up. He probably would get free cloud cream sundaes and chocolate-covered honey drops. Big-eyed girls would crowd around him wanting to hear how he fought off the destroyers. He would have to get used to signing autographs, of course, but that would be okay.

When Erec appeared, Zoey was eating Flying Count cereal in the kitchen. She ran to his side. "Tell me about the destroyers in the dungeon again. Did you almost *die*?" Erec laughed. Since he had been back, his younger siblings, Trevor, Nell, and Zoey, couldn't get enough of his stories.

Trevor downed a mouthful of Magnon Fiber and leaned forward eagerly.

Erec sat down and Zoey climbed into his lap. "It was nothing. I just threw paper on all their noses with a wooden arm, and they dropped like flies."

Zoey's eyes were big, but June rolled hers. "All right, hero. Eat some breakfast, we'll hop a train to Grand Central in New York, and I'll walk you to FES Station."

Danny and Sammy were glued to the television. A reporter blared, "The latest developments of the multinational organization, Eye of the World, have raised concerns. Unnamed sources report that, under various names, Eye of the World is purchasing fleets of ocean liners, railroads, and trucking companies across the globe, as well as many important bridges.

"In an unprecedented move, Eye of the World has just purchased the famous Chunnel connecting Great Britain to the European continent. The Channel Tunnel, previously not for sale, was won after billions of dollars filtered to the controlling governments. Many are expressing fears about Eye of the World having too much control. Its leader, the elusive Crown Prince of Peace, already owns Sky Limit, the megacorp controlling most of the world's air traffic. He explains, 'Eye of the World is taking the mission of peace into its own hands. Governments have abused the trust of their people long enough, using their power over transportation to wage wars as they please. We are simply creating a network of safety and peace that is unbreakable for the good of all.'"

June switched off the television, a sour look on her face. Danny and Sammy huddled, whispering, then insisted on walking with Erec and June to FES Station that led to the Kingdoms of the Keepers and Alypium. Eleven-year-old Nell pushed aside her walker to hug Erec good-bye, then came skinny red-haired Trevor, and finally Zoey squeezed him too, flinging her long blond curls in his face.

June slipped thirty dollars to the short, pudgy hot dog vendor at Grand Central Station. "I'll check in with you as soon as I can get those glasses off your alarm clock," she told Erec. "And e-mail me. If you need anything, just come home through a Port-O-Door."

"All right, Mom."

Danny took sixty dollars out of his pocket and handed it to the vendor. "Two more, Gerard."

"Oh, no you don't," June said. "You're starting school soon, and you need to stay with the family." She snatched the money from the vendor's fist. "Where did you get this?"

The twins stared at her coldly. Sammy produced another sixty dollars and handed it to the vendor.

June's eyes narrowed at the now confused Gerard, who dropped the money back into her hand. "Hey, this isn't family therapy," he said. "I'm running a business here." He looked over Sammy's shoulder at the next customer in a growing line. "Yeah, whadda ya want?"

June's face was red with embarrassment. "We'll talk about this when we get home." She threw withering glances at Danny and Sammy. "We discussed this, and I said no. You start school soon and we don't have a tutor lined up for you in Alypium. There is no reason for you to go there."

Sammy's steel blue eyes swung to her mother. "Mom, we need to stay with Erec. Someone has to keep an eye on him." She grabbed the money out of her mother's hand and shoved it back at the vendor. "We're going too."

"Sammy!" June spun her around. "We will discuss this later. It's time you two pulled yourselves together. Everyone's home now. We're all okay. Let's have a fresh start." She held her hand out to Gerard for the money.

Danny's voice raised a notch. "Listen, Mom. We're going and you can't stop us." He shoved her away from the money Gerard held out.

"What?" June looked shocked, holding her arm where Danny had pushed her.

Erec couldn't believe it. What was wrong with them? "Listen, guys. I'll visit soon. Just stop making a big deal about this."

Danny sneered. "Shut up, Erec. It's none of your business." He turned to Gerard. "Keep the money. We're going with him."

Gerard looked back and forth confused. Finally he shrugged his shoulders. "Password?"

June stepped forward. "No!"

Suddenly, the world around Erec vanished. Instead, he found himself standing in the middle of a green cyclone, rooted to the earth by his feet. His hands stretched into the swirling vortex around him. Everything glowed an unreal shade of green, like he had stepped into a comic book. Thin cobwebs filled the air. He was dizzy and sick, and his stomach rose into his throat.

It was almost as if . . .

It was.

A cloudy thought. But not like any he had ever experienced. Something was happening with his dragon eye. It was making his cloudy thought different. Wild and out of control. He felt changed, morphed into some kind of green monster.

Fire felt like it was shooting from his fingertips. He was strong, energized. He could do anything. It was like the power of the trident was inside him.

Then the command came to him. He knew what he had to do.

Run at Danny, full speed. Knock him down. Use all of your brute force. Then tie his hands with a belt.

What kind of craziness was this? Hurt his brother? Just because he wanted to come to Alypium? No. He wouldn't do it.

But if it had been hard in the past to fight his cloudy thoughts, it was impossible now. His body raced forward, fists up, straight for his brother. He felt sick. Sick with himself, sick with what he was doing, yet unable to stop.

And then he saw it. There was a glint in Danny's hand. Something sharp flew from his fingers as Erec tackled him. He shoved Danny onto the sidewalk, held him down, heart pounding. What was that thing he had been holding? Danny stared at him wildly, a thin trickle of blood running from his lip.

A woman walked by wearing a belted skirt. She looked down at them in horror. Erec closed his eyes. No. But he could not fight it. He yanked the cloth belt from her waist, tied it around Danny's wrists, then sat on his knees. The woman clutched at her skirt, gasping in shock.

It was over. Erec rubbed his eyes, the green light gone. His dragon eye must have switched around to his regular eye.

June's mouth hung open. She rushed over to help Danny up, handing the woman her belt back with an apology. "Erec," she said, "what is wrong with you? Why did you do that?"

Danny sat up and rubbed his head. Erec stared at the ground, ashamed. "I'm sorry." He looked at Danny. "What were you holding?"

Danny glared at him. "A mirror. I had something stuck in my teeth."

Erec dropped his head into his hands. "I am so sorry." He helped Danny up. How could this have happened? Were his cloudy thoughts turning on him? He looked at his hands, disgusted with what he had done.

June laid her hand on his arm. "Are you going to be okay?" Erec nodded. "Maybe Danny and Sammy should keep an eye on you, after all. Come home, you two, and we'll talk about it. Erec." Her hand tightened its grip on him. "Be careful. After that stunt I have half a mind to keep you home. But you have a big job to do. I'll check on you soon with the glasses." She sighed. "Good luck with your first quest to be king."

Little did Erec know how much he would need it.

The swarm of activity in FES Station came as a jolt after the four weeks Erec had spent in quiet, predictable Upper Earth. A thick, lifeless feeling penetrated the air. It was from the Substance, the invisible network that held all magic. Substance ran through Aitherplanes throughout the world, but more of it was in the Kingdoms of the

Keepers, which made it easier to do magic there. For some reason, in the Kingdoms it gave off a sad ache that surrounded everyone, weighing on hearts and minds like an unsolvable problem. Erec knew from before that he would adjust to it in a day or two. After that, he would only notice it on occasion, with melancholy twinges.

People bustled everywhere. Sorcerers and apprentices wore black and blue cloaks; some others sported shiny silver "UnderWear" from Aorth. Interesting shops lined the walls, like Neither Fish nor Fowl Vegetarian Diner, Swim with the Fishes Scuba Shop, and Under Grounds Coffee.

Even with the heavy feeling from the Substance, Erec still grinned at the people flying under the sixty-foot-high ceilings. Women and men raised their arms and sailed up into the wind tunnel of the Skyway, the passageway for people who could fly. Erec had flown before with the help of dragon-scale dust, and Bethany had too, by using heli powder. Everyone in the Kingdoms of the Keepers was born with a magical gift. Erec wished his was flying; he would love to do it all the time. But then again, his gift of cloudy thoughts had helped him quite a bit.

Thin wooden doors appeared and vanished all around the walls of the station. Erec immediately recognized them as Port-O-Doors, magical doorways that took people where they wanted to go, and vanished when they returned. Some of the doors shrunk to fit under food counters. Erec saw a woman stumble out of a shrunken door straight into a luggage rack, spilling coffee on herself and muttering.

Erec had a little money with him, enough to splurge on a cloud cream nectar fizz at United Pollen Farmers. Before he slurped the last drop, it floated and vanished into the air. Without looking, he grabbed his suitcase and headed toward the white neon ALYPIUM sign. He lost his balance as his suitcase wiggled and jerked to the side. He grabbed for it, but it lurched out of his reach.

A tall man with hair greased over a large bald spot appeared in front of him, clearing his throat and squinting through his monocle. "And *what* do you think you are doing? Stealing my luggage, I presume?" He crossed his arms. "You look familiar. I better call the police."

"No, please." Erec looked at the suitcase more closely. It was dark blue like his own, but taller and without wheels. The thing happily trotted to the man's side. "I'm sorry. I thought it was mine."

"Hmmph. Likely story." The man frowned. "If it belonged to you, you wouldn't need to grab it like that. It would have come with you on its own. Stay here." His clawlike hand gripped Erec's shoulder, and he spoke into his index finger. "Police? I'm in FES Station, by the Super A King fastaurant. I've caught a young thief here, trying to steal my suitcase. Yes, thank you." Erec's stomach sank into his knees. He remembered that people here had microscopic cell phones implanted in their fingers.

The man glared at Erec. "Just you wait. President Inkle has gotten a lot tougher on criminals. You'll sit in a dungeon, or at least get a nasty memory implant for this."

Erec remembered how King Piter, the king of Alypium, had punished Earl Evirly with a memory implant. He did not want to spend the rest of his life with terrible memories of rotting away in a cell, sure that it really happened even though it had not. "But I wasn't trying to—"

Four odd-looking, armless men in uniforms appeared. Instead of limbs, they had long, snakelike bodies. Their blue uniforms looked like tube socks with star-shaped badges and brass buttons stuck on. One of the officers wore a hat that looked like a blue bowler with a black band and a star in front, like a cross between an English bobby's hat and one worn by the Keystone Cops. Another wore a taller black hat with a wide brim and a gold buckle, which made him look like a pilgrim. The third sported an ornate silver Spanish conquistador helmet, and the fourth wore a tall white pointed hat with broad wings that looked like it came straight off a Dutch farm girl.

All of the officers eyed Erec harshly, swaying back and forth like snakes. "Ssssso, thissssss is the thief?" the cop in the conquistador helmet asked. "Tssssssk, tssssssk, young man. You will learn sssssoon, crime does not pay."

"B-but . . ." Erec looked back and forth between the men. He could not believe this was happening. They were not even asking him his side of the story. The men's torsos started waving wildly, as if they were about to strike. One flicked a forked tongue from his mouth. Erec's breath caught. What would happen now? He had to get to Alypium to stop Balor, not be thrown in a dungeon somewhere.

A sudden flash of light surprised Erec. The tall man who'd called the police had just snapped his picture. The police officers slid closer on their tails, hissing. Erec wondered how they could catch him without arms. Then the one in the Dutch farm girl's hat tilted back his head and opened his mouth wider than seemed possible. Two long fangs jutted from under his top lip, and a terrible sizzling sound came from his throat. His head wagged in excitement, tilting sideways as he approached Erec.

That's when he realized how they were going to catch him. By biting him.

Thoughts of snakes and poison tumbled through Erec's head in the split second before he turned and ran.

He hoped the officers would not be able to run fast with only one thick leg. When he glanced over his shoulder, he could not see them at all. But then a woman behind him screamed and jumped. The police officers appeared, slithering across the floor right behind him.

A scream gargled in the back of Erec's throat as he pushed his way past people, leaping on his toes across the room. The snake men slid behind him, knocking people out of their way. Erec ran faster, flinging himself behind the counter of a coffee shop.

A girl making coffee yelped. Erec apologized, then dove out of the way when the officer wearing the Keystone bobby hat slid over the counter. The girl looked as terrified as he was, and dumped a pot of hot coffee onto the snake man's back.

The officer hissed loudly and looked back at her, furious. Erec leapt over the counter and ran toward an UnderWear shop. He wished he could fly to escape the snakelike officers. But what he saw next changed his mind. Two of them were soaring toward him, wiggling through the air like worms in dirt. Their fangs glistened in the light.

As he was looking over his shoulder, Erec tripped over a walking duffle bag and crashed to the floor. The snakes slid closer, mouths open. He scrambled to get away, but they were faster, closing in on him. One of them opened wide, fangs poised above Erec's leg.

There was nothing he could do. The snake thing would bite him and whatever happened then would happen. He hoped it was not poisonous.

He squeezed his eyes shut, jaw clamped tight, but he felt nothing. When he dared to sneak a peek, he saw the officer's snakelike mouth frozen over his calf. He jerked it away, but the snake mouth stayed where it was. Silence now filled FES Station. He noticed everybody was frozen, like statues.

A chuckle burst out over his head. "It's a good thing I was here, Erec. Wouldn't want to lose you now. You have too many things to do."

The man who approached him made the snakelike officers look normal. His piercing green eyes were surrounded by thick olive-colored scales, scattered over blotches of pink skin. The scales covered most of his head, making him bald. His wide nose protruded forward along with his jaw, causing him to look like a reptile, and his mouth was long and wide.

The man cleared his throat. "I suppose you're gawking because of my looks?"

Erec shook his head, stunned.

"I understand," the man said. He paced, his hands fluttering in constant motion like birds. "It's the first time you've seen me like this. Nasty, isn't it? A wicked boy did this to me a long time ago. This is a great improvement over the crocodile head he gave me, though. Did you know that if your looks are changed, you can never go back to what you were before?" He grimaced. "I'm sorry. Let me introduce myself. My name is Rosco Kroc. I'm your friend Oscar's tutor."

Erec dumbly shook his hand.

"Well, you better hurry. I've just learned how to stop time, and I can't keep it up much longer. Let's get you out of here."

Erec found his suitcase, which he had left by the United Pollen Farmers. Rosco tossed it on the luggage counter and walked him to the front of the line for the Artery to Alypium. "Are you ready to go? The police will think you vanished. Good thing they don't know your name."

Erec nodded. In a second, everyone around him was moving again. He heard screams from the far end of the station, where it sounded like the officer might have accidentally bit somebody else.

He wasn't sticking around to find out.

CHAPTER THREE

The Real Erec Rex Is Dead

ROUPS OF TEN people entered the pellet-shaped compartments that shot forward in bursts into a dark tunnel. Erec was soon ushered into a large capsule with a clear window in front. He sat in the second row next to a round woman with a blond mustache. His head lurched back as the capsule shot into the tunnel. A small headlight showed whirlwinds of liquid dirt whizzing by.

Erec turned to the woman next to him. "What's in this tunnel, mud?"

She raised her eyebrows. "You've never traveled before, boy? This is a subterranean river. Some of it is mud, and some is the plasma they pump through here to keep it clean."

Erec winced at the sight. It looked anything but clean. They hit a rocky spot, and the capsule bounced roughly against stones jutting from the wall. The woman tutted, shaking her head. "That's plaque building up on the walls. They'll have to fix this artery soon or abandon it. Every now and then a pod gets stuck in a tight artery. It can be hours or days before it works itself free," she complained. "Last time that happened, there was a huge earthquake in Japan."

Within minutes the little ship shot into the daylight and slammed to a stop. Erec staggered, feeling seasick, into Alypium Station. He found the luggage counter and pointed to his suitcase. The luggage clerk poked it and looked at him sadly. "Sorry, mate. It's not moving. I think it's sick."

Erec held back a laugh, and lifted his suitcase off the rack. He dragged it behind him amid the other frolicking and leaping bags. He exchanged his money for three silver shires and seven paper Bils, then found the bus in the outskirts of Alypium.

The cloudy citadel, that huge wall of clouds that surrounded and protected Alypium, shot into the skies ahead of them. Erec's bus waited for a green light before it drove through a long tunnel in the clouds.

When it burst through into Alypium, the sun shone hot. The picturesque town gleamed brighter than he remembered. The grass looked impossibly green, and the sky glowed like a cornflower in bloom.

His thoughts turned back to the letter from his secret admirer. She said they had huge celebrations in his honor. He wondered if people would crowd around asking for his autograph. Of course he would sign, no matter how tiring it got.

Maybe he should write her back. The worst that could happen was she wouldn't answer. He wondered if he might be encouraging somebody completely unappealing to fall for him. But no. Who was he kidding? Nobody would fall for him from a letter. Plus, his admirer seemed appealing enough, judging from her flowery handwriting and scented stationery.

He took out the pen and paper from his pocket and wrote:

Dear admirer,
Thank you for your letter. I'm glad you've heard good things about me. [He stopped and wondered how many people—okay, how many girls—had also heard good things about him.] *I hope things are going well for King Piter now.* [He paused, hoping this didn't sound too dumb.] *I'm coming back to Alypium today to begin my first test to be king.* [Erec sat straighter after writing this.] *Maybe I'll run into you.*
Erec

He folded the paper fast and stuck it into the shell envelope which instantly sealed itself shut. The directions about throwing it into the dirt seemed odd, but Erec had become used to odd things this summer. He opened the bus window and tossed it onto the grass. The envelope glommed into a thick white blob and disappeared.

There was no taking it back now. Oh well, he hadn't said much to worry about. Might as well forget about it.

Two signs twinkled with lights on the lawn of the Green House, where President Inkle lived. One read FREEDOM, LIBERTY, AND JUSTICE: IT'S THE ALYPIAN WAY. The other sign glittered PROTECT YOUR RIGHTS. THEY ARE ALL YOU HAVE. Farther on, swarms of people marched with signs in the yard of a golden turreted building.

He turned to a man with a high, wrinkled forehead who sat next to him. "What's going on there?"

The man winked. "Not from here, eh? That's the Labor Society, where the Bureau of Bureaucrats is located. A long time ago, the old sorcerers worked there—the ones that watched over King Piter, Queen Posey, and King Pluto when they did their twelve quests. Now it's a government building." He laughed. "I'm sure glad I'm not doing one of those quests. They were never easy, but I've heard they are going to be deadly this time around. Of course, *someone's* got to be weeded out." He laughed. "Let's hope it's that smarmy imposter."

Erec nodded and said, "Balor Stain." Balor was one person Erec dreaded seeing again. He had competed against Erec in contests to become king and cheated every step of the way. Erec had won the contests, and the scepter and a stone called the Lia Fail had identified him as the next true king. He alone should be allowed to do the twelve quests that were the path to becoming king. It was ridiculous that Balor and his friends would be allowed to do the quests with him—or against him.

The man next to him murmured something about Balor Stain being all right, but Erec's eyes were drawn to some of the banners as the bus sped by the picketers. Their signs were confusing, and he only caught a few words: ... DOZED FOR TEN YEARS, AND NOW HE WANTS TO BULLDOZE *YOUR* RIGHTS ... Who could that be about? Not King Piter?

Erec's breath caught as he saw Castle Alypium towering over the city, glowing and sparkling like he had never seen it. It looked impressive and royal now that it was upright. King Piter had set the castle on its side right before he was hypnotized, which had made it look like a huge comb dropped from outer space. After Erec rescued him, the king had set it upright again.

He dragged his suitcase past the six stone statues in front and through the immense doors that stood wide open. Inside, the entry room sparkled. Before, grime had coated the chandeliers and the tapestries, and the hardworking maids could not scrub it clean. He smiled. Now that King Piter was himself again, everything was all right.

"Ewec . . . ? Ewec!" An unfamiliar voice squeaked from across the room. A little pasty-faced man flew toward him. Wild, fuzzy brown hair rimmed his shiny bald head, and huge, thick black glasses seemed almost connected to his lumpy nose and bushy mustache like a bad costume. The man, whose eyes only came up to Erec's chin, grabbed his hand and shook it vigorously.

"So glad to finally meet you. So, so glad." The man sounded like a congested saxophone. "I've waited here since I got the word. It's been weeks now. My name is Pimster Peebles, call me, um, Mr. Peebles." He smiled and cocked his head, mussing Erec's hair like a long lost relative.

"Hi." Erec was confused. It seemed rude to ask why this man had been waiting for him. "How . . . should I know you?"

Peebles's high voice shot up and down like a wobbly roller coaster. "Oh, no, no. But you will. I'm to be your sowcery tutor." He stuck his thumbs in his armpits and puffed his chest, face glowing with pride.

"My sorcery tutor?"

"Yes. I wequested the job as soon as I heard about you. Insisted on it, actually. It will be my utmost pleasure to serve he who will be king."

Erec felt even more uncomfortable as the man's chin jutted high into the air. He cleared his throat. "Nice to meet you. I better find my room now, and my friends. Maybe I'll see you later."

"But of course. Follow me, Ewec." The man swiveled on his heel and led Erec down the hallway into a large atrium where the corridors leading to the north, south, east, and west wings met. Nothing seemed to have changed, except it was much cleaner. Erec followed Mr. Peebles into the ornate south wing and up to the second floor, not far from where Balor and Damon Stain had stayed during the contests. Erec remembered with disgust how Balor had hung him upside down in the air in his room, and even tried to kill him.

Peebles gave Erec a key to a room that was a far cry from his old dorm. Three thick mattresses were piled high on the bed, and a step stool to climb up on top of them stood nearby. Plush plum-colored carpets covered the floor, and the windows overlooked the castle gardens. A table was set with sandwiches, lemonade, fruit, and a tray of desserts on white cloth. The only thing missing that Balor's room had had was a large screen and video game chairs. Erec played with the dimmer on the chandelier until Mr. Peebles cleared his throat.

His nose twitched like a rabbit. "Ahem. Once you are settled may we begin your formal tutowing? I am eager to start, but you may want a day to adjust. You are a complete beginner, wight?"

Erec nodded. His mother had told him she had arranged a tutor, but he had assumed it was just for regular subjects like math, not magic. He smiled. This would be great. "How often do we meet?"

A broad grin spread over Mr. Peebles's face. "That, of course, vawies widely from tutor to tutor, but I like to take up a lot of my appwentices' time. You will meet with me evewy afternoon from one to four. In the mornings from nine until noon you will work with Miss Ennui, your academic tutor. Let's meet tomowow at the fwont castle entwance at one. I will accompany you to buy your first wemote contwol." Mr. Peebles beamed.

"My what?"

"Your wemote contwol. Don't you know what that is?" He made flipping motions with his fingers in the air.

Erec nodded. A remote control of his own! Remote controls tapped into the powers deep within people and let them do magic easily. He never thought he would get one, but why not? "Do you know where my friend Bethany is staying?"

"Yes. I believe she's been looking forward to seeing you. She's had her own little mansion built off of the west wing near King Piter's chambers." A frown briefly lit his face. "She dines with the king every evening in the west wing." Bowing, he shook Erec's hand weakly. "I am so honored to tutor you. So honored. Thank you, Ewec Wex." He backed away, bowing and thanking Erec again and again until Erec shut the door.

After Erec unpacked, he wandered through the castle. The dormitories were gone. At the entrance to the west wing, where the king lived, a whiskered man sat behind an ornate desk. He let Erec right in.

Erec had taken only a few steps into the west wing when he stopped abruptly. A large dark shadow appeared before him. His eyes followed an ornately carved wooden walking stick up past a scarab amulet—into the dark brooding eyes of Balthazar Ugry, King Piter's AdviSeer.

There was something nasty about Ugry that made Erec want to keep his distance. Ugry did not look happy to see Erec, either. "You're back. You haven't messed around here enough? Time to cause more trouble?"

Erec's nose twitched. Ugry smelled as rancid as usual. "I think I made things a little better around here," Erec said. "I certainly helped King Piter snap back to normal."

Ugry snarled. "You got lucky. Don't count on it a second time. I might not be so ready to help you, especially seeing as how you're so eager to lay your hands on the king's scepter and throw him off of his throne."

Ugry wasn't going to scare him this time. "I don't want to throw anybody off of anywhere. I just want to make sure the wrong people don't end up in power."

"And you're the right person, of course." He glared, eyes boring into Erec. "Be warned. I'll be watching you." In a swoosh of black, Ugry disappeared.

"Erec!" a familiar voice squealed as he passed the huge fountains outside the castle. A drenched Bethany popped out, followed by Jack Hare and Oscar Felix. Before Erec knew it, wet arms were flung around his neck.

"Awesome."

"We've been waiting for you."

Bethany looked great. She had come a long way from wearing the only patched dress Earl Evirly, the man who had pretended to be her uncle, would buy for her. The sun glinted off her dark eyes and tanned skin, and her long, wavy, dark hair hung wet around her face.

"In you go!" Amid grins and giggles, the three tossed Erec into the water. He stumbled to his feet and spit a small fountain into the pool. "What are you guys still doing here?"

Jack smiled, brushing his blond hair from his eyes. "I'm starting my apprenticeship in magic. The best tutors are in Alypium, and my dad says I should learn things right. We're staying at an apprentice boarding house."

Oscar, short and slim with spiky red hair, looked just as happy. "My dad let me come too. My tutor at home stunk so my dad signed me up with one named Timber Bellows here. But he *died* the day we were supposed to start. Nobody even knows why." Oscar grinned, which Erec thought was odd, considering what he had said. "I thought I'd have to go back home . . . but of all people, Rosco Kroc happened to be in Alypium. He heard my tutor died and he offered to take his place. I am so lucky. Rosco is huge. He's famous. He represents Aorth in the Green House. Rosco is kind of a hero in Aorth."

Jack squinted. "I'm not sure hero is the right word."

Oscar glared at him, then smirked. "Anyway, that means we'll see you every day. All the magic tutors meet with their apprentices in Paisley Park right outside the castle grounds. I'll look for you there."

Jack rolled his eyes. "Stay away from Oscar when he's with his tutor," he warned Erec. "He likes to practice on his friends."

"I met Rosco," Erec said. "He saved me from the . . . Well, I had a small problem with the police on the way here."

"What?" Bethany's eyes widened. Erec told them what had happened.

"Cool!" Oscar said. "Rosco is the best."

"Why don't you all have dinner with me and Piter tonight?" Bethany grinned. "I know he'll want to see you."

"You're kidding." Oscar scratched his head. "I've been hinting at this all month. My tutor, Rosco, keeps saying you'll invite me, but I didn't believe him. I thought you'd hog the king to yourself forever."

Bethany blushed. "Erec's back. It's a special occasion."

Oscar shook his head. "Funny how Rosco is always right."

Bethany trailed a lock of hair behind her ear as she looked at Erec. "So, are you ready to do the first quest?"

Erec nodded. He was still worried about what might happen. "I guess. I can't let Balor, Damon, and Rock win and destroy this place." He shuddered. "I don't have much choice. I just wonder which I dread more, them winning or me." Bethany looked confused so he explained. "If I get one of those scepters I could end up more evil than Balor Stain. I don't stand a chance with those things. They changed me already, just from the little bit that I used them. I crave them every day."

Bethany shrugged off his concern. "If you win we'll bury the scepter somewhere. Or we'll melt it down or get rid of it. Don't worry. I'm just glad you are going to try." She patted his shoulder. "Balor won't stand a chance. You are the rightful ruler anyway, right?"

She grinned and fell with her back stiff into the water, then swept an arm across it, spraying droplets into everyone's faces. She seemed much happier than Erec remembered her.

He wished he felt that way. "I've got that heavy, awful feeling from the Substance, like when we first came here. I hope it goes away soon." He splashed his feet in the water. "You happy here?"

"Loving it." Bethany flung her hands to the sky, sending showers of drops raining down on them. "Look at me. I'm swimming. Playing in the water. Not slaving day and night for Earl Evirly at his dumb newsstand and waiting on him hand and foot." She closed her eyes with a big smile. "I have everything I never had. Piter gave me a whole suite in the west wing, and he even built a mansion for me attached to the castle. Servants buy me dresses and books. They'll make me hot chocolate in the middle of the night if I want. I have my own hot tub with different-smelling bubbles in it every day. And I got the fanciest remote control from Medea's. There is even a slide in my room that takes me down to a special library filled with . . . the hardest math books I've ever seen!" She jumped up and down and squealed.

Oscar rolled his eyes and Jack laughed.

"No wonder you're so happy," Erec said. She was unbelievable at math. "You have everything."

Bethany waved away all she had. "I'd be happy with nothing as long as I had Piter. I know he's not really my father, but he's as close as they come. Sure, the stuff I get is great, but it's so much better to finally have someone want to *give* me something. He said he's starting to think of me like his own daughter." She beamed, then turned serious. "You know, Piter found out some things about me. I was born in Alypium, like you, Erec. My parents were Ruth and Tre Cleary. Ruth Cleary was King Piter's old AdviSeer. My parents were both killed the night King Piter's wife, Queen Hesti, and their triplets died. And I have an older brother named Pi. He's on the Alypium Sky springball team." Erec's jaw dropped in amazement. Springball was his favorite sport. He remembered Pi Cleary, and he was great. "I haven't met him yet, but I will when the team gets back in town."

"Wow, I had no idea." Erec paused, thinking about what she had said. "That's awful about your parents. Are you okay?"

Bethany nodded. "I've known my parents were dead since I was little. At least now I know who they were. They sound like they were great. And now I know where I get my love of math. My mom was a whiz. I guess that's what made her a good seer. King Piter says I'll be just as good, so I have a special tutor."

Jack looked quizzical. "I wonder if you could be related to that famous prophetess, Bea Cleary. She was the one who sent word that Piter, Posey, and Pluto would be born and were destined to rule the Kingdoms of the Keepers."

Oscar rolled his eyes. "Yeah, March thirteenth, 1510. We had to learn all about it in history."

Jack grinned. "It's not a common last name, and she was a great seer too. I bet she's in your family! She gave the Lia Fail to Alypium—that stone that screamed to show Erec was the rightful ruler during the coronation. Plus she told everyone how the scepters fly to the future kings and queens too. And then when Piter, Posey, and Pluto showed up on April eleventh, 1510, as babies, it all happened just like she said. So everyone knew they were the true rulers."

Erec was glad Bethany had such an illustrious past and wished he knew half as much about his own parents.

As if reading his thoughts, Jack said, "Did you ever find your father, Erec?"

Erec shook his head. He had spent most of his life hating his father and was not sure that he wanted to find him. "He's probably somewhere in the Kingdoms of the Keepers. He can find me if he wants. My only memory of him is a recurrent nightmare from when he deserted me on the streets. His boss found me under a bush and called my father an idiot. His boss said, 'The child is useful.' Real heartwarming."

But Aoquesth had told Erec that his father was kind and generous. His father had saved the dragon eye for Erec to have. It didn't add up. He tried to think more pleasant thoughts and remembered his dog. "Where's Wolfboy?"

Bethany clapped her hands. "He has his own room inside now, full of dog toys, and he has a house in the gardens, too." She lowered her voice. "It's padded, and it locks from the outside. His servants bring him there before a full moon." She plunged into the fountain and popped up, water streaming from her eyebrows and nose. "He even has a tutor now, Ms. Frinley. She says he's super smart. She might start to teach him to communicate."

Erec splashed into the water. He was happy for Wolfboy, but shouldn't he have made these decisions? Shouldn't he be the one teaching Wolfboy and setting up his doghouse? "Well, now that I'm back, he can stay in my room."

Bethany frowned, then shrugged. "Okay, but he might not want to. All his things are in there."

Erec sank into the water, bubbles streaming from his nose and exploding at the surface.

The heavy, sad feeling from the Substance still weighed on Erec, but it was easing. He looked through his bag of gold, silver, and bronze coins Bethany had saved for him. Soon he would bring some money to his mother. She needed it.

He found Bethany in the west wing dining hall. Light from the glittering crystal chandeliers glinted off the ornate glass goblets on the table.

Bethany giggled. "Maybe later we can explore the catacombs under the castle. They were covered up for ten years when it was on its side. I hear it's spooky down there." She sat down. "How is your mom? Will she be safe on Upper Earth now?"

Erec hoped so. "She said she'll be fine. King Piter sent me home with chalk for her to draw around our apartment building. It's supposed to protect her from being found."

The chalk line had been faint at best, and on the areas where she drew over the grass, Erec couldn't see it at all. He hoped that it would work. If King Pluto or Baskania captured his mother again, he doubted he could save her.

A man walked into the room wearing a white high-collared dress shirt, a black tie, a gray vest, and a long black dinner jacket with tails. He carried a tray of raw vegetables with white gloved hands, placed it on the table, and bowed low. "Modom. Sir."

"What did he say?" Erec whispered to Bethany.

"This is Jam," Bethany said. "He calls me madam."

The man stood up. His dark hair was slicked tightly against his head, parted way to the side, with little curls dancing around the bottom. Gray-green eyes sparkled in his otherwise composed face. He spoke with an English accent. "Young sir, my name is Jam Crinklecut. I am the majordomo, the butler in charge of the house staff of the west wing. It is my pleasure to serve young sir and modom. If you need anything at all, please ring me on the house phone in your chambers." He bowed again.

King Piter, the king of Alypium, walked in. His white hair bounced neatly behind him as he surveyed the room with his sprightly eyes. It felt great to see him alert and normal instead of slumped over, hypnotized like he had been for ten years before Erec had saved him with the king's own scepter. He no longer looked fifty years older than his sister, Queen Posey of Ashona, or his brother, King Pluto of Aorth. It was hard to believe that the three of them had ruled for 485 years, kept alive by the power of their scepters.

Erec, Jack, and Oscar rose to their feet, and Bethany toppled her chair backward, ran to the king, and flung her arms around him. As he ruffled her hair, he lifted his eyebrows at Erec and waved him over. Erec shuffled closer, unsure what he was supposed to do. King Piter knuckled his head and grabbed him and Bethany in a bear hug. Erec gave him a slight squeeze back, feeling odd about hugging the king instead of bowing.

Bethany shot Erec a strange look as they all sat down.

"Um, could I have your autograph?" Oscar's voice shook.

A deep chuckle erupted from the king. He tapped his finger twice on the table. At the first tap a pen appeared, followed by paper. King Piter signed and handed the paper to Oscar with a smile.

Oscar stared solemnly at the signature. "I'm keeping this forever."

"Erec." The king's blue eyes blazed. "I'm glad you're back. I'll notify the Bureau of Bureaucrats." His face turned sour and he cleared his throat. "I'm sure they'll contact you soon with your first quest."

Servants rushed in with platters of hamburgers, grilled cheese, pizza, and desserts, along with healthier but more austere Alypian specialties. The king's plate was filled with unidentifiable green mush.

"I remember my first quest," he chuckled. "Four hundred ninety-one years ago. We had to save a dragon gone mad from disease. Pluto, Posey, and I researched how to save him, with help from our tutors, of course. We made a healing formula and threw a huge net over him while he was asleep—not so easy, I can tell you. Of course he woke up. Pluto distracted him so I could rush from behind and inject the formula. Posey had a spray to knock him out if we needed it. We thought we had it covered. But he sent me flying with his tail, and Posey's spray sailed into the bushes." He shook his head. "We were nine years old. It's a miracle we survived. Pluto ran away. Luckily he tripped over a huge snake, and he screamed and jumped so wildly that the dragon stopped to watch him. Then Pluto fell face-first in the mud. I think the noise he made when he got up scared even the dragon. Pluto saved us in his own funny way, although he never would see it like that. Aoquesth didn't even notice when I injected the medicine."

Erec's eyebrows shot up. "Did you say Aoquesth?"

King Piter winked. "Yup. The dragon that gave you your eye. Funny, isn't it? That's the odd thing about Al's Well. Its waters are fed from a deep spring with the fountain where the three Fates bathe, so interesting things and coincidences usually happen."

Bethany looked confused. "What Al's Well?"

The king's eyes crinkled. "Al's Well and Ed's Well are our only two taps into the waters of the Fates. Ed's Well gives visions of the future, but it is highly guarded in a place called Earth's Edge, where the Fates live. Al's Well is where you'll draw your quests to become king. I hear they have new fixtures there." King Piter's eyes sparkled. "You will find that the things you must do become entwined with you. They are a part of your fate." He shook his head. "It's a miracle, really."

Oscar said, "My tutor Rosco can tell the future too, I think . . . at least my future."

King Piter frowned. "There are only a few people who can truly tell the future, gifted people like Bethany who will someday be a great seer." Bethany beamed at the praise. "Anybody else who says they can see the future is a little suspect. And speaking of suspect . . . Erec, the Bureau of Bureaucrats will oversee your twelve quests. The process

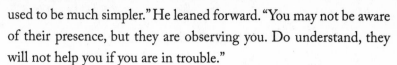

used to be much simpler." He leaned forward. "You may not be aware of their presence, but they are observing you. Do understand, they will not help you if you are in trouble."

Erec was not looking forward to it. "What will I have to do?"

"Your quests may include anything at all. There is no way I can prepare you for them. They are not contests but are steps that will make you stronger on your path to becoming a king. The waters from Al's Well will see into your past and future and direct you as necessary. Normally, the three future rulers do the quests together. Since you are the only one known to be the next true king, you may take two friends to help with each quest, but they will not join you as rulers."

Oscar's eyes widened. "What if I solve the quest myself? Could I be king?"

"No, but I'm sure Erec would thank you for your help. To rule you must be identified by a scepter and the Lia Fail."

Erec frowned. "It seems silly that I'm supposed to be the true king just because I won those contests."

The king chuckled. "Is that why you think you are meant to be king?" He set down a spoon on the table. "Well, I can understand that. It's best that you don't know the real reason now. But the contests were fake, staged as an excuse to make the Stain boys rulers. Being king is your destiny."

The idea made Erec's head begin to hurt. What was Piter talking about? He was just a normal kid. Well, maybe not. Normal kids didn't get slammed with information like this every other minute. His stomach tightened. He was sick of people keeping things from him, and it was happening again. He said to King Piter, "Actually, I don't care what is best for me. I'd like to know right now why I'm destined to be a king." He slapped his hand on the table.

Oscar's eyes widened, and Bethany bit her lip. Erec wondered if he had gone too far, but he didn't really care. He had enough mystery in his life, and he wasn't going to put up with any more.

The king looked uncomfortable. "All will be revealed before too long, I promise. Let's just say you come by it genetically."

Erec could not believe it. "That's all you're telling me? What do I come by genetically? I don't feel like waiting to find out who I really am."

"The only problem," said the king, "is that this knowledge is dangerous."

Erec glared daggers at King Piter. The king cleared his throat and smiled apologetically. Oscar slurped his pizza and Jack munched on cloud loaf in silence.

Suddenly, there was a knock at the door, which flew open a moment later. Behind a befuddled Jam Crinklecut stood Danny and Sammy. Their eyes fixed on Erec with relief.

"These two insisted on finding you right away." Jam nodded to Erec. "They said they are your brother and sister."

Erec looked at them in wonder. "Does Mom know you're here?"

"Sure." Danny shrugged. "She wants us to watch you."

Sammy added, "We missed you." She gave Erec a stiff hug.

The king motioned for them to sit. "Please join us." He signaled the servants, and they brought plates for the newcomers.

Sammy blinked at the king. "Since we are Erec's brother and sister, can we help him with the quests?"

That was odd. Erec wondered how she knew he could have helpers. Maybe they had overheard at the door before coming in.

"That is up to Erec," the king said.

All eyes turned to Erec, who busied himself eating his third piece of cake.

King Piter twiddled his thumbs. "Your siblings may have a room

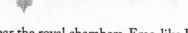

near yours in the west wing near the royal chambers. Erec, like I told Bethany, if you need anything at all, let me know."

"But I'm staying in the south wing," Erec said.

Smiling, the king turned to Bethany and raised a fuzzy gray eyebrow. "You took care of Erec's room?"

Bethany turned red. "His magic tutor thought he should stay in the south wing near him." Her face fell. "I thought the west wing was only for family . . ."

King Piter smiled at Erec. "You may move into the west wing, and your brother and sister are welcome too."

Bethany's eyes widened. "My stomach hurts. Excuse me." She ran from the room.

Erec could not find Bethany the next morning. He had a bad feeling she was upset. Danny and Sammy followed him like ducklings after their mother. Danny even walked with him into the bathroom, staring with empty eyes until Erec shooed him away. Their silence made the situation even stranger. Danny usually never stopped talking. Erec bit his tongue and tolerated them. Maybe Alypium was so foreign that it would take them a few days to get used to it.

He snuck out of the bathroom, took the Port-O-Door in the west wing into his mother's kitchen, and dumped half of his gold, silver, and bronze coins onto the counter. "Mom, I didn't think Danny and Sammy were coming to Alypium."

June pursed her lips. "We discussed it, and it made sense. After what happened here before you left, it seemed a good idea for them to watch out for you, just in case."

"But they follow me everywhere. And now they want to do the quests with me. I thought Bethany and Jack or Oscar might be better, since they've been there awhile."

June sighed. "Do what you think is right, but try not to hurt their feelings. E-mail me on the MagicNet if you have any problems, okay?"

Erec returned to his new room in the west wing and covered his face with a pillow. It was bad enough that he had to compete against Balor, Damon, and Rock to become king and be awarded a scepter that he dreaded having. Life was getting too complicated.

Erec's morning tutor, Miss Netta Ennui, had thick wire-rimmed spectacles that matched her silver hair perfectly. With a grim expression, she made the twins sit to the side while Erec took pretests in math, English, and history. All of the tests were either ridiculously easy or too difficult to do at all, so he finished them quickly.

At one o'clock, Erec found Mr. Peebles by the front castle doors. Peebles flew across the room, a toupee flapping on his head, and nearly crashed into him. "So good to see you, so good, so good. And your bwother and sister, too. Now let's all go get you that wemote contwol, shall we?"

This was Erec's first walk into Alypium since he'd been back. His stomach tightened. Would adoring fans crowd him, taking pictures and asking for his autograph? Maybe the store owner would insist he take the remote for free.

On the walk, however, nobody even looked him in the eye. Erec cleared his throat in front of passersby, but nobody seemed to notice him. He swallowed his disappointment, reminding himself that privacy was a good thing.

"You are so lucky your bwother and sister are here," Mr. Peebles squeaked. His toupee had flown away, and the wind blew the scraggy curls rimming his shiny head. "Family is of the utmost importance. I expect you to include them here."

Mr. Peebles led them into a shop called Tricksters at the edge of the agora. The walls, ceiling, and shelves were black, and bright lights made the objects and people in the shop glow like wraiths. Mr. Peebles approached a silver ghost who gazed from behind the counter. "Do you have a special wemote contwol for this fine young man, Circe?"

"Oh, yes I do, Mr. Peebles." Her words slid like slugs sledding on the icy winds of her breath. She reached below the desk and laid a thin metal box with black buttons on the dark counter. "This should fit your needs. Of course it's expensive. Five gold rings."

When Erec looked through the ghost's eyes, he saw worms wiggling in a jar behind her, which bothered him enough that he could barely think about the cost. He counted five gold rings from his pocket and set them in her outstretched silver hand, then took the remote.

"Caweful, Ewec," Mr. Peebles snuffled. "You may not use this until you've had pwoper instwuctions." He sniffed loudly and pulled the remote from his hands, herding the kids out the door. "This is a very powerful wemote contwol."

On the way back to the castle, Mr. Peebles led them past the Labor Society, the turreted building where the Bureau of Bureaucrats was located. Picketers lounged in the grass waving signs and drinking Flying Donkey Nectar and Snail Trail Lichen Ale. A woman with long red hair to her knees walked around with trays of snacks.

Erec's breath caught as he spotted his name on a sign. No, on several signs. One in the shape of a crown read DON'T SHOVE THE ER SCAM DOWN OUR THROATS. Others stated THE REAL EREC REX IS DEAD, and I'M NOT AFRAID OF EREC REX—TRICKY MAGIC TRICKS NO ONE! Other signs stated BALOR, DAMON, AND ROCK: THREE HONEST WINNERS, and FAIR PLAY, and CONSPIRACY: DON'T LET THE CROWN AND THE KID CONTROL YOU!

Erec's heart sank. What were these people talking about? A thin young woman with short blond hair and pixie green eyes bounced off the lawn and pushed papers into their hands. The flyers read THE ER FALLACY: THE MYTH THAT GIVES THE CROWN A STRANGLEHOLD ON POWER.

Erec felt sick. "Why do you think Erec Rex is a scam?" he said weakly.

The blond woman seemed not to recognize him at all. She laughed at the question. "Obviously you weren't there the night of the coronation. A few here saw it for themselves. Right when the winners were about to be crowned, some sorcerer that *looked* like a kid froze the whole roomful of people and made a scepter and crown come flying to him. Then he made it look like he saved the king from that stupor, or whatever was wrong with him.

"At first people thought the kid had hypnotized King Piter himself. Then he woke the king when he was ready to claim power." She sneered at the scam being played on them. "But King Piter is backing this fraud completely. It looks like they were in on it together, so King Piter can control who the crown goes to. Sick, isn't it? The fake Erec even broke poor Balor Stain's remote control during one of the contests."

Erec could only stare at her blankly. That was not what had happened at all. She shrugged and continued to tell more passersby her information. This was all wrong. He had saved the day. They should be thanking him. What about the snail mail from his secret admirer? What about the "huge celebrations" she talked about? Was she that clueless about what was going on?

Erec was trembling, much too shaky to speak. Mr. Peebles bowed his head. "I'm still honored to teach you, Ewec," he said.

Erec backed away, then turned and ran. He had to get away. How could everything have gone so wrong?

CHAPTER FOUR
Erida

EREC RAN ONTO the castle grounds, past the fountains, the gardens, and the maze, without stopping to think. He was vaguely aware that Danny and Sammy trailed him awhile, but he lost them in the woods. The rhythmic pounding of his shoes and his sharp breaths lifted him above his anger and cleared his head. When the ache in his legs and the fire in his lungs had cleaned him out enough, he sat by a trickling brook. Still unhappy, he threw sticks and stones into the water and watched them splash.

It wasn't fair. Maybe dreaming of admiring fans was crazy. But this? Everyone thought he was a lying cheater and that Balor and Damon Stain and Rock Rayson were good guys he'd wronged. How did this happen? Did Bethany know about this? He could not find her that morning. Maybe she was avoiding him. Maybe she hated him too.

Erec's head was swimming as he wandered back toward the castle. In his daze he tripped over a stick and landed chest-first on the ground. A chirpy rumble behind him sounded like a choking woodpecker. Erec turned and saw a man's face poking through a thick shrub. The stick, slowly receding, now was clearly the man's scrawny leg. Only his big black eyes, hooked nose, and red lips were visible through the bush, giving him the appearance of having wild green shrubby hair and beard. He made the peculiar rumbling noise, and Erec realized it was a laugh.

Erec wondered how he fit so neatly through the bush. "I'm sorry I stepped on you. Are you okay?"

Eventually the man stopped laughing. "A little upset, Erec Rex?"

Erec was startled. How did the man know his name? He wondered if this guy also thought he was an evil scam artist. "Everyone thinks I fixed the coronation ceremony . . . and even fixed the Lia Fail and the scepter."

The man laughed so hard he choked, slapping his sides. "Maybe you did, Erec Rex. Maybe you did."

Fed up, Erec stumbled to his feet and walked on, wiping his eyes with the back of his hand. Nobody understood him at all. Not even the weirdo who took naps in bushes.

In the garden he spotted Bethany and her magic tutor, a young woman with light brown hair. Seeing him, Bethany galloped over, waving her arms, long dark hair blowing in the breeze. Erec walked on, ignoring her, staring down at the grass.

"Hey, slow down! I hope you're not mad at me."

Erec spun around. "Mad at you? I thought maybe you don't want to be seen with me anymore."

Bethany burst out laughing. "No, you kook. Because I was such a jealous idiot last night and because I put you in the south wing? I should've asked for you to stay in the west wing even if I didn't think King Piter wanted you there." Her dark tanned cheeks grew pink. "I thought hard about it, and I guess I wanted King Piter all to myself. But I'm okay with it now. I mean, who keeps their dad all to themselves? It's good that he gets to know my friends, right? And where people sleep doesn't make them family."

Erec was relieved, and he told her what had happened. "I walked by the Labor Society today. All these people were marching with picket signs that said terrible things about me, like I was dead and a phony."

Bethany made a face. "Yeah. Even worse, they think Piter is corrupt. It's pathetic."

"It's worse that people think badly of King Piter than of me?"

"Of course! He's their king. They need to trust him." She stopped and corrected herself. "Well, I think a lot of people do trust him. But Thanatos Baskania has been stirring things up."

Erec shuddered when he thought of Baskania's many eyes bursting through his skin. The thought of running into him again made his teeth clench. "What's he doing?"

"A lot of people like Baskania," she said, shaking her head. "He is the one that created the Kingdoms of the Keepers. Folks think he pulled Alypium through when Piter let them down. He's telling everyone that Balor, Damon, and Rock won the contests, so only they should go on the twelve quests to be kings. Of course, Piter is backing you up, but the Bureau of Bureaucrats is under Baskania's influence. President Washington Inkle passed an emergency law so that the quests will be open to Balor's group as well as you."

A glob of pink materialized in the dirt by Erec's foot, sprouting from the earth like blooming bubble gum. Purple swirled through the odd disk, which was dotted with red hearts and flowers. A pair of antennae waved at one end.

"What a weird snail." Bethany bent down to look closer. "Look, it has your name on it."

The snail crept onto Erec's foot and fluttered its eyes toward him expectantly. Erec picked it up. Pink paper emerged from under the shell. When Erec pulled it out, the snail hid its head, and its shell flattened.

Bethany gasped, her face pale. "What did you do to that poor thing?"

"It's a letter. I've gotten one like this before." Erec hesitated before opening it. He wondered if it was from his secret admirer. It probably was, as the stationery was the same. His heart pounded and his stomach clenched, but he wasn't sure if it was because he was getting mail from a girl who had a crush on him or if it was because she had misled him so completely about what people thought about him here. Maybe it was just a mean trick. Maybe there was no secret admirer. He gripped the letter tighter and stuffed the shell in his pocket.

"What's it say?" Bethany hopped on her toes, eyes flashing.

Erec shrugged, staring at the paper like he didn't know how to unfold it.

"Come on!" Bethany gently extracted the pink, perfumed page and opened it.

My dearest Erec,
I can't tell you how excited I was that you actually wrote me back!
I never thought you'd have the time, as I'm sure you're crowded by
fans constantly. But I will treasure your letter forever. You sound

THE MONSTERS OF OTHERNESS

as cute as your picture! Maybe someday if I'm lucky I'll get to meet you. But, until then, you'll always be in my dreams.
Love, your SA

Bethany's face darkened and she stared at Erec. "You have a girlfriend?" She shoved the letter toward him, but he stuffed his hands in his pockets. Confused, she managed a shaky smile. "That's great, Erec. I'm happy for you. When do I get to meet her?"

"Bethany, I haven't even met her."

"Yet," she said sharply.

"She's not my girlfriend." Erec grabbed the letter, crumpled it into a ball and threw it into a clump of purple flowers. The flowers grew smaller and bent away from the crumpled paper.

"Why are you hiding this from me?" Bethany ground the tip of her shoe into the dirt. "You've obviously exchanged letters and sent your picture. You're her dearest Erec, aren't you? And she's your . . . whatever her initials were."

Erec smirked. "SA. That's secret admirer. But that's not even true. The whole thing is phony. Someone's dumb idea of a joke. Look around—where are all my admiring fans? And I never sent anyone my picture. It's probably from one of the millions of people who hate me here." Erec pointed at the purple flowers, bent away from the letter as if they were terrified of it. "Look, it's probably poisoned."

A grin spread across Bethany's face. "Those are shrinking violets." She tossed a handful of dirt onto some broad purple blooms. They grew tiny and trembled under the torrent. "You should write back. Figure out who wrote the letter and we'll get them back. Nobody messes with Erec Rex and gets away with it!"

Erec smiled. Who cared if people thought he was a big fake? Bethany knew the truth, and so did Jack and Oscar, King Piter, and even Mr. Peebles.

"I'm done with my tutor for today," Bethany said. "Let's go inside and write your SA back."

My dearest SA,
I am so excited that you wrote back too! You sound like a really sweet girl. I think that since we are writing each other, you should tell me your name. You know mine! And I do want to meet, too. Let's set up a place and time.
Erec

"You should write '*Love*, Erec.' They'll think you totally fell for it," Bethany giggled.

"No way. But when I meet whoever it is, you can pop out with your remote control and freeze them. Maybe I'll learn to use mine by then too."

Bethany was shocked. "I couldn't do that. Remote controls are not for revenge or hurting people."

Erec crossed his arms. "Well, what good are they, then?"

She laughed. "My tutor said I should study magic for the sake of learning and to help others. You shouldn't use magic for selfish reasons."

"Obviously not everyone thinks so." Erec felt his ears redden as he remembered Balor Stain hanging him upside down in the air. He wondered if Mr. Peebles would teach him how to use his remote for his own purposes.

"I thought we'd show up with rotten tomatoes." She laughed.

Erec sighed and flopped back onto the carpeted floor of his new room. "It's such a relief to be away from Danny and Sammy. They follow me everywhere. They're probably searching for me now." He immediately felt guilty for saying it, though. They thought they were supposed to keep an eye on him. Well, when they found him, he'd take them to the agora for a cloud cream sundae and chocolate-covered honey drops.

They wandered outside with Wolfboy and Cutie Pie, Bethany's pink fluffy kitten, to toss the snail with Erec's letter into the grass. Before it hit the ground, however, a hand reached from behind a bush and plucked it from the air.

Erec and Bethany scrambled around the bush and found a skinny, dark-skinned man with a thick white turban wrapped around his head, no shirt, and a thick white cloth wrapped around his waist. Laughter bubbled from him like a brook. Erec immediately recognized him as the man who had popped through a shrub in the castle gardens. Wolfboy stared at him, ears up. The man held the snail on an outstretched palm. "Ahh, young love. So bitter, yet so sweet." His whoops of laughter irritated Erec. The odd man was surely making fun of him. "You fools have no clue who it is you really love. And you, sir, will discover soon that those you love are not who you think."

Erec snatched the snail mail from the man's palm and dropped it to the ground, where it sank into the earth. The man stood up and faced Erec and Bethany. Feathers flapped behind his shoes like odd wings. He whipped off his turban, a rectangle of white terry cloth that fluttered in the breeze, revealing a shiny bald head. "Dry now." With his other hand he yanked off the cloth that was folded neatly around his waist. Bethany screeched and closed her eyes, but a baggy bathing suit covered him. The man flung a towel over each shoulder and waddled, pigeon-toed, to the castle.

"Who was that?" Bethany squinted after him. "He sounded like he knew something about your letter. 'Those you love are not who you think.'"

"No," Erec grumbled. "I don't love whoever wrote the letter. That guy was crazy, that's all."

Danny and Sammy appeared down a row of hedges. "Where were you?" Sammy's eyes fixed on Erec.

"We were worried about you." Danny sounded more bored than worried.

"I'm fine. I just got upset . . . the picketers . . . never mind. Let's all go to the agora. I guess Mr. Peebles has given up on me for today."

Danny perked up at the mention of the tutor's name. "Mr. Peebles said you could choose any two people to do the first task with you. Will you pick us?"

Erec shrugged. "I haven't thought about it. It might be better if I picked people who are more used to Alypium and give you time to adjust here."

Bethany added, "It sounds like the quests could be dangerous. Piter had to tackle a sick dragon for his first quest, and he almost didn't make it."

Erec's stomach clenched. With all the excitement of coming to Alypium, he had not given much thought to the actual quests he had to do.

"We want to be with you to protect you. We insist," Sammy said.

Sighing, Erec closed his eyes. "We'll see."

When they got back to the castle, a loud screech made Erec jump. Danny whipped around, pulling a remote control from his pocket. A creature with a large black vulture's body and a woman's head screeched in the air. Her black hair was combed into a tight bun, and thick black eyebrows hung over a beaklike nose and black lipstick. She grasped a parchment roll in her talons, which she held out to Erec, letting out a cry that was as much a squawk as a scream. "Erec Rex . . . Erec Rex . . . Erec Rex . . ."

"That's Erida," Jack whispered. "She's a Harpy. President Inkle brought them out of Otherness to help with law enforcement and to run the Bureau of Bureaucrats."

Erec took the parchment as Danny slipped his remote control back into his pocket. "Where did you get that?" he asked Danny.

"I bought it when we were at Tricksters magic shop."

Erec had not noticed that. He would have to find out why Danny bought it and if he could use it, but first he unrolled the parchment, which read, "The Committee for Committee Oversight formally invites Erec Rex to the Labor Society this Wednesday at 1 p.m. to accept his first quest."

At the bottom was engraved a smiley face next to the words, "Our Mission—POPS: Prompt, On-time, Punctual Service."

Erec squinted at the page. "What does the committee do?"

The bird woman howled a piercing shriek and said in a shrill voice, "A committee is a group of people organized for a purpose, you idiot." She rolled her eyes.

"But what does the Committee for Committee Oversight do?"

The bird woman bared her talons at Erec. "You ask a lot of questions. It's the committee that oversees the other committees to make sure that none of the other committees are overlooked, or if a committee has overlooked anything then whether a new committee should be formed."

Erec and Bethany exchanged a puzzled glance. "A new committee formed for what?" he said.

The woman's face turned red and her black lips clenched as her wings beat faster in the air. "For anything. Like . . . like the Committee to Formulate Mission Statement Opinions and Ideas."

"Like POPS?" Bethany pointed to the bottom of the parchment.

The woman tossed her head, but her hair was pulled back too tightly to move. "Of course. And like our last mission statement, PUPS: Patient, Understanding, Pleasant Service." She flew away, shaking her head and muttering rude comments under her breath.

CHAPTER FIVE

Al's Well

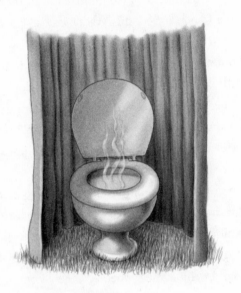

DANNY AND SAMMY were standing as silent as sentries outside Erec's door when he awoke. They followed him to breakfast—nectar, ambrosia, and other foods set out each morning in the west wing's dining room—then to meet Miss Ennui, Erec's academic tutor. The twins stared at him vacantly, making it hard to concentrate on the math tests that filled his morning hours. He couldn't wait to meet Mr. Peebles at one and learn how to use his remote control.

When Mr. Peebles led them into Paisley Park, just outside the castle grounds, Erec's eyes widened. The park was filled with apprentices, many wearing blue cloaks, and their tutors. Kids waved remote controls at leaping lizards, which then froze in midair and tumbled onto the grass. Others levitated rocks and each other. Some kids meditated, unaware of anything around them. Stone benches and odd paisley-shaped shrubs were scattered over the grass, giving it an almost mazelike look.

A boy with snowy white hair and black eyes looked familiar. As Erec passed, he overheard him talking to a girl. "I'll tell you a secret. That guy, the one who claims he's Erec Rex, I know he's a phony. Y'know why?"

The girl shrugged him off, not interested. He continued, "Because *I'm* Erec Rex. If anybody should be doing trials to be king, it's me. But I don't want to be king anyway."

Both the girl and Erec rolled their eyes. Erec was amazed this kid was pretending to be someone that everyone hated. Well, it took all types.

Mr. Peebles sat at a stone table and set down a thick book called the *Manual of Ethics and Magicological Statistics and Standards, Level VI*. "Ethics are most important in the pwactice of magic. You will outline this book to get a good basis before you begin." He plopped *The Math Behind the Magic*, another heavy tome, on top. "This will also be key to your understanding, so you will outline it next."

Erec stared at the thick books, confused. "Can I learn to use the remote control, too?"

"In good time." Mr. Peebles set Erec's remote gingerly on top of the stack. "You may look at it now, I suppose, if you're quite careful. Do wemember, it is hard to use in the beginning."

Erec picked up the remote and turned it around in his hands. "When I learn to use this, can I do whatever I want?"

"Of course, Ewec." Mr. Peebles's fuzz-rimmed head nodded eagerly.

"Even defend myself or get even?"

"Why not? You'll need to know how to do that, won't you?"

Erec nodded.

A concerned look filled Mr. Peebles's face. "Are you, ahem, wecovered from yesterday?"

Erec nodded. "I don't care what they think."

"Good, good. The whole thing was entirely my fault. I should never have walked you by the picketers. King Piter would not be pleased. I take it you were not supposed to know about any of that. You might find out more then. Can't have that. Although I can't say I entirely agree . . ."

Erec pinned the little man in his gaze. "Is King Piter keeping things from me?"

Mr. Peebles crossed and then uncrossed his legs. "Dear me. Dear me. I did hint at that, didn't I? Well, I couldn't actually *say* if I did know, now, could I?"

"What don't I know? Tell me."

Mr. Peebles's eyes fluttered at the sky. "Oh dear. I weally hate to be in this position. As your tutor, looking out for your best interests, I do want you to know who you are and who your father is. But I have to obey orders." He sighed.

Erec grabbed the remote control, pointed it at Mr. Peebles and pressed the green button, wanting him to tell everything he knew. Nothing happened.

Mr. Peebles tutted and patted Erec on the knee. "I understand. I weally do. Let's just say . . . I can't tell you what you seek or I'd jeopardize my position here. But if, say, you were to go into town more, you might just happen to find out." His voice dropped to a whisper. "During your afternoons with me you may either outline your books or sneak into Alypium." He tapped the books. "Now get started on your outlines."

Erec looked sadly at the huge texts. "Tomorrow I find out my first quest at one o'clock."

Mr. Peebles smiled at the news. "How exciting. I want the three of you to tell me all about it."

Jack and Oscar joined Bethany, Erec, Danny, and Sammy for dinner that night in the west wing. Servants brought roasted quail, barbecued salmon, whole grain cloud loaf, and loads of vegetarian dishes and desserts served along with the meal.

"Alypium is heaven for vegetarians." Jack sighed, loading his plate.

Oscar popped a donut in his mouth. "I'm thinking of becoming a dessertatarian."

Jack rolled his eyes.

"How did your magic lesson go?" Bethany asked Erec.

He sighed, thinking of the heavy volumes he had to outline. "Awful. It's going to be forever before Peebles teaches me how to use my remote control." He remembered seeing Bethany using hers with her tutor. It didn't seem fair. But then again, maybe learning his tutor's way would be better in the long run. "Peebles said I could use it for anything. Even revenge if I wanted. So maybe your tutor is wrong."

Bethany shook her head. "You can't use magic on people for those reasons. It would corrupt you." She held up her index finger. "My tutor says that once you start using remotes for fighting and revenge, the next thing you're trying to kill them. You can get power mad."

"That's ridiculous." Oscar laughed. "My tutor, the famous Rosco Kroc, says that some people are too afraid to use the gifts they've been given. Get a new tutor, Bethany," he suggested. "We levitated objects and turned them in the air for only a few hours, then went straight to people." He giggled. "It was so fun at Paisley Park the other day. People didn't know what hit 'em. Rosco had more fun than I did, I think. We've been working on making people warm, cold, ticklish— that one's real fun. I guess I'm just lucky that someone as famous as Rosco is my tutor. And I'm learning so much better now. He's skipping all the dumb stuff. He said I'm too good for that garbage. We're working on killing bugs now. Rosco said I'm the best student he's ever had, and he gives me cloud cream sundaes every day."

Jack stared in amazement. "You're killing bugs? How could you? I guess people must be next, right?"

Oscar rolled his eyes. "Please."

King Piter walked in and sat at the head of the table, nodding to the kids. Bethany took the opportunity to ask him, "What's really correct? Is it okay to use magic on people for whatever you want, like Erec's tutor says? Or does it corrupt you?"

The king fixed Erec with a penetrating gaze until Erec squirmed. "Every time you use magic for your own personal gain, you become more tangled in the dark shadows inside yourself. As you learn more, you will know how to untangle yourself, but that is not easy. Of course, there are times that we all use magic to help ourselves or those we love, times when it's necessary. But each time the choice must be weighed heavily, for the consequences run deep. Look at what happened to Baskania. He can do nearly anything—replicate any magic around him—and he does. He was born able to manipulate the Substance, and he's learned so much and used it for such bad reasons that his sanity is gone."

Throughout his entire speech, the king ignored the others, talking only to Erec. "When you are training, a healthy respect should be taught along with the knowledge. Using magic at a whim for your own gain is very dangerous indeed. Erec, it seems I should have interviewed your tutor more thoroughly. When we originally talked, he seemed like he understood what I wanted from him."

Erec knew what the king wanted Mr. Peebles to do—hide things from Erec, like who he was and who his father was. "Mr. Peebles is just fine. He's making me outline an ethics book, so I'm sure he's not overlooking any of what you said."

The king looked relieved. "That's better. Say, I hear you're getting your first quest tomorrow. I will stay to find out what it is, but the next day I must go take care of a big problem in Otherness, the wilds that lay outside of Alypium. Something terrible has happened there. The dragons' babies, their hatchlings, have all disappeared. All that is left is one nest of eggs." He rubbed his head. "I wish I knew what to do."

Bethany's eyebrows narrowed. "The dragons' children are missing? That's terrible. Can I help?"

"No," the king shook his head. "It's best you stay here. Plus, Erec may need your help." He looked at Erec. "If you need anything while I'm gone, my AdviSeer, Balthazar Ugry, will be keeping an eye on things here."

Bethany's face fell. "But he's . . . he's—"

King Piter stood to leave. "He has his difficulties, yes. But Balthazar is nothing but loyal. Ask Erec. Balthazar saved his life."

That was true, Erec thought. But Ugry had just threatened him, told him, "Be warned." Something was not quite right about him, and Erec did not want to find out what it was.

The next day, Miss Ennui did not let Erec out one minute before noon, even though he had finished the science testing early. Bethany and Jack met him with lunch in a bag, and Oscar joined them with the man who had rescued Erec in FES Station. He nodded at Erec, green eyes winking between his thick olive scales.

"Um, this is Rosco Kroc." Oscar puffed his chest. "My tutor." Rosco was small and wiry, but in good shape. Under his black sorcerer's cape he wore a neatly pressed suit that looked very expensive. "You don't mind if he comes along, do you, Erec?"

"Of course he doesn't." Rosco's voice was deep and oddly familiar. "I thought it would be interesting seeing you draw your first quest again." He laughed a high-pitched titter.

"Again?" Erec looked at him in confusion, then turned away from his scaly face so it wouldn't look like he was staring.

Rosco's cheeks reddened between his scales and he shrugged. "Just a turn of phrase."

Erec smiled at him. "Thanks for saving me from those snake police."

More people followed them as they walked closer to the gleaming, turreted building, until finally the streets were full. The crowd parted to let Erec's group pass across the wide lawn to the small side door.

Someone shouted, "I hope you fall on your face, kid."

Another murmured by his shoulder, "Don't worry, he'll never beat Balor, Damon, and Rock in a fair fight."

Another's voice dripped with sarcasm. "Even if he says he is Erec Rex."

Out of nowhere, someone shoved Erec, and he stumbled. The crowd grew noisier, shouting threats. Bethany, Oscar, and Jack guarded Erec's sides. Rosco held Oscar's remote control out to ward people away.

Balor and Damon Stain, Rock Rayson, and Ward Gamin stood before the closed door.

Ward said to Balor, "What's up with your brother Dollick? Why isn't he doing any of these quests?"

Balor shrugged. "He's a little sheepish." He spotted Erec and grinned. "Well, well. It's my old friend. Glad you could make it, Erec Rex. That's who you're supposed to be now, isn't it?"

Erec sneered in reply. "I wouldn't have missed it, Balor. Especially since I found out this nice place would be ruled by *you* if I didn't come."

Balor laughed. "This nice place actually likes me, which is more than it can say for you. You give yourself a lot of credit, like your being here could actually make a difference." He flipped his silver remote control out of his pocket and spun it in his hand, shooting Erec a knowing look. "Just five minutes with you, and this time you won't live to tell about it. I see you don't have those glasses anymore. Those were the only thing that saved you the last time."

Erec pulled his remote control out of his pocket and tapped it in his palm. "We'll see what happens this time."

Balor's eyes widened and he quickly slid his remote back into his pocket. Luckily, Balor had no clue that Erec couldn't even use it to turn on a television.

Erec heard a click, and the small wooden door into the building popped open. He walked through, followed by the others. The door slammed shut on its own before the crowds outside could pour in.

Erec's eyes adjusted to what looked like a dimly lit antique shop. A little man rushed from behind the counter straight into Erec's face, looking him up and down with wide eyes. Everything in the room was covered in a thick layer of dust, including the man himself. His bony knees and elbows jutted out of skinny limbs, and his unkempt, stringy gray hair and beard hung to his waist. He wore a shaggy gray smock, like a prisoner in a dungeon. Deep wrinkles furrowed his brow. Otherwise, he looked ageless.

He got uncomfortably close, studying Erec's face and chest as if Erec was some kind of artifact. Erec stepped back, unnerved. The man noticed the confusion on Erec's face and cackled wildly. He laughed so hard that he fell on his bottom, which was padded by his unruly hair and the equally shaggy carpet covering the floor.

"Oh . . . oh, excuse me." The man gripped his side and choked his laughter down. "I haven't seen a person in here in four hundred and seventy-five years. I forgot." Laughter burst from his nose. "I forgot how funny you all look." The man clenched his jaw, but his chest shook and tears streamed onto his wild beard as he looked over the group.

Finally, the man took deep breaths and his chuckles subsided. He climbed to his feet. "My name is Janus. Please don't mind if I stare. It's been so long, and this job does get boring. I oversee the shop." He waved a hand at the odd collection of items on the shelves. "But there are never customers because it's always closed. It's silly. Everyone knows this isn't a closed antique shop; it's the old Quest Control Center. That darn Committee for Suppressing Change has seen to it that I sit here like a prisoner. 'Be always prepared,' they say. 'You never know when the next rulers will come through.'"

Janus was so excited, he jumped up and down on his wiry legs and clapped. "But now you're here. And I have a job to do." Looking satisfied, he sat down behind the dusty counter.

Suddenly, Janus burst into tears. Sobbing, he laid his head on the counter, wrapped in his skinny arm. He choked and snorted, pounding his fist so ferociously that a dust cloud rose and several people sneezed. Erec and Bethany exchanged looks.

"Are you okay?" Bethany asked.

"N-no . . ." Janus wailed. He looked up, face soaked. "My job will be over too quick. You'll be gone in a minute and I'll be all alone again." He broke down into more sobs.

It seemed that nobody would ever find out the first quest. Balor snorted. Damon pointed at Janus and said, "Want me to smack him one, Balor?"

"Not yet, bonehead."

"How long will it be before you see people again?" Bethany asked.

Janus sniffled. "I don't know. I guess for the second quest."

"See?" Bethany said. "That won't be so long, now, will it?"

Janus sniffed and shook his head. "No, no. Not really." He cheered a bit, and straightened himself up in his chair. "Okay," he announced. "Only those may come in here who know those asked to participate in this quest. And only those may go in there," he pointed to the door at the back of the shop, "who may draw the first quest from the well."

Balor pushed his way to the counter. "That would be me. I won the contest to become king, you know."

"And your name is?" Janus stroked his beard, suddenly sounding officious.

"Balor Stain."

Janus shook his head, looking over his paperwork. "No. Only if Erec Rex was not here today. Then I believe he would have forfeited his natural rights, and the contest winners could take his place."

Rock Rayson smirked. "I'm Erec Rex."

Erec shot a look at him. "He is not. I am."

"Oh, really? I have an identification card. Do you?" He laughed.

Erec had no identification whatsoever. "My friends can vouch for me."

"Mine too." Rock grinned.

Janus sighed and slid a pad of paper across the counter. Dust shot up like a mushroom cloud. "Come on, sign your names. Let's go now."

Rock Rayson scrawled Erec's name on the paper. Janus pushed it to Erec, who signed his name, then handed the pad back. In a moment, the letters in Erec's signature darkened and seemed to crack open. Bright light shone from the words on the paper, beaming into the dusty shop.

A moment later, the rim around the door at the end of the room glowed with the same light. Smiling, Janus nodded to Erec and gestured at the door.

Erec went over and opened it. Filling the door frame was an odd material that shimmered and waved with the same light, like a giant bubble. Erec could not see through it, but he passed an arm in and out.

"Move it, loser." Balor shoved Erec aside. He thumped against the glowing substance and bounced back like it was rubber. Balor punched it, then kicked it, cursing, while Erec walked right through.

Behind the bubble material stood an enormous, spotless lobby, as different from the dusty antique shop as Erec could imagine. It seemed much bigger than the entire building looked from the outside. Rows of fluorescent lights lit huge banks of elevators against the walls. Glass cases listed offices and departments. The building looked cool and efficient. People with briefcases rushed by, not noticing Erec at all.

He waited until a heavy man at a large desk hung up a phone. "I'm Erec Rex. I'm here to get my first quest to become king."

The man pressed a few buttons on his phone. "Kid's here. Yup, I'll send him up." He pointed. "Elevator C to the sixth floor, room 612."

Erec looked through the walls of the glass elevator as he rode up. He could have been on Wall Street. The building seemed at odds with the quaint character of Alypium. In Room 612, a woman at a desk ushered him to a row of seats. He sat down and she continued working.

After nothing happened for what felt like an hour, Erec got tired of fidgeting and asked if he was in the right place. She adjusted her glasses, which hung from a chain around her neck. "It'll be just a moment." She waved him back, looking annoyed.

For another long stretch of time, Erec watched her make phone calls and file papers. He remembered the mission statement, "Prompt,

On-time, Punctual Service," wondering why he had rushed to get here.

Finally the woman approached him with a clipboard. "Do you have your Stroke 5C form?"

"My what?"

She adjusted her glasses. "Your Stroke 5C. I can't give you your paperwork until you show it to me."

Erec took a breath to calm himself. "Where do I get that form?"

"In Room 613."

Erec left the room, shaking his head. Couldn't she have mentioned that form two hours ago? Plus, it turned out that room 613 was locked. Erec pounded, but nobody answered. He went back into room 612, exasperated. "Nobody was there."

The woman looked at him calmly. "Helen Masterson is on vacation. You'll have to get the form here today."

Erec bit his tongue as she handed him a packet of paper. He wanted to strangle her. She was lucky she was not dealing with Balor Stain.

"Sign here." The woman pointed. She flipped through pages of small type. "Sign here, here, here, and here. Now your thumbprint." Erec did as he was told, hoping he wasn't signing his future away.

The woman filed the packet and handed him a clipboard and pen with another packet of papers. He answered a long list of questions, providing details about his family and even telling his favorite color. At the bottom was a statement that he had to sign. "I agree to complete the quests to the best of my ability and to follow the ethical guidelines listed below." The extensive list included such things as not dropping people down elevator shafts or wells, not killing cats more than eight times, and not eating the last cookie in the jar unless he was really hungry. He signed the paper and the woman motioned him back to the waiting area.

After another hour, the woman gave him a gold slip of paper and took him down an elevator to where a janitor waited. "Take him to Al's Well. He's got the pass." She turned back to the elevator banks.

The janitor put down a garbage can and unlocked a door in the back of the building. Erec was surprised that none of the crowds from the front were back here. In fact, there was nothing but an empty grassy field leading to a hill. Atop the hill sat a small, circular stone well. Erec followed the janitor to the base of the hill, where a small gravestone bore the single name JACK.

Erec pointed to the tombstone, but the janitor shook his head. "We don't talk about that much."

Shuddering, Erec climbed the hill after the broad-shouldered janitor. A big man wearing overalls and a tool belt and carrying a large plunger, appeared at the top. AL was embroidered above his pocket.

"Ey, what's dis? Is it time already?" Al looked and sounded like a Brooklyn plumber. "Ya got yer pass, buddy?"

Erec nodded and handed the gold slip to him.

"All right, den." Al unlocked a door in the stone and swung it open.

Once Erec was inside, the enclosure no longer seemed so small. The stench was awful, though. Flies immediately buzzed around Erec's face.

Al laughed. "Got ya, don't it? The smell? Ah, ya get used to it. It's the smell of life, bud. People's fates aren't always so sweet."

There was nothing in the enclosure except what looked like a round shower curtain and a few servants scurrying around with tools in their hands. Al pulled a cord and the curtain flew open, revealing an oversized toilet. A row of servants all dropped to their knees and bowed dramatically before it.

The toilet stood in the center of the grassy ring, gleaming white.

Al waved his plunger in pride. "There she is. I keep 'er in perfect condition, just as my three lovely ladies, the Fates, demand. All right, you go ahead and pull out your little job. I'll wait here."

Erec stared at the toilet in disbelief. "You don't actually mean . . . ?"

Al laughed. "Of course I do. How else ya gonna get it out of there? Aw, don't worry. Nobody would dare pee in there, if that's what you're thinkin'."

This was how he had to get the first quest? Erec gulped and walked toward the wide toilet bowl. At least it looked clean. A large hole in its bottom led straight into blackness, making the toilet look like an outdoor latrine. Some green steam escaped from the hole.

Erec's stomach knotted. Whatever quest he got would not be easy. He might die doing it. But if he didn't try, Balor certainly would. He would hand the royal scepters to Baskania, and the Kingdoms of the Keepers would suffer the consequences.

He got down on his knees and, after a moment of hesitation, plunged his arm deep into the toilet. His eyes squeezed shut in anticipation of what he might grab. He felt his hand go through an icy mist, then submerge in a liquid that felt like it was both boiling and freezing at the same time. His first reaction was to yank out his hand, but then he realized the heat and cold did not hurt. He fished around in the liquid until he felt a thick, warm piece of paper, and he pulled it out.

Hands dripping, Erec did not want to look at it. He was happier not knowing. What would it say? Kill a lion with his bare hands? Fight the ferocious Hydras he learned about once in the MONSTER contest?

Trembling, he lifted the dripping paper. The printing was clear, unsmudged by the liquid. "You must open Patchouli's eggs in Nemea."

CHAPTER SIX

Imposters

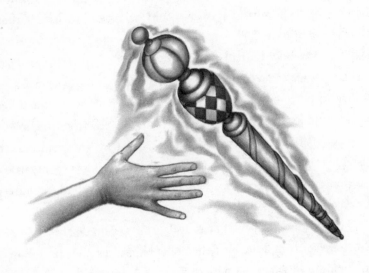

EREC READ IT again. This didn't sound right. Open eggs in Nemea? What was Nemea, some grocery store in Alypium? Below it read, "Tomorrow at one o'clock."

Al read it over his shoulder. "Opening eggs? Sounds like an Easter party." He chuckled. With a nudge, he ushered Erec out of the enclosure. A fly followed him all the way down the hill, buzzing around his head. "Careful, someone fell down here once and died," Al said, pointing at the gravestone. Erec hurried through the back door of the Labor Society building, then through the bubble shield into the dusty shop.

Bethany, Jack, Oscar, and Rosco Kroc were waiting, smiles on their faces. Oscar beamed. "Rosco's like a seer. He knew you'd be back here in four hours."

Erec waved the paper he had pulled from Al's Well. "I'm supposed to crack open eggs in some place called Nemea." It sounded pathetic. What kind of a quest was this? He wasn't sure if he was more relieved or disappointed that there wasn't something dangerous to do.

"I'll take that paper, boy," dusty old Janus croaked. "This will be posted in front of the Labor Society. It's public information. You do know there will be another team—Balor and Damon Stain and Rock Rayson—competing against you? It's never been done before, but a law was passed and it seems like that's the way the quest is going to go."

"You're going to compete to crack open eggs?" Bethany laughed. "Who are you going to pick to help you?"

Oscar stood up a little taller, trying to be noticed.

Erec shrugged. "There are three of you. I don't know."

"What about Danny and Sammy?" Bethany asked.

"No way. I need someone dependable."

Erec had put this decision off as long as he could. No matter who he picked somebody was bound to feel bad. Well, he might as well just pick who he wanted. "I can choose different people each time, so I'll get you next, Oscar. I guess I'll start with Jack and Bethany. Is that okay, guys?"

Oscar's jaw fell. Rosco put an arm around him and Erec heard him say, "Didn't Rosca' tell ya? You had to see it for yourself. Listen, so what if Erec will be a king? You'll be a hero, and that's much better. Wait and see, you'll even save my life someday. Everyone will worship you." He led Oscar away.

Erec shook his head. "I can't win. Now Oscar's all upset. And I'm sure the twins will be mad."

"You better tell them now," Bethany said.

"Now? You're kidding. I'm putting that off as long as I can."

Bethany sighed. "They'll feel much better hearing it directly from you. You owe it to them. They did follow you all the way out here."

He knew she was right.

Erec found the twins' adjoining rooms in the west wing of the castle. It was funny; he had never come to get them before. They always found him before he could think about looking for them anywhere.

He stopped short just outside Danny's door. Two men with deep voices were talking in the room.

"All right, you tell him your feelings'll be hurt if he doesn't let us do the first quest with him. Make yourself cry. If that doesn't work, I'll clobber him. That will persuade him."

"Make myself cry? Why don't you try that, Bruno?"

"It's a chick thing. You gotta figure out how to do it."

Erec listened in shock. Who were these strangers planning on doing the quest with him? Did the whole world want to join him? And what were they doing in Danny's room?

He pushed the door open a crack and peeked inside. His heart skipped in fear. There was Sammy, perched on a bed, but out of her mouth came a deep man's voice. "Yeah, luckily the twerp has no clue about us. When we're out there with him we'll make things go our way. Maybe he'll slip and cut his own throat."

Out of Danny's mouth came another unfamiliar deep voice. "Stop getting ahead of yourself. The boss wants him fresh so he can cut out the dragon eye. Then we can kill him. And before he finishes any quests and gets more powerful."

Erec slammed the door open and walked in. They looked at him

THE MONSTERS OF OTHERNESS

in surprise. The person disguised as Sammy started talking in her high voice. "Hi, Erec. We missed you. Did you get your first quest?"

Erec was seething with anger. "I got my first job, and that's to kick you guys out of here."

The men who looked like the twins sprang to their feet. Danny's look-alike pointed a remote control at Erec. "Okay, we thought this would go easy, but now we are going to have to take a little walk." He muttered, "Akamptos." Erec's body instantly froze. "Aeiro." Erec's feet lifted in the air, and he sailed between Danny and Sammy out of their room. He tried to yell, but his voice was gone. Erec closed his eyes and prayed. *Help me, somebody.*

As Erec floated down the hallway with his feet near the ground like he was walking, Jack appeared around a corner. "Hey Erec, is this a good time to talk about the quest?"

Sammy waved to him. "Maybe later," she said. "Erec said he'd spend some time alone with us."

Jack nodded knowingly and walked on.

Around the corner, as they drew near the west wing entrance, Danny stopped. King Piter loomed before them. His broad shoulders swelled under his red robes.

"And where are you going?" His voice boomed.

"We're going for a walk," the fake Danny explained. "Erec is going to tell us about the first quest. We get to help him do it."

"Is that so? It seems it would be difficult for Erec to talk to you at all the way he is right now." The king pointed at Erec, who then settled to the ground. His body loosened, including his tongue.

"They're imposters," Erec gasped. "They were going to bring me to Baskania, take my dragon eye, and kill me."

"Let's see." The king winked. In a flash, two paunchy men stood where the twins had been. They whipped remote controls from their pockets and pointed them at King Piter. The king chuckled, flicking

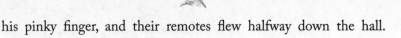

his pinky finger, and their remotes flew halfway down the hall. "Where are the real Danny and Sammy?"

"Kidnapped," the phony Danny snapped. "You'll never find them."

"Oh, yeah?" Erec eyed King Piter's scepter. "Make them tell where the twins are."

"Not now, Erec." In another blink, Danny and Sammy's doubles were gone. "They are in my dungeons," King Piter explained. "I'll deal with them later."

"But why didn't you use your scepter? We could find them now."

King Piter shrugged sadly. "I can't, Erec. As you will soon learn, scepters are dangerous. I can only use one in extreme circumstances. I shouldn't have used mine as much as I did when you so kindly woke me up. I wasn't fully myself yet, and I'm still paying the price."

Erec looked at him, confused. "What price?"

"It's a kind of madness. A craving so deep I can't describe it, for power and all that it brings. You may understand somewhat. You have used it yourself. The scepter makes you feel like a light shines on you and you alone. You bask in its rays. It makes you strong, confident, complete, perfect. You become a better person . . . for a while. But all around you, the things you love and care about fall to the wayside. You crush them in your quest for more of what the scepter brings you. Even worse, your path changes. Subtly, for the scepter is your friend, but it is a friend you cannot trust. You start on the path of evil.

"So you see why I may not touch it until I've mastered my feelings. My whole kingdom could crumble. I would destroy it, you see."

Erec understood more than he admitted. "But aren't there times when you have to use the scepter, even with those dangers? My brother and sister are kidnapped. We have to do something."

The king shook his head. "If I could use the scepter now, I would find all the baby dragons that have disappeared in Otherness. If I'm right, their lives aren't worth a crumb in the breeze right now." His face softened. "I know you're worried about your brother and sister. I will alert my plants, they're my extensive system of spies, and of course the Alypium police." He sighed. "Your mother's Seeing Eyeglasses will be the best way to find them. And I will postpone my trip another day."

Erec's stomach sank. How stupid he had been to leave those glasses near that horrible alarm clock. He hoped his mother had been able to pry them off of it.

The king looked concerned. "I heard about your quest, Erec. Be careful there."

Erec shrugged a shoulder and looked down. "Opening Patchouli's eggs in Nemea?" It sounded ridiculous. "I suppose I should find out where Nemea is tomorrow, and where that Patchouli's egg shop is."

"Don't you know?" The king looked at him oddly. "Nemea is one of the great dragon reserves in Otherness. Patchouli is a mother dragon who has been badly hurt. And the eggs you are to open, her hatchlings you are to save, are the last known baby dragons in Otherness. Their mother is missing, and they can't get out of their shells without her help."

"Oh." Opening eggs didn't sound like a joke anymore. He had to open dragon eggs. Dragon mothers were very protective. If she showed up he would be stepping into the jaws of danger after all.

Sitting on the castle lawns, Erec told Bethany about his quest. He flopped onto his back. "I should have known something was up with the twins. They didn't have *L*s on their foreheads like we did at first here."

Bethany laughed. "That Loser Identification Law that President

Inkle passed is so obnoxious. I can't believe we walked around with *L*s until we got used to this place."

Erec shook his head, thinking how Upper Earth people who did not remember magic were labeled "losers" here. He was frustrated that King Piter would not use his scepter to find Danny and Sammy. The solution lay in his grasp, but he wouldn't use it.

But Erec would. And he knew he could, too. All he had to do was grab the scepter when the king wasn't paying attention.

"You have to trust the king, Erec," Bethany told him. "He knows what the right thing is to do."

"Trust King Piter?" Erec cried. "Bethany, I have to tell you something. Peebles said King Piter is keeping things from me. And they sound big, like who I am and who my father is. He won't let Peebles tell me either. He obviously doesn't trust me." Erec started plucking blades of grass, almost mad at them. "But I'm going to find out. I'm sure if I work on Peebles I can get the info. He didn't seem happy to be keeping it from me anyway."

Bethany was worried by that idea. "If King Piter doesn't want you to know something, maybe you shouldn't try and find out. There has to be a reason."

Erec flung aside the grass he had gathered. "I don't care what his reason is. I need to know who I am. Why was I born in Alypium and taken to Upper Earth? Why does Baskania have it out for me? He wanted to kill me even before I got the dragon eye." He spread his arms wide. "Bethany, I want to know who my birth mother is and why I remember my father being so horrible when he did great things like saving Aoquesth and giving me the dragon eye."

She nodded her head in agreement. "You're right. You deserve to know. I'll talk to King Piter about it."

Erec was not sure he believed her promise. He knew why Bethany trusted King Piter so much. She felt like she finally had a father and she'd never see past that. He decided not to tell her about his plan to grab the king's scepter at dinner and use it to save the twins.

"Anyway," she said, "tonight I'd love to check out those spooky catacombs under the castle. I'm up for some adventure!"

Erec was going to reply when the smell of perfume wafted to his nose. A pink blob pushed through the soil by his feet. He watched with irritation as it became a flowery envelope with his name on it.

"Well . . . open it!" Bethany leaned forward in anticipation.

Erec did not want to touch it. The last thing he was in the mood for was this practical joker, whoever it was. "You read it. I don't want to look at it." He kicked it toward Bethany.

"Easy, there. It's not this little guy's fault." Bethany picked up the shell envelope and slid out a letter.

My darling Erec,

My heart pounded when I read your last letter. It was a dream come true. You actually want to meet me! You seem like such a nice person for a famous hero, but then again I would expect no different.

Then my heart sank. I should never have expected we could meet. I'm not allowed to come to Alypium, and it would be so hard for you to come to Lerna, where I live. And why would you just for me? But you are right about not knowing my name. It's Tina Amymone. I suppose for now I'll have to live on my dreams and your wonderful letters. Please write back!

Yours faithfully,

Tina

Erec flopped back in the grass, exasperated. "This jerk won't stop at anything. He's making himself sound pathetic."

Bethany studied the letter. "Erec, I think this is the real thing. Tina doesn't even live in Alypium. What if wherever she is, in

Lerna, you do have lots of fans? She sounds pretty convincing."

Erec narrowed his eyes at her. "You're kidding. You saw the way people think of me here. Don't tell me I have a fan club hiding somewhere. This is just some jerk chickening out from meeting me."

"Well, I say you write back and find out where Lerna is. There's no return address on the shell. Maybe it's in Aorth. The snail does go underground."

"Why bother?"

Bethany shot him a look. "What if some poor, lovesick girl is waiting for your next letter? And if this is a hoax, we can at least get more clues to who is sending these."

Erec flipped his hand in the air. "Okay. Whatever."

They went into the west wing to get some paper. Erec thought that if, on the very small chance there actually was a lovesick girl involved, making her more lovesick by writing her back might not be a great idea either.

Bethany handed Erec a piece of paper and a pen and dictated, "My darling Tina . . ."

Erec didn't like the "darling" part but jotted down the rest of what Bethany told him to write because he couldn't think of anything better to say.

Dear Tina,
It is so good to finally know your name. But now I want to know more about where you are from. Who knows? Maybe we will meet one of these days. How old are you? How did you get my picture? And I'm curious about the huge parades in my honor you describe. Do you really think that's going on in Alypium?
Erec

Bethany told him to close the letter with "Love, Erec," but he didn't like that, so he just folded the letter into the shell. He and Bethany ran outside and watched the shell disappear into the dirt.

King Piter was sitting alone at the head of the table when Bethany and Erec came into the dining room. His scepter was resting against the table at his side. Erec spotted it and sat in the chair closest to it.

The king's large shoulders were hunched, and he looked up at Erec with sad eyes. "I took the liberty of calling your mother. She would like to speak with you over e-mail after dinner." He paused. "She does not want you to rush home. In fact, it's better you stay here to help look for the twins in Alypium. She will search in Upper Earth." The king made it sound like searching Upper Earth was simple. Perhaps he didn't believe they had been taken there.

He sighed. "Unfortunately, my AdviSeer help is limited now. Ruth Cleary, Bethany's mother, was an exceptional seer, but that Spartacus Kilroy who took her place couldn't even see what was before his own nose." He started ticking off his fingers. "Balthazar Ugry used to be something of a seer, but something happened to him when I was bewitched, and now he's more . . . limited. I am consulting another seer. They call him the Hermit. He is very good, although he may not stay in Alypium for long. He says the twins are alive and well."

Jam Crinklecut and his assistants brought in heaping plates of food. Ignoring the sprouted wheat berry and quinoa salads, Erec reached straight for the pizza. He hoped the Hermit was right.

The king pulled thin-framed wire spectacles from his pocket and set them on the table. "Your mother is still unable to remove her Seeing Eyeglasses from . . . an alarm clock, I believe?" He cleared his throat. "You may use these. They are mine. You will find they work in the same way."

Erec took the glasses from him. They looked like normal glasses.

"Use the glasses to check on Danny and Sammy, but don't talk to them," the king said. "If their kidnappers realize you are there, they could block your ability to see the twins. Just spy on them and pick up what you can." He put out a hand in apology. "I'm sorry I can't help. I have to get to Otherness. Things are looking bad. The dragons are quite upset. They have had no luck finding their children. The only babies that will be left are in Patchouli's eggs that you are to open. I hope you can do it." He shook his head. "Also, there's trouble brewing in Aorth. We might need reinforcements."

"What's going on?" Bethany asked.

The king looked troubled. "Just rumors, actually. And my own gut feeling. I think that Thanatos Baskania is closer to learning the Final Magic. Or at least where its secrets are hidden."

"What's the Final Magic?" Bethany asked.

"Unnatural magic," he said in a hushed voice. "Magic that was never intended for people. Learning a little magic can be easy, and learning more gets harder. Breaking past the barrier of needing a remote control takes discipline, and it only gets more difficult from there."

Not if you had help, Erec thought. His hand slid under the table near the scepter. He could feel a slight warmth coming from it. His desire to pick it up was so tremendous that he almost forgot why he wanted it.

"Magic skills are like a path from one room to another," King Piter went on. "Walking the first half is easy. Then divide the rest in half. The next part is harder to walk. Then divide what is left in half, and the next part is even more difficult. Each time it gets tougher to take smaller and smaller steps. And, with each step, if magic is learned for the wrong reasons, insanity grows right along with the magical knowledge."

Erec let a finger touch the king's scepter next to him. Its electric power surged through his body. "If you keep dividing what's left in half, you'll never get to the end," he said.

"Exactly right. Baskania is so close that he's completely obsessed with that final step. But magic is designed so that cannot happen. Nobody can know all, control all, have no limits. Each step he takes now is extremely tiny and impossibly difficult."

Erec's fingers stroked the golden scepter more boldly.

Bethany grinned. "That's Zeno's paradox. You can never leave the room you're in because each step can be halved into infinity."

"So like your mother." King Piter smiled.

In a flash, Erec grabbed for the scepter. Yet his fingers closed on nothing but air. King Piter held it out in his other hand, a warning look on his face. Erec swallowed his embarrassment. Was he that obvious? He tried to play it off. "But you said Baskania found out how to learn the Final Magic."

"Not yet, he hasn't." The king frowned, and deep worry lines appeared on his face. "If he does, we will all know it. His madness, as well as his power, will become complete, and nothing will remain as it was. My plants tell me he is planning on raising his grandmother from the dead." Erec and Bethany both recoiled in shock. "I am not sure this can be done. The only way requires a flowering plant that is no longer in existence. It's a shame I cannot use my Aitherpoint quill to tell me where the dragons are, and Danny and Sammy. It's like the scepter. I'm not strong enough to use it yet without it taking me over."

That reminded the king of the trick Erec had just tried to pull. "Be careful with your decisions in Nemea."

Erec tried to pass off what he'd done with a shrug. "I only have to open the dragon eggs."

"It's not as easy as it might seem. Your quest from the Fates will affect many people in different ways, depending on your choices. You see, the quests are not contests but situations that need fixing, by you. To be honest, I don't know how Balor's group can compete against you. It is quite possible that he could open the dragon eggs faster than you and you could still win as far as the Fates are concerned because of the way you handle the situation. That's the key. The quests are things you need to do for others so that you can learn. For example, once you hatch the dragon eggs, do you walk away and let them die? Their mother, Patchouli, is missing. She won't be there to help them. Do you figure out how to save them? There are no rules, only your own conscience." He was reminded of something he had to tell them.

"The sign posted outside the Labor Society says that Patchouli's eggs will be ready to hatch tomorrow at one o'clock. I will take you and your two friends there in the morning."

Balor would probably be waiting with his remote control, ready to smash open all the eggs at the stroke of one o'clock. If only Erec could use his remote control. Well, he would just have to use his wits instead.

Before e-mailing his mother from the computer in his room, Erec put on the glasses that King Piter gave him. Bethany sat on a chair and waited. His mother appeared before his eyes in their small apartment. She was crying quietly over a cup of coffee, staring at her computer.

"Mom?"

June jumped, spilling her coffee. "Erec? Is that you?"

"Yes. King Piter gave me some Seeing Eyeglasses like yours. I was going to check on the twins, but I found you instead."

June looked around the room, unsure where to address Erec. Her eyes were red with tears. "Those glasses will show you who you're missing most. To see the twins you need to think about them first, miss them. Tell me everything you see. Pay attention to what's around them, for clues to where they are."

"King Piter said not to talk to them. The kidnappers could make it so the glasses don't work."

"That's a good idea. Check on them, then e-mail me right away. I'll wait here." She pointed at her computer.

"Wouldn't it be better if I could talk to you?"

June looked surprised. "That's right, you can. You haven't used MagicNet e-mail, have you?"

Erec shook his head. "Okay. I'll be right back."

He took off the glasses and thought hard about the twins. How they had been gone long enough that he missed them. He definitely was worried about them.

He put the spectacles on his eyes and blinked. Bright sunlight was streaming through large glass windows, falling upon the tables and chairs in a small shop. Two large cloud cream sundaes sat on a table, slowly disappearing bit by bit. A spoon clanked onto the table from thin air, and one of the water glasses vanished.

Sammy's voice giggled. "Good thing I can't see you getting chocolate syrup all over your shirt."

"Right, Miss Perfect. Who was the one who stuffed so much candy in her mouth she choked? You're just jealous that I beat you Rollerblading today."

This was the old Danny. There was no doubt in Erec's mind. Someone must have made them invisible to hide them. Erec had to bite his tongue to keep from shouting out. He looked all around the shop. It must be in Alypium—that was cloud cream they were eating—but he didn't recognize the place. A poster of a clown holding a large umbrella hung on the wall. Erec would search for a shop with that poster as soon as he got back from his first quest. He wished he could go right away, but by the time he found the shop they would probably be gone.

He took the glasses off. Bethany showed him how to e-mail his mother by typing June's full name and clicking on her picture. Her face appeared on the screen.

"Erec? Did you see them?"

"They were invisible, but they were eating huge cloud cream sundaes, and I could hear them. It was definitely them."

June's voice cracked with worry. "Did they seem okay?"

"More than okay. They were giggling and talking about Rollerblading and eating candy."

"That's good," June said, confused. "I don't understand what's going on, but I'm glad they're okay. Piter told me the Hermit said they were fine too."

"I'll find the cloud cream shop as soon as my first quest is done, and I'll track them down. I promise, Mom. Don't worry."

June nodded, lips tight. Whatever was going on, Erec would find out.

Erec closed the e-mail and looked at Bethany. "First, all I have to do is walk into a dragon's nest. I'll just break open the eggs hoping the mother doesn't pop back. And if I can't do it, the last known baby dragons in Otherness will die, since all the rest are missing. And I don't even want to think about what will happen if the mother comes back. I wonder how angry a dragon mother can get."

CHAPTER SEVEN
The Nevervarld

A S THE SUN set, Erec and Bethany headed to the library tower in the castle. They didn't have much time to find out about the care and feeding of newly hatched baby dragons.

The librarian's nameplate read, "Carol Esperpento." Her granny glasses were as narrow as her eyes, but they shot far past her face on both sides. She pointed to the third floor, where the books on beasts were kept. "The books must stay here," she warned sternly.

The section on dragons was at the top of the wide spiral staircase. They browsed through section headings such as "Dragons and Dungeons," "Delectable Dragon Dung Dishes," "The Many Uses of Dragons in the Healing Arts," and "Hiding Dragons' Disguises." Finally Erec found the section labeled "Raising Baby Dragons" and pulled out a thick book called *No More Sea Monkeys: How to Talk Your Parents into Buying You a Dragon Egg, and How to Survive Once It Hatches.* Bethany picked up *The Total Loser's Guide to Bringing Up Dragons.*

Erec read, "The most important ingredient to feed and protect newborn baby dragons is Nemean lion skin. While everything else has its place in their safety and development, without the fresh lion skin, baby dragons will not be able to live unless they have their mother's milk." He shook his head.

"Uh, bad news, Bethany. It looks like baby dragons need to eat lion skin in order to survive. And it has to be fresh. I doubt we'll find that for sale on the MagicNet. And I don't think either of us are up for hunting and killing a lion tomorrow morning."

Bethany's face fell. "I see the same thing in here, too. I don't know which is worse, killing a lion or letting the last baby dragons in existence die. Maybe we should look up how to hunt lions."

Erec raised an eyebrow. "Am I hearing things right? You would actually consider killing an animal?"

She crossed her arms. "Well, dragons are meat eaters. And if they are the last ones left . . ."

"And I have to kill the lion with my bare hands, I guess?"

Erec had no idea how to hunt a lion. Both of them kept on reading. It seemed, in the end, the lion would have the last laugh.

On the next page there was a recipe:

Dragon babies do best with their mother's milk, but this formula will work nicely for those raising dragons on their own

Baby Dragon Formula (enough for a brood of six)

6 fresh Nemean lion skin flowers, chopped with a lion claw

6 cups *Daemonorops draco* berries

3 *Amanita muscaria* mushrooms

4 [50 ml] tubes animal blood

6 drops nitrowisherine

10 stinging nettles, ground to a paste

12 Thai dragon chilis

6 dashes each of cinnamon and black pepper

Erec laughed. "Look, it's not the skin of a lion they need, just lion skin flowers. I think we can handle that. I'm sure we can get a lion's claw off the MagicNet. Maybe we can find the other things in Hecate Jekyll's old storeroom under the kitchens."

Bethany turned pale. "Animal blood? That's disgusting. How would we get it anyway? Here we go with having to kill an animal again."

"Maybe we could just buy it."

"But someone still had to kill the animal," Bethany pointed out.

"Oh, there's more here about animal blood," Erec said. "Mammal blood is recommended. Human blood is considered the best. It gives the developing dragons insight into what will be both their deadliest enemy and closest ally," he read.

Erec and Bethany shared a smile. "Well, I guess we won't need to kill any animals," he said.

Bethany laughed. "That's a relief. I think. I guess we can go to the royal hospital and get our blood drawn."

"I'll do it," Erec said. "We don't both have to get stuck."

Bethany didn't argue with that. "We better write these ingredients down. Some of them are pretty interesting. This says *Daemonorops draco* is a palm tree that grows in the Indian Archipelago. The berries make a paste called dragon's blood. And *Amanita muscaria* are a kind of poisonous toadstool."

"I hope we can find them."

"Oh, look," Bethany exclaimed. "This book also says that biting beetles are good for the dragon hatchlings to eat with their formula."

They copied the list, then went to the royal hospital wing. Dr. Ezzy Mumbai was packing up for the night. Blond curls flowed loose around her face, and she batted long eyelashes at them. "Long time no see. You having any problems?"

Erec shook his head. "Could you please draw some blood from me? I need to make a formula to feed baby dragons."

Dr. Mumbai laughed. "It's always something with you. I don't know what you kids are up to, but I can't do medical procedures without a real indication."

Bethany was surprised. "It's just drawing blood."

The doctor put her stethoscope in a drawer. "I'm sorry, kids. Time to go. I'm closing up now." She ushered them from the room and locked the door behind her.

Erec leaned against the wall, arms crossed. Well, he thought, he didn't need a doctor to draw blood. "I'll just get a knife from the kitchen."

"What are you thinking?" Bethany's eyebrows narrowed. "Are you going to slice yourself? You could bleed to death."

"I'll just nick my finger, I guess." The thought made his fingers ache, but what was a little pain compared to the life of the last baby dragons in existence? "Maybe you should do it for me."

There was a shuffling noise, and the door to the royal hospital opened. A girl with stringy brown hair, gray eyes, and glasses poked her head out. "Rick Ross? Is that you?"

Erec immediately recognized Darla Will, the girl whose gift, or curse, was that if anybody got sick or hurt around her, she got the same thing, only twenty-four hours earlier. "My real name is Erec Rex. Sorry . . ." Erec felt bad that she remembered his fake name, like he had lied to her. But the last time he had been in Alypium it had not been safe to use his real name.

She smiled. "I heard something about that. It's just that I'm usually in here." She waved around the room. "I'm sometimes late on news. I couldn't help overhearing. Do you need some blood drawn?"

A smile spread over Erec's face. "Do you know how?"

"Do I ever. Hospital stuff is all I've known since I was a kid, growing up in places like this. C'mon in. I know where they keep everything."

Darla wiped rubbing alcohol over Erec's arm, put a tourniquet around it, and stuck a syringe into his vein, pulling back thick, dark red fluid. "How much do you need?"

Bethany looked like she was about to pass out.

"Four fifty-milliliter tubes," Erec said, amazed the needle didn't hurt. "You're good at this."

Darla shrugged. "It's easy." She pulled out the syringe, pressed a spot on his arm with gauze, then injected the blood through the rubber stoppers of four test tubes. "Here you go."

Erec felt dizzy and weak. He pocketed the vials of blood and thanked Darla. He and Bethany headed to the west wing. "Well that was the easy part. I hope we can find the other ingredients on the MagicNet."

They went online in Bethany's room. It was as easy as Erec

remembered. A woman's face appeared on the screen, her dark hair pulled into a tight bun. "Yes?"

Erec checked his list. "I need six fresh Nemean lion skin flowers."

The woman nodded briskly. "Nemean lion skin flowers."

The screen split into eight boxes, a different person framed in each. A box at the bottom of the screen said, "Next eight of forty-six." The vendors in the boxes were silent, shuffling through their files and looking suspiciously at each other.

That wasn't a good sign. "Last time they were all trying to outshout each other, wanting me to buy their stuff." Erec said to the screen, "Don't any of you have Nemean lion skin flowers?"

A woman with more brown hairs sprouting from her chin than from the top of her head lifted a white lacy flower. "I have a lion tail flower from Lerna."

Encouraged, a few other vendors began to wave flowers at Erec. "A lion hair flower grown in Bangor, best quality for you."

"Here's a nice toad skin flower you'll like."

Erec crossed his arms. "Those aren't any good. I need a Nemean lion skin flower. Who has one?"

A few of the vendors disappeared from their screens. The woman with the hairy chin clucked at him, "Don't you know? Nobody can get those flowers. They can't grow in our world." Her hands fluttered around her head. "They're the only living things that need to grow where there is absolutely no magic. No Substance. No Aitherplanes. Everything else in this world needs some magic around it. They say the Nemean lion skin flowers grow outside our realm, in the Nevervarld beyond the Substance."

Bethany crossed her arms. "So nobody's ever seen one? How do you know they exist?"

"Oh, we have seen them," she said with a sly smile. "An explorer found some once and brought back a lot, sold it for a high price. Made him very rich. And we who bought it from him made some good money selling it too, but now it's all gone. Even he couldn't find it again."

"How did he find it the first time?"

The woman laughed. "There is a hole in the Substance somewhere in Nemea. They say it was made by the searing power of a dragon's eyes. It's not marked though. It's invisible. You could spend your whole life feeling through the air in Nemea and never find it."

"And the flowers are in the hole?" Erec asked.

"To get them you have to crawl through it," she explained, like he was a small child. "But you can't stay in there too long because, aside from the lion flowers, nothing can live there. A human would die in a few hours in that world. The only thing that can last in there at all is a dragon, and even then only for a few days."

Erec shook his head in dismay. "Someone must have some of those flowers left."

"Good luck finding them. Most of them got used up when it was trendy to raise your own baby dragons." The woman chuckled darkly. "Stupid fad. Half the dragons ate their owners within a month."

Bethany had an idea. "Hecate Jekyll kept everything in her storeroom. Maybe we could find some in there."

Erec brightened up. "You're right. I'll get a few other ingredients here, then we'll go check it out." Looking down at his list, he turned to the woman. "Do you have a lion claw?"

The vendors that had remained on screen immediately started shouting out prices and waving claws. Erec bought one for nine shires from the woman, handed the money into the screen, and took out a claw in a small bag.

Next he asked about the *Amanita muscaria* mushrooms. Other vendors returned to their boxes, all wildly waving huge red-capped toadstools. Erec bought three from the woman who spent time telling him about the flowers. They were huge, with bright red caps, and were covered with white warts. They looked like they were straight out of *Alice in Wonderland*. "If I eat one side, will I grow tall?" he joked.

The woman handed him the mushrooms in a bag. "Don't eat those at all. Who knows what would happen to you. Need anything else?"

"Six cups of *Daemonorops draco* berries."

Bethany tapped him on the arm. "Don't you think you might find that in Hecate's storeroom? Maybe you don't need to buy it. Especially since we might be missing the key ingredient."

Hecate Jekyll had been the head cook at the Castle Alypium. She now resided in the dungeons, after it was found that she was the one who had been bewitching King Piter for the last ten years. But her storeroom in the kitchens was packed with more odd ingredients than Erec could imagine.

Erec looked at Bethany, then at the vendors waving clusters of small red berries. "How about I get these, and we'll check the storeroom for the rest." He studied the ingredient list. "The other things look more common anyway."

He bought the berries for four shires from the woman, who now was gloating because she had gone out of her way to talk to Erec. The other vendors were giving her nasty looks, and some began imitating her in cloying, nasal voices.

With the claw, mushrooms, and berries, Erec and Bethany headed for the castle kitchens. When they arrived, a tall woman with ultrashort, steely gray hair, gray eyes, and gray skin was shouting at the kitchen staff.

"That's the new head cook, Greta Minster," Bethany whispered. "She's not as nice as Hecate was. But, then again, I guess Hecate didn't turn out so nice. I don't think we should ask her for help. Let's sneak into the storeroom before anyone sees us."

They stole across the room and hid behind huge tubs of butter and barrels of olives. Bethany grabbed a large glass jar off the top of a barrel. "Bet we'll need this."

Erec searched for a large round plaque with a closed eye carved into it. Finally he spotted it, glimmering in the floor. He bent down and whispered into it, "One eye sees all." The eye opened wide and the thick metal disc slid across the floor, uncovering a hole. Erec and Bethany scrambled down a ladder and into the lit storeroom below. "I'm glad that still works."

The narrow room was packed with shelves full of ingredients, most of which were so gross Erec didn't want to look at them too closely. "It's alphabetized." They looked under *N* for Nemean lion skin flowers, but none were there.

"Maybe they're under *L*."

That brought no better results. Bethany and Erec searched under *S* for skin and *F* for flower to no avail.

"Oh, man." Erec sat down heavily. "This stinks."

"Well, we might as well put the rest of the ingredients together. That's better than nothing."

Erec nodded. Pulling out his bags, he dropped the *Daemonorops draco* berries into the glass jar, as well as the three mushrooms, then pulled the rubber stoppers out and poured the tubes of his blood into it. The mixture made him sick. "This is disgusting."

"It's for a good cause." Bethany found a huge jar of stinging nettles and added ten into the mix. "Ow," she cried. "My fingers hurt now."

Erec counted out twelve Thai dragon chilis, then put in six dashes of cinnamon. He sneezed wildly when he added the black pepper. Wrinkling his nose, he said, "It's good she kept regular spices down here too."

Bethany looked at the jar suspiciously. "I bet that's not regular pepper." Erec examined it more closely, and saw the black grains whizzing in the air like tiny pilots. "Hey, look at this! I found a jar of biting beetles!"

"Great, let's take it with us. Now for the nitrowisherine." Erec remembered where it was on the shelf. "Hey, the last time I used this, a drop spilled on the floor and I got a wish." He stood straighter and grinned. "I can wish for the lion skin flowers! Perfect."

He opened the dark round jar of nitrowisherine and fanned the rancid smell away from his nose. Six drops slid gently from the dropper as he squeezed them into the glass jar. "You ready?"

Bethany nodded, holding the jar of biting beetles. Erec picked up the formula jar, then released a drop of nitrowisherine onto the floor.

A huge explosion shook the room. Even though he was expecting it, the noise took Erec's breath away. They both slammed into the shelves behind them, rattling the rows of boxes and glass jars. Erec announced, "I wish Bethany and I would find the hole in the Substance in Nemea so we can get the lion skin flowers."

In a flash, Erec and Bethany were transported to a tangle of trees. Stars were blinking in the night sky over their heads. Erec still held his glass jar in his arms. "Are you okay?"

"Yeah. Where are we?"

The forest stretched as far as Erec could see. He tried to get his bearings. It had all happened so quickly. But, then again, he hadn't known what to expect. "I guess this is Nemea. King Piter said it's a dragon reserve." Erec shivered. He wondered if this was where Aoquesth lived. "I guess the hole in the Substance is somewhere around here."

Bethany shivered. "I thought you were going to wish for the lion skin flowers to appear in the castle."

"Oh, that would have been easier, I guess."

She seemed glad to have come anyway. "It's pretty cool here. Mystical. Okay, we might as well look for the hole."

"I wonder where it is." Erec felt blindly around the grass near the trees.

Bethany reached up, touching leaves. "We don't even know what we're looking for." They both waved their hands through the emptiness around them. She laughed. "If somebody saw us now, they'd think we were crazy."

"Maybe it's closer to these trees." Erec kneeled close to the roots of a large fir tree, and Bethany tripped over him. Both of their hands shot out together into a space that felt tingly and dry. Startled, they turned to look. Their hands were invisible past their wrists.

"It's a hole." Bethany rose to her knees, and her arm disappeared as she pushed it farther in. "It feels awful in there."

Erec fought the urge to yank out his hand, which felt mostly numb, with occasional little pinches and jolts. "Well, I wished that we both would find it. So I guess it makes sense that we found it together. Ready to go in?"

As he stepped further into the void, the glass jar in his hand stopped short, like it had hit a wall. When he put the jar down next to the tree, he could pull his arm through easily.

"Maybe we can't bring anything with us there," Bethany said.

"No, I just put a leaf through." Erec held it up to show her. "I think it's only the jar that won't go in."

"It might be because of what's in it. Remember, the woman said that the Nevervarld can't have any magic in it at all. Nitrowisherine is magical."

Erec thought for a moment. "Why don't you keep an eye on the jar out here? I'll find the flowers. That way we'll know everything is safe."

"You sure?" Bethany waved her hand through the opening. "It doesn't feel too good in there."

"Yeah," Erec said, shuddering. "Tell you what. Just leave your hand through the hole so I can see it."

When he tried to swing his foot through the hole, it would not go in. It took him a moment to remember his Sneakers were magical, and he took them off.

When he tried to slide further, something in his pocket seemed to catch. He pulled the magic glasses out and set them on his shoes. Barefoot, he decided to get it over with quickly before he had time to get nervous. He stuck both arms through the gap and plunged his head in.

Erec's breath caught and his chest felt frozen. Everything around him was . . . nothingness, a gray swarming nothingness that had no substance to it at all. No . . . Substance. He was surrounded by what seemed like television static, a seething world of black-and-white flecks. Little sparks flicked and stung him. His knees still rested on the ground outside, but his arms and hands were floating in a strange sea. He could see nothing other than the moving specks on all sides.

Control, he thought. *Be calm. You can do this.* He climbed all the way into the abyss of the Nevervarld, then gripped Bethany's hand for dear life. All sense of gravity was gone. There was no up or down, no sounds, and nothing to see except for Bethany's hand, the one vision of reality left. He remembered that humans could only survive here for a few hours. How long would it take to find the lion skin flowers? It didn't seem like he could find anything in this huge gray void.

Somewhere in the back of his head he heard echoes that sounded like *Thank you* and *Yummmm.* Slowly he released his grip on Bethany's hand. He tested letting go and reaching for it again a few times before he finally edged away. Going anywhere in the Nevervarld was difficult, a combination of swimming and willing himself through the static. The strain of trying to move made him

THE MONSTERS OF OTHERNESS

tired. The energy in his body seemed to be absorbed by the particles around him. He searched, felt all around for something that could be a flower. Bethany's gleaming hand began to look less and less real.

His eyes adjusted to the whirling nothingness around him, or maybe it was his mind that was adjusting. Shapes gradually began to form within the chaos. Rocks? Statues? No. The forms were something he knew he would never understand, because there was nothing similar on earth. It was so confusing. He wondered how long he had been here. It could have been minutes or hours.

Erec focused hard, looking for any sign of plant life. All the while he made sure not to wander out of sight of Bethany's hand. A crackle of energy struck his wrist and he drooped, exhausted. He realized that the sparks striking him were his own energy leaving his body.

Where are you? he called to the plants in his mind. *I need you.*

Why couldn't he have a cloudy thought now? He became so tired, he wasn't sure if he should keep looking for the flowers or try to make it back toward the hole before he could no longer move. Then he heard the noise again. It was louder this time, and it seemed to come from inside his head. Something was speaking to him. *Thank you. Your energy is delicious.*

His life energy was flowing out of him fast, disappearing into the particles whizzing around him. It was suddenly clear. Erec knew it and the Nevervarld knew it. He would never get out of here. It was a trap.

He tried to talk to the voice in his head. *I need some lion skin flowers to save the dragon hatchlings. I have to go back.*

The space around him echoed in his mind. *No human gets out of here alive. It's impossible. Surrender yourself.*

But I can't, he thought. *I heard an explorer came here and brought out lion skin flowers once.*

Swirls of nothingness washed through him until he was lost in their haze. *That is not true,* the voice said. *Once a man came here looking for lion skin flowers. He got a few in his hand before he died. We pushed his body through the hole and he brought them out with him. His friend took the flowers away from there. That same friend brought others back, pushed them in here to their deaths, hoping they would bring more flowers out with them, but none of them did. Others have come here hoping to find various things, but never made it out alive.*

Erec knew this was true. It was the end for him. Well, he decided, he might as well die holding the flowers in his hands so the dragon hatchlings could live. He called out to the flowers in his mind, *I need you. Please come help.* His mind fuzzed until he could barely remember why he needed them.

A faint echo reached his ear. *I am here. I am next to you.*

Just then, a Nemean lion skin flower appeared right next to him. He couldn't exactly see it, but somehow he could sense its presence, its spirit. *Thank you.* It drifted into his hand. It was his now. Then another came in. And another. Six flowers came to him by their own will, giving themselves to him, knowing. By now he could not recall why he even needed them. He could barely remember where he had come from and where he needed to go. But they were in his grip.

He was losing consciousness fast. A dim hum buzzed around him. The last bits of his life were soaring away, gone forever. Blackness grew around him, filling his being. There was something wrong . . . or right . . . he couldn't tell. The voice spoke to him again, but it was so very dim now. *You are not dead. We do not understand. There is something in you that is stronger than human. A part of a dragon. You will be dead soon, though, if you don't think fast.*

Think fast? Erec could not think at all. What was that about a part of a dragon in him? It was a dream. Not real. Nothing was real. Why was he here? What was the reason to go on? But then he saw Bethany's hand, shining almost too bright to look at, glowing colorfully in the gray swirl.

That was it. Bethany.

He floated back, pushed and pulled by the flowers somehow until he reached her.

And she pulled. In one yank his head popped through, gasping in the sparkling air. With another tug he was lying on the ground and gazing at the stars, which were impossibly bright.

Bethany looked down at him in horror. "Erec, are you okay? You're ice cold." She laid a hand on his cheek. "You don't look good."

But Bethany sure did. She radiated with more vibrant color than possible, a world of color concentrated in one small person. He was glad it was dark. In the light of day, her brilliance would have been blinding.

She bit her lip. "Can you talk?"

Erec shook his head. All the feelings, sensations, life, were too much. Energy rushed into him so fast he was dizzy. Finally he took a deep breath and raised his head. "You know that scene in *The Wizard of Oz*, where Dorothy walks into Munchkinland and everything changes from black-and-white into color? I'll never watch that movie the same way again."

Bethany laughed with relief. She felt his arm, testing. "You're warming up."

The Nemean lion skin flowers rested in Erec's hand, motionless. Their energy had drained out, for they couldn't survive here. He knew what they must have felt like, energy leaving them like it did from him in their world. Yet they came willingly. Here they looked like clusters of thick beige furry petals, very much like lion skin. He stared at them, fascinated. "The only reason I survived is because I have a dragon part in me. It must be Aoquesth's eye. Every other human has died in there." Saying that, he was thankful that Bethany had not gone in.

"Well," she said, picking up the glass jar, "I guess we should cut them up with the lion's claw and throw them in."

"Cut them up?" Erec realized he was still in a daze. "You better do it."

He managed to get the claw from his pocket. Bethany took it, chopped the flowers against a rock, and dropped them in the formula.

The mixture looked lumpy and disgusting as she stirred it with a long stick. The flower petal pieces began to fizz, and bubbles raced through the mixture. In moments the solid bits melted and the concoction took on a glossy brown texture.

Satisfied at last, she stopped stirring. "Now we have one other small problem. How do we get back to Alypium?"

Trees towered above them, making Erec feel like a small lump of earth. He could barely hold his eyes open.

"Erec? We can't wish ourselves back, can we?"

"No." He hadn't thought about returning. Plus, the ground was so warm and comfortable. "Tomorrow. We'll figure it out tomorrow. Okay?"

He was asleep before he could hear her answer.

CHAPTER EIGHT

The Amulet of Virtues

S OMETHING POKED EREC'S face and neck. He turned over and shooed it away, but it kept prodding him.

"Erec. Erec! We've got to get moving. You don't want to be late for your first quest."

That woke him up. He raised his head off the ground, feeling stiff.

"You've been sleeping forever." Bethany was walking around holding the jars of formula and biting beetles.

"All right." Erec pulled himself to his feet and looked around. "Maybe if we wander around we can find a way back. If only I had a scepter."

In a rush, the craving was back. He wanted one. Badly. It was worse now after touching King Piter's scepter last evening. He had felt its power again, and it was too much for him. The king was right. There were always reasons to want to use it. If he did, he would soon forget the reasons and use it for the feeling of power it gave him alone.

"If only I could magic us out of here." Bethany wistfully eyed her remote control. "I only know how to use it for little tricks. I can move small things in my sight, freeze them, turn them, and I'm working on moving small people, but I can't even move myself yet."

They started to wander through the woods. A thought occurred to Erec. "I bet there are dragons around here." He looked into the sky.

A flash of green light filled Erec's eyes. Everything around him was green. Thick bands of netting and wide white ropes filled the air.

But something in the sky caught his eye. A darkness there was growing closer. It began to form a shape as it zoomed toward him, fast.

Suddenly he could see it clearly. It was a dragon. The thing roared and screeched at him, talons bared, sailing through the sky right toward him. Fire shot from its mouth as it zoomed in for the kill. Erec screamed and fell back.

Then the green light faded. He was sitting on his behind, no dragon in sight.

"Are you okay?" Bethany leaned over him. "That was so weird. Your dragon eye came out, but now your regular eye is back. What happened? Is it something from the Nevervarld?"

Erec shook his head. "It's a cloudy thought. Well, it's not exactly that anymore. It's more like a premonition. It happened before at home. I could see myself tackling Danny and then later on I did tackle him." He trembled, thinking of the fury in the eyes of the dragon he saw attacking him. Would this happen too? He didn't see himself stopping the dragon, though, or doing anything at all. But that didn't make sense. Cloudy thoughts always told him what to do to save himself.

This couldn't mean he ...

What if it meant he would die?

A bitter taste filled his mouth as he scanned the skies. "Let's get going." He rose to his feet, and they set off again. With each step, Erec's heart sank more. It must be close to afternoon. He would never get to Patchouli's nest in time to open the eggs. Balor would win the quest hands down. There went the kingdom. And the scepter. His desire to win almost surpassed his fear of owning the scepter now.

As he kept walking, a feeling of deep sadness filled him. Even worse than losing the quest, he would not be able to save the baby dragons. The only dragon he had ever known, Aoquesth, had been so nice to him.

"Ah, there you are," a deep voice boomed. "Come to Nemea a little early, I see?"

King Piter appeared before them, scepter in hand. Erec immediately stared at it with longing. He was amazed at the strength the king must have to hold it for so long and resist using it.

"Well," the king said with a smile, "I thought I'd find you in Alypium. It's a good thing I brought Jack with me so you three can make it to your first quest together. It's not too far from here. I needed to come here anyway to meet with some dragon elders." He cocked his head to one side, and all four of them began to rise in the air. They kept floating upward until they stepped onto the top of a large cliff jutting from a mountainside. Near them, a huge black nest of fused iron shavings and tree branches sparkled with gems and gold. In the middle sat ten green eggs, each the size of a watermelon.

Balor and Damon Stain and Rock Rayson sat on the other edge of the nest, glaring.

"You're not allowed to help," Balor shouted to the king.

"I wouldn't think of it." The king winked at Erec. "I'm sure things are under control."

Erec wondered where the king's confidence came from.

"Good luck." King Piter twinkled his fingers at Erec, then vanished.

Erec, Bethany, and Jack all smiled. That was a nice magic trick right there.

Balor was talking quietly to Rock. The nest was so large, Erec couldn't hear them.

"I wonder what their plan is," Erec said.

"Why don't you use your watch?" Bethany said. "It lets you hear from a distance, right?"

Nodding, Erec played with the dials. Damon's voice rose quietly from the watch as he said, ". . . and we're the ones that get to see Biscottia bring back his grandma from the dead!"

Balor glared at him. "It's Baskania, you bonehead. The Shadow Prince to you. Now don't forget your job, all right?"

"Yeah, I know," Damon said. "Fight Erec's team. Knock 'em out."

"That's right," Balor said. "Rock will use the blowtorch, and I've got my jackhammer remote." Hearing that, Erec remembered how Balor's remote had sliced through a stone anvil in the Tribaffleon contest. Balor checked his watch. "Three minutes to go."

"Let's start now, dude," Rock said.

"No, idiot." Balor glared at him. "That Harpy, Erida, is coming to announce the contest. You'll get us kicked out."

Erec turned off the watch. "Aw, man," he moaned. "They're gonna kill us. I bet these eggs are hard to open."

"Here's a sharp rock," Jack offered. He fished around in the dirt and handed it to Erec. "I'll use my hands."

"Damon's planning to fight us." Erec glared across the nest. "I'll take him on while you guys open the eggs."

"I think you should open the eggs," Jack said. "If I open them it might not count as much as you doing it."

"Nobody knows what's going to count."

Erida, the creature with a woman's head on a black vulture's body, flapped in on a breeze, four other Harpies behind her. They each had black hair pulled into tight buns and lustrous black feathers. Their only distinguishing features were the sharpness or fatness of their bitter faces. Their pale skin looked stark under the blackness of their lips, scowling eyes, and coarse eyebrows.

Erida screeched, "The Committee for Committee Oversight is formally overseeing the first quest for kingship." She looked around with wild eyes as if daring anyone to challenge her. "This is in the spirit of our new mission, PIPS: Positive, Inspirational, Peaceful Service." The Harpies all nodded.

Bethany whispered, "They seem to like making up those things more than actually sticking to them."

Erida announced, "The team of Erec Rex will be competing against the team of Balor Stain, winners of the first contests to be kings. The quest is . . ." She flourished a small piece of paper. "You must open Patchouli's eggs in Nemea."

Erec knew the "you" meant him. He was the one who pulled the quest out of Al's Well. He hoped all these people interfering wouldn't make the Fates angry and mess it up for everyone.

"Of course," Erida squawked, "the Stain boys are expected to have an advantage as they are thirteen and Erec Rex is only twelve, according to his forms." Erec could not imagine that would make a difference. Maybe it would be a convenient excuse to account for Balor's cheating.

A shrill whistle blasted through the air. Balor, Damon, and Rock ran into the large nest. Erec dashed to one of the eggs himself and pounded on its shell. It felt like thick, cool plastic. He could feel the dragon scratching and moving inside. The shell bent very slightly when he pushed it, but it would not break.

Someone yanked him onto his back. He looked up, and Damon was standing over him. "I'll get you, you Erec Rex dummy ball." Damon pulled his floppy gray hat over his ears, but part stuck up on top, making him look even goofier. "Take that!" He kicked Erec hard in the side.

Though his ribs smarted with pain, Erec grabbed Damon's other foot and pulled. Damon tripped over Erec and fell next to him, then smashed him in the side with his fist. Erec looped a leg over him, trying to hold him down, but Damon sprang up and grabbed Bethany's ankle, yanking her away from the egg she was trying to crack open.

In the meantime, Jack was pounding an egg to no avail. Erec finally managed to pull Damon away from Bethany, but Damon easily pushed him aside and tackled Jack.

Feeling the time pressure, Erec scratched the sharp stone that Jack had given him against one of the eggs. Nothing happened. He shoved it harder into the eggshell, and bent over it, jamming it in with his foot. No matter how hard he tried, though, the rock did not make a dent. Erec looked up to see how the Stain team was doing. Rock's blowtorch and Balor's jackhammer remote were not working either. Then his jaw erupted in sharp pain. Damon had kicked him in the face. He toppled over, the stone flying from his hand.

The taste of blood flooded Erec's mouth. He put his hand to

his face and felt wetness from his bleeding tongue and lip. A wave of anger surged through him. It was bad enough that nobody could crack the eggs open, but Damon keeping him from trying was too much. Growling, Erec dove on Damon, and the two of them rolled over the sharp sticks and iron filings of the nest.

Seeing that Erec needed help, Jack, an egg under one arm, stepped on Damon's chest. "You don't think you're stronger than all three of us, do you?"

Erec held Damon tight against the nest with Jack's help. "Hey, Bethany, bring me an egg."

Bethany brought an egg over and dropped it into Erec's free arm. She scowled at Damon. "If you just tried to open the eggs and let us work in peace, maybe we'd all get something done. And, by the way, you really hurt me when you grabbed my ankle, you jerk." She ripped his floppy gray hat off his head.

Erec, Jack, and Bethany froze when they saw what lay under Damon's hat. A huge bone, very much like an oversized dog bone, projected from the top of his head. Damon sat up and rubbed the bone. "Where's my hat?"

"Um, sorry." Bethany handed his hat back. No one knew quite what to say. Damon looked like he wasn't going to attack again, so they let him get up and walk away.

It was clear that nobody was going to be able to crack the eggs open, so there was no reason for Damon to fight them. Balor used his remote control to try to smash the eggs against rocks, burn holes in them, and slice them, but nothing worked. He kicked an egg in frustration. "Stupid dragons. I hope they all die."

They all tried different methods. Bethany scratched one of the eggs with a fine twig and mumbled math equations softly to herself. Erec scratched an egg against the sharpest things he could find in the nest. He pushed it against rubies, gold spikes, and iron. Then he scraped it on the nest below him and heard a noise. It was kind of a squeak, and the egg shivered at the same time. Faint lines appeared on the eggshell. He looked down and saw a diamond jutting out of the nest.

Erec jiggled the diamond and found it was loose. He eagerly worked it out of the nest and ran it over the egg. A crack appeared in the shell. He pushed harder, and the shell tore open in his hands. Inside, a tiny dragon hatchling peered out with a faint mewling sound. Little green slitlike eyes looked up at Erec. Its sharp teeth bit the air as if it expected food. Green slime rolled off its head.

Everybody stopped what they were doing.

"Aw, it's so cute!" Bethany said. "Look at its little tail." Blood red spines like little thorns ran in a line down its back. Its scales were a shimmering green. Erec was so focused on the dragon that he was surprised when he was suddenly knocked sideways by Balor. The baby sailed from his hands onto the hard nest. In an instant Balor grabbed the diamond from Erec. "Get him, bonehead," he commanded.

Damon took off running as if he'd been waiting for the order. Tackling Erec, he flattened him on the ground. Erec shoved him off, but Damon grabbed his leg before he could get up. Jack tried to pitch in and pull Damon away, but Damon grabbed him and he went down too.

"Stop it!" Bethany screamed. "Leave them alone." She whisked Damon's hat off, revealing the huge bone jutting from his head, but this time he did not let up.

Meanwhile, Balor had opened two eggs and sliced into a third. "Eew. This one just has goo inside." Green slime dripped down his fingers. He threw it to the ground in disgust and grabbed another.

Bethany found a small diamond attached to the nest and sliced another dragon egg open with it. "Oh, look!" She stopped what she was doing and peered at it. "It's so sweet. It's trying to lick my finger . . . ouch!" She shook her hand. "I don't know if it bit me, but something in its mouth really stings."

Erec tried to pull Damon away, but Damon grabbed the dragon out of Bethany's hand and squeezed it. "You're not getting this one. It's mine now. Ouch!" He threw it hard onto a rock. The dragon hit with a cracking sound and made a sad little noise.

"What did you do?" Bethany cried, enraged. "Why did you have to hurt it?"

Balor laughed nearby. "It's done! And they're all cracked, and I opened eight of them. I won!" He put his hands on his hips and walked around the nest with his chest stuck out. "Give it up, Rex. I'll be the next king, and there's nothing you can do about it. You don't have what it takes. C'mon, Damon."

Balor, Damon, and Rock strutted off, heading around the corner of the cliff. Erec pointed his watch at them and heard Balor talking to someone. "All right, Dad. Let's go. We creamed him, of course. I told you we wouldn't need help."

The Harpies flew away as well. Erec looked over the nest. Six baby dragons were strewn about making crying noises. "Are some missing?"

"Some of the eggs didn't have hatchlings in them," Bethany said. She sat down with a lost look on her face.

"Well," Erec said, "I'm glad we brought the formula for these guys, whether or not we won this stupid thing. Look at 'em. They're so little." He opened the glass jar and picked up a dragon baby. Its tiny black jointed wings opened and shut. Then he realized that he had no idea how to feed it. He tried tipping the jar and putting the dragon's mouth into the liquid. The dragon coughed and sputtered, but it did not get anything down its throat.

"Here, try this." Jack handed him a small stick.

Erec dipped the stick into the formula and put it in the hatchling's mouth, but the baby turned his head away. "C'mon, little guy. This is good for you." The dragon would not let the stick anywhere near its mouth. Instead it kept trying to nibble on Erec's fingers. "Ouch, that hurts." Erec picked up a stone and tried to dribble formula from it onto the hatchling's tongue. The dragon would have nothing to do with the stone.

Bethany laughed. "It wants your finger, Erec."

"Oh, all right." Erec dipped his finger into the formula and put it in the hatchling's mouth. The dragon sucked happily. "Ow!" He whisked his finger away. "That stung." He tried it again. This time he filled his palm with the liquid and let it run down his finger into the dragon's open mouth. He tried to keep his fingertip away, but the dragon proved very good at reaching out and nipping him. Soon the liquid itself began to sting his sore finger. When he put the dragon down, it raced perkily around the nest. "Well, it did him some good."

They looked around at the other dragons. They lay helpless, mouths open and waiting.

"I'll feed this one some of the biting beetles." Bethany reached into the jar and jerked her hand out. "Ouch! These things really do bite, hard." She shut the jar and put it down, unsure what to do.

"I'll try it." Erec took a beetle out of the jar and fed it to a dragon lying near him. The pinching beetle hurt, but he blocked the pain from his mind. These were the last dragon babies left, since all the rest of the dragon hatchlings in Otherness were mysteriously missing. He wasn't going to let a little soreness stop him from doing what he needed to do. "Jack, you have the gift of talking to animals. Can you tell what these guys are saying?"

Jack took the jar of formula and sat next to Erec. "I tried talking to them, but they're too young. They just make crying noises." He put some of the formula onto a finger and put it in one of the dragon's mouths, then yanked it out. "Ow, man. How do you do it, Erec? That really hurt."

Erec shrugged. "I don't have a choice, I guess." He popped a few biting beetles into the waiting mouths of the hatchlings, trying to ignore his red, swelling fingertips. *Breathe steady. Mind over matter,* he told himself. "I'll take care of it, guys. My fingers are shot already."

Jack winced as Erec took the jar from him. "Look at your fingers."

"I'd rather not."

For twenty minutes, Erec took turns using different fingers of both hands until all the dragons had swallowed a few handfuls of the liquid. They tumbled happily around the nest.

"Wait a minute." Bethany bent over a rock. "Another baby is trapped in here. I think this is the one that Damon threw. It looks hurt."

Erec peered into the crack. A little dragon was twisted under an iron filing. Its neck was bent, maybe broken, and Erec could see that it was breathing very slowly. "This thing's not going to make it. Unless . . ." He slowly straightened its body under the rock, cupping it in his hand, and it began to breathe easier. Its neck was still pinned down, though. "As long as I hold its back up like this, it's okay. Maybe if I give it some of the liquid, it'll get stronger and I can set it down again." He dipped a hand into the mixture, ignoring the searing agony racing through him. The dragon bit weakly at his finger, sucking the formula slowly. Erec steadied his breath, clenching his teeth against the pain. He could take it. It wouldn't be much longer. He would find some medicine to make his fingers heal. But he wouldn't let this little guy die.

A shadow appeared overhead in the sky, slowly growing larger. Ignoring it, Erec stuck his hand back into the liquid, squeezing his eyes shut because of the sting. He carefully held the baby and cupped his hand to its mouth. "Aaagh," he cried as fiery pain filled him.

Suddenly everything around him became a green whirlwind. Thick white ropes hung in the air like netting. Erec reached to touch them, but he could feel nothing. The nest, the dragons . . . everything glowed a bright green. And he was spinning now, dizzy. It was a cloudy thought. But where was the command? His stomach clenched.

The shadow above him began to take on a shape. It grew larger, more birdlike until . . .

It was a dragon. The same dragon he had envisioned when he was walking through the woods with Bethany. Teeth bared, its talons stabbed toward him. It had a wild look in its eyes. It was out for the kill.

"Run!" Erec shouted. Bethany screamed as she saw it too. She and Jack stumbled backward out of the nest. The dragon didn't notice them though. It focused on Erec as if he was attacking the hatchlings.

Erec felt strong, energized in the green vortex, like he could do anything. Yet what was he supposed to do? There was no command, no order from his cloudy thought. And even though he felt strong, he knew he was no match for the dragon. He looked down at the helpless creature in his palm, then up at the beast whizzing toward him in the sky. His body shook, and he wanted to drop the baby dragon and run. But he couldn't. If he let it go, its neck would twist again, and it would die. He looked up again, desperate.

The dragon in the sky was screeching at him. Fire blazed from its mouth. It must have been one of the parents, attacking to protect its babies. And Erec was lost in a cloudy thought, but for the first time there were no instructions. Just like in his premonition. There was nothing he could do. It was over.

He kneeled in the nest and looked up, pleading with the angry dragon to understand. The baby licked his hand harder and he did not even feel the sting.

The massive creature soared down fast, fury in its eyes. Erec stared up at it, mesmerized. Then, for some reason, he knew who it was. He knew this was the mother dragon, Patchouli. She was flying to protect her hatchlings from an intruder—him. She was terrified by the human in her nest. Dragons were worth a fortune to humans. Their scales, blood, bones, and claws were priceless, used for magic and medicine. She wanted to kill this intruder before it was too late.

Erec barely realized he was reading Patchouli's thoughts. He was terrified. His life would be over in seconds.

Patchouli dove at him, staring with wide eyes. His mind blanked as her talons reached for him, slicing the air, touching his shirt.

At the last moment she swerved away and lit on the edge of her nest, looking at him hard. Erec could sense her thoughts through his foggy haze. She realized he was helping her children, could see right into his thoughts.

He knew they were reading each other's minds because his dragon eye was looking at her dragon eyes.

His cloudy thought, his dragon eye, had saved him.

Suddenly the green light and white ropes faded away. His dragon eye rolled back to reveal his normal one.

Patchouli was a little smaller than Aoquesth, and her scales were redder. Her jointed black wings stretched and closed over her back, and her red spines shone in the sunlight. She was beautiful.

"Thank you for saving my babies, Erec. I was caught in a trap for days, and I would not have made it back in time. Dragon babies have to hatch right when they're ready. They would have died if you hadn't fed them."

He smiled, still too shaken to speak. His hand that held the injured dragon shook.

Patchouli came close and nuzzled the little being in his hand.

"He would never have lived without your care. I'm going to name him Erec after you. Not a normal dragon name but very fitting, I think."

Little Erec was sucking away on his finger. As he relaxed, the pain returned and he winced, pulling his finger away.

"Set him down. I can take care of him now." With her long talons, Patchouli lifted the iron from around its neck and scooped her baby up. "Give me a moment with him, then I'd like to talk to you."

Bethany and Jack crept back around the corner and sat with Erec on the side of the broad nest while Patchouli tended to her child. Erec found that as his breathing steadied the pain in his fingers grew almost unbearable. He lifted his hands to examine them. They were purple and swollen, lined with bites and jagged lacerations.

Bethany leaned away. "I can't look at them." As her eyes met his, she noticed something strange. She lifted it off the top of Erec's shirt. "What's this? I don't remember you wearing it before."

Around his neck hung a thick chain with a large round medallion etched into twelve segments. One of the pie-shaped segments glowed a deep red, while the other eleven were gold like the chain. He shook his head. "I don't know where that came from."

In the next moment, the acute pain returned, and he squeezed his eyes shut. "I have to go to the royal hospital, quick. My fingers are killing me."

Patchouli crossed the nest toward Erec. Her other six children raced excitedly around her. "You have used your own blood to feed my children. They will always be indebted to you. I cannot thank you enough." Steam gushed from her nostrils. "I can see you are in pain. Let me help you." She poked a claw through her thick scales. When she drew it out, a drop of purple blood was on the tip. "Excuse me for not having a cup to offer you. Would you sip this off my claw? It will help."

THE MONSTERS OF OTHERNESS

Erec took Patchouli's large claw in his hand. Any doubt about drinking the dragon blood was washed away by his desire to stop the intense pain he was feeling. He put his mouth on the claw tip, careful not to let it poke him. The liquid tasted of metal and hot peppers as it dissolved on his tongue. Instantly, his pain vanished even though his hands still looked terrible. He felt alert and stronger than he ever had.

Patchouli was watching his face. "That is Aoquesth's eye you have, isn't it? So you are Erec Rex. It's a good thing I saw your dragon eye. It let me read into you, see who you were and what you were doing. I hate to think what I would have done otherwise. I was so afraid for my children. With all of the other dragon hatchlings missing, I have been so worried that something would happen to these little ones. Now that I'm back I'm not letting them out of my sight."

Erec shook, thinking about what almost happened. "I could read your thoughts too."

"Dragon eyes let you do that with other dragons."

"I can see things so clearly through Aoquesth's eye. But it makes everything green. And I see ropy stuff all around."

"That's the Substance, Erec. Dragons can see it everywhere."

Erec paused, shocked. He never had thought what the thick netting was. So this was the stuff that made everyone feel so sad in Alypium. He tried to remember if he could see it when he had the cloudy thought at home. "I think in Upper Earth the Substance looked different. More like cobwebs . . . thinner."

Patchouli nodded. "It is thinner there. The Substance from Upper Earth is now mostly in the Kingdoms of the Keepers."

The Substance that carried the magic . . . Erec guessed that made sense.

"Erec, I want to give you something to thank you."

Erec held up the medal on his chest. "Is this from you?"

"Oh, no. Don't you know? That is the Amulet of Virtues. You got it for completing your first quest to become king."

Erec eyed it more carefully. A symbol glowed in the red segment of the pendant. "What does this mean?"

"It's in an ancient language. That word means 'self-sacrifice.' That is what you showed in this quest. Each segment of the amulet will fill in when you complete a quest." With a talon she pointed. "To earn them, you must prove you have the twelve virtues befitting a ruler. I'd say you showed your self-sacrifice well today."

Erec stared down at the Amulet of Virtues. So he had succeeded in the first quest after all. Balor thought he had won, and the Harpies from the Bureau of Bureaucrats likely did too. He wondered if Balor's team had gotten amulets. If not, what would they all think when they found out?

That led to a new thought. Maybe the people of Alypium would accept him now. He knew Bethany was right, he shouldn't care about pleasing people who didn't really know him. He just couldn't seem to help it.

Steam spouted from the dragon's nostrils. "Don't take the amulet off, Erec," she warned. "It will protect you more with each quest you complete."

"But . . . did I win this quest because I fed your hatchlings? I didn't have to crack open all of your eggs like I was told?"

"Were you told to crack open *all* my eggs? I believe you succeeded because you did what you were meant to do. The Fates were surely aware of exactly what would happen here today." She sighed and smoke streamed from her nostrils. "I have something for you. It is a treasure I have kept for centuries, but I think you may have more use for it than I do. Come into my cave. I had to move my nest out here to keep my eggs warm, but if you follow me . . ."

Erec followed the beautiful creature into a cavern lit by an unseen source. Gold bricks paved the floors, and huge piles of gems surrounded tables of mysterious artifacts, gilded swords, magical talismans, and ornately carved marble statues. Patchouli carefully lifted a small scroll from behind a glittering screen with her claws and set it before Erec.

"I want to give this to you. It is called the Archives of Alithea. It's a magical scroll that has been passed down from a realm that vanished thousands of years ago. The society that created it valued truth above all else. So this is a scroll of truth. It may be used only one more time, and I am sure you will know when that time is right. When you open it, you will see the full truth, and show the full truth to anyone within sight of you."

"The truth about anything?" Erec immediately started thinking of unanswered questions about himself he wanted to know.

"Anything you ask it. And you may use it for selfish reasons, but from what I know of you, you'll save it for something really important." Her eyes twinkled. "This was created by strong magic, and only those that possess a magic touch can use it. Most humans could not make it work—but you can now."

"Why me?"

"When you fed my hatchlings, some of their essence entered into your fingers, just as you gave them some of your essence. I know it hurt, and you did it to save them, but it also left you with a special touch. You may notice that something happens to your fingers when you get your next vision through your dragon eye."

Erec regarded his swollen fingers in a new light. "How do I ask it to show a certain truth?"

The dragon handed the scroll to him. "The scroll is sentient. It knows what is happening around it, what you are thinking. Just untie it and pull it open, and it will answer what needs to be answered. This use will be its last, though. It has been employed by many people for many reasons, some good and some bad. But it's old and worn now. Once you are done with it, it will no longer be of value."

"Thank you very much." Erec put the scroll into his pocket.

"There is something you should know. Not that it should be a problem . . . well, not a big problem, anyway."

Erec looked up at her.

"When you are carrying the scroll, while it is on your person, it will compel you to tell the truth."

Erec could not see the harm in that . . . yet.

CHAPTER NINE
A Monstrous Mob

T HEY HAD NO sooner left the nest when Erec realized he was starving. "How are we going to get back?" They walked down a sloping path, hoping it led somewhere.

Jack shrugged and looked around. "Maybe King Piter will come get us."

Bethany whispered, "Do you think Patchouli could fly us back to Alypium? I'm hungry."

"I don't know," Jack said, glancing back. "She probably doesn't want to leave her hatchlings now." He gazed down from the top of the high cliff where they were stranded. "This is crazy."

"Crazy?" a voice asked. "Well, it's all how you look at things. Give me an insane world and I'll give you a happy Hermit."

Erec snapped around to see a thin brown face poking between two boulders. It was the strange dark-skinned man who had popped out of the bush. "What are you doing here?"

The man giggled. "I'm charged with watching you, so get used to me following your sorry backside." He exploded in a fit of laughter, the only one who appreciated his odd joke. "Oh, the crafty Erec Rex, the wily Erec Rex, the one who will destroy our world as we know it." Although what the Hermit was saying was far from complimentary, he was grinning widely.

Bethany whispered, "Maybe he says the opposite of what he means."

The Hermit laughed with glee. "Oh, the clever Bethany Cleary, the sneaky Bethany Cleary, the one who would save our world to destroy it."

She raised her eyebrows. "Ohh*kay*. I think we better get back before you shake a screw loose."

Giggling, the Hermit gave a sharp nod, and the four of them were transported to the castle grounds.

"Toodle-loo." The Hermit waved. In another flash he had disappeared.

"Strange guy." Erec lifted the Amulet of Virtues that hung around his neck. "I wonder what would happen if I won all of the twelve quests—or did them right, anyway—and nobody ever found the other two people who were supposed to be the 'rightful rulers'? Maybe then I could pick who I wanted to rule with me." He thought a moment. "I'd pick you two, I'm sure."

"Don't tell Oscar you said that." Jack glanced over his shoulder. "After you left, he was pouting that you didn't care about him. I told him you said he could help with another quest. Oh, and Rosco has been saying he'll never get to do a quest with you. You will let him . . . won't you?"

"Sure I will. I could only take two."

"Poor Oscar." Bethany shook her head.

They went into the castle kitchens, and one of the staff made them a tray of sandwiches and cookies, with bowls of cloud gruel and fresh berries. She stared at Erec's fingers which had now turned a cherry red with little white boils.

"I have to go into Alypium and look for Danny and Sammy," Erec said between handfuls of chocolate-covered honey drops. "I saw with King Piter's Seeing Eyeglasses that they were in a cloud cream shop, and I need to find it. Maybe someone there knows where they went."

"At least they seemed okay," Bethany said.

"They seemed more then okay. They were happy," Erec said, puzzled. "I don't get it. If they're not being forced to stay there, why don't they come home? And if they are, why would kidnappers give them candy and sundaes and take them Rollerblading? They were joking about how fat they were getting from all the treats."

"Why don't you see what they are doing now?" Jack suggested.

"That's a good idea." Erec took King Piter's glasses from his pocket, sliding them out past the Archives of Alithea. He focused his mind on his brother and sister and put the glasses on. This time, Danny and Sammy were clearly visible. They were goofing around on a beach, eating cakes and cookies. Why didn't they run away, or at least call? Erec wondered. They must know June would be worried sick. Erec resisted the urge to shout out to them. He wanted to tell them to quit what they were doing, to come home. But one false move and he might lose his connection with them for good. No, he would play it safe for now.

He took the glasses off. "They're on a beach, of all places. I have no idea where."

Bethany finished her nectar drink. "I think you should still start with the cloud cream shop. Maybe a little detective work will give you the answer. If you want, I'll go with you, and we can walk Wolfboy and Cutie Pie."

Erec smiled at her. "Sure, I'd love to have a pretty girl go with me to the store."

Bethany blushed and raised her eyebrows at him. Erec could not believe he had said that. What had come over him? He could not have felt more embarrassed and was sure his face was as red as hers. "Uh, sorry. Don't know why I said that."

The Archives of Alithea, which made sure he would tell the truth, tingled in his pocket.

They ran into Oscar near Paisley Park by the castle grounds. "Oh, there you guys are." He pointed at Erec. "Your morning tutor, Miss Ennui, was upset you missed your class with her. I heard she said that you'd forfeit your chance at the crown if you missed any more."

Erec could not believe his ears. "But I had to do the quest today."

Oscar shrugged. "Wasn't the quest at one o'clock? I don't think that gets you out of your morning work."

Pimster Peebles appeared, waving wildly from a distance, and waddled toward Erec. "Oh, hello, Ewec Wex. I hope you don't feel too bad that you lost. What's this?" He lifted the amulet off Erec's chest. "Hmmm. Well, well." Peebles was fascinated. "The Amuwet. That's intewesting." He looked at Erec with new respect. "Would you like to spend a little time going over the books with me since we missed our session today?"

"Not now, thanks. I have something to do in Alypium."

"Can I help?"

In truth, Erec very much wanted help. But the one who should have been helping, King Piter, was off on some trip. "My brother and sister were kidnapped. I need to look for them."

Mr. Peebles wrung his hands. "Not Danny and Sammy. They seemed so sweet."

Erec cocked an eyebrow. "Sweet? Those two were not Danny and Sammy. They were imposters."

Mr. Peebles looked shocked. "Spies? No. Well, by all means you look for them. I fully allow you to go into Alypium during your afternoons instead of studying with me. And while you're out," his voice lowered to a whisper, "you may want to ask awound about the Memory Mogul. You might learn something intewesting. But if you do, let's keep it a little secwet. Understand that I am going against King Piter's wishes by mentioning this."

"What do you mean?"

Mr. Peebles squirmed. "Let's just say I don't agwee with the king tweating you like a baby. I know he just wants to protect you, but you have a right to know." He headed back to the castle.

That left Erec with a big question. What did Peebles think he had a right to know?

The framed poster of the clown holding an umbrella was unmistakable. Cloud Nine Flavors, the cloud cream shop that the twins had been in, was smack in the middle of Alypium.

A soda jerk stood behind the counter, hands on his hips. "Can I help youse?"

Erec asked, "Did you work here last night?"

The man was annoyed. "Yes, I own the joint. I'm here all the time. You want something?"

"I just wondered if my brother and sister might've been here. We were supposed to meet, and I missed them."

"Well, that great description and a dime will get you a chocolate peanut. 'Two kids—'"

"They might have been invisible," Erec added.

"Oh, that's rich. Then I wouldn't have seen them, would I?"

He had a point. "Did any adults order two cloud cream sundaes and not eat them themselves?"

The man stared as if Erec took him for an idiot. "My shop was closed last night. There was only one adult here, and I don't question him. He does what he wants."

Erec's heart began to race. Only one adult was in the shop when the twins were here. "Who was it?"

The soda jerk shrugged. "Rosco Kroc."

On the slow walk back to the castle, Erec's mind raced. Rosco, Oscar's tutor, must have been the kidnapper. "We better warn Oscar," he said. "He might be next."

Bethany nodded. "I thought Rosco seemed strange, but I never expected this."

They kept walking until someone popped off a sidewalk bench and came toward them. "Hey," the man said, "you're the one who set up the scepter and the Lia Fail during the coronation ceremony this summer." He made an ugly face. "We won't be ruled by a *phony*, do you hear?" His friends nearby nodded and made noises of agreement. Erec ignored them and walked on, but a crowd started to gather around them.

"Go home, phony. Leave us alone. You can't push us around . . . phony . . . phony . . ." The crowd around him shouted and pointed fingers at him like a single creature with many heads.

Erec wanted to get out of there. They didn't know what they were talking about. He was trying to help them, save them. He took a deep breath and tried to remember what Bethany had told him. It didn't matter what these people thought. If they weren't going to bother to find out the truth about him, then who cared? He glanced over at Bethany, filled with shame that she should see this. She marched straight forward, face red, with her hand on Erec's shoulder.

Three young men stepped right in front of Erec, blocking him so he couldn't pass. One of them screamed in his face, "You disgust me. All you care about is yourself and your little girlfriend here. You want power so bad you don't care who you step on. Why don't you let Balor, Damon, and Rock do their quests in peace?"

Erec felt his face get hot and his hands close into fists. "Balor would give the scepters to Baskania, and they would make you all slaves or worse. I'm trying to stop them."

The man laughed. "Did you hear that?" He looked around at his friends. "This guy is doing us a favor. Mean old Balor and Baskania are trying to hurt us." He gave Erec a hard shove. "Do you think we are idiots?"

"Yeah!" the crowd shouted, pressing closer like an angry beast, like a monstrous mob. Someone stuck a foot out and tripped Erec.

When he stood back up, Bethany whispered to him, "Get out of here. Run." In one quick motion, she ducked under someone's arm and disappeared.

Erec burst through the crowd, heart racing, and ran down the street. Several people trailed after him, shouting names, but most of the crowd stayed behind. Everywhere people were sneering at him. Now that people had seen him going to the Labor Society to draw his first quest, they knew what he looked like. He was totally humiliated. Why didn't anybody believe him? Who was behind these terrible rumors?

Erec turned into a candy shop that had its doors propped open and watched to see if anyone was still following.

"Yes, I'll take those, too."

He spun around. Balthazar Ugry was standing in front of the counter.

Erec backed into a corner, bumping his sore fingers. He hid behind a rack of spun-sugar bird's nests, cherub puffs, and divinity. He wished he could hear what Ugry was saying. After a moment, Ugry paid the clerk and walked toward the door, stuffing a bag of candy in his pocket.

Was Ugry the one feeding the twins candy? Erec put on King Piter's glasses. There were the twins, in full sight, eating cloudsicles. Standing right next to them was Rosco Kroc.

Erec had to find Rosco now. He stuffed the glasses into his pocket and asked the clerk, "Did that man, Balthazar Ugry, say anything about twins to you?"

The man's eyes narrowed. "That man happens to be King Piter's AdviSeer. You think I'm going to repeat what he said to some kid?"

Erec wondered if it would help if he told the clerk he was the twins' brother. Probably not. At least this guy didn't recognize him. "What kind of candy did he get?"

The storekeeper grinned, seeing the chance for a sale. "Chocolate rain from Cinnalim, in Otherness. Want some?"

"Sure." Erec paid him and took a brown paper bag full of small chocolate pieces.

"Be careful," the man said. "Sometimes a few bugs get in with the rain." A new, meaner expression crossed his face. "Hey, aren't you that kid who's been messing with Alypium, trying to rule everybody?"

Erec darted out of the shop before the man could say any more.

CHAPTER TEN

The Memory Mogul

EREC HAD NO idea where to find Rosco Kroc, but he was sure that King Piter or somebody at the castle could tell him. He ran onto the castle grounds between some hedges. Bethany was resting on a stone bench, her head in her hands. He took a seat next to her. "Are you okay?"

She nodded. "Don't let them get to you, Erec. People like that are stupid. They let themselves get sucked up in a crowd's madness and stop thinking on their own." She frowned at what had just happened. "Mobs like that are really dangerous. They can do anything. Things that people would never do on their own. I really hope you don't care about what people like that think."

But Erec did care, even though he wasn't sure why. He said, discouraged, "I want them all to look up to me, respect me. I want girls to line up for my autograph. Pretty girls." He listened to his own words in horror. What was he saying? He sounded like an idiot. Why was he . . . ? He felt a tingling in his pocket. The Archives of Alithea. Patchouli had said they would make him tell the truth. Great.

Bethany was not happy. "So that's what this is all about for you? I thought you were in this to help people. But if you just want girls . . ." She stopped short. "Maybe that crowd was right about you."

Erec wearily closed his eyes. "No, Bethany. You're the only girl I really care about." He grinded his teeth. This was ridiculous. He was making it sound like he loved her, and that was not what he was thinking. Could this get worse? He snuck a peek at Bethany. She was staring into the distance with a slight smile. Well, at least she felt better. Changing the subject, he said, "It's getting late. Tomorrow I'll go find Rosco. I think I'm going to get some sleep." And he would definitely take the Archives of Alithea out of his pocket and stash them in his room before he made a complete and utter fool of himself.

Miss Ennui glared coldly at Erec the next morning. "Do you know what will happen to you if you miss our classes? You will be kicked out of the castle and sent home. If you did not truly want to be king, then you should not have bothered coming here. Kings are principled people, not lazy oafs. There is no excuse for missing yesterday."

Actually, he had a pretty good excuse. "I'm sorry. I ended up in Nemea early for my first quest. Now my brother and sister are missing. I know where they are and I have to find them. Can I please go early today?"

"I am sure the authorities can handle the situation better than a thirteen-year-old boy."

Erec blinked. "Twelve." He sank into his chair, realizing he was stuck.

Three hours dragged by as Miss Ennui droned on about the history of the Middle Ages. His fingers throbbed a little, but they seemed to be getting better. She had finally reached a subject that interested Erec, the Black Death of 1347, when she announced, "Our time is up."

At noon, he set off for Paisley Park. Mr. Peebles ran up to Erec and pumped his hand up and down. His toupee was on today, but upside down with the hair part against his head. "Congwatulations, boy. Congwatulations. You're still in the quests. When Pwesident Inkle and the Committee for Committee Oversight found out that Balor and Damon Stain and Rock Ward had won the egg-opening quest, they tried to pass a law so that you would be out for good. But Al's Well doesn't seem to be open to anybody but you." He pointed at the chain around Erec's neck. "And nobody else has gotten one of those."

Erec's hand went to his Amulet of Virtues. He was relieved that he could do the next quest, but also worried about it.

"I have to go into Alypium to find Rosco Kroc," Erec explained, "so I can't meet with you now."

Mr. Peebles wrung his hands. "Oh, you won't find him there today. He had to go back to Aorth, and he took his pupil with him. They're coming back early this evening, I believe."

"Do you know where he lives? He kidnapped Danny and Sammy."

Mr. Peebles laughed at that notion. "Now, that's widiculous. Wosco is on our side. I'm sure he'll do everything he can to help you. I don't know where he lives, but I'm sure your fwiend Oscar could tell you tonight."

Erec clenched his fists. He hated the idea of waiting until tonight. In the distance he saw Bethany lifting rocks with her remote control and sending them flying into a pond. When would he learn to use his remote control?

Right as he was about to ask, Mr. Peebles winked. "Are you going to outline books today or are you going to find the Memory Mogul?"

Erec sure didn't want to outline books. What he really wanted was to learn about his remote control and use it tonight on Rosco. He pulled it out and pointed it at a stone, pushing a button. Nothing happened.

"Now, now. Put that away," Mr. Peebles tutted. "We haven't even started learning about that yet."

Erec fired back, "But that's what I want to learn."

He walked away, thinking he'd seek out the Memory Mogul. On his way, he stopped near Bethany and her tutor. At least he had left the Archives of Alithea in a drawer in his room so he wouldn't have to worry about making a fool of himself.

"Rosco is in Aorth with Oscar today," he reported to her. "I'm going to try and find him tonight."

He watched Bethany try to lift a stone bench with her remote control. It moved about an inch before falling down. She saw how interested he was. "What's wrong?" she asked.

Erec shrugged. "I just want to be able use my remote control. I don't know a thing about it."

Bethany's tutor Clarus smiled. "It's easy. Just say 'aeiro,' point your remote at a rock, and press the big green button."

Erec tried that, but his rock did not budge. "How long does it take before I can do it?"

Bethany looked at him funny. "It worked the first time for me. Remote controls make magic easy. Doing it *without* the remote control is hard."

Clarus said patiently, "It's not easy for everyone. People have different ability levels, you know."

"You mean, I might never be able to do magic?" Erec felt a chill. He remembered that Oscar could not use a remote control at first. Then again, he was learning much better now with Rosco. The name made Erec clench his teeth.

It was not easy finding the Memory Mogul's shop. Most of the people Erec asked simply glared at him and turned up their noses. Finally a blind woman told him the store was near the edge of town, close to Medea's magic shop.

Inside the store, a counter stretched across the entire room. Behind it were racks of shelves covered with tiny packets. A small, spindly man hunched over the counter. His wild white hair and beard projected from all angles of his face, making him look like a dandelion gone to seed. He seemed to be in a daze.

The man remained still as Erec walked up to him. Erec cleared his throat, but the man seemed to take no notice. "Excuse me."

The man jumped. "Oh! How's that for sneaking up on an old man? You should be ashamed of yourself, boy. Scaring me like that." His wispy hair and beard waved around in the air as he spoke. It made him look so comical that Erec had to bite his lip to keep from laughing. "Now," the man said, "what were you saying, sonny? You have a memory to get rid of?"

Erec pointed at the shelves behind the man. "What do you sell here?"

"You don't know?" The man looked indignant. "Memory chips, of course. Splices. I cut, I take out, I add in. Anything can be altered." He coughed. "What was the question?"

"You were telling me about the memory chips."

"Of course. Memory chips. I've got all types." He waved a hand across the huge racks. "I've got bits of memories from all over the known earth and beyond. Want a bit of African jungle safari? Wild nights in the ogre bars? Dungeons? I've got plenty of dungeons," he said happily. "Of course there's no guarantee that the memory will be fully pleasant. But what fun would it be if it was all nice and safe, right? So what would you like, boy?"

"I'm not sure I want to buy any memories right now."

"So you're here to get rid of one? No problem. Would you like a replacement, or do you want to leave an empty gap where it was?"

Erec had to stop to consider. Why did Mr. Peebles suggest he come here? He said he might find out something about himself.

"Can I help you?" The man turned to him with a smile, white hair wagging around his face. He seemed to have forgotten their entire conversation.

"Do you happen to have any memories in the name of Erec Rex?"

The man chortled. "Oh, ho, ho! Erec Rex, eh? Even I remember the day I got the memory of Erec Rex. And I do admit my memory isn't exactly what it once was." He mused in silence a moment, then looked at Erec. "Can I help you?"

"I'd like the memory of Erec Rex. Tell me about it."

"You and everyone else, kid. I still remember the day his mother brought him here." His eyes sharpened, gained focus as if he could see her still. "He was real little, three, I think. And he was in trouble, hiding for some reason. He was here with another kid, and his mother had just changed their looks. They both got a chunk of their memories taken out that day. I talked his mother into giving Erec a replacement memory to take its place. It's usually easier on a kid to have some past to remember, I told her. It also doubled the price. And I happened to have a memory I had just gotten from a girl about his age. It was a short one, but who cared? It was something, right?"

The Memory Mogul's eyes danced as he relived old times. "His mom was real worried his replacement memory might be a bad one, but I told her it would be fine. The girl had looked nice enough. How bad could it have been, right? But then he started crying as soon as he got the memory, darn kid. His mom wanted me to erase it, but I couldn't do it for a week—too dangerous—so she had to leave it in." He shrugged. "Aw, don't worry about the kid. It was no big deal. His new memory was so short and hazy, and at that age it would only really come out in his dreams. The other kid there that day never got a memory replacement," he recalled. "The mom was too upset."

Erec gripped the counter, mind spinning. He couldn't believe his ears. He had known his mother changed his looks, but now this. And what was the memory replacement he got? Some memory discarded from a girl? What could it be? He squeezed his eyes shut. Something that would only come out in his dreams.

In the next moment he froze. His dreams? He remembered the nightmare he always had about his father. It was his only memory he had of his father. But what if—Erec felt sick—what if it wasn't really his own memory? So that wasn't his father, then? It was someone else's father?

Erec's breath became heavy and he felt faint. He looked around the shop, but there were no chairs. He wondered if he should be glad that his memory of his terrible father wasn't his. He hated the memory, hated the man. But he had grown up with that memory nonetheless. It was all he knew.

The man tapped the counter, white wispy hair waving. "Can I help you, sonny?"

Erec stared at him. "I'd like to buy the memory of Erec Rex. Do you still have it?"

The man smiled. "Ah, Erec Rex. I still remember the day his mother came in the shop—"

Erec interrupted. "Do you still have it?"

"Oh, goodness no. I sold it the next day to a young man his age who had another memory problem to get rid of. But I wish I kept it, I'll tell you. You and everybody else that's been in here want it. I could've gotten a good price on that one, yes sir. If I'd known how popular it would be, I'd have checked it out myself, too. It's hard to resist trying out some of the memories I get in here, especially the more exciting ones. Of course, they can mess with your own memory if you're not careful. Not that I would ever let that happen to me."

Erec thanked the man, who settled back into a glassy-eyed stare. He didn't seem to notice when Erec left the shop.

Before dinner Erec found Bethany in her suite and told her what had happened at the Memory Mogul's shop. She turned pale at the news. "I can't believe it. How creepy. Whose memory do you have?"

"Who knows? The awful thing is, it's not mine. Not that I want that memory to be true, but my whole life has been based on it." He kicked the wall in frustration. "I don't understand why my mother never told me this before. I've been upset for years about that stupid guy deserting me, whoever he was. Every time I complained about him she would just say, 'Your father loves you,' which I thought was a huge lie. Now I don't know what to think. I guess maybe my father did love me. But what happened to *him* then? Where is he?

She said he's still alive." Erec thought of his dragon eye. "I guess this fits with what Aoquesth told me about my father being so great. He's not the guy I was remembering."

Bethany rubbed her chin. "I guess it would have been hard for your mother to tell you your memory was fake unless she told you she had a chunk of your real memory chopped out. And she did that so you wouldn't remember who you were, I guess. Like she changed your looks to hide you."

"That's supposed to make me feel better?" Erec could feel anger spread from his stomach through his whole body. "Just like she made all my old friends forget about me—remember that?" He closed his eyes. "I can't take this anymore. Can you even imagine what it's like to grow up thinking you know who you are, then find out you're someone altogether different?"

Bethany didn't have to answer the question. Of course, he thought, she knew exactly what that was like. Only she was glad to be a different person than she thought. She'd have to be happier now than stuck with Earl Evirly.

Maybe he should feel relieved. If he could ever get used to it. And yet there was one more problem.

"You know the difference between you and me, Bethany? You know now exactly who you are. Your parents were Ruth and Tre Cleary. You have a brother, Pi, on the Alypium Sky springball team. Your mother was the king's AdviSeer, and you have a distant relative, Bea Cleary, who was some great prophetess." He pointed both index fingers at his chest. "What do I know about myself? I know that my mother and King Piter are hiding my history from me. My memory was erased when I was young, and now it's gone. I'll never get it back. My father and my birth mother are alive, and I have no idea who they are. I'm supposed to be destined to be the king here, but I don't know why . . ." He trailed off, afraid if he said more his voice would start to shake.

They walked into the royal dining hall in the west wing, where Jack and Oscar had already sat down to eat. Jack was munching wheat berry salad and cloud loaf. Oscar seemed to be waiting for Jam Crinklecut to bring in the stacks of cheeseburgers and pizza.

"Oscar!" Erec was glad to think of something else. He was ready to rescue the twins. "Your tutor kidnapped my brother and sister. We need to find him, tonight. I thought maybe he captured you too."

Oscar reddened slightly. "You're wrong, Erec. Rosco would never hurt anyone. He's the best teacher in the world. He's already teaching me how to do magic without a remote."

Erec felt a twinge of jealousy. "I don't care what he's teaching you. He's a criminal. Do you know where he lives?"

Oscar nodded. "He lives in Aorth, but I know where he's staying in Alypium." He shook his head in wonderment. "A criminal? No, Erec. But Rosco is brilliant. He *said* you'd come with me to his house one night soon."

Erec didn't think it was so brilliant for Rosco to realize that Erec would be tracking down his stolen siblings. "Will you take me there?"

"Sure." Oscar shrugged. "But I've been with him, and I know he doesn't have the twins."

"He has them, Oscar. He must have hidden them from you." Erec dropped his head into his hands. "This has been quite a day."

Erec and Oscar walked through the castle grounds. Erec was glad the sun had begun to set so that he would not be mobbed again by Alypians who thought he was a con artist. He was wearing the magical Sneakers his mother had helped him find the first time he was in Alypium, making his steps smooth and silent.

A swoosh of black swept by the street in front of them. AdviSeer

Balthazar Ugry was gliding toward them. When he saw Erec, his eyes narrowed. Erec felt chilled inside, but he made himself stare back. It felt like he was looking into the face of death. Ugry flipped up the hood of his black cape, becoming invisible as he sped by. Erec saw he had dropped something, so he reached to pick it up.

It was an empty candy wrapper.

Erec stared at the wrapper, then stuffed in his pocket. He didn't know why, but he had the feeling that Ugry wasn't eating the candy himself. In fact, the candy made him think about his brother and sister.

But there was no time to worry about him now. He knew exactly where Danny and Sammy were, and he was going there to free them.

Rosco Kroc was renting a small house on the Avenue Rue. The door was locked, but a window was cracked open. "Stay here, Oscar. If I call for help, pop through the window with your remote control out. It'll help if he's surprised."

Oscar laughed. "Fine, but Rosco's not doing anything wrong. Don't forget to let me in when you find out for yourself."

Erec climbed through the open window. He stepped onto the kitchen counter, then slunk onto the floor. There was no noise in the house. Suddenly, he realized that Rosco might not even be home. His Sneakers let him walk soundlessly through the house. He peered around corners until he spotted Rosco reading papers at a desk facing away from him.

Erec slipped back into the kitchen and found a rope plant hanger. He quietly pulled the plant out, lifted it from the ceiling hook, then entered the study behind Rosco without a sound. In a flash, Erec dropped the woven rope circle around Rosco's chest and yanked back, hard.

Rosco's mouth flew open, and he struggled to his feet, kicking the chair behind him against Erec. Erec did not let go. He yanked the rope harder, struggling against Rosco's weight until Rosco tripped to the floor and fell on his back, eyes seething with hate.

Erec put a foot on Rosco's face, wondering what to do next. He grabbed the chair and set it on Rosco's chest. Maybe he could pin him down and make him talk.

That didn't work so well. Rosco shook off his surprise and pointed a finger at Erec. Erec flew back and smacked the wall hard with his head. Rosco pushed the chair off and stood glaring down at Erec. The green scales on his head glistened.

"Here already? You're a regular bag of tricks, aren't you?" He pointed at Erec, walking closer, seething. Erec felt his chest being crushed inward as if Rosco's anger was filling him, pushing on his lungs. He could barely breathe.

"Thought you could overpower ole Rosca', did you? You always thought you were something special, huh?"

Erec's chest caved in completely. Everything looked gray. He could not breathe at all now, let alone call for help.

Rosco stepped closer, sneering. "I should kill you right now, do the world a favor, but . . ." He squinted, then stepped back. Erec fell to the floor and gasped for air, his chest suddenly freed. Rosco kicked him in the side, though not too hard. "That's for even thinking you could overpower me. Just because you fought a few destroyers doesn't mean you're a big man. Don't look so surprised. I know all about you."

Erec's head throbbed and he fought back the urge to throw up. "Where are Danny and Sammy?" he gasped.

Rosco started to walk away. "Persistent little devil, you are. Well, get up if you can and we'll go ahead and have ourselves a chat. I assume Oscar showed you how to get here? I'll call him in." He left the room.

Erec struggled to get up. He felt like an idiot coming into Rosco's house with a half-baked plan, thinking he could rescue the twins. He had been sure they would be sitting on Rosco's couch eating candy, and that when he gave the signal the three of them would run to safety.

Erec doubled over when he tried to sit. His stomach and his head ached. Only sheer anger gave him the will to stand, fighting off his dizziness and pain. He struggled out of the study, bent slightly at the waist.

Rosco and Oscar sat on the couch in the living room. Rosco gestured to a chair. "Glad you could make it. I was just explaining to Oscar that although you broke into my house intending to kill me, I will spare your life, out of the kindness of my heart." An angelic smile settled on his face, and he blinked a few times with wide eyes. "I am sure this was a big misunderstanding. You will pardon my behavior when you attacked me, of course."

Erec nodded. "Where are the twins?" His eyes danced furtively down an unexplored hallway.

This was one of the few times Erec had seen Rosco sitting. The man usually paced incessantly. Even now his leg bounced up and down as if sitting was a struggle. He smiled at Erec. "I think I am beginning to understand why you came here, attacked me, and are demanding to know where your brother and sister are." He stared at Erec expectantly as if waiting for him to answer.

"Isn't it obvious?" Erec stepped toward the hallway, but the movement was so painful he dropped into the chair.

"Yes, I'm afraid it is. Something happened to your siblings, I take it, so you have gotten paranoid, and who is better to blame than someone who looks different, who has scales on his face instead of skin. Green ones, no less."

Rosco made him feel a twinge of guilt, even though it wasn't true. "No, that's not it, Rosco. I saw with King Piter's Seeing Eyeglasses that you were with the twins today when they were eating cloudsicles. And you were with them in Cloud Nine Flavors the other night too. I asked the clerk."

Rosco raised his eyebrows. "First of all, why don't you tell me what happened to Danny and Sammy? Did they run away?"

Erec shifted painfully in his chair. "They're missing. And you kidnapped them."

"Hmmm. So we're back to blaming the freak." Rosco touched a purplish red spot on his neck, rubbed by the rope Erec had attacked him with. "Look, if there's one thing I can't stand, it's someone hurting kids. If Danny and Sammy were kidnapped, I will gladly help you find them. Any friends of Oscar's are friends of mine." He tapped his hand on the sofa cushion. An ice pack appeared and he put it on his neck. "Even if Oscar wasn't your friend, I'd still want to get my hands on any slimeball that steals kids."

"But I saw you with them yesterday," Erec said.

Rosco pursed his lips. "I did see them yesterday, come to think of it. I went into a snow cone shop and they had just gotten cloudsicles. I wish I had known they were missing, I could have done something. But they seemed fine at the time. Not like they were upset, from what I can remember."

"But what about the other day in Cloud Nine Flavors?"

Rosco tilted his head in thought. "I went there at night after it was closed for a snack. I'm friends with the owner, and he lets me in when I want. I didn't see them there, though. Maybe they had already left."

Oscar pulled out his remote. "We'll track them down, right, Rosco? Then we'll make whoever took them eat dirt."

Rosco grinned and mussed Oscar's hair. "That's what I like about you, young 'un. You've got spunk. You want to be the best, so you will be. Trust me, you will." Oscar and Rosco gazed at each other with unmasked affection, until Erec cleared his throat.

Rosco said, "I'm not going to rest until I find this joker, I promise you. It's going to take a lot of hard work and spunk." He tapped Oscar on the head, then looked at Erec. "But in the meantime, I'm keeping my eye on you, too. You can't be safe enough around here with everyone so worried about who will be the next king. And I'm sure you're going to keep poking your nose into the search for your brother and sister. I would too," he added, as Erec's back stiffened. "It's just, you may want to learn a little more magic first. Nothing against Peebles. He's a good man. But he moves a lot slower than me. If you'd like, I could teach you a few basics in your spare time."

Erec's jaw clenched. He wanted to believe Rosco. It would be so nice to finally learn some magic. But he needed to be sure. Erec pulled the spectacles that King Piter gave him from his pocket and put them on. He discovered Danny and Sammy asleep in double beds in a small room. They looked comfortable and snug, while here Erec was, beat up, searching for them. He wanted to wake them up and demand where they were, but that would be a mistake. If someone was listening, they would know Erec had the glasses, and they would make certain he couldn't use them anymore.

But who would be listening while they were asleep? Erec called softly, "Danny . . . Sammy." There was no answer. They slept without twitching a muscle.

Oscar looked around, surprised. "What was that?"

Rosco shook his head. "Nothing, Oscar. Just Erec checking for the twins."

Erec took the glasses off and flinched at his sore back.

"Sorry, is this better?" Rosco pointed at him, and in a moment the soreness faded away.

"Thanks." It seemed Rosco was right. The twins weren't here. And Rosco had offered to teach him some magic. Erec thought about that. To finally learn some magic! He was tired of being the only one in Alypium who couldn't point a remote control at something and pick it up. "I would like to learn from you." The other voice in his head suddenly came back, and he frowned. "Don't you have any idea who might have the twins?"

Rosco sighed. "No idea. Except . . ." The skin around his scales turned pale.

"What is it?"

Rosco's eyes grew wide. "I just remembered who I also saw at the snow cone shop yesterday. Didn't think much of it at the time. Seemed like he was taking the twins out for a treat."

Erec leaned forward. "Who was it? Tell me."

"It's somebody we call the Hermit."

CHAPTER ELEVEN
Erec's Song

BETHANY WAS PACING back and forth in the breakfast room when Erec arrived Saturday morning. He heaped a plate full of ambrosia and slid a pancake alongside, then sat down.

"Aren't you eating?"

"I can't." Bethany chewed her lip. "My brother Pi sent a snail letter. He's coming to Alypium tomorrow afternoon." She stopped pacing, her face filled with worry. "What if he doesn't like me?"

"How could he not like you? If you were Damon Stain, you might worry, but—"

"No, really." Bethany collapsed in a chair. "I'm a math dweeb. I'm not sure what he'll think about that."

"Even if he hates math, he'll still think you're great."

Bethany fidgeted, bending and unbending her fingers. "You like me, but that doesn't mean Pi will." She laid her hand flat on the table and took a breath. "Sorry. I'm just a little nervous. What happened with Rosco last night?"

"He doesn't have the twins. He's going to help me find them though, which is a lot more than King Piter is doing," he added.

Bethany winced at the accusation.

"Sorry." Erec reminded himself that she thought of him like a father. He wished he knew his father. If his father was brave enough to rescue a dragon and save its eye for Erec, then he would definitely find the missing twins.

"You're right. King Piter should have been able to do something." Bethany's attention was drawn to Erec's swollen fingertips, which were now dark purple with black fissures. They looked worse than yesterday. "Would you come with me to meet Pi tomorrow? I'd really appreciate it. I don't know if I can handle it myself."

"Sure. I better go to the royal hospital now and get something to help with these." He held his hands up.

"Those dragons sure did a number on you," Bethany said, rising to her feet. "Want some company? We can take Cutie Pie and Wolfboy for a walk after."

Dr. Mumbai was in the royal hospital. She jumped when she saw Erec's hands. The ends of his fingers looked like purple fans, or some kind of poisonous mushrooms. "Look at you. What happened? Have you been springing mousetraps? Here, you sit down."

She started mixing a solution that fizzed and foamed. As Erec waited, he told her about the dragon hatchlings. "Now I understand," she said. She dipped his fingers into the warm liquid that smelled like perfume. In a few moments, the stinging eased. "If it gets worse, come back and I'll give you some pills, but they might make you sleepy."

Erec liked this world, where doctors could fix things so quickly. He thanked her and joined Bethany outside with Wolfboy and her fluffy pink kitten Cutie Pie. The cat jumped on Wolfboy's back, making him run wildly in excitement. Cutie Pie hung on, enjoying the ride.

A raucous shriek from behind them made Erec jump. "Erec Rex . . . Erec Rex . . . Erec Rex." Erida, the Harpy, flapped toward them, a rolled parchment in her claws. Her black lips scowled at Erec. She squawked, "Against our better judgment, the Committee for Committee Oversight is forced to give you this invitation to the second quest. It seems you have some sort of ill-gotten deal worked out with Al's Well. Once we figure out why the well will only accept you, we'll correct the matter immediately. Most irregular, I am sure."

Erec took the parchment. "You want to kick me out just because you think Balor opened more eggs than I did? Would you kick him out if I was winning?"

Her black eyes burned into his. "We have been kind enough to include you at all, despite the general disapproval of you, and of what you have done here in Alypium and despite the doubts of your integrity. Most people want you banned from the Kingdoms of the Keepers altogether."

Erec shrank away. Her words hurt. Why did the people he wanted to save hate him? Couldn't they see the truth? Seeing Bethany standing right by him, he silently recited his mantra, *Don't care what they think . . . don't care what these kinds of people think.* She was right: He was too sensitive. "I guess you would ban me if you could figure out another way to get the quests from Al's Well. You just want to move things along so Balor, Damon, and Rock can be kings sooner."

She glared at him silently while he unrolled the parchment. "The Committee for Committee Oversight formally invites Erec Rex to the Labor Society tomorrow at ten a.m. to accept his second quest."

At the bottom was engraved an angry-looking face next to the words, "Our Mission: PEPS, Put-out, Exasperated, Pissed-off Service."

Erec couldn't help smiling. "Interesting new mission."

The bird woman flared her wings, clawing the air with her talons. "You can congratulate yourself for that one, Erec Rex." She flew away, shaking her head and muttering rude comments under her breath.

They walked Wolfboy, Cutie Pie riding on his back or Bethany's shoulder, into the agora to get cloud cream sundaes. Erec looked around, hoping to see a sign of Danny and Sammy. The clerk handed them the sundaes with a scowl. "You're the kid who's trying to mess with the new kings."

Erec ignored him. So what if he met one more person who wasn't a fan? They went outside and found a quiet spot in a patch of trees.

"I'm so glad Rosco is going to help me find the twins," Erec said. "I don't know how I'd do it on my own." He pulled out King Piter's glasses. "That reminds me. I better check on them."

Bethany nodded. "You should talk to your mom, too. Let her know what's up."

Erec wasn't crazy about that idea. "I guess. Of course she doesn't tell me anything. Why should I tell her?" Dark feelings flooded through him about losing his only memory of a father, even if it was a bad one. It was her fault, just like all the other secrets. Why wouldn't she trust him with the truth?

Erec focused on the twins and put on the Seeing Eyeglasses.

Suddenly, it seemed like he was gliding down a street in Alypium. The feeling was disorienting, that he was moving when he really was sitting still, and he wobbled a bit in his chair. The twins were nowhere in sight, but he heard Sammy's voice as plain as day. "Get off! You *ate* your whole bag of candy. Leave mine alone."

Danny laughed. "You don't need it, sis. Have you looked at yourself lately? One more candy bar and you'll rip through your clothes like the Incredible Hulk."

"Oh, yeah? Well, you look like you could be a springball ball without needing any padding."

"C'mon, gimme that bag. You know, there's always more candy in President Inkle's office." Erec saw where the twins were headed. The door to the Green House swung open, and Erec followed their voices inside and down a hall.

A disturbing, loud, oddly familiar voice said, "Well, look who's here. It's Erec Rex. Fancy meeting you here."

Erec looked wildly around, but the few people he saw in the Green House hallway were rushing around with briefcases, not noticing him at all.

"What, are you blind now, bright boy?" The voice sounded just like Balor Stain's. But what was he doing in the Green House? And how could he see Erec if he was only looking through the glasses? Unless . . .

He slipped the glasses off, and there was Balor Stain smirking at him. "More fancy glasses, huh, bright boy? You think you're such a big shot because you got that amulet, don't you? Well, let's take a look at it." Balor tried to yank the Amulet of Virtues off Erec's neck, but like his mother's Seeing Eyeglasses, it would not come off. Balor's smirk vanished, replaced by a look of pure hate. "You're not getting away with any more of your tricks, kid. We won that last quest fair and square, and it's recorded by the people that count." He got right in Erec's face. "I want to know how you worked it so only you can draw the quests from Al's Well. Did you bribe someone?"

Erec grinned. "I don't have to bribe anyone. I guess the well knows who is really supposed to be the next king."

Balor squinted at him meanly. "I guess if you weren't around, Al's Well wouldn't be so picky then. Meanwhile, when you're drawing the next quest, make sure you tell the well not to let the timing interfere with the Monster Bash."

"The what?"

Balor's cheek pulled into a half smile. "Typical bright boy. Knows a lot about one thing, clueless about everything else."

Damon appeared behind Balor. "The Monster Bash? Now? Can I go? Can I go bash the ugly Hydras?" Damon straightened his floppy gray stocking hat, and sang, "Damon had a Monster Bash, Monster Bash, little lamb. Brother is a—" He stopped when he saw Balor sneer.

Balor pulled out his remote control and pointed it at Erec. The king's Seeing Eyeglasses jumped out of Erec's hands and into his. "That was much easier than last time. Thanks." Balor put them on his face and frowned. "What's this? This isn't funny." He pulled the glasses off. "Good one, bright boy. It's all black. Well, they're mine now. I'll figure out how they work."

As Balor turned away, Erec shot toward him. Balor ducked behind Damon and said, "Bye, bye, bright boy." With a flick of his remote control, Balor vanished along with his brother.

Erec kicked the dirt in frustration. "I can't believe it. How am I going to track down the twins now?" He paced back and forth, trying to think of a plan. "I guess I'll search where they've been, ask around there." It sounded hopeless. Who in Alypium would help him if he asked? They all thought he was a criminal.

Bethany's jaw dropped. "Oh, no. Now Balor can use King Piter's glasses to spy on people."

A sour laugh popped out of Erec. "I don't think so. The glasses only show you the person you miss the most. I think that's why Balor saw black. He doesn't care about anybody else enough to miss them."

"Hey!" Bethany pointed. "Is that a snail?"

Erec knelt down to the dirt. Sure enough, what looked like a pink and purple rock grew before his eyes until it became a large snail with his name on it. He pulled two pieces of paper out and put the shell in his pocket.

My dear Erec,

How are you doing there? Alypium must be a terrible place if they don't appreciate what you've done for them. How can they be so blind? I don't understand. You are a hero here.

It feels like we are getting to know each other much better. I'll try and answer your questions. I am fourteen years old and have a sister who is nine. I love to read and play soccer, and I'm a cheerleader for our high school springball team. I don't actually have your picture, but everyone here has seen it. You are on all the banners for the parades and parties in your honor, and you've been in the newspapers too.

There is one question I am afraid to answer: where I am from. I live in Otherness. My people have been misunderstood, Erec. We've been kicked out of one place then the next, shipped here and there, and finally made to settle out here in the wilds. We built Lerna out here. It's a beautiful city, and I am happy to live here, but I wish we had the freedom to live wherever we want. You seem like such an understanding person, I hope you are not prejudiced. I'm afraid to find out.

Now you have to tell me the things you like to do. I love that you said we might meet some day. It cheers me up, but then reality sinks in. I think about it a lot. I even wrote a song about it. I hope you don't think it's too stupid.
Love always,
Tina

Erec's heart pounded when he handed the letter to Bethany. Maybe Tina wasn't a joke. Maybe there was a real fourteen-year-old girl somewhere in love with him. He read the next page.

EREC'S SONG, BY TINA
SOMEWHERE IN OTHERNESS A GIRL WEAVES A SONG
THE NOTES ARE SO SWEET BUT THE SOUNDS ARE ALL WRONG
HER FINGERS ARE FLYING BUT THE MELODY SLIPS AWAY
SHE GIVES IT HER ALL, BUT THE TUNE IT WON'T PLAY
WE'VE NEVER MET, GUESS WE NEVER WILL
WE'RE WORLDS APART, BUT THEN AGAIN, STILL
WHAT GOOD IS MY MUSIC, JUST WHAT IS IT WORTH
IF IT CAN'T CHANGE A THING IN THIS CRAZY EARTH

THE CHORDS ARE THRILLING, A DREAM TO ME
MY HEART IS SPILLING, OH LET ME BE
I'M AFRAID IT WILL ALWAYS BE
AN UNFINISHED SONG

YOU ARE MY HERO IN THE CLOTHES OF A FOOL
WE LOVE YOU HERE, BUT ALYPIUM'S CRUEL
MY HEART IT STOPPED WHEN I LEARNED THE NEWS
AND AFTER THAT, THE JAZZ TURNED TO BLUES
THE WORDS "YOUR KIND" AND "MY KIND" ARE SO UNKIND

IF WE MET WOULD OUR SONG UNWIND?
EVEN THOUGH TO ME YOU'RE A STAR
MAYBE OUR NOTES ARE NOT ON THE SAME BAR

THE CHORDS ARE THRILLING, A DREAM TO ME
BUT IT IS CHILLING—WE CANNOT BE
I'M AFRAID IT WILL ALWAYS BE
OUR UNFINISHED SONG

Bethany pried the paper from his hands. Erec's face was hot. She gasped as she read the song lyrics, hand on her mouth. "This girl is head over heels. Did you see this? 'My heart is spilling . . .' Oh, Erec. The poor thing."

"I better stop writing her," he said, embarrassed. "I'm getting her hopes up, and she'll never even meet me. It's making her sad."

"No, you don't understand. If you stopped writing her now, after she bared her soul to you with that song, she'll just die. Be her pen pal, okay? That's all she wants. This will fade away on its own."

The next morning before ten o'clock, Erec and Bethany walked to the Labor Society so he could draw his second quest. Jack and Oscar met them on the way, this time without Rosco. The streets were full of people hissing and booing him. Jack, Oscar, and Bethany tried to surround him and keep the crowd away. Erec wished Rosco was there to ward people off with his remote control, but Rosco probably didn't want to be seen with him.

Clamors filled the streets. "Ba*lor*! Ba*lor*! Ba*lor*!"

Erec wondered why he was bothering at all. These people didn't want his help. And he'd probably be better off at home, out of harm's way. A swell of anger rose in him. This wasn't right. He looked down at the Amulet of Virtues clanking around his neck. The small red segment glowed faintly with the symbol that Patchouli had said represented self-sacrifice. Well, if he had put himself out for the baby dragons, that felt like nothing compared to this abuse. Troubling himself for these people reached a whole new level in self-sacrifice. He smiled faintly, wondering if the waters of Al's Well somehow knew he would be proving this virtue again. Well, like it or not, he was not going to let these people be taken over and destroyed by the Stain brothers and Baskania.

Jack and Oscar nudged people out of the way to let Erec cross the lawn of the Labor Society. The angry mobs shouted "Cheater!" and "You *lost*! Quit now!" A woman cried, "I heard he escaped from King Pluto's dungeons. He's a hardened criminal." A man nearby shouted, "He's a phony. He made himself that necklace thing to fake people into letting him stay in the quests." Somebody threw a rotten apple at his chest. It slid off, leaving a mark over his heart.

Erec tried to keep his face blank. Why did it hurt so much? Why did he care what they thought? What mattered were the people who knew him. He couldn't please everybody. If only he could make himself believe that.

They finally reached the side door of the Labor Society. The small wooden door did not seem to fit with the rest of the building, which shined silver with beautiful turrets and flags. A sign on the door said "Back at ten o'clock." Erec's watch showed one minute until ten. It had taken him longer than he thought to get through the crowds.

Balor and Damon Stain, Rock Rayson, and Ward Gamin stood before the closed door, grins on their faces. Balor wagged his eyebrows at Erec. "The crowd loves ya, kid. You think they're ever going to let you be king here?" He laughed. "I think when we're done using you to get these stupid quests out of the well, you'll end up in somebody's dungeon."

Erec wished he knew how to work his remote control. He was

sure he could think of a good way to use it now. "You got my glasses, Balor?"

"No way. Like I'd carry them around so you could try and get them back."

A clicking noise came from the door. Erec turned the knob and opened it. They all went into the Quest Control Center, which was supposed to look like an old antique shop. Erec wondered if the Committee for Suppressing Change ever thought about why they did things. The doors slammed shut. Janus, the little man with the huge wild hair and beard, leapt from behind the counter and jumped up and down in unadulterated joy. Dust flew off him as he ran up to Erec and Bethany, threw his bony arms around them, and then shook everybody else's hands up and down.

"Welcome back!" Tears glowed in his eyes, and his hands covered the part of his face that showed through his long, scraggly gray beard and hair. He looked like he had been stranded for fifty years on a desert island. Janus gazed at Bethany, hands over his heart. "You were right. You all came back so soon. I am so glad." He began weeping into his arm.

Damon scratched the bone on his head through his hat. "Duh . . . should I sock 'im one, Balor?"

"No, you idiot." Balor leaned toward Janus and pulled out his remote. "You see here. I won the last contest. I want to be able to get into Al's Well myself. How do I do it?"

Janus chuckled. "Ah, drama. Excitement. I love all the little ins and outs of being with people. I'd forgotten how emotional they get."

Balor got angrier, eyes flashing. "You've forgotten what they can do to you too, if you don't cooperate."

Janus giggled. "So cute. So funny." Then he became serious. "I guess you should know that Al's Well's choices of who to accept are not up to me at all. Oh, no. Al gets that information straight from the Fates through the well. So any complaints need to go right to the top."

Balor paused, finger over his lips. Erec could tell he was scheming about how to get his way.

Janus straightened himself proudly. "Only those may come in here who know those asked to participate in this quest. And only those may go in there"—he pointed to the door at the back—"who may draw the second quest from the well. Erec Rex?"

Erec stepped forward. "Yes?"

"Come sign your name here." Janus sniffed and whispered, "Would you kids stay here a while after he goes? I can't bear the thought of this ending so soon."

Erec signed his name on a pad of paper and watched as the letters grew thick and black, and then broke open, letting rays of light gleam through. They shone on his face and lit the shop. Soon, the molding around the back door glowed with the same light.

When Erec opened the door, the shimmering bubble again filled the door frame. "See you later." He waved.

In a last attempt to have his way, Balor charged at the bubble. He smashed into it headfirst and bounced back, rubbing his bleeding nose. "Damon, Rock, see if you guys can do it."

Erec patiently waited as Damon and Rock ran into the bubble, then walked away rubbing their shoulders and necks. He waved to them and passed easily through it.

The huge glass and steel lobby again took him by surprise. It looked so different from the warm, dusty shop. He asked the man at the desk by the elevators where he should go.

The man picked up his phone. "Kid's here again. All right. I'll tell him." He put the phone down. "Elevator C to the sixth floor, room 612."

In room 612, the same woman sat at her desk. She smiled, but her eyes were hard as she handed him a stack of forms. "You need to sign these."

Erec flipped through the stack of papers. Most had lettering so small he could barely read it. When he reached the last sheet, his eyes settled on some boldfaced type that read, "...and I understand that I will not, under any circumstances, be given a scepter or be allowed to rule as king in any of the Kingdoms of the Keepers, no matter what the outcome of the quests ..."

His palms pressed into the papers. This was it. Everybody was against him. Well, he was not going to sign anything like this. No way. He handed the papers back to the woman.

"That was quick," she said. "Did you sign them all?"

"No, I didn't sign any of them. I read enough of what they said, and I won't do it. I'm the rightful ruler. If I do the quests, it's so I can be the king." He crossed his arms, not willing to give in.

The woman seemed unsure what to say. She mouthed something, waved the papers at him, and then got up. "So, you're saying you won't participate at all if you have to sign these?" A smile broke out on her face. "This may be just what we were waiting for. I'll be back."

Erec did not care what they were waiting for. This was the limit. He sat for an hour until the woman came back into the room, a scowl on her face. "Well, you lucked out this time, you scoundrel. I've heard from enough people about you, and now I've seen it for myself. A real rule breaker, all right. It looks like the Fates aren't as clued in as the rest of us, though. Al's report is that they still didn't change their mind."

Yeah, right, Erec thought. The Fates were clueless, and the street mobs knew what was going on. He shook his head. The woman made Erec wait while she counted her fingers and the cracks on the wooden desk before shoving a gold pass toward him.

Erec remembered how to get to where the janitor waited

in the basement. It figures, he thought. The person with the lowliest job would be the one to take him to Al's Well. The more he thought about that, the better he felt, though. The janitor probably had the most integrity of anyone who worked in the Labor Society.

Erec and the janitor walked through the grassy field, and Erec climbed the hill to Al's Well, avoiding the small gravestone. Al stood atop the hill in his overalls, hands on his hips, plunger hanging from his stuffed tool belt.

"Ehhh, good ta see ya again. Glad you survived that first one. I heard you almost got attacked there."

"How did you hear that?"

"Aww," he said, and blushed. "I'm not supposed to say anything. The girls like to gossip, and I overhear sometimes."

"The girls?" Erec was confused. Only his close friends knew what had happened in Nemea.

"Yeah, the Fates. You know." Al shrugged. "Anyway, I'm glad you're back. They were pretty impressed too."

Erec's spine straightened. Impressed? Did he hear right? This was practically the first compliment he'd gotten since he came to Alypium. "Did you say the Fates were happy with me?"

"Oh, yeah. They love ya, kid. Real fans, I think."

A smile crept onto Erec's face. Somebody out there appreciated him. Maybe things weren't so bad. "Do the Fates decide who gets to be king?" he asked hopefully.

"Oh, no. You decide that, I guess. The Fates just hang out in the waters and get to know about everything. They have a ball gossiping, drinking cosmos ripples, lounging in the pools."

"Don't they decide who lives and dies?"

"Who, them? They wouldn't have the heart to kill a fly. They do a few things, not too much . . . don't even cut the threads anymore—you know, the threads of everyone's lives. Got a tigress to do it. Usually gets it right, she does."

Erec handed Al the gold slip, and he nodded. "Your wish is my commode, as the girls like to say." He unlocked the door to the enclosure. Erec immediately recoiled from the stink. Al sniffed in a deep breath. "Ahh. The scent of life. Stinks, don't it?"

Erec agreed, but was not inclined to enjoy a huge whiff. Workers buzzed around along with the many flies. Al pulled the cord of the shower curtain, and the servants all dropped to their knees and bowed before the gleaming, oversized white toilet in the center of a grassy ring.

Al grinned. "You know what to do, bud."

Erec nodded. Even though he knew it was clean, it still creeped him out to reach into what looked like a latrine with green steam blowing off the top. He rubbed his hands together. It occurred to him for the first time since he was invited to draw the quest that he had no idea what he would have to do. He hoped it wasn't life-threatening.

Well, no use putting it off. He kneeled and stuck his arm deep into the toilet. Cold mist swirled around it. When the liquid that felt both hot and cold washed over his hand he jumped. Where was it? It was in here somewhere.

A thick, warm paper slid into his fingers. Even though part of him wanted to leave it there and not deal with what it said, he pulled the slip from the well. The paper dripped green water onto the grass, but the printing was clear. "You must stop the monsters in Lerna."

CHAPTER TWELVE
Another Premonition

EREC GAVE THE paper to Janus to post on the front lawn.
It was dated Friday, September 10, at one o'clock.

Bethany's eyebrows went up. "Lerna? That's where
your secret admirer lives. I guess we'll get to meet her
now."

"We?" Erec had not thought about who was coming with him
on this quest. He did tell Oscar it would be his turn. Maybe it would
be fair for Bethany to wait this one out. Plus, if Tina really liked him,

she might get the wrong idea if she saw him and Bethany together.

As if she read his mind, Bethany's face went pale. "Or maybe not. I don't want to cramp your style."

Balor and Damon waited outside the Quest Control Center, peering over Janus's shoulder as he posted the second quest. "What?" Balor shouted. "It's the date of the Monster Bash! The quest is to bash the monsters, Damon. And we get to lead the festivities!"

"Whoo-ee!" Damon danced around and broke out in his usual tune, "I'm gonna lead the Monster Bash, Monster Bash, little lamb. Brother is a little lamb whose fleece is white as snow." He looked around, gloating, and then seemed confused about what he had been singing.

"This is perfect." Balor rubbed his hands together. "Dad's going to love it."

"So will the Shadow Prince," Ward Gamin added. "He's the one that planned the Monster Bash. It's his baby. This couldn't have worked out better for him."

Rock Rayson giggled. "And after we visit the Fates it will work out even better for us."

Erec felt his fists clench. The Fates were the only people other than his friends who were on his side. It figured Balor was planning on strong-arming them to get his way. Erec swung toward Balor. "You leave the Fates alone."

Bethany looked at him, surprised.

Balor chuckled, hands up in mock surrender. "My oh my. Sensitive, aren't we? Worried that you might not be the only one who gets unfair treatment?"

Rage poured through Erec, and he took a threatening step toward Balor. Erec knew enough about unfair treatment, all right. "You're going to leave the Fates alone and butt out, Balor. Do things the right way for once. And give me my glasses back. They won't do you any good."

"Listen to this, boys," Balor smirked. "Poor little Erec wants his glasses back. Maybe he should ask his girlfriend Bethany to beat us up for him."

"Leave her out of this." Erec lunged at Balor, but he vanished. Instead, Damon stepped forward, swinging. Erec dodged his punch, but Damon came at him again.

"C'mon, Erec," Bethany said. "These idiots aren't worth it. Let's go."

Not listening to her, he pushed Damon away, but Damon shoved back harder, and Erec stumbled. He knew he should walk away, but he was past his limit. Dodging another blow, Erec grabbed Damon's hat and felt the large tubular bone inside it. He grabbed it and forced it toward the ground. Damon's head went down with it. Erec let go only when he was lying on the grass. "You get me those glasses back, hear?"

Damon's eyes flashed at Erec. He sprang from the ground and knocked Erec over. Together they rolled on the dirt. Erec could overpower most kids if he had to, but Damon was stronger than him. He held Erec's arm on the ground and punched him in the nose. Erec tasted blood. Trying to get him back, he kneed Damon in the stomach, but Damon didn't wince. He hit Erec in the nose again, harder.

Furiously, Erec grabbed the rocklike bone in Damon's hat, his Achilles' heel. Damon's head jerked to the side. Erec yanked it again, and Damon screamed. Oscar and Bethany stared as Erec got up and walked away, leaving Damon moaning and cursing on the ground.

Bethany rushed over to him. "You look terrible. Let's get you to the royal hospital and get that nose fixed." She put her hand on her head. "Oh, no, I'm sorry. Pi is supposed to meet me in Paisley Park soon. I have to wait for him."

"I'll wait with you, like I said. I feel fine. I'll take care of it after." Erec wiped his face off and tried not to look at the smeared blood on his hand.

"Don't go to the royal hospital," Oscar said. "Rosco will fix it better than the doctor. I'm pretty sure he's home."

"And I'm supposed to walk through Alypium looking like this?" Erec laughed bitterly. "That's all people need is to see me bleeding from my nose. They'll all be convinced how right they are about me."

"Who cares what they think?" Bethany said. "Let it go, Erec." They walked toward Paisley Park, Erec keeping his face down so nobody would notice him.

"Hey, Oscar," he said, "what's the Monster Bash?"

"It's really cool. A lot of people from Alypium are going into Otherness in a few days to show the monsters what's what. We're not letting them scare us anymore."

"What kind of monsters? What have they been doing?"

"All kinds of nasty beasts. Hydras, ogres, Cyclopes—they're awful creatures. President Inkle says that their very existence threatens our way of life here. They'll tear us to shreds given half a chance. So the Monster Bash is our way of striking back until we can find a way to get rid of them completely."

Bethany crossed her arms, not liking the idea. "Why don't people just leave them alone? They're out in Otherness, not here bothering us."

Oscar explained patiently, "Oh, they used to be here, and they're trying to get back to kill us all. They hate us, think they're better than us. Those monsters are polluting our world just by being here, lowering us, because they're so nasty."

"Wow." Erec was glad the monsters were in Otherness now, not here. But then he remembered that it would be his task to stop them. He wondered what "stopping them" meant. Killing them? He hoped not. Maybe just stopping them from doing something. He wished the quest instructions had been more specific.

Just like that, everything around Erec turned bright green. Big chunky white webs hung in the air: the Substance, which carried all the magic in the world. He stopped in his tracks. Was he having a cloudy thought? Or was it another premonition?

A crowd of people stood around him in the green light. Erec could feel a deep anger swelling within him, growing out of control, unstoppable. He ducked down and grabbed the feet of a young blond-haired man. Then he stood and swung the horrified man around him in a circle by his ankles, knocking over everyone around him. Hatred and rage filled him so powerfully, he could barely think.

The people watching him in the green light were horrified. He knew they thought he was out of control, a monster. Worse than that, he agreed with them. He had turned into something else, something awful.

Finally the green light faded away. Erec was left pale and shaky. Stumbling off the sidewalk, he threw up under a bush. Bethany and Oscar watched him, jaws agape.

"Are you okay?" Bethany said hesitantly. "You want to sit down?"

"Wow," Oscar said. "You turned green, dude, like all green. Your skin was green, like a lizard or something. And your dragon eye came out and it was glowing—"

Bethany cut him off. "Leave him alone, Oscar. I don't think it's so cool to Erec." They both waited expectantly for Erec to tell them what had happened.

Erec didn't know what to say. How could he admit what he

saw? Because he knew it was going to happen sooner or later. Ever since he got the dragon eye, each time he had a cloudy thought he had a premonition of it first. First when he jumped on Danny, then watching Patchouli zoom in to kill him, and now this. What on earth was he doing here? There was no questioning the shock in the eyes of the people around him, the people he was hurting. He hated to think of the expression of the poor blond guy he was swinging into everyone else.

And that deep, ferocious anger that overtook him. That also had never happened before in a cloudy thought. Nor had the feeling that he was becoming something else altogether, something monstrous.

Erec merely shook his head at Bethany and Oscar and walked on toward Paisley Park. His friends followed him in silence.

As they passed a bush, Erec was startled. Danny and Sammy's voices rang out clearly from behind it. Danny said, "What ya staring at, sis? Never seen a world-class athlete before?" Sammy giggled. Erec ran to the bush and then backed away, amazed at the odd sight before him. A llama with the head of a bald man faced away from him. Could this be one of the monsters that had snuck back into Alypium to destroy them? Where were Danny and Sammy? As he stared, the head turned around. It belonged to none other than the Hermit. Erec blinked, then realized the llama was standing behind the Hermit, and only the Hermit's head was visible over the bush. He was feeding something to the llama.

But where were the twins?

Erec lunged forward to grab the Hermit but only succeeded in grabbing the bush and stabbing the purplish skin on his fingers. He cried out in pain.

The Hermit nodded at Erec's fingers. "I see you've come far."

Erec could not tell if the Hermit was being sarcastic. "Where are the twins?"

The Hermit cackled with glee. "Only some of us can see. Only few of us can know. And on that note, it is time for me to go." He snapped his fingers and was gone, as were the voices of the twins.

Erec ran around the bush. The tall llama was munching grass, and it looked up at Erec with bland eyes. Then it spit its cud onto his shirt, making a stain near the one from the rotten apple. Even the llama didn't like him.

"I'm nervous about meeting Pi," Bethany said as they sat on a bench in Paisley Park. The sun glinted red off her dark, wavy hair. She cringed as a bad memory came to her. "What is the deal with that bone coming out of Damon's head? I've never seen anything like it. Maybe Pi knows." As she mentioned her brother's name, her brow knitted. She pulled out a notebook and began scribbling illegible letters and numbers all over the page, glancing occasionally up the path.

Erec leaned over her work. "Whatcha doing?" His nose ached worse then ever. After she met Pi, he would find a Port-O-Door and go see if Rosco could fix it.

Bethany shrugged. "I'm trying to distract myself. This is like doing crosswords for me, takes my mind off things. It's really fun. I'm proving that set theory is wrong." She jabbed the different numbers with her pencil. "I've shown that one equals infinity, so ordinal numbers are not real, which totally messes up set theory as we understand it. It's pretty exciting because . . ."

Bethany's voice faded away as a gangly young man with flaming red hair walked up the path. He looked as nervous as she did. Finally he raised a hand in a wave.

Bethany shot off the bench and threw her arms around him. Her head only came up to his chest. She broke away and looked into his face. "Pi . . ."

"Hiya, Bethany." A goofy grin broke across Pi's face as they sat on the bench. He squeezed his knobby, freckled knees together, then looked at Erec with his dark brown eyes. "What happened to your nose? You okay?"

"Yeah," Erec said. "Just got in a fight."

Pi eyed Bethany up and down. "You look like Mom." His voice caught, and he glanced at his white knuckles.

Erec thought Pi and Bethany could not look more different, except for their dark brown eyes.

"You remember Mom and Dad?" Bethany's hand shot to where Erec knew an invisible locket hung around her neck, holding her parents' pictures.

Pi nodded. "You have one too?" He pointed at Bethany's hand, and she dropped it, surprised. Pi fumbled with something unseen around his neck that opened to reveal the same pictures that were in her locket.

Bethany's eyes misted over. Pi grinned at her. "I hear you take after Mom. Kind of a math whiz?"

She nodded. "Do you like math too?" she croaked.

Pi laughed. "It's my gift. I can see arcs and calculate angles automatically. It's a sport, really. A big game. Helps a lot with springball when I want to know where to throw the ball for the right trajectory, that kind of thing. So you like math?"

Bethany nodded. "I just proved that one equals infinity."

Winking at Erec, Pi grabbed Bethany's head in the crook of his arm and mussed her hair. "That's great, Bethany. My little sis is learning about math too. So you already know there is an infinity between zero and one? I'll teach you a few math tricks. That'll be fun." Pi seemed to relax now that he had found common ground with Bethany. "Do you know about the continuum theory? I can teach you how to figure angles in a second, and that'll help with any sport you play."

Bethany's lips pressed together. "I know all that. I'm not saying there is an infinity between zero and one. I actually proved that one equals infinity. I disproved the existence of ordinal numbers. And now I'm working on set theory." She held up her notebook sheepishly. "I almost have the whole thing disproved."

Pi's eyes widened as he stared at her. He shook his head. "That's impossible. I don't believe it, sis." He leaned over her notebook and whistled. "You're a sharp cookie. What have you done here?"

As Bethany and Pi began to discuss concepts that were as high over Erec's head as the cloudy citadel itself, Erec snuck back to the castle.

Erec pulled the letter from Tina out of his pocket. He still could not believe a girl had written a song for him. And he would be going to Lerna now so he could finally meet her. She already thought he was a hero. Just wait until he stopped the monsters there. He thought about it. Poor Tina and her family must be living in terror of those monsters. It was a good thing he was going there to help them. This time he would write Tina back himself. Bethany didn't need to help. It really didn't involve her anyhow.

Erec wondered how he would find Danny and Sammy without King Piter's Seeing Eyeglasses. Maybe the king had another pair. So many thoughts swarmed in his head that he almost walked into a bush. Why were the twins acting as if they were having the time of their lives? Couldn't they call home? Who ever heard of kidnappers loading kids with cloud creams and candy and taking them to beaches? And what were they doing in the Green House? It sounded like they had met President Inkle.

That was it. He had to get into the Green House and see if anyone there knew where the twins were. But first he'd go see Rosco. Hopefully he could fix Erec's nose. It was starting to throb. And maybe Erec could learn how to use his remote control. It would be nice to know how to use when he was spying in the Green House.

Erec checked his e-mail before taking the Port-O-Door to Rosco Kroc's house. Ten messages blinked on his computer, all from his mother. A tide of anger rose in him again. He was tempted to ignore the messages, but he e-mailed her back.

June's face appeared on the screen. "Erec! I'm so glad you caught me at home. What happened to your nose?"

"I got in a fight." Erec didn't feel like softening it for her, not today. "Don't worry about me."

"I am worried," she said with her usual motherly concern. "And I thought we'd find Danny and Sammy by now. The Alypium police are useless. I suppose I shouldn't expect King Piter to work miracles, but . . ."

"He's useless too. He left town, more worried about the missing dragon hatchlings than Danny and Sammy." Erec added, with lots of sarcasm, "I guess there are a lot of people I can't rely on."

"Erec, did something happen?"

"You could say that. I found the Memory Mogul. Remember that guy? What he had to tell me was very interesting." Erec felt his face get hot.

June was quiet. After a moment she said, "What did you find out?"

"Just what you'd expect. That I had a chunk of my memory taken out when I was young. And you put a replacement memory into my head, a memory that's not really mine about my father, or someone

I thought was my father." Erec's voice rose to a shout. "All these years, Mom. All these years I had nightmares about that guy. I hated him. It's caused me grief my whole life. I thought I had a lousy father who deserted me. And you let me keep believing it." He tried to calm his breathing. "Did you ever, once, think about telling me the truth?"

June answered in a long, drawn-out sigh. "Erec, how could I have told you about your memory implant unless I told you everything? I am so sorry about this. But there are reasons you shouldn't know more. Hey, you got to be a normal boy most of your life, and that was important."

"No, Mom. I never got to be normal. What normal kid moves from town to town constantly, with all of his friends' memories of him erased each time? How do you think that feels?"

"I know," she said solemnly. "I've told you how sorry I am about that. I needed to keep us from being found." She paused, searching for words. "Look, I know how hard this is for you. I've felt terrible your whole life when you talked about that memory of who you thought was your father. I never knew what to say. When you were young, you wouldn't have understood, and later there never was a right time."

"Well, the right time is now," Erec said hotly. "Let's hear about the memory that you erased from me."

June wrung her hands. "I can't."

"What?" He could not believe his ears. "I think you can, Mom. Tell me."

"I . . . promised King Piter that I wouldn't."

King Piter? He was the cause of all of this? He didn't want Erec to know anything. Thank goodness Peebles at least had pointed him in the right direction. "Do you mean you would tell me right now if it wasn't for King Piter?"

June considered that. "I might. But that doesn't matter now

anyway. You'll find out everything when the time is right."

"When King Piter thinks the time is right, you mean. What about what I think?" Erec paced back and forth, livid. His breath shot in and out in spurts. "I can't go on like this. The only tiny thing I knew about my birth parents turned out to be a hoax. What do I have left? Nothing. No history at all. A big blank. And not only do I not know about my parents, I don't know about my own self. King Piter said I was destined to be a king, but I have no clue why. Who cares what he thinks about this. It's none of his business."

"Yes, Erec, it is." She rested her head in her hands. "I'm sorry."

It's okay, he told himself. He didn't need his mother or the king to tell him what he needed to know. He would find out for himself, as he had done all along.

June looked up. "Have you seen the twins lately?"

"They're fine. Each time I check they're eating fistfuls of candy, hanging out at a beach, or Rollerblading. Get this, they've even been in the Green House and met President Inkle. It sounds like they're having a blast."

"Why wouldn't they call?" June hugged herself. "Someone's lying to them, telling them something to keep them from calling me. Maybe they think I know they're there and said it was okay. Maybe someone told the twins I was dead."

"I don't think so, Mom. They looked too happy."

"I think you should put on the glasses and tell them to call home, that we're all worried about them. They need to hear it from you."

"It's too late, Mom. King Piter's glasses are gone. But don't worry. Rosco Kroc is looking for the twins, and he's good at tracking people. And we may have a clue where they are." Erec realized his voice sounded cold, like he wasn't even related to them. He tried to sound softer. "I'm going there now. Did you get the glasses off the alarm clock?"

"No, it's been harder than I thought," she said crossly. "The clock is useless now that it's staring into the Seeing Eyeglasses all the time. I have to keep it in the sink. It keeps crying so much it makes a huge mess. I hope I can figure out how to get them off." She sighed. "Let me know about anything you find out right away. And be careful." She blew Erec a kiss.

Erec felt a little better after he talked to her, even if she had lied to him. Yet he still had no clue about his past. The aching in his nose returned. He had to see Rosco. As he was reaching for the Port-O-Door, he had a funny thought. Maybe Rosco could find out who he was.

CHAPTER THIRTEEN

Learning Magic

THE PORT-O-DOOR BECAME shorter and skinnier. As Erec opened it, a terrible stench poured into the vestibule, along with a black banana peel, wads of crumpled paper, and a rotting fish head. It would not open far, pushing against a pile of trash up to Erec's knees. He crouched to look through the door. The lid of a trash can was above his head.

His luck, opening a Port-O-Door straight into a trash can on

Rosco's street. He slammed it shut, kicking a filthy cloud cream box and plum pit out of the way. The vestibule stunk now, the garbage on the floor mingling with blood from his fingers that he had scraped on the bush, or was it his crushed nose that was bleeding now? Erec's stomach rose into his throat. He quickly selected another spot on the street, slightly farther from Rosco's house.

The door grew very short. Erec opened it straight into an empty doghouse. He kicked the trash from the vestibule into the dog's humble home and stole out onto the street.

The streets tilted dangerously one way, then the other. Erec nearly fell before he realized it was not the street but he himself that was swaying. He stopped to catch his breath. The pain from his nose and fingers had been getting steadily worse, and the smell of garbage seemed to have tipped his sense of balance. He crossed the street. What if Rosco wasn't home? He guessed he would just lie on the bench on his front porch.

Embarrassment mixed into Erec's daze as he remembered breaking into Rosco's house and attacking him with a plant hanger. He rang the bell.

Rosco's face peeked out of the door under a green leather cowboy hat. He looked stunned. "Hold on right there. I'll be back." He shut the door and returned a moment later. "Pardon me if I don't invite you in yet." He gestured to the blood splashed on the cement porch floor and helped Erec sit on the bench. "What in Keeper Kingdom happened to you, kid?"

Erec examined his fingers, red and swollen with torn skin. "I got like this from feeding the baby dragons in the first quest. Then they got cut up more when I tried to catch the Hermit through a bush."

"And your nose?"

"I got in a fight."

Rosco picked up Erec's hand and peered at it closely. "Looks like someone tried to fix your fingers. Was it Ezzy Mumbai?" Erec nodded. "She's no healer. If Ippocra Asclep was still there, you'd be fixed. She disappeared ten years ago when the triplets and queen were killed, along with a bunch of other people. Nobody found Dr. Asclep's body, so I wonder if she might be alive somewhere. Anyway, you came to the right place. I can fix anything. It's cake, if you're taught right."

Rosco disappeared, then came back with a steaming mug. He sprinkled a dark powder in it and murmured something that sounded like, "See ya later, krocogater." The mixture sizzled and then grew quiet.

The drink burned like sharp cinnamon in Erec's throat. Every muscle, bone, and sinew in his nose seemed to jump to attention, each with its own agenda. His skin rippled as pieces rearranged themselves under its surface, fighting for position. It did not hurt, although it itched terribly. He sneezed repeatedly until finally the rumbling movement stopped. Erec felt his nose. Totally normal. No pain at all.

Erec held his hands out. The open cuts had healed, but his fingertips remained red and swollen.

"No problem." Kroc grinned. He took a deep breath and put each of his fingers on Erec's. Jolts of pressure pushed through into Erec's bones, but he felt a stubborn resistance push back. Rosco grimaced, forehead wrinkled and sweat popping out. Finally he dropped his hands.

"Well, I'll be hanged. Let me try this." He stood Erec next to him and then raised his hands with a ferocious look, like a wild beast. Erec stumbled back in shock. White sparks flew from Rosco's fingertips toward Erec like small fires, but they sizzled on his skin and went no deeper.

Rosco dropped his hands. Rage appeared in his eyes. "What is this? Rosca' can fix and destroy *anything*." He glared at Erec as if it was his fault. Erec dropped onto the bench while Rosco regained his wits. "Finish that drink. It'll make you sleep, and it might fix your fingers more."

Erec gulped the rest of what was in the mug. Almost immediately, a velvety peace enveloped him. He forgot about his throbbing fingers and fell asleep on the bench.

Erec felt much better when he woke. Dusk was creeping over the rooftops of the town. His fingers looked fine, only faintly red. Rosco was nowhere to be seen so Erec rung the doorbell. Rosco peered out, eyed him up and down, then let him in.

"Thank you. Whatever you did really helped."

Rosco winked and motioned for Erec to have a seat.

"Any news about the twins?"

Rosco shook his head. "I've been asking around. I'm sure they're still in Alypium, but I keep missing them. They hang around the ice skating and roller skating rinks, the miniature tennis courts, and a lot of sweetshops. The Hermit is always close by." He shook his head again. "I keep thinking about the food, though. It's almost as if . . ."

"What?"

Rosco contemplated his fingernails as if he didn't know how to answer. "It's just a hunch. I don't want to scare you. I could be totally wrong."

"What is it?" Erec's heart began to pound.

"Now don't get all worked up, okay? This is just a feeling I have. Although my ideas tend to work out more often than not. You see, there are these monsters that live out in the wilds of Otherness . . . well, they're ferocious beasts, they are. Word is, they're demanding a sacrifice. Two children. They're bloodthirsty things, and if they don't get the children as a gift from us, they'll kill a lot more than that.

Someone might've figured your brother and sister are easy victims. They don't belong to anyone around here. Nobody to complain. Anyway, it would explain why someone was fattening them up."

Chills washed over Erec as Rosco's words sank in. So this was what his quest was about. "Are these monsters in Lerna?"

Rosco nodded. Erec felt sick thinking of all the candy Danny and Sammy had been eating. He heard them saying how they were both outgrowing their clothes. If he didn't do something they would be monster food. "If only I still had the glasses King Piter gave me I could warn them."

"You don't have those anymore?"

"Balor Stain stole them."

Rosco shook his head, and Erec remembered what Balor had said about the Monster Bash. "Will there be other people there helping us stop the monsters in Lerna?"

Rosco spoke quietly. "There are two factions. One wants to give the monsters what they want. The other is ready to fight. The Shadow Prince is working with President Inkle to draft soldiers from the Kingdoms of the Keepers to march on Otherness. General Moreland will lead them, and I think they could succeed, but I don't know if they'll make it in time." He made a long face. "If they don't, it seems a lot for you to handle yourself."

Erec drew back, uncomprehending. "The Shadow Prince?"

Rosco smiled. "Yes, your old friend, Thanatos Baskania. You seem surprised he is gathering an army to fight the monsters and save the children."

Erec nodded, mouth open. That didn't sound like him at all.

"I know you didn't get along with him, but you didn't think he was all bad, did you? Nobody is all bad, or all good either, are they?" He let the question hang in the air, then went on. "I hear he was real disappointed that you turned down his friendship. Well, there is still time to make amends, I'm sure. I remember my own father used to be disappointed in me once upon a time, just because it took me a while to get started doing magic. And look at me now."

"And you made up with him?" Erec asked.

"Well, he died." Rosco looked away.

"Oh. I'm sorry." Erec was confused. "But Baskania is trying to help? To save Danny and Sammy?"

"Apparently, yes. Oh, I'm sure it's not all for innocent reasons. He wants to be a hero, you know. Save the day, all that."

Erec could picture that. "But what if he doesn't make it in time? The twins might be fed to the monsters first."

Rosco sighed. "I wish you still had those glasses. I'll do my best to track them, see what the Hermit is up to. He is from Otherness, knows it like the back of his hand. When he disappears from Alypium, we can really worry."

This wasn't the way it was supposed to be. How could Baskania be doing more to save the twins than King Piter was? Was Baskania not all bad and King Piter not all good?

"On Upper Earth, Baskania is called the Crown Prince of Peace." Erec thought about Baskania working for world peace. Maybe he wasn't all bad.

Erec shook his head. It was too confusing to think about. Baskania used magic for his own ends, for evil ends. Erec stopped short. Thinking about magic reminded him of one of the reasons he had come to see Rosco. "Say, would you teach me how to use a remote? I better learn as much as I can so I can stop the monsters."

"Well." Rosco sniffed at that idea. "I guess I better teach you the basics. Got it with you?" Erec shook his head. "That's the first lesson. Always keep it in your pocket until you're good enough that you don't need it. Not everyone can use one, you know," he pointed out. "Only about half the people here can, and much fewer can do magic without one. If six months go by and you still can't use a remote control, you're pretty much booted out of training, good-bye and thank you."

Erec wondered if Peebles would have taught him anything in six months, given how much time it would take to copy those huge books. Then what would have happened to him? "So some people take a while to learn?"

Rosco nodded. "You can never tell how far someone will go with magic because you don't know what is inside them, making them tick. Sometimes fear holds them back. Acquiring magic takes a special strength, deeper focus. But," he continued on a brighter note, "if you have any at all in you, a remote control will pull it out at the push of a button. It's easy. You learn a simple command, press a button, and the equipment does the rest. A monkey could do it." He dug through a drawer, found a silver remote control, and tossed it to Erec.

"Don't you carry one in your pocket?" Erec asked.

Rosco laughed heartily. "I haven't needed one in ages. I'm teaching Oscar how to do real magic now. Soon he won't need one either. You can only do so much with these things. True power lies far beyond this hunk of metal."

Erec closely studied the remote control. At the bottom right was a button with the number three on it. Other small buttons dotted its center, with odd symbols on them. A large green button glowed brightly at the top, surrounded by four buttons with arrows pointing in different directions.

"Press the button on the bottom right corner until it shows a one. You'll have to start at level one, of course."

Erec pushed it as instructed. "What's level one?"

"It's the simplest magic. If you tried to move a pencil set on level three, it would throw it clear through the walls of a house. If you had the power, that is."

Erec thought that would be cool. "What can you do with level two and three?"

Rosco sighed and shook his head. "I forget how little you know." He raised his hands, indicating a high and a low. "There are six levels of magic. The first three can be done with a remote control; the others are for the experts only. Everything exists within a network of magic called the Aitherplanes. The particles that flow through it are called the Substance. If you can manipulate the Substance then you can have effects on the elements that are in it." He waved all about them. "Everything around us. Some tricks are easier to do than others. For example, level one has to do with moving things. The easiest are the smallest things, inanimate things and close things." Rosco lifted a finger, crooking the knuckle. The lamp next to Erec began to bounce up and down. Rosco's finger began to twirl and the table under the lamp spun so fast that a book on it crashed into a wall. Erec's stomach lurched as the couch he sat on shot up toward the ceiling. He ducked before his head hit, and then the couch dropped, freezing in midair before it hit the floor. Objects sailed around the room. Erec turned upside down until Rosco let him drop headfirst onto the couch. In one bang everything crashed back where it was.

"Level two gets harder," Rosco said mildly. "A lot of this level has to do with sensations, making people feel things. Not hard stuff to do, really." Without warning, Erec burst out laughing as he felt tickled all over. Then he broke out in a sweat, boiling hot, and a moment later he was freezing, teeth chattering. "It's convenient. Once you get good at this, you'll never feel sick anymore. Also, at this level you can destroy objects and kill things. This is easier to do than fixing them, of course."

Erec held his breath for a moment, hoping Rosco would not demonstrate this part.

"Lots of magic fits into level three. When you get to this level, you are officially a sorcerer. Used to be sorcerers wore black robes to show off and scare people. Not so much anymore. This level includes flying without heli powder." He snapped his fingers and vanished, then reappeared, fire spurting from his fingertip. "Starting fires, making water, breezes, and waves, teleporting objects long distances."

Rosco pointed at the device in Erec's hand. "Level four can't be done with a remote. Too hard. At this level you can change the appearance of things or people, but you have to be careful with this one. You can never get it back quite right again." Rosco gestured at his own face. "Healing people falls into this level, and that's not easy to do. Making things grow. Multiplying people, things, or even yourself. You can create a force field at this level.

"Level five is really cool." Rosco rubbed his hands together and grinned. "I'm starting to work on it now, and I'm not sure how far I'll get. That's not because I'm a dunce, either. Very few people get this far. At this level, you can talk with animals and even plants. You can enchant objects to serve you or have their own personalities. You can even control time, within limits, making things move faster or slower, if you learn to have enough of an effect on the Aitherplanes and the Substance. Seeing the future is often classed into level five, but you have to have special math abilities and need seer training. So I might overlook the future bit, but I'm going to do my best to tackle the rest of this level. Then watch out, world."

Rosco fell silent, lost in a dream of magic and domination. Erec cleared his throat. "What about level six?"

Rosco snapped back to life. "Almost nobody has reached this level, except the Shadow Prince. The years of studying it requires—most people don't live that long. You have to really understand the Substance, make it work at levels that most people could never grasp. I'm talking the quantum, atomic, cosmic, and mathematical structure of how everything works, and how to change it. Of course, that's

Baskania's gift, being able to manipulate the Substance. At this level you could do anything that is anyone's inborn magical gift. You can read people's minds. It's amazing, really."

"So you can do anything at level six that you can do with a scepter?" Erec asked. The very thought of the scepter warmed his insides, and he craved it again. Maybe level six could give him everything the scepter would without the downside of it controlling him.

Rosco shook his head. "No, unfortunately for the Shadow Prince. King Piter's scepter is the strongest force in magic, and the Shadow Prince wants it for his own. That scepter gives you unearthly power. With it, you can change people's memories of the past. You can control their minds, make them tell the truth, lie, be happy, sad, or scared. You can make people follow your commands, mentally and physically. The scepters will also give you advice; they know everything that's happening in the Aitherplanes. And, of course, keeping one lets you live forever—another nice advantage."

"So with the scepter you can do anything?"

"Well, some things are always out of bounds. But, with enough willpower, I say people can do anything. A scepter can't bring someone back to life, but someone has worked out a way to do this with a potion. A scepter can't change our atmosphere, create things or beings out of nothing, but the Shadow Prince is working on these things on his own. So who knows what we may be able to do in the future."

Rosco's voice trailed off, like a dream had ended. Eyeing the remote he had given Erec, he motioned for Erec to aim it. Rosco then set a pencil on the table. "To move this, just say 'phero' and push the green button. See if you can do it."

Erec focused on the pencil and pushed the button.

"Phero." His finger felt a little sore and weak where it had not fully recovered from the dragon bites, but the pencil shot into his lap.

"Hey, I did it." He put the pencil back and tried it again, then did it three more times, figuring out how to control how far it went by how hard he concentrated. "What do the other buttons do?"

"The right and left arrows around the green button let you reverse and redo the magic you have just done. The up and down arrows let you control the power you're sending out. It's best not to rely on those. Learn to control the power with your mind. Then try to use the remote without word spells. It teaches you more mind control that way."

Erec pointed to the smaller buttons that had funny symbols. "What are these?"

"Special features." Rosco shrugged. "They're not on the basic remotes you start with. Those hook you up to the MagicNet, cell phones, timers, clocks. Why don't you keep that remote. I just got it to use with Oscar, and he has his own."

"Thanks." Erec put the remote control in his pocket, glad to have one he could work. He stretched and let out a long yawn. Despite the fun he was having, it was getting dark and he was hungry. "Before I go, I want to ask you something. I need to find out more about my history, who my parents were, that kind of thing. Can you help me?"

Rosco snickered. "Must be rough not knowing so much. Too bad I can't help you, kid. King Piter wouldn't like that at all."

Erec sizzled with anger at mention of the king's name. "C'mon, Rosco, I won't tell him."

"Oh, I know that," he said. "But the king's right. Knowing this would affect you badly. And I'm afraid to change too much. Erec, has Oscar told you I can see some things in the future? I can tell you this. You will find out soon enough the answers to all of your questions. Sooner than you should. And it won't be good for you either."

Erec absorbed this, not sure what to think. "Thanks, I guess. Oh, I forgot to tell you. The last time I saw the twins, they were visiting the Green House. I think they met President Inkle."

Rosco's face broke into a grimace. "I have a bad feeling about this."

Erec instantly became worried. "What is it?"

"Why would the Hermit try to get the twins to meet President Inkle before feeding them to the monsters? Don't you think that would make the president look bad, if he meets the kids who end up getting eaten? The Hermit is playing a political game. I don't like it at all."

Erec didn't like it either. He scratched his head, thinking of the dangers. "What kind of monsters are they?"

Rosco shuddered. "The worst, most feared kind of monsters in all of Otherness. The dreaded vogum."

CHAPTER FOURTEEN
Escape to Otherness

Putting the port-o-door in the doghouse had been a mistake, Erec found out. Its canine resident, a mud-colored German shepherd, had come back, and it barked loudly when Erec tried to climb into its house. The dog eagerly sniffed at Erec's fingers and growled deep in its throat.

"C'mon, boy. Come on out. Sh . . . shh . . ." Erec tried to sound soothing, but the dog snapped at him. A light switched on in the house nearby. Fearing he'd be caught, Erec grabbed the dog's collar and pulled. The dog snarled and lunged at him, teeth bared. He let the dog sail over him and dove into its house. Turning right around, the shepherd tore into Erec's side, scraping his skin with its teeth and getting a wad of Erec's shirt in its mouth.

In a panic, Erec punched the code numbers into the Port-O-Door. A man in the house shouted, "Poopsie? Here, Poopsie. Did you trap a rabbit in there?"

Poopsie yanked Erec's shirt harder.

"Poopsie. Come here. Now," the man called. Poopsie looked at Erec with disgust, probably at her own name, before letting go and trotting to her master, barking all the way. Let loose, Erec flung himself through the Port-O-Door and slammed it shut.

The vestibule still smelled like garbage. Even so, Erec was relieved to be back in the west wing of the castle. He found all the food in the dining hall was gone so he called Jam Crinklecut for room service.

"Yes, young sir?" Jam sounded eager to please. "Why, of course. And what would young sir like to eat?"

Erec asked for two hamburgers, fries, apple pie, and brownies, although he knew he should start eating the Alypian food so he could perform better at the next quest.

His mind was in a whirl. He had actually worked magic, used a remote control. Who needed King Piter's help, anyway, he thought. He could do everything himself, like find his father and save the twins. If Rosco would teach him the basics, he hoped he could move on to level two soon.

Before Erec went to sleep, he decided to answer Tina's letter.

Dear Tina,
Guess what? I just found out I'm coming to Lerna, so I'll get

to meet you for sure now. In fact, I found out that you guys are having some problems there, and my quest is to help you! So if you think I'm a hero, maybe I'll get a chance now to prove it. [Erec hoped he didn't sound like he was bragging. But, then again, he knew how Tina felt. What was wrong with impressing her a little?] *The first quest was cool. I got to save the last known baby dragons in Otherness. Hurt my fingers a little when I fed them, but that was okay.*

I have to tell you, Alypium stinks. Everyone hates my guts here and thinks all kinds of crazy things, like I enchanted King Piter's scepter to come to me and faked everyone out that I should be king. I'm just doing what I think is right. It helps to know that people where you live are supporting me.

That's so cool you have a high school springball team. Where I come from it's only a pro sport. The uniforms, padding, and arena would be way too expensive. I guess you don't use arenas in Otherness, though. [Erec remembered the springball game he saw in Alypium where a force field kept the balls from sailing into the stands.]

Tina, don't feel bad about telling me about your people. [He thought about what she had said about her family. It sounded terrible, being forced to live out in the wilds, among vicious monsters.] *It sounds terrible what happened to them. From what I know about the people of Alypium, though, it doesn't surprise me. They seem ready to gang up on anybody. They sure went against me. It sounds like Lerna is a great place and I can't wait to see it. And I am not prejudiced.*

I am almost thirteen. [Erec erased this when it sounded too young, then he rewrote it.] *I like learning magic, which I'm just starting to do. Do you know how to use a remote control? And I like to hang out with my friends and read books when I get a chance.*

By the way, I liked your song. Totally not stupid.

See you soon,

Erec

The next morning, Miss Ennui glared at Erec over her spectacles. "Because of the recent events in Alypium, I will change our topic today to discuss the problem of the monsters." She spoke of the dreaded Hydras who loved to devour humans, the feared ogres who loved to snap people in two, the ferocious Cyclopes whose look would paralyze their human prey, and the nasty Chimeras whose goat, lion, and snake heads would fight over who got to devour their victims first.

Then she began to speak of the dangerous dragons of Otherness. "One must always fear the unleashed wrath and wild hysteria of the dragon. They are stupid creatures, poorly formed and ugly, and only too eager to shred their prey into pieces without any reason other than sheer love of destruction. The grotesqueness of the dragon has almost no match—"

"Wait a minute," Erec interrupted. "That's not true at all. I've met dragons. Aoquesth gave me his eye, and he was wonderful. And Patchouli was too. She was beautiful, and she gave me—"

Miss Ennui leaned forward. "A dragon gave you something, and you took it? How foolish! Erec, you need to turn it over to a responsible authority. What did she give you?"

Erec hesitated. He was not about to hand over the Archives of Alithea to anyone, any more than he would give his Amulet of Virtues to Balor. "She gave me advice, that's all," he lied. "And it was good advice too."

She appeared satisfied with that answer. "Any advice that a dragon gives is bad advice, I'll tell you that. They would never help humans. They are too stupid and evil."

Erec couldn't believe his ears. "Why do you think that? It's not true."

His tutor tapped a large stack of books on her desk. "It's all right here in black-and-white. You'll just have to take my word for it."

Erec found it hard to listen to the rest of her lecture. After grabbing a quick lunch, he met Pimster Peebles in Paisley Park. Peebles came flying at him so fast that his latest toupee sailed away in the breeze. When he reached Erec, he flung himself on the ground at his feet. "Oh, Ewec. Tell me it isn't twue. I hear you have to single-handedly slay all of the monstews in Lewna? This can't be. Oh, you are too good, sir. To lay your life on the line like that for the pwoud people of Alypium."

Peebles's words hit hard. Single-handedly slay all the monsters? Erec wasn't sure he could slay anything—or that he wanted to. How did somebody go about single-handedly slaying ferocious creatures anyway? And do this all for the people of Alypium, who hated him? This wasn't exactly what he had in mind.

Peebles pulled himself off the ground and folded into a low bow. "I am at your service. May I teach you? Or would you rather spend the afternoon in Alypium?"

Erec took out his remote control. "I'd like to learn some magic."

Peebles threw his hands up in the air. "Oh no, sir. We cannot do that yet. You are not weady, and I won't have you jumping in over your head."

"But if I'm supposed to kill the monsters, don't I need to know how to use a remote control?"

Peebles threw a few sly glances to the side. "If that were the case, we would have been given specific instructions. I suppose you will have to slay them in other ways."

This sounded ridiculous to Erec. It looked like Rosco would have to help him. In fact, Erec decided, he would find him right now. He should be in Paisley Park with Oscar. Erec backed away, smiling. "I think I'll skip my lesson today, if that's okay."

Rosco and Oscar were taking turns levitating each other near a fountain. When Rosco spotted Erec, his face dropped. "I was going to go find you. Bad news. The Hermit is gone. I think he's taken Danny and Sammy to Lerna."

Erec's breath caught in his throat. "He's gone? Are you sure?"

Rosco nodded. "My guess is he's going to give the twins to the monsters soon. When the monsters attack on the day of the Monster Bash, he can tell everyone how it didn't work. That would make the government look bad, especially since the twins have spent time with President Inkle."

Erec stiffened in surprise. "But I thought he was going to try to feed the twins to the monsters on the day of the Monster Bash. Isn't that what I'm supposed to stop them from doing, eating the twins?"

Rosco gave him a funny look. "No, Erec. The monsters demanded two children a while ago. Your quest is on the day of the Monster Bash. That is the day we think the monsters are planning an attack on humans. I think the twins will be given to the monsters before that."

This didn't sound right. Erec shook his head. What was he going to do? He didn't have the glasses to find the twins. At least he knew where they were going. He had to get to Lerna fast. He was sure he could travel to Otherness from Alypium Station.

That meant he needed to know as much as possible before leaving. "Can you show me any more magic right now?"

Rosco glanced all around for Peebles. "I don't think your tutor would appreciate that. Come to my place this evening and I'll help you out."

Erec thanked him politely, but he planned to be long gone by then.

On his way back to the castle he spotted Bethany. He ran over to say good-bye. "The twins are on their way to Lerna now, and I need to go there before anything happens to them. Take care of Wolfboy for me, okay?"

Bethany was having none of it. "I'm coming with you, Erec. I'm sure it's dangerous out there. You might need some help." She paused, looking uncomfortable. "That is, if you want me."

As appealing as saving Tina on his own was, the thought of Bethany going with him sounded really good. Her help might make a difference. Plus, Bethany would make Otherness less intimidating. "That would be great, Bethany. Is it okay with your tutor?"

Clarus closed her eyes and concentrated, then looked at Bethany and winked. "Sure, kid. See you soon!"

Bethany and Erec walked out of the park. Trumpets blared in the distance, followed by the deep thrum of bass drums. Soon a marching band tramped before them on the street, followed by a huge parade. Posters of Baskania decorated the sides of huge wooden crates, and on top were effigies of the monsters of Otherness. Some of them were being hacked to pieces by the people riding on the crates. Erec spotted a replica of a Hydra with many snakelike heads, like the one he had seen in the MONSTER race the last time he was in Alypium. He was also surprised to see the likeness of a dragon that somebody was happily chopping up. The dragon was made to look stupid, with big, dull eyes.

Erec winced. "Don't people understand that dragons are smart and beautiful? What is the deal?"

Behind the crates, soldiers in green khaki uniforms marched with high goose steps in tight rows. Erec and Bethany's eyes met. A man who was no taller than four feet led them. He was covered from head to toe with ribbons and medals. "Death to the monsters!" he shouted, his voice rising above the crowd.

"Death to the monsters!" the army echoed.

"Well," Bethany said, "at least it looks like you'll be getting some help with the monsters. I think that's General Moreland."

"Rosco mentioned him. He said they might not make it in time for the Monster Bash, let alone to save the twins."

They darted around the back of the parade and into the city toward the bus stop. Signs dangled off buildings. One that read KEEP ALYPIUM FOR THE ALYPIANS, showed a family standing together in front of a small white house. Another that said READ THE PROTOCOLS OF THE ELDERS OF VOGUM, IT COULD SAVE YOUR LIFE showed a painting of a book within the open jaws of a serpent.

"These signs give me the chills," Bethany said. "Why do you think everyone's getting so riled up?"

"Do you think it could be because of the quest I drew from the well?"

"Oh, I don't know." Bethany sighed. "Maybe it's just because the Monster Bash is coming up and because of all the problems they've been having here."

A few people began pointing at Erec and shouting. Before long, a huge crowd was following them, shouting threats and insults. A man yelled, "He's with the monsters. He's helping the monsters." Like a match to a flame, the idea made the gathering crowd go wild.

Angry voices yelled, "He's on their side!" "He wants to kill us!" The crowd closed in fast. Erec could see the bus stop, but it was still several blocks away, and there was no way they could outrace the crowd, let alone wait for the bus. People appeared out of nowhere, closing in. Everybody was looking at him with hateful eyes.

Erec's fists clenched. Someone shouted, "Grab his chain! Get the amulet!" Hands grabbed his shoulders and yanked the Amulet of Virtues on his neck. He batted them off and ran, but soon a wall of people blocked him in on all sides.

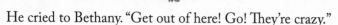

He cried to Bethany. "Get out of here! Go! They're crazy."

Hands clawed him from all sides. Angry shouts blended into a deafening roar. Somebody pushed him. He slammed into a young man, who pushed him into a sneering woman.

In a jerking spasm, Erec's back arched. Energy zinged through his body, shot out of his fingers and toes, and shone from his eyes, ears, and nose like fog lights. Everything around him turned emerald green. Thick white webs filled the air as far as he could see. Clouds spun in the sky like a cyclone, blending with the buildings around him, and he was spinning too. He felt sick, dizzy, deranged.

The hatred of the mob of people fed into the powers racing inside him. It grew, and grew.

He was strong now, invincible, enraged.

His head tilted back, and a violent roar emerged from his throat, reverberating in the air around him. Even to him it sounded unearthly, unreal. More like a lion or thunderclap than a human sound. Another roar ripped from his throat, and his arm shot out like a cat clawing prey. Talons had burst through his fingertips. He tore them through the air, snarling, to the horror of those around him. The people nearest to him stepped away, shocked expressions on their faces. A spotlight shined on the people he looked at, and he realized the light was coming out of his dragon eye.

Rage seethed through him. How could these people do this? How could they gang up on him? People around him retreated, pushing others away from him. "He's a monster," someone murmured. "He's in with the monsters."

He heard a voice call from the back of the throng. "Get him!"

Five or six people pointed remote controls at Erec at the same time. Erec ducked before they fired.

The cloudy thought command rang through his head. *Swing the blond man by his feet before he captures you. Knock everyone down with him.*

Crouched down, Erec lunged forward and grabbed the ankles of a young blond man holding a remote. Without a thought, he stood and swung the man around in a circle, wiping remotes out of hands and knocking people over. People toppled, shouting in anger. Erec let the man go and he sailed into the crowd, people falling around him.

With space cleared, Erec fled toward the castle. The green glow faded along with his feeling of superhuman strength. This was the strangest cloudy thought he'd ever had. Erec could not believe what had happened. He looked down at his fingers. Thankfully the claws were gone. It was almost as if he had turned into another creature, or that another creature had come out of him.

A creature like a dragon.

Erec ran faster. The crowd closed in behind him, more determined then ever to catch him. Shouts like "String 'im up" and "Grab his amulet!" made his blood race.

What good did that cloudy thought do? he wondered. It might have saved him for two seconds from being attacked by the mob, but he seemed no better off now. Then again he wondered what might have happened to him if he didn't have the cloudy thoughts. Would he have made it out of there? He tore faster through the castle gardens, the horde of people at his feet.

"Storm the castle!" someone shouted. "Take no prisoners."

Now he was bringing destruction into the castle with him. He had to leave Alypium now, try to find Otherness, and warn Danny and Sammy before it was too late. Bethany was nowhere to be seen. He must have lost her in the crowds.

He ran toward the west wing, not knowing where else to go, footsteps hot after him, until he got to his room. He flung himself inside and locked the door, but he knew it was only a temporary solution. His pursuers were ready to bash down anything in their way.

Erec threw on his Sneakers and threw Rosco's remote control

and the Archives of Alithea in his pocket, along with a few handfuls of gold, silver, and bronze coins. He couldn't think of anything else he needed. Right before he opened the door, someone pounded on it. He stomped hard with his Sneakers, making a loud crash sound down the hallway. He could hear the person outside run toward it, shouting, "This way!"

Erec bolted out his door and ran for the Port-O-Door near the royal chambers. Right in front of it stood Jam Crinklecut holding a silver tray with cookies and hot chocolate. He looked at Erec, gray-green eyes wide. "Modom Bethany likes an afternoon snack after her tutor is done. Would young sir like some as well?"

"Not now, Jam!" Erec darted past Jam into the vestibule of the Port-O-Door.

"There he is!" Three men appeared at the end of the long hall, pointing. "Get him." They ran toward Erec.

Jam sized up the situation quickly. Then he winged the tray at the men. Hot chocolate splashed the walls, and cookies flew like Frisbees, but the tray steadily spun toward its target, clattering into the men and knocking them down.

Jam hurried into the vestibule with Erec and slammed the door. "Where to, sir?"

"Otherness." Erec could hear footsteps pounding toward them. The screen on the Port-O-Door was divided into a white section labeled "Alypium," a blue one labeled "Ashona," a red one that said "Aorth," and a yellow one that said "Otherness." Jam poked a finger onto the yellow section. Before Erec could find Lerna on the screen, Jam pressed the map somewhere in the middle. A click resounded. Jam threw the door open, shoved Erec through in front of him and pulled it shut.

"Thanks, Jam." Once through the door, they found themselves deep in the woods somewhere in Otherness. He wished Jam had asked him where he wanted to go. Then again, they probably would not have had the time to find Lerna on the map, wherever it was. Anyway, he was glad to have somebody with him out here in the wilderness. "I wonder where we are."

Jam looked around. "I don't know, sir. From the appearance of the fauna, it seems we may be in a jungle in Otherness."

"Yeah, thanks, Jam. I kinda figured that." Other than the Port-O-Door leading back into the castle there was no sign of civilization in sight. "Can those people figure out where I went through the Port-O-Door and follow me here?"

Jam nodded his head from side to side, thinking. "It would take them a while. Unless we get rid of it on this end. Then they'll never find us. Would young sir like me to get rid of the Port-O-Door?"

What did he have to lose? He could not go back into Alypium now, or even later. That crazy mob of people would find him, and then who knows what would happen? He could end up in a dungeon or worse. Then how would he find the twins? How would he get to Lerna for his second quest and stop the monsters?

No, his way was forward. He gazed wistfully at the Port-O-Door, then agreed. "Let's get rid of it. They'll be out here chasing me soon otherwise. If you want to go back to Alypium, it's okay."

"And leave young sir out in the wilderness all alone? I don't think so." Jam straightened himself and dusted off his gray vest. "I go where I am most needed, sir."

Erec smiled. "Thanks, Jam."

Jam typed a code into the keypad of the Port-O-Door and it vanished.

They were adrift in a strange dark jungle with no idea where they were nor where they were headed.

Erec pointed straight ahead. "Should we go this way?"

"You're in charge, young sir."

That was just what Erec wanted to hear.

CHAPTER FIFTEEN
The Cyclopes

I T WAS QUIET in the jungle, the kind of quiet that rings in your ears. Gone were the shouts of the frantic mob that had chased Erec. His ears adjusted to the crickets, soft twitters of birds, little breezes playing games with leaves . . . and what sounded like a loud belch.

Erec and Jam looked at each other, eyes wide. Someone else was out here with them. Nobody was within sight, but they heard heavy footsteps crunching leaves and twigs, moving away from them.

"Oh, my." Jam shook his head. It seemed to be sinking in that they really were in the wilds of Otherness, with no idea what lay before them.

"Do we follow the footsteps?" Erec asked. "Or run the other way?" It was a coin toss. Civilization could be a good way to find how to get to Lerna—as long as it didn't mean getting eaten. He shivered, thinking about what he had heard of the vogum and other monsters that lived out here.

Jam looked uncertain, eyes darting back and forth between where the footsteps had come from and the opposite direction. "Whatever young sir thinks, sir."

"Let's go that way, carefully, and see what we can find there." They set out toward where they had heard heavy crunching footsteps. Whatever had made them must have been big.

Jam caught his breath. "I entirely forgot. We haven't been inoculated. There are all kinds of diseases one may catch from traveling in Otherness. One usually must get shots before coming here."

That was the last thing Erec needed to hear. "Like what?"

"Well," Jam said with a sigh, "there is the dreaded hat head. It's a terrible affliction, they say, similar to another called helmet hair." He shuddered. "Then there is something called the drenchers. Not nice at all."

Erec wished they'd had the shots, but they'd just have to take their chances. Instead he asked, "Jam, what was wrong with those people in Alypium? They were all acting so crazy."

"It's been getting worse there, with everyone riled up over the monsters. We in the Kingdoms of the Keepers have always been more vulnerable to that kind of craziness, since the Substance is disturbed here. Makes us all a little crazy sometimes."

They soon came to a clearing. In it stood a huge stone hut with a peaked red wooden roof. Smoke issued from a small chimney in the center. Erec sighed with relief. Here was someone to help them find their way to Lerna. Maybe even give them some food. Erec realized he was hungry.

Suddenly, a raging, beastlike growl reverberated from inside the hut. A man in the house began sobbing, screaming, but the roar of the beast overwhelmed him. Erec and Jam looked at each other in terror. What was going on here? Maybe one of the terrible monsters in Otherness had broken into some poor man's house. Maybe it was even the vogum. Erec wanted to run, but he couldn't leave the man to an awful fate.

Jam pulled Erec away, but he broke free and ran under a bush by the house. Jam followed him and whispered, "Has young sir gone mad? This is not a safe place for us."

"I know," Erec whispered. "Tell me, what are the vogum like?"

"Not good." Jam's forehead wrinkled. "The vogum are a term for the two most hideous, dangerous creatures on earth. The Hydras and the Valkyries. When they get together, their powers grow and combine into a terrible force. We call that the vogum."

Erec jabbed his thumb toward the house. "We have to help that guy, Jam."

Jam's face filled with determination, and he nodded. The windows were too high to peek through. Another earthshaking holler rattled from inside, with bloodcurdling growls following it.

"No!" the man cried. "No! No!"

"Rrraaaaaauuuughh!" the monster bellowed.

The situation seemed dire. There was no time to waste. Erec had his remote control with him. He barely knew how to use it, but now was the time to try. Maybe he could lure the monster away from the poor man and then figure out what to do.

He wanted to throw open the door and burst inside, but the

thick wood of the huge door was heavy and hard to move. After prying it open, he ran in with his remote control out.

On a huge couch before him sat two of the strangest creatures Erec had ever seen. They were human in form, yet enormous, each with a single large eye bulging from their foreheads. A male one was dressed in a huge sarong tied over one shoulder that looked like it was made of animal skins. The septum of his nose was pierced with a large bone. He clutched a large, pointed spear in one of his hands.

The female creature next to him was wearing an ornate dress festooned with more silk, beads, and buttons than Erec had ever seen in one place. Muscular calves, the color and texture of tree trunks, extended from her dress to the pearl-emblazoned high heels encasing her huge feet. She held a dainty china teacup with her pinkie finger extended.

Neither of the creatures noticed that Erec had burst into their room, remote held high. Their eyes were glued to a large television set, showing more creatures that looked like them on a talk show. One of the hideous things on the television was sobbing, and another talked about how every relationship it had went sour.

Jam whispered into his ear, voice shaking, "Cyclopes, sir. Back out slowly."

Erec took a step back, but froze when the male Cyclops let loose another earsplitting roar in response to a Cyclops on television saying, "Love isn't easy, love isn't kind, but I am willing to give it all up to just have one more taste of love again." The female Cyclops put her arm over her eyes. "No," she said, in the voice that Erec had thought was the man's, "it's just not fair. I can't take it."

The male Cyclops sniffed. His voice was a deep growl. "Something smells good, honey. You cooking?"

"No," she said. "I thought we'd carry out some ginglehoffer."

"Funny." The male sniffed again. "I smell the blood of an Alypian man."

Erec stiffened. Jam yanked him back toward the door. Then both of the Cyclopes swung around and looked at them. "Loook! Aaaarrrggghhhhh!" The male Cyclops sprang to his feet and ran at Erec and Jam. Erec scrambled toward the door, shaking. Before he could escape, it slammed shut in front of his face. He looked up to see the Cyclops's hand on the door. A second later, Erec and Jam had been scooped up in each of the Cyclops's hands.

The Cyclops seemed to go mad, running around in his hut holding Erec and Jam, roaring wildly and screaming, "Food! Food!"

Erec thought he was going to faint. It was all over. No second quest. No saving the twins. He was caught in the grip of a terrible beast who was racing around his house with him so fast that Erec's head was spinning. Jam looked green.

Please, Erec prayed, *let me have a cloudy thought. Let me turn into a dragon and scare this creature away.*

The Cyclops plopped Erec and Jam onto two small stools, fists tightly clamped around them. He eyed them greedily with a terrifying smile. Erec frantically tried to remember how the MONSTER contest had said to escape from Cyclopes. Tripping them? No . . . bribing them. That was it.

He remembered something else. Miss Ennui had said Cyclopes loved to crush humans' bones for sheer pleasure. But then again, she also said that one glance from a Cyclops would turn a human to stone. That didn't seem right. Neither he nor Jam had been changed.

"Food!" the creature roared. "Vaerna! Bring these visitors some food!"

"Calm down, Haenry," the woman Cyclops with the deep man's voice answered. "I'm getting some now."

The Cyclops let Erec and Jam go, and plopped himself on a stool. Erec wondered if he jumped and ran, would the creature catch him again? Haenry looked at Erec and smacked his lips. "We don't get a lot of guests out here," he growled. "Who are you?"

Erec was afraid to say his name. Maybe the thing had heard about him from Alypium and hated him too.

Jam said, "I'm Jam Crinklecut, kind sir. Please accept our visit as a sign of goodwill extended from our simple home to yours."

"Jam," Haenry chuckled. "Sounds like you'd be good spread on toast."

Jam gulped.

"And who are you?" It turned its gaze to Erec.

Nothing came from Erec's throat. If he lied, would this thing be able to tell? His lips moved silently.

"Wait a minute," Vaerna said. "He looks just like this picture." She held up a black-and-white picture of Erec surrounded by a black border with some words printed beneath. "Haenry, he's Erec Rex."

If Erec had any doubt that Haenry had heard of him, it vanished now. Haenry let out a wild roar, pounding his chest and shaking his hair in abandon. He stomped so hard the room shook. "Erec Rex! Erec Rex is in me house?"

Erec and Jam traded glances, sure this was the end. Jam smiled apologetically as if to say he had tried his best.

Haenry bowed low with a big grin. "I am honored by your visit, Erec. You are more than welcome in me house."

Erec looked Haenry in the eye and said, "You are hideously ugly." Jam looked at him in shock. Erec gulped, body frozen, jaws clamped shut. What made him say such a stupid thing? Then he remembered. He was carrying the Archives of Alithea. Why had he brought them? The wretched scroll made him say the dumbest stuff. He shook his head, eyelids slowly closing.

Haenry laughed so heartily that Erec's ears rung. "You think I'm ugly? That's a good one, Erec Rex. I like you, even though you look worse than a Hulder man."

Vaerna set huge plates of unidentified meats on their laps and sat down. "Eat, please." The floppy gray items in front of them had smells Erec could not identify. "So, are you here to save the dragon babies?" she asked eagerly. "It's the talk of Polyphemus and all of Otherness, I hear. It's a disaster that they're all missing. Nobody knows what to do."

Erec felt bad. "I'd like to help with that. There is something I need to do first, though."

Haenry said, "We are thankful to you, Erec. You saved King Piter, and therefore you helped us. How may we repay you?"

Erec's jaw dropped. Did he hear right? Were these the first people that understood what he had done and didn't think he was a liar and a cheat? His breathing eased.

"Well, I need to get to Lerna and find my brother and sister. Can you help me get there?"

Haenry roared, making Erec jump. "Of course I'll help. Anything for Erec Rex, hero of Otherness."

Erec started feeling pretty good. This was working out much better than he'd expected. His stomach growled, and he realized how hungry he was. He sipped a steaming drink in front of him. In the next moment he slammed the cup down. His mouth was on fire. Vaerna raised the massive eyebrow crossing her forehead. "Don't like root scotch?"

"N-no," Erec said as politely as he could. He hesitantly picked up a piece of slimy meat. It tasted like gooey metal, but he was starving, so he ate a little more.

"Sorry," Vaerna said. "All I had left over was giant mosquito liver."

Erec dropped the rest back onto the plate and gagged.

Erec and Jam spent the night on the floor on pillows, each the size of a mattress. In the morning, they graciously turned down more giant mosquito liver. As always, Jam parted his hair far to the side and slicked it down with some gel he carried in his coat. Erec wondered why. It made him look silly. He had just started looking more natural, too, after most of it had worn off.

Jam excused himself and returned a few minutes later with berries and wild chicory leaves on a small silver tray he had stashed in his dress coat. "A good butler is prepared for anything." He pointed at bushy green leaves with a round orange fruit. "*Solanum macrocarpon.* The gboma eggplant. Leaves are good for boils and throat difficulties, sir."

Erec looked at the tray in awe. "How did you know about this stuff? And have the tray?"

"It's my gift." Jam's eyes twinkled. "I'm always prepared to serve."

The wild vegetables and fruit tasted so good Erec finished the whole tray. Immediately, he felt bad he had not saved some for Jam. "I'm sorry."

"No problem at all, sir. Young sir must eat first. Jam will help himself outside."

Haenry kissed Vaerna good-bye with a sound like a truck hitting a tree, then walked outside with Erec. "Well," he growled, "let's see your map. I'll try and figure out where we are and how to get to . . . Where did you say you are going?"

"Lerna." Erec's heart sank. "You don't know the way?"

"No, never been out of Polyphemus. No reason to go." Haenry shook his head. "People look too strange other places for me taste. But Cyclopes are very good at tracking things. I can follow almost any footsteps if I need to. So let's see your map."

Erec held out his empty hands. "No map. I guess we'll have to walk until we find something."

They walked through the trees until Haenry suggested that Erec and Jam each ride on one of his shoulders. From then on they moved much faster. Even so, Erec wished they knew where they were going. They could well be walking straight away from Lerna and out of Otherness as far as he knew. Hopefully they would find someone soon who could tell them which way to go.

Out in the middle of nowhere they came upon a huge metal box with a glass front that glistened between the pine trees. Haenry walked close, and Erec could see it was a vending machine filled with small gray balls. A sign at the top read, "Worm aniballs. Three for a gand." Erec laughed. Why would anybody want worms out here? He couldn't see a lake to fish in sight.

Soon after, they came to another vending machine in the woods, this one selling animals of all shapes and sizes. The sign on the machine said, "Pets. One for two shires." These were not aniballs, but real rabbits, dogs, cats, mice, birds, and turtles sitting on little shelves. They looked like they were talking to each other, but Erec could not hear what they were saying. For a moment he was tempted to buy a pet hamster, but he quickly realized that this was not the time. Haenry nodded toward the animals. "Snack anyone?"

"Uh, no," Erec said. "I don't think so."

Before long, they found yet another vending machine in the forest. Erec looked into it with curiosity. An old man sat scrunched up inside on a small shelf. His legs were crossed, barely able to fit in the tight space. A long limp gray beard and mustache hung down his face, and he gazed into the distance as if the sight of Erec, Jam, and Haenry wasn't worth a glance. The sign on the top of the vending machine said, "Advice. One for a shire."

One advice for a shire? This was too good to pass up. Erec had a pocketful of change and saw no reason not to try it. "Why don't we each get some advice?"

He handed silver shires to Jam and Haenry. Jam put his shire into the advice machine first. The old man inside took a puff on his pipe and tilted his head. "You should stop waxing your hair down. You look stupid."

Jam's face dropped. Erec looked away, embarrassed. The old man was right, though. Jam had a pleasant face, but he did make himself look ridiculous the way he slicked his hair to the side.

Haenry eagerly put his shire in, not in the least put off by what had the old man had said to Jam. The old man gazed at the Cyclops with a bland look and said in an uncaring monotone, "Your daughter, Vaeronicae, loves you and Vaerna. She ran off to find true love, but now has learned that the truest love is in the hearts she has known all along." Erec thought it was funny to hear the man say such flowery things with such a dry voice.

Haenry, on the other hand, threw his hand over his heart and howled so loud that Erec jumped. He ran around screaming like a wild man for a minute, then threw himself onto the forest floor, sobbing. "Me Vaeronicae, me dear daughter. We have sent her from our hearts, ne'er to return. We are such fools in the world of love, such pathetic wastrels." Haenry really did look pathetic, howling and sobbing. It was odd to hear such a gruff-looking creature nattering on about, well, the same kind of things that made him holler at the talk show he had been watching. Erec decided that Cyclopes, even if they looked tough, were ridiculously sentimental.

It was his turn. He dropped a shire into the machine. The man's stare bored right through him. "You are trying to find your way around in Otherness. Since you are very absorbent, you can ask the pointing pines to help you find your way."

The pointing pines? Erec looked around him. Plenty of pine trees were scattered among the other trees. Were these the pointing pines?

He asked the man, "How do they work?"

The man rested calmly, not batting an eyelash, as if he had not heard Erec.

"I see." Erec pulled out another shire and put it in the machine. "How do the pointing pines work?"

The man answered with a tinge of sarcasm, "You shouldn't care so much what people think about you."

No kidding. It was a problem, he knew, but it was not what he wanted to hear. He needed to know how to get around Otherness. "How do the pointing pines work?"

When there was no answer, he kicked the machine.

"That's it." Yet he knew what the old man wanted. He dropped another shire in. "How do the pointing pines work?"

"The Archives of Alithea will make you embarrass yourself by forcing you to tell the truth." The old man wore a satisfied gloat, as if he was aware that Erec already knew. The advice was getting worse and worse. Erec almost had forgotten what the man's original advice was, about the pointing pines.

"Haenry, Jam, do either of you know about the pointing pines?" They shook their heads. He thought about what the man had said about him. "Jam, what does he mean that I'm very absorbent?"

Jam was pleased to help. "Young sir, being absorbent is a great thing. It means you are in touch with the Aitherplanes and the Substance that runs through them. The more absorbent one is, the more power one has inside. You could say you are at one with the energies around you. Absorbency lets you work with the Substance. King Piter is ultra-absorbent. He also has a device given to him by the Fates that makes him even more so."

"Oh, really?" Erec was curious. "What's that?"

"An Aitherpoint quill. If he thinks a question and starts to write with it, the quill will write an answer."

"He mentioned that quill before." Erec's eyes widened. "He said he wasn't strong enough to use it yet. But if he could have found out where Danny and Sammy were . . ."

"I don't know." Jam's brows knitted. "The quill doesn't always give direct answers. It can be pretty cagey."

Erec didn't care about King Piter or his cagey quill. As usual, he would find his own way.

He glanced at the old man inside the vending machine. He'd said to use the pointing pines. By now Erec had dealt with enough things himself, including his wild dragon eye, that he felt confident. He'd make the pointing pines show him the way.

CHAPTER SIXTEEN
The Pointing Pines

EREC WANDERED THROUGH the trees, staring at the pines. Most of them did have long, green fingerlike points at their tops. Erec focused on one of them. "Which way is Lerna?" The pine did not move.

Instead a swirl of pink appeared in the dirt by his feet, growing quickly into a snail covered with red hearts. He was sure it was another letter from Tina. Her snail mail seemed able to find him anywhere when he was outside. He pulled a sheet of scented pink paper from the shell.

My dearest Erec,

I can't tell you how excited we all are that you are coming here. But I guess the most excited one is me. And you're going to help us? That is so amazing. We always knew you were brave, but what you are going to do is the bravest thing I can think of. Those monsters are coming to attack us. It scares me what will happen when they get here. And it takes about the most selfless, honest, caring person I can imagine to stand up to them, especially knowing what could happen.

But, because I know what may happen, I really am afraid for you and don't want you to do it. I would rather you be alive, and still a hero to me, than dead. You are such an amazing person, and one of the few not from Lerna that sees things the way we do here.

I am so proud that you saved those baby dragons on your first quest. I hope you might even be able to save the rest of the baby dragons that are missing from their families. Why shouldn't I wish for that? You seem to be taking on every other problem in the world!

Alypium does stink. It once was a great place. I used to live there before my family was thrown out for not being the same as everyone else. But if they don't appreciate you there, know that you'll always have a place that really wants you here in Lerna.

When you come, you can stay at our house if you want. I asked my mom and she would love it. And if you like springball we'll get a game together while you're here. That would be a blast—and I'll put on my uniform and cheer just for you! And no,

I don't use a remote control. And I'm totally psyched you liked my song. I'm learning it on guitar. If you want, I can sing it for you.
Love and waiting,
Tina

Erec reread the letter five times, then stuck it in his pocket. Tina was so great. He wondered what she looked like. She sounded pretty from her writing, girlish from the hearts and pink perfumed stationery. She probably had long blond hair and blue eyes, or maybe wavy red hair, but no, he pictured her blond. Anyway, he couldn't believe he'd be able to try a pickup game of springball there, and that Tina would cheer on the sidelines for him. He couldn't wait to get to Lerna. It was true that he had to face the monsters—he had no idea how he'd fight off the snarling Hydras and dangerous vogum—but the army from Alypium should be there, and hopefully he'd get a cloudy thought.

He tried not to think about that part. Anyway, he wouldn't get there at all if he didn't figure out which way to go. He gazed up at the pine tree tips, full of hope and excitement about Lerna. *Show me the way, pines,* he thought. *Show me the way I need to go.*

Before his eyes, the pine tree tips all started bending in the same direction like rows of fingers pointing toward his destiny. "Look! Jam! Haenry! Check it out!"

They all gazed in wonder as the pine trees bent slowly, silently, as if bowing to a king.

Haenry took huge strides with Erec and Jam on his shoulders. Over their heads appeared an immense dragon sailing through the air, breathing fire, black wings flared against the blue sky. Its scales shimmered a dusky red.

"Wow," Erec said. "That was beautiful."

"Look." Jam pointed. Behind some trees was a huge cavern entering a jutting rocky cliff. "Dragon territory."

Haenry looked ill at ease and walked faster. "I'm getting hungry," he growled. "Let's get out of this dragon settlement and I'll catch us a ginglehoffer. It's dangerous here."

They passed a rocky cave on a hill. It looked familiar. Could this be Aoquesth's cave? Erec felt that it was. "I think I know the dragon that lives there."

Haenry growled quietly, not wanting to attract attention. "Thinking you know a dragon won't save you from it. Let's get out of here." He raced through the woods, trees whizzing by in a blur. Erec and Jam had to duck low on his shoulders to not get whacked in the head by stray branches.

Eventually Erec heard music ahead. Yes, he was sure it was music, a sign of civilization. Lerna! He sighed with relief. Maybe he could find Tina's house in time for dinner so he wouldn't have to eat spit-roasted ginglehoffer.

As they grew closer, they could see the spires and turrets of a village. The music, which sounded like it came from a carnival, grew louder as they approached. There must have been a special event going on. Maybe it was a parade in his honor. Tina did know he was coming. . . .

Circus music flowed from a big red-and-white-striped tent, filling the town. The streets were desolate, except for one passing car that was jammed with about twenty people. It seemed like everyone was in the tent watching some show. They walked through a folded fabric opening and all heads turned to look at them. Someone ran from a giant ring on the floor in front of them. Erec kept walking, barely noticing that he, Jam, and Haenry had stepped into the ring. Suddenly, spotlights were on them. A mass of balls rolled onto the

THE MONSTERS OF OTHERNESS

floor. Trying to get a look at the crowd, Erec was blinded by the spotlight, and he stumbled on the balls. He fell into Haenry, who knocked over Jam. The audience was laughing and applauding as he tried to get up, but he slipped on a mat covered with soapy water. He fell, his face splashing into a bucket of water someone shoved there at the right moment.

The audience roared with laughter. Erec was not sure what was going on. It all happened so fast. Haenry said, "This is a clown settlement. Unless Lerna is only clowns, this ain't it."

Erec squinted into the audience. Everyone's skin had a white sheen and circles of bright makeup. This wasn't Lerna. Tina wasn't a clown, that was for sure. He wondered if the clowns might help him find his way, but they were having too good a time laughing at him, and he did not trust them. It was time to get out and keep going toward Lerna.

The three stumbled toward the exit, but before they got there, each was hit square in the face by a gigantic pie. Erec blinked, and huge chunks of pie fell to the floor. He wiped another chunk off his cheek and licked it. It was chocolate cream pie, and it was good. He scooped the large chunks off his face and ate them. He picked the rest of the tin off the floor. It was better than ginglehoffer, anyway.

Outside the tent, Jam produced white cloths for everyone to clean their faces with and found more berries and edible leaves. Erec looked up at the pine trees, asking them in his mind which way he should go. At first there was no response, but after he concentrated and relaxed, the pines began to bend, pointing in the same direction as before.

Haenry helped Erec and Jam back onto his shoulders and started off. They trudged through the woods at breakneck speed.

"Thanks, Haenry," Erec said. "I would have never made it to Lerna in time on my own."

Through the trees, Erec could see a building on a distant hill. Suddenly, the whole building sprang into the air on four thick, wiry legs. It fell onto one pair of feet, then the other, and in this way it leaped and hopscotched down the hill and across a field.

"Look at that!" Erec pointed.

Jam squinted. "Ah. That would be a Vulcan store, sir. Hard to spot, those are. Before the MagicNet was invented, very few people could buy things from them. They're hard to find when you need one, and they can be a nightmare to track."

The store leapt over a brook and bounded out of sight. "I wonder if that is where my mom bought our alarm clock, toaster, toothbrush, and coat rack."

"If they are animated objects, then likely yes, but she probably ordered online. Vulcan stores prefer Otherness, but one can occasionally find them in Alypium or Aorth. On rare occasions they have been seen underwater in Ashona as well."

Haenry stopped so suddenly that Erec and Jam shot from his shoulders into the leaves and bushes of the forest floor. Haenry sniffed. "I smell dinner. I'll be back." In five minutes he returned with an ugly carcass slung over his shoulder. The ginglehoffer looked like a gigantic crab with one large, protruding eye and a huge circular mouth with rows of sharp teeth. Its body was round and six feet across.

Jam raised his eyebrows. "How did you catch that thing so fast?"

Haenry reached into his pocket. "I use these as bait. Never fails." He pulled out a few marshmallows. With the help of a large stone, Haenry soon cracked the ginglehoffer open and began stuffing large handfuls into his mouth. "Have some," he said.

"Uh, no thanks," Erec said.

Jam nodded briskly. "Not hungry anymore, kind sir."

There was a stirring in the bushes, then a loud snorting sound.

Leaves thrashed and a guttural noise filled the air. "Hruunkhh, hruunkhh, mooorrrhh." Two huge bulls appeared behind the leaves. When they stepped forward, Erec could see they had giant, hairy human legs. One wore something that resembled a red skintight bathing suit, and the other white cotton underpants.

Minotaurs.

Erec remembered the minotaur that had attacked the kids at a party in the agora. Luckily he had gotten a cloudy thought then and stabbed it in the eye with a shard of glass. But there was no glass here and no cloudy thought. And the minotaurs looked hungry. They pawed the dirt with their human feet and waved their hoofed front feet in the air.

Haenry did not look concerned. "Hey, fellas. Leave these guys alone. This is Erec Rex, here. He saved King Piter. We all owe him one."

The minotaurs did not look impressed. They snorted again and charged.

Erec and Jam jumped and ran behind Haenry, who lifted them onto his shoulders. He kicked the minotaurs away with his foot. "Dumb animals. Let's get going." He took off across the forest with huge strides.

Erec looked behind to see the minotaurs who had apparently given up and were now running at each other at full speed and bashing their heads together.

It seemed they would never find Lerna. "How big is Otherness?" Erec asked.

"It's huge," Jam said, "although I admit I have never been here before, sir. It's all the protected wilds for the creatures that long ago were exiled from Upper Earth, and then from the Kingdoms of the Keepers."

"So are we on Upper Earth, then?" Erec was confused.

"Yes, in a sense. Alypium is smaller, up in the Himalayan Mountains. There is a golden dome of mist around it that keeps anyone that is not familiar with magic from seeing or entering it, and it keeps the climate nice too. Otherness is spread through parts of Nepal, Tibet, and Myanmar, up through the Tien Shan Mountains of China and parts of Russia. It is in areas where Upper Earth people can't go. Either the wilderness is too rough in those parts or Baskania put spells on those lands to keep people away."

"And where is Ashona?"

"Why, in the Pacific Ocean, sir. Of course. Another protected area. And Aorth is underground, with segments under each of the earth's seven continents. Very large, indeed."

Great. If Otherness was that large, they would never get to Lerna, let alone in time to save the twins and stop the monsters. Finally, Erec saw clusters of mud-colored huts amid some hills. This was not how he pictured Lerna, but at this point he didn't care what it looked like. It was getting dark, and he was only too happy to climb off of Haenry's shoulders and walk toward the little settlement.

A very small man darted out of the shadows and looked them up and down suspiciously. He could not have been taller than two feet. The man had glowing amber eyes, which mischievously peeked through the long white hair that settled over his face. A red pointed cap sat on his head. Erec was amazed to see long cat whiskers growing from his nose.

"Eeh?" The man looked them up and down. "Watch yee all doing here? Did the trolls sent ya's? Well, tell 'em we know how to keep our mouths shut. And stop sending us threats or, or . . ." He shook his fist at them.

Erec fought the temptation to pick the little man up. "The trolls didn't send us. We are looking for Lerna. Do you know where it is?"

"What-a?" The little man asked. "Never heard of it. And I've heard of everything around these parts."

"Which ain't much." Another little man with a pointed blue hat, cat whiskers, and glowing amber eyes poked his head around the corner. He ran to Erec, Jam, and Haenry and looked them up and down, shaking his head with disgust. "They're biggies, all right. And no tails on 'em either. Let's take them to our biggies then, see what cooks up."

The two small men led Erec, Jam, and Haenry into the cluster of mud huts. Two normal-sized men were talking on the corner. When they turned around, Erec could see they both had slim brown tails like cows.

Around a corner stood two tall women who looked perfectly human, until they turned around, and Erec saw they had long white cow tails poking through holes in the backs of their skirts. The man looked at them suspiciously, and Erec noticed a few of the women were poking their heads around the corner.

The little man in the red cap grabbed Erec's and Jam's wrists as if he had captured them himself. He made his voice extra gruff. "I found these creatures hanging around and acting all suspicious. They say the trolls didn't send them."

The little man in the blue cap grabbed Haenry's wrist and puffed his chest up like he was proud of his capture. Then he glanced up at Haenry and must have thought twice, for he slowly lowered his hand and backed away, bowing in apology.

"Thank you," one of the human-sized men said. "Who may you be, then?"

"Just travelers," Jam said. "We are looking for a city called Lerna. Do you know where it is?"

The men shook their heads, as did the women who had come out to stare with interest at these individuals with no tails.

It seemed Erec would never find Lerna. "Do you have a place we can stay tonight?"

After much chattering and nodding, a man spoke up. "We are the Hulder people. Welcome to our little village. It seems Tomte and Nisse, our gnomes, brought you here, so we owe you a good meal and a place to sleep."

At the mention of this, Tomte and Nisse hung their heads in shame. "Are you sure you're not with the trolls?"

After Erec, Jam, and Haenry reassured the gnomes that they were not, the Hulder folk brought them steaming plates of delicious meat, scrambled eggs, cheeses, and breads. Erec was so hungry he practically inhaled the food, making a point of not asking what it was. "Your tails look funny." Erec bit his tongue. There went those annoying Archives of Alithea again. Real smooth.

The women giggled, pointing at him and whispering, he was sure, about his lack of a tail.

Haenry had just asked for his fourth helping, when he growled, "This is Erec Rex with us here. You all should know you're helping a very important person."

At once, the Hulder women shrieked, running away, hands over their mouths. One dropped an entire platter of cooked apples on Jam's head. The men stepped back, looking pale. One asked, voice trembling, "What are you doing here? We can't tell you anything. We don't know anything. Just go away and leave us alone."

Erec and Jam looked at each other. Well, that was interesting. If there ever had been any reason to think these strangers were hiding a secret from him, this was it. It seemed about the most suspicious thing he had heard anyone say. And Erec was through with secrets. "You know who I am?"

The Hulder men and women who had gathered back around him, staring in curiosity, all vehemently shook their heads. "Oh, no. No."

"No!" "No." They looked like they were trying so hard to convince Erec that he almost laughed.

"But you went nuts when you heard my name. You must've heard of me somewhere."

"Oh, no. Never." "Not at all, no." "No."

"Yeah, right." Erec glanced at Jam. "What secrets are you keeping from me, then?" he asked them. "Do they have to do with the monsters in Lerna?"

The cattle-tailed people looked at each other in confusion and shrugged. "Monsters in where?"

Erec frowned. "Do your secrets have to do with who my father is?"

"No." A man waved him off. "We don't have any secrets, okay? We'll give you a place to sleep tonight, then you'd better leave us alone."

Erec was not satisfied. "I want to know any secrets you have about me now. I'm tired of people keeping everything from me." Nobody seemed to be paying any attention to him. "Do you know where my brother and sister are?"

The Hulder folk shrugged and walked away. Jam cleared his throat. "Does your secret have to do with the trolls?"

The tailed people reacted with shock, shaking their heads in a frenzy. "Absolutely not." "Trolls? Never heard of them."

Jam winked at Erec. "Methinks they doth protest too much." He tilted his head. "So the trolls are planning something, then?"

"Oh, no." The Hulder people waved their hands in front of them wildly, shaking their heads. "Absolutely not."

"I see." Jam pondered a moment. "Does this something have to do with Erec's second quest?"

The men and women tilted their heads as if they had no idea what Jam was talking about. "Hmm," he murmured to Erec, "I guess not." He squinted, eyes roaming over the small crowd. "Have the trolls threatened you, then, if you told their secret?"

Again, there was an uproar of denial, making it clear that they had, indeed, been very much threatened. Although this seemed like a way to get answers out of the Hulder folk, it took a long time. The villagers seemed to sense that they were revealing too much, and they began to disappear into the buildings. One of the Hulder men offered Erec a bed in his house that evening, and another offered one to Jam. Somebody told Haenry he was welcome to sleep in the barn with the gnomes.

Erec followed a Hulder couple to a small hut made of packed earth and straw. They pointed him to a tiny room with a bale of straw for a bed. Erec was frustrated. What were they hiding? How could he find out? Then he remembered something that he was carrying.

He took the Archives of Alithea out of his pocket and stumbled, letting the scroll slip through his fingers onto the floor. The Hulder man picked it up and held it out to Erec, but he did not take it back. "What is the secret you're keeping for the trolls?"

The man crossed his arms. "The secret is that they're hiding the baby dragons in Trollebotten Cave in Jotnar. Baskania is going to kill them all two days after the Monster Bash in Lerna." The Hulder woman looked at her husband in shock, mouth hanging open. "Kajsa, what are you saying?" She put her hand to her forehead.

Kajsa looked to be in as much shock as she was in. "I don't know. I just told him."

Erec asked, "Why is Baskania going to kill the baby dragons?"

Kajsa straightened and said, "He's harvesting their eyes so he can have many dragon eyes to make himself more powerful. Their eyes were too young to work right at first, but now they're ready." He looked sick and started to walk in circles. "Why am I saying this to you? You must have put a spell on me."

Erec looked sternly at him, as if he had indeed worked some kind of spell. "And why did you want to hide this from me in particular?"

"You are Erec Rex." Kajsa looked defeated, as if it was not worth even trying to resist. "You are setting things right. You saved King Piter from Baskania. You will probably save the dragons too."

"Don't you want the baby dragons saved?"

Kajsa's wife piped up, seeming now resigned to telling Erec everything. "Of course we want the dragons to be saved. We're afraid, that's all. The trolls come here and take our food and treasures. They tell us things and then threaten us if we spill their secrets. If you race off to save the dragons, and the trolls find out we told this to you . . ."

"Don't worry," Erec said. "Nobody will ever find out that you told me. I think I'd better go now."

The man nodded, handing Erec back the scroll, completely unaware of its power over him.

CHAPTER SEVENTEEN
Trollebotten Cave

BALOR AND DAMON Stain walked through the thick oak doors of the Inner Sanctum of the Green House. Balor pushed against one of the doors as he went in. As he thought, it would not budge. Only Baskania, the Shadow Prince, could open and shut them. The doors slammed shut behind them.

The room was dimly lit and twinkled like a firefly convention. Hundreds of candles around the room threw glittery light on the gems encrusting the walls and the gold furniture. Baskania enjoyed sparkling images, fine artwork, clean lines, and modern design. Balor guessed that was because he had so many eyes.

"No, Balor." A hoarse whisper echoed from behind a large desk. "It's because I'm old. I'm sick and tired of looking at ugly junk and pathetic people. You'll understand someday. The only things worth anything are beauty and power."

A collection of eyes glowed behind the sculptured desk. As Balor walked closer with his brother, he saw that the eyes belonged to Baskania. He sat in a velvet chair, eyes covering his face, neck, arms, and hands. Slowly, the eyes melted into his flesh. They left deep pits, making him look like a sea of holes. Then skin stretched over them, swallowing them, until his face became a flat expanse of skin. Looking at him made Balor gulp. A sharp, bent nose erupted, followed by a deep gash that formed thin lips and a twisted smile. His black cloak fell over his arms.

One steely, sunken blue eye with dark bags under it popped out, but only a deep dent sat where its matching one should have been. Baskania had removed his own eye to make room for Erec Rex's dragon eye. But instead, Erec Rex had managed to get away with it. Unforgivable, but it would soon be corrected.

Balor much preferred to look at the Shadow Prince as he was now, silver gray hair flowing into a sharp widow's peak, sneer lines around his mouth. Beside him stood President Washington Inkle, so thin and trembling that it seemed he could be blown over like a leaf. He was tall and had a few gray hairs scattered over his bald head. His lips bore bright red scabs from his habit of biting them.

Balor crossed his arms in front of him. He was important, chosen by the best, raised to the top. It was only a matter of time before he would be at Baskania's side. Baskania had assured him of that. Then, before long, he would be Baskania's boss. Nobody would keep him down. He was glad that the men posing as Danny and Sammy Rex were discovered. Now he had the chance to prove his worth, do an important job.

Baskania's voice was cold. "You know, Balor, this will be much easier once you and Damon give me one of your eyes. Then I can see what you see and know what you are doing, wherever you are. If you are going to spy on Erec Rex for me, I will need to look through your eye whenever I want."

Balor grabbed his brother's arm in fear, but quickly let go, hoping Baskania didn't sense his fear.

"Don't be afraid, boy. It won't hurt . . . for long, that is. Your pain is my gain, right?" His cackle made Balor's stomach rise into his throat.

Damon swung around to look at Balor. "Should I whack him—"

"Shut up!" Balor interrupted. He looked at Baskania and the president. "Sorry. He's an idiot."

"We know," Baskania purred. "But, luckily for him, a precious idiot. Now tell me about Erec Rex." At once, he bared sharp teeth, and his eye darkened with anger. "I don't like what I see in your mind. Out with it!"

Balor found himself shaking. "Erec Rex is missing. He disappeared from Alypium without a trace. Bethany Cleary is still at the castle, though." Who was this jerk to make him feel stupid like this? He had done a good job. It wasn't his fault that the stupid kid was gone.

Baskania eyed him silently. He stroked a silver eye in his hand. A coal center showed through the hole that was its pupil.

Suddenly, pain crushed Balor's body. A great force shoved him onto his knees, and then threw his face onto the floor, arms outstretched in front of him in a deep bow toward the Shadow Prince. Damon bowed on the floor at his side.

Baskania tittered, looking at President Inkle until he joined him with an uncertain giggle. Soon they both roared in laughter. "You," he snorted to Balor, "actually think you are worthy of my presence." He sniffed, a cold eye staring through his mirth. "You flubbed the simplest task I could have given you. And I'm training you fools, with your lamb of a brother, to follow in my footsteps? I need to know where Erec Rex is. We no longer need him alive. I'll deal with the Fates myself if I have to, so you can draw the next quests from Al's Well yourselves."

He sneered at President Inkle. "Find Erec Rex. Do whatever it takes. He is an obstacle. It's time to kill him, now, before he gets more power from that Amulet of Virtues. Plus, he has my dragon eye. I want it back."

Erec found Jam after pounding on a few doors. "We have to get Haenry. I just found out what the Hulders' secret is."

Jam rubbed his eyes. His hair was beginning to perk back to life after some of the wax had rubbed off. Erec thought he looked much better. "But, young sir, what can we do about it? We don't even know where Lerna is. It's certainly nowhere in sight."

"True, Jam. But I know exactly who needs to know this information right now."

Haenry was asleep in a stable. They woke him, which was no small task, and involved throwing rocks into his side and jumping on his stomach. "Haenry, the dragon hatchlings are in danger. We have to run back into dragon country, and fast."

Haenry jumped up and helped Erec and Jam back onto his shoulders. Then Haenry ran through the night, branches whizzing by and occasionally scraping Erec when he wasn't careful. They passed the clown village and continued deep into the wilds.

"I hope this is the same way we came." Erec heard loud wolflike howls that did not seem too far off. He noticed the moon was full and had a bad feeling that the cries might not be from wolves. At least

Wolfboy would be safely locked up in his padded doghouse tonight. He thanked Bethany in his head for arranging that.

The night became blacker as Haenry ran nonstop. He was excellent at tracking, as he had said, and was following their old path with ease.

As they ran near rocky cliffs and outcroppings, Erec squinted, looking for Aoquesth's cave. "I think that's it." He pointed at a dark cave on a hill. "Let's check it out."

They tiptoed up to the dark cave entrance. Erec could hear a low rumble from inside. "Aoquesth?" he called into the blackness. There was no answer. He tiptoed in, chills running through his shoulders. It seemed like ages ago that he had been here, getting the very eye that he was looking through right now with Aoquesth's own eye attached to its back.

"Get back here," Haenry quietly growled, grabbing his shoulder. "What are you thinking? That thing will slash you head to toe and ask questions later."

"He knows me. It's okay." Erec hoped Aoquesth remembered him. It seemed he would, after guarding a dragon eye for ten years for him. But he also remembered Aoquesth had evened the score with his father by giving Erec his eye. Maybe now there would be no reason for him to treat Erec differently than anyone else. Well, the lives of the baby dragons of Otherness were on the line. Erec had to warn him.

Jam stepped into the cave behind Erec, but Erec turned and held his hand up. "No, Jam. You better stay out with Haenry. Aoquesth doesn't know you, and I'm not sure what he would do to you. Plus, if there are more of us it might startle him, make him attack or something."

"Young sir," Jam whispered, "please let me go in for you. I will explain to Ao . . . the dragon that I am with you and tell him about the hatchlings. There is no need for young sir to risk his life."

"Really, Jam, it's okay. Thanks for offering to put your life in danger for me. But he doesn't know you, and he has all these rules about humans. You don't have a chance in there." Haenry did not need any persuading to stay back with Jam.

It was dark in the narrow passage that led from the cave entrance, much darker now at night than it had been before. The rumbling noise sounded like a snore. It grew louder as Erec felt his way down the rocky tunnel toward the huge cavern. Then the rumble stopped.

A dead silence filled the cave. The dragon must have sensed his presence and woken. Erec was struck with fear. What if this was no longer Aoquesth's cave? What if he remembered it wrong? What if another dragon lived here now, one that would not care who he was or what he had to say? He remembered Aoquesth asking if he preferred to be lightly toasted or deep fried, saying that humans were good snacks.

He closed his eyes and steadied his breath. The dragon hatchlings were in danger. Baskania was going to kill them all at once and take out all of their eyes for his own. He couldn't imagine how much power Baskania would have then. Erec still didn't know how to fully use his own dragon eye, but he was sure Baskania would know exactly what to do with his.

He took another step. This time he had no Magiclight, and there was no light streaming from the inside of the cavern. The dragon could be waiting for him at the end of the tunnel, mouth open.

A stream of fire raced toward him in the tunnel. Erec dodged out of the way, pressed against the cave wall. A snort of steam filled the passage, making it so hot Erec broke out in a sweat. Fire raced through the tunnel again, this time singing Erec's sleeve.

"Aoquesth?" Erec's voice trembled.

"I see somebody knows my name. Do you think that will save you from your fate, foolish human?"

"It's me, Erec Rex." Erec held his breath, praying Aoquesth would remember him and that it would matter. He thought about what happened with Patchouli. He had looked at her with his dragon eye and they could read right into each other's thoughts. If only he could get a cloudy thought now he could look at Aoquesth.

"Walk closer to me," the dragon said. Erec thought it sounded like Aoquesth's voice. He hoped it was. "I want to see you."

Shaking, Erec walked up the tunnel. A light began to fill the huge, gem-encrusted cavern, falling on countless tables of treasure and magical goods. Enormous stacks of gold bricks lined the round room. On display was an amazing collection of suits of armor and weaponry that had obviously been taken from humans who had overestimated their own abilities. Aoquesth must have peeled off all this gear like the shells of peanuts before being eating the hapless humans who wore it.

And there was Aoquesth. There was no mistaking him. Gigantic muscles rippled under scales that shone a deep red and purple-black hue. Blood red spines cascaded down his back to the tip of his tail, and huge black wings rippled beside him, unfolding slightly and closing over him again. His immensity and sheer power took Erec's breath away.

The dragon tilted his head. "Erec Rex. My, this is a surprise. And waking me up in the middle of the night, too. I don't suppose you think you're free to come marauding through my treasure just because we have once met."

Erec shook his head, tried to force words out before it was too late. "N-no. I came to warn you. I found out where the baby dragons are."

"Hmm. Do come in, Erec." Aoquesth backed into his cave and sat by the same onyx table where Erec had once played chess with him. "Please, have a seat. I promise I won't harm you until I hear you out. Then we will see what riddle I will give you. An easy one or a hard one."

Erec remembered Aoquesth's rule about giving a riddle to humans that entered his cave. Only if they could solve them would he spare their lives—and usually the riddles were too hard to answer. He took a breath. "I've been trying to find my brother and sister. They've been kidnapped. I think they're in Lerna and will be fed to monsters unless I get there fast enough to save them."

Aoquesth nodded.

"So a Cyclops has been helping me and we were looking for Lerna. But we found this little village. The people there knew a secret, and I tricked it out of them with magic. They told me where the baby dragons are. I found out Baskania captured them to harvest their eyes. The hatchlings are old enough now, and their eyes are ready for him to take. The trolls are hiding the hatchlings for him in Trollebotten Cave, in Jotnar. Baskania is going to kill them all two days after the Monster Bash in Lerna. We ran as fast as we could to tell you."

Aoquesth breathed out steam in silence. "Erec Rex, you are like your father." They sat awhile looking at each other. "Thank you. Unfortunately, most of the dragons are out on hunt, looking for signs of the hatchlings. I would be out too, but I haven't been well. There is likely nobody here but me, and we don't have the time to hunt other dragons down. We should act now. Am I correct to assume you will help me?"

"I will." Erec's mind spun. He wasn't sure what good he could do. He wasn't nearly as powerful as Aoquesth. But then he thought about Danny and Sammy. "If I help you free the baby dragons tonight, will you help me fight the monsters in Lerna tomorrow?"

"It would be my pleasure." Steam poured from his nostrils.

Haenry fell backward in shock when Aoquesth emerged from the cave. Jam looked frozen, mouth agape.

Aoquesth nodded at them and then said to Erec, "Oh, I almost forgot your riddle. Let's see. I don't really have time to help you, so I'll give you the simplest one I can think of. Please consider it well, and do your best. I would really hate to have to eat you, given what we are setting out to do."

At the mention of eating Erec, Haenry fainted into the grass. Jam rushed over and fanned his face. Haenry's eyes slowly opened, looked at the dragon, then slammed back shut.

"Okay." Aoquesth sat on a large rock and extended his jointed wings fully. They glistened a deep, velvety black. "Who thought he was one thing and found out he was another, received a dragon eye, then went to save baby dragons, and used to look different until his mother changed his appearance?"

Erec was afraid to answer even though it seemed obvious. If he was wrong, for any reason, would Aoquesth really eat him?

Jam piped up. "Why, young sir, he must be talking about you."

Aoquesth nodded. "I'll accept that as a correct answer."

Erec sighed in relief. Everything would be fine now. They would save the baby dragons and rescue Danny and Sammy, all with Aoquesth's help. There would be no more worries about how to deal with the terrible monsters in Otherness with a powerful dragon on his side. "Do you know where the Trollebotten Cave is in Jotnar?"

"Yes. Jotnar is right next to Lerna." Aoquesth pawed the ground. "I'll be able to take two of you on my back there now. Preferably the smaller two." Haenry looked immensely relieved. "We'd better leave now."

Aoquesth lowered his head to the ground so Erec and Jam could climb onto his back.

Erec asked, "Will you be okay, Haenry?"

"Oh, no problem here," Haenry bellowed. "I'll follow me tracks back to Polyphemus real easy."

"You go run along then," Aoquesth said. "And if I find anything missing from my cave I will track you down."

Haenry took off at a run. "I'm going now, see? Far away from your cave. I'll sleep under a tree."

"Oh fine, then." Aoquesth sighed. He turned to Erec. "Just wait here." Aoquesth grabbed a shocked Haenry in his talons and flew off the ground. Haenry turned white. "I'll take this one to Polyphemus so he won't have to sleep under a tree. Right back, kids."

Erec told Jam what Aoquesth had said. Jam frowned. "I wonder why he's not well."

Erec shrugged. "He looks okay to me."

In minutes, Aoquesth appeared empty-handed. He lowered his head to the ground. "Now climb on."

Erec stepped onto the dragon's wide head, holding his horns. Then, holding one spine at a time and stepping on others, he scaled the steep climb on to the dragon's back. Jam followed him up and sat behind Erec, and the two of them squeezed between Aoquesth's spines and held on tight.

Aoquesth lifted his head. "You do both understand that this is highly irregular, don't you? I wouldn't normally be caught dead doing this."

In a wondrous arch of his back and swipe of his wings they lifted off the ground. Erec stared at the ground below him, amazed. He could not believe he was riding a dragon.

The earth dropped below them and they climbed through the air like a balloon that was finally let loose, like a shooting star. Trees sunk lower until they disappeared into a swirl of the night sky. It seemed almost as if Erec was the dragon himself, a part of that immense, beautiful creature he was riding. He gripped on to the spine before him for dear life. Behind him, he heard Jam say, "Ohh, sir, it's so beautiful."

Clouds brushed by them, then shot downward as Aoquesth climbed higher than Erec thought possible. It almost seemed as if he was heading straight for orbit. The full moon glistened bright before Erec's eyes, sparkling in more patterns and colors than Erec thought possible. It was as if its face radiated pure goodness into the atmosphere of the earth, and there was nobody else but them to feel and see it. Then, in a moment, the dragon turned and dove, spiraling downward in a controlled free fall. Erec closed his eyes, then pried them open, not wanting to miss a thing. He held Aoquesth's spine so tight his hands went numb. Clouds swept past them and the ground rose up so quickly that Erec felt sure they would crash straight into it. But Aoquesth climbed upward again and then settled back down for a smooth landing.

He put his head down and Erec and Jam climbed off. They were on a grassy knoll in a small clearing in the woodlands. The dragon's wings sagged and he panted a little. "I'm sorry. I shouldn't be tired this easily. I haven't been myself lately."

"What's wrong?" Erec asked.

"Oh, just five hundred years of wear and tear. It wouldn't be so bad if I hadn't lost my dear Nylyra a hundred years ago. That changed everything, you know."

Erec looked around. "Is the cave near here?"

Aoquesth nodded. "A short walk. When I flew over it I saw two trolls guarding it in front. No surprise really. We better see what's happening there before we decide what to do."

Erec was surprised the dragon did not want to burst into the cave, flames flying, and rescue the hatchlings right away. Maybe five hundred years had snuffed his fire a bit. Or maybe he really wasn't feeling well enough. Erec tried not to think about that.

Around a hillside was a cave, very different from the rocky one in which Aoquesth lived. It was more of a deep pit in a grassy hill that looked like it went straight downward. Aoquesth was right. Two unusual-looking men stood before the pit opening.

Very unusual men.

One of the men had three heads crammed next to each other on short, tough necks. The head on the left had wild black hair sprouting in all directions and an equally dizzying beard. The head in the middle was clean-shaven and bald with gruff features and a single, thick eyebrow. The third head had delicate features and green hair sticking straight up. Erec thought he looked slightly out of place. The other man looked more normal, except that he had white spiky hair and was carrying another head under his arm that joined in the conversation. Both men were huge, thick, and looked like cavemen in their filthy, sleeveless, cloth tunics.

"Are those trolls?" Erec whispered.

Aoquesth nodded, and steam rolled into the night. "They'll do anything for a pocket of gold. It's their weakness."

Erec thought about it. "What do they spend it on?"

Aoquesth whispered. "They just hoard it. Not that there's anything wrong with that, of course." Erec thought the piles of treasure in Aoquesth's den would put any troll to shame. "But one must have values, you know. Rules. Ideals. Trolls have none of those things. They'd sell their grandmother for something shiny."

The two trolls with five heads between them were having a great time yelling and arguing with each other. Erec could hear the one with green spiked hair growling, "It's three o'clock. Time to take them out for their exercise."

"Oh, shut up," said the bald head. "You don't know how to relax."

"Yeah?" The first one turned to fully face the bald one, a fierce look on his face. "You don't know how to not relax, you lazy bum. Always making us sit on our duffs, lounging around."

The bald one looked pleased, and spit at the first one. "It's not my fault if our body listens to me when we have disagreements. I just have the best suggestions, that's all."

"The laziest suggestions." The first head bit his ear.

"Can't youse two ever shut up?" the hairy head roared. "I can't get a moment's silence here." He turned to commiserate with the head being held in the other troll's arm.

Jam whispered, "Three in the morning doesn't seem a nice time to exercise the hatchlings."

"It's not," Aoquesth said. "But trolls can't be out in the sunlight or they turn into stone. Plus, this gives them more protection from the hatchlings being seen."

"So," Erec said, "in the daylight they won't be guarded?"

Aoquesth snorted. "Oh, they will be all right. Just from the inside of the cave, not in the sunlight. The trolls will be in there sleeping near them all day. But they wake up in a flash, don't doubt that."

The troll holding the head began to toss it up and down, much to the amusement of the other heads. "Cut it out. Let me alone!"

The hairy head growled, "It won't be long before we get paid and will be done with this smarmy job. Standing here with the likes of youse."

"Buts we better do it right," the green-haired head offered, "or the Shadow Prince will put us all out of our misery for good."

Suddenly Erec felt sick. His stomach clenched and he was overcome with dizziness. In a flash, everything was green. It looked like daytime. Huge webs of Substance hung around him. He waited with dread to see a preview of what would happen to him. Something in Trollebotten Cave with the trolls? A fight with the monsters in Lerna?

There was no fighting, no trolls, nothing at all. Only green, and the Substance, and it was closing in, zooming up to him. It was like the nothingness around him was growing and swelling until it swallowed him up. He felt fainter, lighter, as if his very life was seeping out of him.

And then it was over. He was back in the night by Trollebotten Cave.

THE MONSTERS OF OTHERNESS

He wiped sweat off his brow. Jam looked concerned. "Is young sir all right? Should I find a tonic in the woods?"

"I'm okay, Jam." Erec did not want to think about what this premonition of his next cloudy thought might mean. This time he had actually felt his life leaving him and had felt powerless to do anything about it.

Aoquesth watched Erec. "You are learning to use your eye, I see."

"Learning to use it?" Erec was not sure he would call it that. "More like it's using me."

"Let it for now. Later you will find out how to make my eye work for you." Erec had almost forgotten it was Aoquesth's eye. "But, as you see, a dragon eye can look into the future."

"You can see the future?" Jam asked.

"Yes," Aoquesth and Erec answered at the same time. Erec laughed. "Only at times for me, and not too well."

"I can also see the future, but it's a bit more controlled. It is actually not something we dragons do much. If you were able to read your future at a glance you would understand too. You enjoy things less when you are always trying to control things instead of just living. Like my dear Nylyra dying. I might have been able to prevent it. Who knows? But had we spent our time together avoiding death we would not have truly lived and loved. The time we did have would have been lessened. Oh, a few dragons do that, I guess, but they're not generally happy. Most of us save looking into the future for important matters."

Jam looked confused. "The future you see is not set in stone then? You can change it?"

"Yes," said Aoquesth. "It is the future that will happen naturally, unless I knowingly alter it. I am given that choice."

"Isn't this important enough to look into the future?" Erec asked. "The lives of all the baby dragons are on the line."

Aoquesth pondered this. "I think you are right, Erec. A few dragons have tried to see the future to tell where the hatchlings were but could not do it. Maybe it was too far away in time then. But we are about to save them now. I will look to see if our rescue will work, and if I must change things, then I will. Pardon me a moment." He rested his head on the grass. Soon, a green light beamed from his eye, shining on the plants and trees ahead of him like an unearthly beacon.

The dragon held so still Erec wondered if he was breathing. Then, at once, he exhaled and his eye shut. Aoquesth shook, rumbling, as if an earthquake was erupting inside of him. Erec and Jam stared. Was he okay? Had this hurt him somehow?

The dragon sniffed and raised his head. He looked calmly at Erec. "I am all right now. I am ready to proceed with this."

"What did you see?" Erec asked.

"No." Aoquesth shook his head. "It's enough that I have seen. There is no reason to discuss it further."

"Can you tell me at least if Danny and Sammy will be okay?"

"No, I can't." Aoquesth seemed resolute, so Erec reassured himself that at least someone knew what to do.

Erec was tired. "What now? Should we break the hatchlings free?"

"We watch them," Aoquesth said. "They'll be brought out for exercise soon. Then we'll make our plan." Erec wondered why they didn't make a plan now, as Aoquesth knew what would happen.

Soon the trolls entered the cave and came out leading a horde of dragon hatchlings in metal collars attached to a long chain. There must have been fifty of them, scales of all colors glistening in the moonlight. They yipped and squeaked, stumbling over each other and flapping their small black wings. One or two lifted a bit off the ground before the chain pulled them back down. They were so cute Erec felt his heart melt. He wanted to go save them now, if he only had a clue how. "Why don't you breathe fire on the trolls, Aoquesth? We'll free them right now."

"I can't, Erec. I am running out of energy, and I need to save it all for something I will have to do. Just watch and think of another way to save them."

This was not what Erec wanted to hear. The dragons tried to frolic as much as they could on their chain, running around in the grass and crashing into one another. One of the little things was upside down in its collar, its feet sticking up out of the grass. Erec resisted the urge to run over and set it upright.

The trolls took little interest in the dragons, their many heads arguing and laughing at each other. Erec noticed a flask hanging off of the belt of the three-headed troll. "What do you think that is?" he asked.

"Ah," Jam said. "I've heard that trolls carry a magic flask of spinacia plasma to make them strong enough to lift huge loads. Is that true?"

Aoquesth nodded. "If I wasn't so tired I could get rid of these trolls right now. I'm afraid I'll have to rest. As I said, it's important that I save my energy for later. But you can steal into the cave when the trolls are asleep and rescue the dragons. I can't tell you how you do it, since I could only see the future from my perspective. I was not able to see what you did in there. But I know you can do it."

"May I go with you to help, sir?" Jam asked.

Aoquesth nodded. "You go too. But for now, both of you need sleep."

Erec was glad to lie on the grass near Aoquesth. He could barely hold his eyes open.

Jam awoke Erec as the trolls walked back to the cave entrance. "Well," said the head that was not attached to a body. "Only one more night of this and we'll get our chunks of gold."

"None too soon." The other yawned. "Time to head in now. I see a hint of color. The sun will be up soon."

They climbed into the cave, pulling a chain attached to a huge boulder which then slammed into the cave entrance, closing it. It didn't seem possible to get into the cave now, but Aoquesth had sounded confident that they could.

Dawn arose and the golden sun gleamed off of Aoquesth's scales. Erec stared at the cave, heart sinking. It was bad enough having to rescue the baby dragons himself, but when he thought about fighting the ferocious monsters in Lerna in two days, it was overwhelming. "I wish Haenry was still with us. We could use all the help we can get with the monsters. If only there was some way I could contact him."

"You could send him a snail mail," Jam said. "Don't you have an envelope in your pocket?"

Erec pulled out the shell envelope from Tina's last letter. "I don't know how to make it go where I want. Won't it just go back to Tina?"

Jam pulled paper and a pen out of his coat, prepared for everything as usual. "The snail will know what to do. It can find anyone when they're outside."

Erec wrote:

Haenry,
Thank you so much for all of your help. I could not have found out about the baby dragons and gotten out here near Lerna without you. Tomorrow we need to fight the terrible monsters that are coming to attack the citizens of Lerna. I wonder if you are able to help us in any way. If you could come here that would be great. Or if it's too hard I understand.

Anyway, thanks again for everything,
Erec Rex

He put the letter in the shell, told it to find the Cyclops Haenry in Polyphemus, and watched it vanish into the soil.

Jam disappeared into the woods and came back with his silver tray full of fruits, berries, and edible leaves. He handed a cluster to Aoquesth. "It's *Portulaca oleracea*. Good for just about everything, even for dragons."

Aoquesth thanked him and munched the leaves. "Not bad. Needs a little hippo meat to go with it."

"Look what I found, young sir." Jam waved a cluster of leaves with excitement. "*Colea zacachi*, the dream herb. A little of this will help us move like we're in a dream. It may keep us from being noticed as easily."

Erec thought about the size of the trolls, and he hoped so.

CHAPTER EIGHTEEN

A Hole in the Substance

EREC AND JAM waited a few hours so the trolls would be in a deep sleep. Then they each stuffed some of the *Colea zacachi* leaves in their mouths. The leaves tasted like thick, hairy caterpillars that squished slime onto his tongue when he chewed them. He managed to swallow, and moments later he lifted slightly off the ground, as if he weighed almost nothing. Jam and Erec jumped and floated easily up before drifting down again, like they were on the moon. Erec was not sure if this would help them rescue the dragons, but it sure was fun leaping up, catching tree branches, and drifting gently back to the ground when he let go.

Aoquesth lay still on the ground. Erec and Jam snuck to the edge of the grassy cave. There was a small crevice on one side where the boulder didn't quite cover the entrance. It would be tight, but they could squeeze through it. The only problem would be getting the dragon hatchlings out through it, or getting themselves out fast enough if there was danger.

"Are you ready, sir?" Jam asked.

Erec nodded. "Let's do it." He squeezed through first, glad he was wearing his magical Sneakers so he didn't have to worry about making noise. After he made it through the crack, he skidded down a steep tunnel, barely landing on his Sneakers. He remembered Aoquesth had said that trolls were light sleepers. Jam tumbled in after him. Erec held his arms out to catch him, but Jam bounced off of him and onto the floor. The Colea zacachi leaves let him drift down silently.

It was dark in the cave, but a chorus of loud snores echoed in Erec's ears. He held still until his eyes adjusted, then walked silently in his Sneakers toward the sound. Jam stayed where he was to keep from making noise.

Around the corner, a very dim light showed the mass of sleeping dragons who were now on the trolls' schedule. The two trolls were asleep, their many heads gurgling and snoring. One of the heads was drooling heavily onto another one's eyes, causing it to wipe itself off in its sleep. Erec looked around the room to see if there was anything that could possibly help him. Other than a small pile of gold that the trolls must have brought here for comfort, there was nothing else in the room. Nothing but his wits, which seemed sadly lacking at the moment. Even though he could step quietly because of his Sneakers, he could not imagine getting the dragons out without the trolls noticing, especially through the small crack at the edge of the boulder. The dream herb he had managed to gag down did not seem like it would help either.

If only he could have a cloudy thought now. But then Erec remembered what his last cloudy thought had been. It wasn't reassuring. He remembered the feeling of doing nothing, staring into nothingness, his energy eking out of him. He pushed that thought out of his mind. There had to be something he could do.

He noticed the flask that was still attached to the three-headed troll's belt. It would give him strength, but how would that help? If he picked up the dragons in one scoop he would still wake up the trolls. Would it give him enough strength to overpower them?

Well, he would not know until he tried it. With long, slow steps, he crossed the cave floor and ducked next to the three-headed troll. The flask was within reach, if he could only unhitch it without waking the troll. He leaned closer and saw that it was in a holster. When he put his hand on it, though, two of the troll's heads grunted, and the troll rolled over, plopping a thick arm over Erec's shoulders.

Erec was pinned to the ground. Well, this was great. Now he would be the troll's teddy bear until evening, when the trolls woke up, at which time he would become the troll's breakfast. What if Aoquesth had seen the future wrong? He pushed as hard as he could, but the arm was like a lead weight. He could not even slide to the side. At least it wasn't lower on his chest or he would have suffocated.

The flask on the troll's belt was now almost under the troll, but Erec could still see it. He strained, reaching as far as he could, until he felt the cool glass. His fingertips touched it, but he could not get it out. He sighed. If only he could do magic. Then he could get the flask, overcome the trolls, and stop the monsters in Otherness, no problem.

Erec's breath stopped. Magic. He had done some magic. There was no reason he couldn't do it again. He slipped the remote control out of his pocket. Let's see, how did it work? He remembered pushing the large button, saying something that could make things move. But how far would it move? And which way? He had not practiced it at all.

He lay for a few moments in silence, trying to remember what word would make things move with his remote. A soft crunch resounded in the distance—Jam's footsteps. No, he thought. Don't come over here now. There's nothing you can do. You will just wake up the trolls.

There was another soft crunch, and the troll squirmed, gripping Erec tighter. It was obvious he had heard the noise in his sleep. There wasn't much time before Jam woke them up. Erec had to act fast, if only he could remember that word. But even if he remembered it, what should he do? Moving the troll's arm with a spell seemed out of the question. Whether it shot off of Erec or floated up high, it would surely wake him, and Erec would be history. No, the only possibility was to try to move the flask closer so he could reach it.

The remote control felt slippery in his hand. It was brand-new. He had only used Rosco's before, and he had absolutely no idea how well this one worked. Erec tried to point it at the flask, but he was not sure if he was also pointing it at the troll's hip. That would be the last thing he wanted to move.

There was another crunch, this time slightly louder as Jam grew nearer. Erec was grateful he was trying to help, but Jam had no idea what danger he was putting Erec in. What was the word? It was on the tip of Erec's tongue.

Then he remembered. He pushed the button. "Phero," he whispered.

The flask lurched from the troll's holster, yanking his belt along with it. "What?" Two of the troll's heads woke up and looked around in shock. Before another moment went by, Erec pulled open the flask and tipped it into his mouth.

The fluid in it was green, and it tasted greener still, like lichen from the forest floor. Erec felt no different at all, but he now easily lifted the troll's arm off of him. The tonic in the flask had definitely had an effect.

All three heads of the troll were now awake and looking around, stunned. In a moment, six eyes settled on Erec, followed by four more from the other troll. "What's this? We have a visitor." The three-headed troll was rubbing his hands together eagerly.

"Nothing like a nighttime snack, I always says." The bald head laughed.

"Save some for me," the bodiless head complained. "You never save any for me."

Jam looked stunned. "Please, take me. Let this young sir go. He's too small for you anyway."

The green-haired head looked at Jam, laughing. "Okay, we'll let him go . . . until after we finish you off. He'll make a good dessert."

Erec picked up the three-headed troll, holding its wrists behind its back. Jam looked at him in amazement, unaware he had drunk the spinacia from the troll's flask. The trolls also seemed stunned. "Well, now, there's no reason for this," the hairy head said. "Set us down and we'll talk man-to-man, seeing as how you've got a little more in you than most other'n."

Yeah, Erec thought, like your spinacia plasma. Erec set the troll down and tried to look menacing.

"Don't look at us like that," said the bodiless head. "We can still overpower you when we want. First we just want to know who you are and why you're here."

Looking at them, it did seem that they could overpower him if they worked together. Maybe if he fought them both at the same time, Jam could sneak the baby dragons out. But, then again, if the trolls were getting a hunk of gold to guard the dragons they weren't likely to let them go. And Jam would certainly be crushed in any fight. There had to be a better way.

Erec fought the urge to blurt out the answer to the troll's question. The scroll in his pocket made him tell the truth, but if he thought hard enough he could choose which truth to tell. Could he could trick them somehow? "I have something that you would want. We can make a trade for the dragons."

All of the heads began laughing at once. "That's a good one." "Oooo-eee!" The troll slapped its side. "And what, pray tell, is this fine treasure you carry that we'll end up with anyway before the day is through?"

Erec pulled the Archives of Alithea out from his pocket. "This is a magic scroll that makes you tell the truth when you hold it. Would you like to see it?"

After some growling and fighting over which troll got to hold it first, the white-haired one took it, setting its other head on the ground. "Doesn't look too exciting to me."

"Just try it," Erec said. "Try to lie."

The troll muttered, stumbling on his words. "I can't. But I don't really know what to say."

"Maybe this will help," said Erec. "Who is paying you to guard these dragons?"

"Why," the troll muttered, "the Shadow Prince. He's harvesting their eyes." The troll looked around in shock. "I can't believe I told you that. Here, try it." He handed the scroll to the three-headed troll.

Erec looked at him. "What will it take for you to give me the dragons?"

The troll that held the scroll answered, "There is nothing you can do to get them. The Shadow Prince is too powerful. If we break our promise to him that will be the end for us." He laughed. "But don't you worry; we'll take this treasure anyway after we eat you for breakfast."

Jam clucked his tongue, shaking his head with a sad look. "If you did, that would be a shame for you, kind sirs. I have something much better to give you, more riches than you've ever seen before. Surely you would like to see what that is before you eat us, or I won't be able to give it to you."

The trolls looked at Jam with new interest. "More treasure?" the hairy head asked. "This gets even better."

Jam looked at Erec, an eyebrow raised. "Yes," he said. "Outside is the most tremendous treasure ever. You just have to step outside to see it. But you need to do it now."

The trolls were laughing and sneering at once. "That's the oldest trick in the book. You want us to step outside into the light of day, make us turn to stone. We're not that stupid."

Jam shrugged. "Daytime is over, kind sirs. You're awake, right? Do you not believe me? Watch, I'll hold the scroll and then you'll know I'm telling the truth."

Erec held his breath, afraid of what would happen next. Jam picked up the Archives of Alithea. Before he spoke, he closed his eyes in concentration, making sure he didn't spout out more than necessary. "Outside is the biggest ball of gold you will ever see. It is the greatest treasure we have on earth. If you wait, it will be too late and it will be gone from view." He put the Archives of Alithea down. "You had better hurry if you want the treasure. I couldn't lie to you when I was holding the scroll, now, could I?"

The trolls foamed at the mouth, overcome with greed. One of the heads shouted, "He said it's night now. He couldn't have lied with that scroll." Another nodded. "Let's go!" The trolls raced to the cave entrance, leaving the unattached head behind, and threw the boulder out of the way without hesitation.

Warm rays of sunlight shone down on the trolls' faces. They quickly turned to stone.

Erec looked at Jam in wonder. "How were you able to lie when you were holding the scroll?"

"I didn't." Jam winked. "The biggest ball of gold was outside, our greatest treasure, the sun!"

Jam and Erec led the chained dragons outside into the light. Jam was looking much better now that his hair wax had worn off. The dream herb helped them bounce easily up the tunnel with armloads of the hatchlings. They were still chained together, so some dangled in the air as others were scooped up, but they got out quickly. The little things looked around, blinking, unused to the sun. Aoquesth was waiting nearby. "Good job, Erec. I am glad to see things have gone as expected."

Erec studied the dragons. "You won't be able to carry them back, will you?" There was no way they would fit on Aoquesth's back, even if he was strong enough.

Aoquesth shook his head. "There is another way."

In the distance, the faint sound of trumpets and snare drums rose over the hills. It grew louder, enough for Erec to recognize the music. It was the same tune he had heard the marching band playing in Alypium the day he was chased by the mobs of angry villagers. He remembered the parade had been led by the tiny General Moreland and wondered if he was in Otherness now.

Erec looked down at the dragons. How was he going to get them to safety, back to their homes far away in another part of Otherness? Baskania was supposed to be directing the army marching into Lerna for the Monster Bash. If he was nearby, how could Erec get the dragons by without him noticing? If only he could safely hide them somewhere until the Monster Bash was over. He and Aoquesth could find their parents then, somehow sneak them back home.

He wondered if there was anybody he could trust to hide the dragon hatchlings. Probably not. Certainly the Alypians had bad views of dragons. He remembered Miss Ennui's lecture and the dragon effigies in the parade.

Miss Ennui. Erec closed his eyes. He had forgotten. She had told him that if he missed another of her classes he would be kicked out of the quests, sent back home. Not that he had the choice of staying in Alypium anyway. But he wondered if he would be allowed to do the second quest, to stop the monsters in Lerna. Well, even if it didn't count for anything, he would still do his best to save Tina's family. And he had Aoquesth to help him, so he really had a chance.

If only there was a place to hide the dragons. Baskania would be here soon after the Monster Bash, and he would not let them go easily. He would uproot every shrub in Otherness to search for his prizes. Where could they go where there was no trace? Not anywhere in this world.

Then Erec realized what he needed to do. The dragons had to hide in the Nevervarld, the place behind the Substance, the place of no magic at all. Most humans could not survive there, but he remembered that dragons could last there for days. And the Nevervarld, with its complete lack of magic, of Substance, would be one place where Baskania would have no power.

There was a hole into the Nevervarld in Nemea, but without nitrowisherine to help him, he would never find it again. He tried to remember what he had heard about the hole, think if there was a way to find it again. The woman in the MagicNet had told him it was made by the searing power of a dragon's eyes.

He looked at Aoquesth. "Can you make a hole in the Substance?"

Aoquesth nodded. "Yes, with your help. You are thinking of hiding them in the Nevervarld, and it does seem the only option now. We would never get these hatchlings home before Baskania began to search for them. And it would take too long to find their parents now. Someone else might find them first."

Erec frowned. "Are you sure they can they live in there?"

"Only a few days, at best. Beyond that I don't know. They will eat the lion skin flowers." He sighed. "After I help you, you must come back for them as soon as Baskania is gone. If you lead them into Nemea and the wilds near where my cave is, their parents will see you are bringing them to safety. I am afraid that if you go to the parents first, they might roast you before they heard what you had to say. We've become pretty skeptical of humans."

"But won't you help me find their parents?"

Aoquesth snorted.

Erec remembered what the Substance and the Aitherplanes looked like through his dragon eye. "Aoquesth? Can you see the Substance all the time?"

"Yes. It's a perk of being a dragon, along with some others you may discover someday, having one of my eyes. Well, I have been saving my energy. Opening a hole in the Substance is no easy task."

"How do you do it?" Jam asked.

"I see it," Aoquesth said. "I see deeply into it until I can cut it with my sight."

Erec frowned. "Why do you need me to help you?"

"Because," said Aoquesth, "you have my other eye."

Erec's mouth dropped. So he would have to cut through the Aitherplanes with his eye? It seemed impossible. He could barely control it, let alone use it for a purpose like that. "How do I . . ."

Steam gushed from Aoquesth's nose. "I will show you. Are you ready?"

Erec nodded, not sure he felt ready for anything.

"It's best we do this now," Aoquesth said. "Jam, do you have a pen?"

Jam produced a pen from a pocket.

"Good. Now mark one of the petals of that small daisy there." Jam dotted a spot on the flower.

Aoquesth motioned to Erec. "Sit next to me. We will both stare at the spot that Jam drew. Concentrate. Bring your dragon eye forward and look through it. See the Substance . . ."

"Wait a minute," Erec said. "I can't just bring the dragon eye out. It does it by itself sometimes. I don't know how to work it."

"Well," Aoquesth said, "it's time you learned." He took a breath. "Dragons are pure, Erec. We are creatures of the air, true to our natures and our hearts. In order to work your dragon eye, you need to think like a dragon. You need to pull from yourself the most pure emotion you have. Love. That is what dragons are, you know, creatures of love. You may not understand, see us shredding our prey, killing those who cross us. But we need to eat and protect ourselves. Inside we are very close to the Aitherplanes and the magic in them. And that is love, too.

"That is why Thanatos Argus Baskania will never get the full use out of any dragon eyes he has. He could use them all right, but only from the other side, the way that is much more limited in its power. He would use them with his hate. And the future it would show him would be warped, and he would destroy that future because of it. It is not only important that we save these hatchlings so they can live. It is also vital, maybe even more so, that Baskania does not get one hundred dragon eyes to add to his power. He would see things he could never understand; change the future without pause. And that would destroy all of existence."

Chills ran down Erec's neck. He had not known what was at stake. "Tell me how to make the hole, Aoquesth."

"First, you must bring out my other eye. Use your love, Erec. Focus, not on people or things that you love, but on the love that is in you. What you have within. Your pure emotion. Focus."

Erec did focus. He closed his eyes and sensed deep inside of him all the love he had in his life. Images of people and things shot through his head, but he dug deeper and thought about what was underneath, and that was himself. He felt good, in touch with the earth and all that was in it. He was at peace.

He opened his eyes, and everything was green. Big wads of white netting shone in the air. This time, Erec felt connected with them, and the magic that lay within them.

"Very good." Aoquesth's voice rung clear. "Now let us both focus on the dot that Jam drew on the flower petal. We will look into it, with our eyes, and see. Really see. Every thread of Substance that is in that spot will show itself to us as we concentrate. And as it becomes fully clear, and we see it for what it really is, we may speak to it. Move it. Change the Substance in this small spot of the world."

It sounded like no small task, but Aoquesth's voice sounded sure and Erec felt confident. He looked at the spot that Jam had drawn. It was a small black mark on a tiny white petal, but it was clear. Erec looked harder. The netting of the Substance hung around it, but did not seem to lie in that tiny spot. It had to be there, he was sure.

He squinted, looking harder. What had Aoquesth said? To really see it. But how? Where was it?

Love. He could hear Aoquesth's voice in the back of his mind.

And that was all it took. The love he felt poured out into the spot. What appeared before his eyes was amazing. It was an unveiling, a giving of something to him, a showing of secrets, an opening. For he could now see the layers that existed in every plane that was there, and they were beautiful. He went closer, not in body but in his mind. As he approached them they grew for him and split into all of their parts, each more fascinating than the next. So this was magic. This was how it worked. It was the lifeblood of the universe.

Erec had no idea how long he had been exploring the Substance, or what Aoquesth might have been doing. But the further he got into its depths, the closer to an end, the more layers separated out into more parts until it became obvious. It was infinite. And it was love.

This realization sprung upon him, changing him somehow. For now he could not only see the gorgeous patterns but he could feel them, understand them. It was time to ask them to change for him, for the dragons, and for the sake of the world.

Without averting his eyes, Erec asked with every ounce of his heart. And the Substance said yes. He pushed into it with his vision, moving things, changing them. He separated out the small webs and the smaller ones, aware that someone else was working alongside him, helping him carve the path. A hole was appearing. He could see it now. And he had to make it grow, make it big enough. And even though the Substance was letting him, it was hard. Because the hole was emptiness. Nothingness. A gap in what was important, and it scared him. But he could not let his fear stop him. He had to push forward.

The nothingness grew around him, sucking the self out of him like a vortex. He pushed further, giving every bit of himself to make the change, but he did not know anymore if the change was inside or outside of himself. Every bit of energy was sucked out of him, burned up in the fire of making and unmaking. He felt fainter, lighter, like he was disappearing altogether.

Then, finally, blackness took over completely.

CHAPTER NINETEEN
Hat Head and the Drenchers

THERE WAS A cold feeling on his face, some kind of wet rag. Erec was not sure where he was. He forced his eyes open. Nothing was green anymore. The sky was beginning to darken.

Jam leaned over him, blotting his forehead. "Is young sir all right?"

Erec nodded.

Jam produced a spoonful of thick brown liquid. "To get your

spirits back, sir." He hesitated, his voice sounding tender and concerned. "You have a white streak in your hair now, from what you've gone through, sir."

The medicine tasted nasty but woke Erec enough that he propped himself up. Aoquesth was lying beside him, eyes open. "Did we do it, Aoquesth?"

"Yes, Erec. Jam marked the hole for us by replanting a fig tree in that spot. You must remember that it is about thirty feet away from the Trollebotten Cave entrance."

"Okay." It sounded to Erec like Aoquesth was not planning on helping him get the dragons back to their parents. That was all right. Aoquesth had helped enough, and he wasn't well. Erec understood. He sat up, feeling stronger as the medicine Jam had mixed took effect.

Erec extended his arm toward the fig tree and watched his hand disappear into the hole. Little snaps of static electricity jolted his skin. He reached around in the hole, feeling the strange, tingly dryness of the Nevervarld before pulling his hand back out. "I don't think we should leave them in here too long. It didn't seem very safe in there. And they're little, too."

Jam smiled. "I wish I could take the dragons in, sir. You have been through enough today."

"It's okay, Jam," Erec said. "No other humans could survive in there. If I didn't have Aoquesth's eye I would have died the first time."

Jam led the small dragons up to the hole in the Substance, patted a few of them on their heads. Erec took his magical Sneakers off and put his feet into the hole, watching as they disappeared from his view. He could not go in past his waist, however. "Hmm. I wonder why?" Then he realized what was in his pocket. He took the Archives of Alithea out, handed the scroll to Jam, and with a push, he jumped in, leaving only his head and arms in the world that he knew. Surprised, he saw the Amulet of Virtues hung on his chest into the Nevervarld. Why could it go in if other magic things wouldn't? Maybe it was because it was almost a part of him. He hadn't ever put it on—it had just appeared on him after his first quest.

Erec grasped the ground with one hand and reached for a dragon with the other. He tried to ignore the way he felt, as if his legs and body were numb and floating in outer space. The earth under his hand steadied him, and he clung to it. The little dragon wandered haplessly up to the hole, and Erec pulled it through. As he did, his own head dipped into the Nevervarld.

He gasped. As much as he was ready, he had forgotten the tingly feeling that surrounded him. Empty nothingness extended forever, everywhere. It was already starting to pull him out of himself. Swirls of black and white flecks encompassed him, moving all over him and even through him. He could feel the lack of magic, of Substance, and it was a vacant, unreal feeling. Like swimming in static, endless seas of black-and-white static, and watching while he turned into static too. In the distance he heard a familiar sound. *Thank you. Yummm.*

The dragon baby looked as shocked as he was. Its yellow scales glowed with more intense brightness than Erec had ever seen. He reached to its face, trying to reassure it.

And then he could hear it. He could hear the dragon's thoughts. *Where am I? What is happening?*

It's okay, Erec thought. *You're in the Nevervarld. You'll be protected here. Soon you will be with your parents.* For some reason the baby dragon trusted him, he could feel it. Sharp little sparks stung Erec's skin. His energy was flowing out already.

I don't like it here, the dragon thought.

Erec didn't either. He closed his eyes, squeezed his fists to get control. The chain felt cool and solid in his hand, something to grip, something real. He pulled it and another dragon fell into the abyss of the Nevervarld, this one glowing a wild green. Erec let go of the ground, and hand over hand, pulled all of the baby dragons through the hole.

The colors and confusion rang like chaos in chaos, swimming reds and yellows, blindingly bright, lighting up the moving sparks of black and white. It was dizzying. Dragon thoughts resounded through the Nevervarld, echoing through Erec's mind. *What is this place? Are we dead?*

No, Erec responded. *You are in hiding here, safe from the trolls. I will bring your parents to you, okay, little guys?*

They calmed down a bit, but Erec wanted to leave them with some of the lion skin flowers to eat. He looked for them, but other than the overwhelming colors of the dragons, he could not make out shapes in the swirls of moving specks.

Okay. Think. How did he do this before?

He was tired now, swimmingly, spinningly tired. Each particle that blew through him seemed to take a piece of him with it. Focus. Why was he here? Oh, yes. The dragons. The flowers.

Where were they? He looked away from the dragons into the particles, hoping to identify something there. He was not sure if he was moving or holding still, but it seemed like shapes were forming and coming closer. What were they? The sparks struck him harder and sharper now, pulling more energy out of him. Where were the flowers?

He tried calling to them over the mental noise of the dragons. *Flowers, please help me again. These dragons need you.* It seemed pathetic, asking the flowers to come and be eaten. But they had come to him before to be taken out of their world, as if they knew . . .

Something soft brushed his hand. *I am here. I will help.*

Erec sensed the flower and sent it toward the dragons. *These will help you here. They will feed you and keep you well.* Lion skin flowers gathered around Erec and the dragons. He could feel their good will.

The voice of the Nevervarld echoed through him. *You are not dead yet. You are the human with the dragon part.*

Erec knew there was not much time before he collapsed forever in the Nevervarld, but he had forgotten how to move, how to get out. Did it have to do with swimming or willing himself? He was so tired. The hole in the Substance shone through like a glimmer, but it could have been inches or miles away. Erec pressed through the void, struggling against nothing at all, moving or not moving. Something he could not identify pushed him, softly and steadily, as his mind began to fade. The hole grew closer, larger, until somebody or something gave him a great big shove and his head popped through.

Erec shuddered with the hugeness of it all. Plants, trees, sky—it all glowed with so much color it hurt. He squeezed his eyes shut, but the colors of the sky pressed through, and the insides of his eyelids, with their red veins and brown shadows, overwhelmed him. At least the last time he had come out of the Nevervarld had been at night. Even then, the stars were too much for him.

Jam leaned over Erec. "Sir, you are ice-cold." He put his coat over Erec and slid the scroll back into his pocket. "Are you all right, sir?"

Erec nodded. "Please whisper." Voices, bird chirps, even the breeze was almost as agonizing as the feeling of the solid ground under him. He took a deep breath. It was okay, he told himself. Soon he would readjust, but for now, sleep was all he could bear.

Erec awoke the next morning feeling much better, except for a strange ache at the front of his forehead. He touched it and felt a huge duckbill-like protrusion coming from his scalp. The enormous swelling stuck straight forward so he could see it if he looked up ... but he could not remember banging his head. In fact, he could not imagine how hard he would've had to have hit it to create a lump that big.

He sat up. Nearby on the grass, Jam was munching some nuts and berries. An enormous disklike protuberance ran in a circle around the butler's scalp, making him look something like a flying saucer. He nodded to Erec. "I'm afraid we've come down with hat head. Could've picked it up from the clowns. It takes a while to incubate. Maybe our resistance is down. Hopefully we'll find a doctor in Lerna."

Erec exhaled. Great. Just when it was time to meet Tina he was going to look like a freak. "I guess we should try to find the twins."

Jam nodded. Erec could not stop staring at his halo of skin. "Aoquesth is sleeping, sir. He said we should go on without him, promised he'll meet up with us when he is needed at the Monster Bash. I think he needs his rest."

Setting off toward where they had heard the parade, they came to a hill. At the top, they could see a city in the distance that looked like a town in Upper Earth. They headed for it, sure it must be Lerna.

After an hour's walk they reached the outskirts of the city where a few houses and business lined the road they were following. Erec knocked on a door. Hopefully this person would be able to help him find Tina Amymone, and then he would figure out how to track down the twins.

A man with a camouflage military hat and a wiry mustache answered the door and stared at them. Erec suddenly remembered that he and Jam looked deformed with their hat-shaped heads. He smiled, hoping to play it off. "Hi. We're new here and I'm trying to find someone."

"Well, come on in." The man was gruff. He puffed on his pipe. "I don't get much company round here. I'll help ya." He looked at Jam. "Looks like someone threw a flying disk through your head."

Jam shrugged. "We have hat head, I'm afraid. If you'd like us to step out so you don't catch it—"

"Nah, I don't care," the man said. "There's a doctor around the corner, anyway. Doc Shandy. You might want to stop by the office."

Erec was relieved to hear there was a doctor nearby. Hopefully this defect would go away before Tina saw him. The man seemed genuinely glad to have company. "Well, not to brag," Erec heard him explaining to Jam, "but I am quite the hunter. Bagged quite a few in my day too. Big and little 'uns, flies of all kinds. Even a few mosquitoes too. Want to see my trophies?"

Erec thought he was hearing wrong, but on the wall hung hundreds of tiny plaques, fly heads mounted on each one. The man walked over to Erec and nodded. "Nice one, huh? I bagged that one with my bare hands two summers ago. Isn't she a beaut? Check out this babe over here." He pointed to another fly trophy. "Killer big, this one. Didn't think I'd be able to get her home. And this one over here is my latest. Shot it in my neighbor's backyard. It kept landing on the dessert so I had to take matters into my own hands." He puffed his chest up. A row of tiny slingshots hung on the wall nearby.

Erec and Jam glanced at each other. "Um, very nice," Erec said. "We were just wondering if you knew how to find someone who lives in Lerna. Her name is Tina Amymone."

"Never heard of her. Of course, if she lives in Lerna proper you can look her up when you get further into town. Phone books and all. Out here we're a little isolated."

Erec and Jam thanked the man for his help and set off toward town along the same road. Suddenly, rain began to pour down. Erec was drenched. He hunched his shoulders, slightly glad that his hat head was keeping the rain off his face. Strange, the sky had been blue and the weather perfect just a minute ago. In fact, it was still quite blue when he looked around.

"Sir?" Erec looked back and saw that Jam had stopped walking. "You have a little rain cloud above you, sir. Following you."

Erec tipped his face up so he could see out from under the brim of his head. There was indeed a very small dark cloud over him, stopping when he stopped and moving with him. Rain poured from it onto Erec alone and left a trail of water on the sidewalk behind him. "Why is this thing following me?"

Jam looked stunned. "I don't quite know, sir. I've never seen anything like it before."

Erec was glad to find Doctor Shandy's office around the corner. They entered and found a tall, young, dark-haired man sitting behind a desk. Nobody else was in sight. The rain cloud followed Erec into the office, soaking the floors.

The man looked up casually. "Hello."

"Are you Dr. Shandy?"

"Why, yes!" The doctor sounded surprised. "May I help you?"

"Um, yes. We have a little problem." Erec gestured to their heads.

"Yes?" The doctor looked at them expectantly.

"Well," Erec said, "we both have hat head. And now I have this rain cloud following me, but I don't know why."

"Got a case of the drenchers, eh? Nasty, they are. Soak you to the bone." He nodded as if he found it fascinating, but he did not appear inclined to do anything about it.

"Is it curable?" Erec asked.

"Oh, yes. Yes indeed." The doctor nodded affably.

"Well?" Erec waited to hear what the doctor suggested, but he just sat looking at them with a smile.

Jam asked, "Sir, would you please cure us now?"

"Oh!" The doctor stood. "I see. Well, let's take a look." Dr. Shandy circled around Erec and Jam with pursed lips, humming to himself.

"Ooh. Look at that." He stared at Erec's forehead. "Such a bad case. Tsk, tsk." He drummed his fingers on his desk, then disappeared into the back, returning with a large hacksaw. "I suppose I'll just chop off those bad spots, then."

Erec and Jam made faces at each other. Jam asked, "Aren't there any alternative treatments, sir?"

Doctor Shandy put the saw down. "Of course. There are always other treatments. Maybe some leeches." He reached for a large bottle filled with fat, black, squirming creatures.

Erec cringed when he brought one close with some tweezers. "No. I'd rather not."

"All right." The doctor put the leaches away. "Yes, I suppose that never really works. How about this?" He pulled a dusty black bottle off of a shelf. Black steam shot out when he opened it. Jam waved it away. "Yes, I guess people generally do die right after that one." He rooted around more on the shelf. "Here are some pills that can make you smart. Too bad they cause rebound dumbness when they wear off. A few university professors are addicted to this one." Erec wondered if this doctor had been the one to prescribe the pills to them.

"Ahh, I know." Dr. Shandy looked relieved. "Some of this wine will be just the right thing. Have some."

"Will it help?" Jam asked.

"Well, no, it never actually helps. But it's a really nice vintage."

"I think we'd better go," Jam said.

Just then, a thin woman with long, wavy red hair floated into the room. She wore a gauzy white dress with a pink belt. Tiny white flowers in her hair matched her dress. "Troy, are you pretending to be the doctor again?" She crossed her arms. "Now apologize to these nice people."

Troy lowered his face and looked up at them, batting his eyes. "Sorry."

"Now," the real Dr. Shandy said, "I see one of you has the drenchers. I'd better treat you both or you might come down with it later." She nodded at Jam. "Oh, you have hat head too. Oh, dear. Well, come with me."

Erec and Jam sat side by side on an examination table. The doctor handed Erec a bucket to catch most of the water raining on him. "Have you been through a stressful situation lately? That can make you more susceptible to the drenchers."

Erec nodded, not wanting to go into it. She handed him a silver pill and a cup of sweet rose-colored liquid to wash it down with. She put on a reflective hat and gave one to Jam. "So the cloud doesn't find us." In moments, the cloud developed a silvery lining, stopped raining on Erec, and drifted from the room.

"Ah, that's better," she said, throwing a towel onto the wet floor. "Now for your hat heads. Put these on." She handed them metal cones that sat on top of their heads. The cones, which looked like old-fashioned hair dryers, blew warm vapor onto them. "They will get rid of the germs momentarily."

Erec felt his scalp ease. Other than the mild ache in his fingers left over from feeding the dragon hatchlings, he felt great. The cone had fluffed Jam's hair, and he looked like a new person.

Dr. Shandy accepted two gold rings as payment and looked up Tina's address for them in a phone book. "It's 111 Scylla Street." On their way out, Erec saw that an unhappy Troy now had a drencher cloud over his head.

CHAPTER TWENTY

The Monsters of Otherness

I T WAS ONLY fitting that Balor and Damon Stain should ride in the plush palanquin with King Pluto and the Shadow Prince, while lowly Rock Rayson had to walk with the hordes from Alypium. Even Balor's father, the great sorcerer Mauvis Stain, was not allowed up here. Balor knew he was superior to the lowly peasants out there. Yes, this was the way it should be.

The palanquin, a silken tent with ornate velvet cushions, was held with long poles on the backs of Baskania's more lowly followers.

Baskania had soundproofed the fabric. As usual, he held King Pluto's scepter, although everybody knew the one he really wanted belonged to King Piter.

The king rested on pillows, layers of fur blankets covering his ermine robes. "Do you think we still need Danny and Sammy Rex, master? It won't be long before the world is at our feet."

Baskania sighed. A third eye stared blankly from his forehead, and several peered from his palms. "They may still be useful. But you are right. I will soon have the power that I seek. After I dispose of Erec Rex, I'll have them killed as well.

"Soon my dear grandmother will come back to me. Her death will no longer separate us. She will tell me the Great Secret, the prophecy revealing where the Final Magic is hidden." A lazy smile slid across his face. "The moon and stars will bow to me then."

Baskania chuckled. The eyes on his palms darted back and forth, seeing what various followers around the globe were seeing. "If that is not enough, I will be filled with dragon eyes, mine to use as I may. My power will be unimaginable from that alone, more than all creatures on earth combined. But the dragon eye I desire most is attached to Erec Rex's eye. I will enjoy extracting it, painfully, before I kill him. Thank you, Pluto, for locating him. He has fallen right into my trap. You've come through as usual. That idiot Washington Inkle couldn't tie his own shoes without help."

Pluto smiled, looking appreciatively at his scepter.

Balor chuckled. Erec Rex had it coming. And he would be there to watch.

As they got closer to the center of the city, Erec noticed that the streets were filled with girls. But these girls looked different from any he had ever seen. They were tall and slender with long silver hair that swayed like molten metal when they walked. Their wide-set eyes flashed a steely blue, and most seemed fond of a glittery makeup that sparkled from the corners of their eyes. The girls were everywhere and all just alike. So this must be what Tina looked like.

Erec thought he would ask for directions. A girl walked by with a swing in her walk that said she knew where she was going and she better not be messed with. He cleared his throat. "Um, excuse me. I'm looking for Scylla Street."

The girl swung around, silver hair sparkling as it floated on the breeze. Her eyes twinkled. "I live on that street. What do you need there?" She wore a short silver skirt, a shimmering white sleeveless top and knee-high silver boots. Her high cheekbones glittered pink. She seemed to sparkle everywhere.

Erec bit his tongue. Don't say it. Please. He knew the Archives of Alithea were trying to have their way with him. He forced the words out, sure he sounded like an idiot. "I . . . want . . . to find . . . Tina Amymone."

"Oh!" The girl laughed. "That's great. We live together. My name is Rowena. Come with me!"

Erec and Jam followed Rowena through the streets. The girls they passed were tall and shining, with an unreal air about them, almost as if they had walked out of a comic. They were beautiful, there was no arguing that. Erec began to worry what Tina would think when she saw him. She might be disappointed. At least she had seen his picture. Anyway, it didn't really matter, he told himself. She appreciated what he had done, and he was there to save her from the monsters.

Now that he was actually in Lerna and going to meet Tina, the whole thing was starting to feel too real. He could not imagine frightening monsters, Hydras and Valkyries, whatever they were, coming here and attacking everyone. This looked like a normal city in Upper Earth. There were movie theaters on some corners, clothing shops, restaurants. They walked onto what looked like a typical suburban street lined with houses, lawns, and trees.

Rowena turned up one of the driveways toward a white Victorian style house with yellow gingerbread trim. Erec guessed Rowena was Tina's sister. She moved with graceful, fluid strides up to the door, opened it, and disappeared inside.

Erec and Jam stood at the open door. It did not seem right to barge in, and Rowena had not asked them. Something that must have been some sort of a servant creature working for the family scuffled up to the door. Erec had never seen anything like it. It was a head taller than him, with spiky horns and small beaded tufts of hair atop its head. Sharp teeth jutted from its mouth, and spikes shot from its long, dangling nose. Thick bumps and polyps covered its greenish skin. Three long tentacle arms hung at each of its sides, decorated with golden bangles, and ending in sharp, curved claws. But, oddest of all, a row of eyes stared at him from under the creature's neck and around its shoulders, above its white dress.

"Erec?" The creature had a surprisingly high voice.

"Yes." He smiled. "Is Tina here?"

"I am Tina!" The thing smiled at him.

Erec's smile melted off of his face, and his jaw dropped. This was Tina? He had no idea she looked like this. It all made sense now, her talking about her people being different. She must have noticed his shock, for she giggled uncomfortably. Erec tried to explain. "I'm sorry, Tina. It's just that you're so ugly, that's all. You're hideous. I thought you were going to look like Rowena."

He could not believe what he had heard himself say. It was that awful scroll again, the Archives of Alithea, messing with him, making him say everything he didn't want to.

Tina threw her tentacles over her face and ran away, sobbing. Jam looked at him sideways, too polite to say "Good job, kid." Erec dug the scroll out of his pocket and handed it to Jam, who looked at it and said, "Ahh, yes. That would explain your . . . behavior, sir."

Erec ran into the house calling for Tina. Rowena looked at him coldly. "She's in her room. Maybe it's best that you go."

"Please," Erec stammered. "I need to talk to her. Give me another chance."

Rowena's icy blue eyes narrowed. "Well, all right. But if you upset her again, I'm throwing you out myself."

He knocked softly on her door. "Tina?"

He heard some sniffing. "Go away."

"Please. I didn't mean what I said. I was holding a scroll that makes me say awful things sometimes. I don't have it on me anymore. I am really sorry, Tina."

The door cracked open and one of her large amber eyes peeked through the crack. "Are you sure you want to look at me again? I might be too painful a sight."

"No, Tina. I'm sure. Please open the door."

The door cracked open more, and Tina stood there with fat tears streaming down her face. The tears fizzed and popped on her bumpy cheeks like they were carbonated. She sniffed. "Let's sit in the study." Erec glanced in her room and saw a huge poster of himself on her wall. He felt terrible.

"Tina." He considered holding her tentacled claw in his hand but then thought better of it. "I really like you. I loved your letters, and I couldn't wait to get them." He wasn't sure how to take back what he had said. "Look, isn't that what matters? I don't mind the way you look, I just need to get used to you, that's all. And I'd like to be friends, if that's okay. That's what this is all about anyway, right?"

Tina nodded. "Okay." She stared at her knees, claws scraping the floor.

"I am such an idiot to have been holding that scroll when I first met you. Just understand that was not me talking. Our first real conversation is here, now, without that scroll. Erase everything you heard downstairs."

Tina sniffed. "Well, do you think I'm ugly then?"

Erec laughed. "No. You take some getting used to because I've never seen anyone like you before. But look at your arms, like octopus legs. Those are awesome. You could do six things at once. And your claws are way cool. Where I go to school, in Upper Earth, all the guys would think you were amazing."

"You mean they would all be in love with me?" She looked at him suspiciously.

"I didn't mean that. Probably not. But who wants to fall in love, anyway? I'd rather be with a cool-looking friend like you."

Tina smiled. "Well, okay then." She crossed a few of her tentacles. "I told the mayor I'd let her know when you arrived. The whole city wants to have a parade in your honor."

"Wow. I don't know about that. I mean, it's nice and all, but it's a little embarrassing."

Tina shifted in her chair and patted down her dress. "So you've never met a Hydra before?"

"No." Erec laughed. "And I have no idea what I'll do when I face them either. I heard that cutting off their heads only makes more grow, and they'll slash you to pieces as soon as they look at you. I remember something about putting a bag over their heads. Anyway, I guess tomorrow is the big day."

Tina was staring at him in shock, her lower lip quivering.

"It's okay," Erec said. "I didn't mean to worry you. I'm sure I'll pull it off. Things usually work out. And I have a dragon that's going to help me, my friend Aoquesth."

Tina's eyes narrowed into tiny, red slits and she burst into more carbonated tears. She clawed at the couch and looked at the door like she wanted to leave if only she could find the strength. Her face screwed up into a wrinkled ball that was lost in her spikes and teeth.

"I don't understand." Erec began to wish he was somewhere else. What was he saying wrong? "Can you tell me what the problem is?"

All of Tina's eyes flashed at him in anger. "I thought you said you weren't prejudiced. I thought you were coming to protect us." A sharp sob burst from her and she covered her face in her tentacles.

"I'm not prejudiced! Why are you saying that? And I am going to try and protect you. I'm sorry I don't know exactly how it will work yet."

Tina's tentacles crossed in front of her. "Well, why are you saying such terrible things about Hydras, then?"

Erec raised his eyebrows. "Because that's what they're like, right? You don't like them either, do you? Aren't they coming here trying to hurt you?" He could not understand why she was saying these things.

"Erec," Tina spoke quietly, head tilted. "In case there was any way you couldn't know this, I am a Hydra. Everyone in my family is a Hydra. The whole city of Lerna is filled with Hydras and our friends the Valkyries. I thought you knew that." She shook her head. "You had to know that. And now you're saying all these terrible things to me. First you tell me how ugly I look, then you say nasty, prejudiced things about Hydras."

It was Erec's turn to be stunned. "But you never said that in your letters. I had no idea. I thought Hydras were different. I really did." He stared at her. "I thought Hydras had lots of heads that were like snakes."

"No." She gestured to the eyes protruding from above her shoulders. "These are remnants of the multiple heads our ancestors

THE MONSTERS OF OTHERNESS

had before us. They're handy. We can see in different directions at once, great for playing sports."

"But I even saw a picture of a Hydra this last summer, and it looked nothing like you."

Tina looked at him crossly. "Was it a photograph? Or a drawing? Because you won't find a photograph like that. Baskania made all the artists in Alypium, Ashona, and Aorth register with him to make propaganda drawings for his cause, which is to make us look bad."

Erec thought about the MONSTER contest where he had seen the Hydra with long necks and big fangs. It looked lifelike, even moved, but from the back it looked like motionless cardboard. Whose decision was it to use those images for that race, anyway? The contest had been arranged by Spartacus Kilroy, who, it turned out, was reporting to Hecate Jekyll, Baskania's follower. They had just been trying to set up a way to give the scepters to Balor, Damon, and Rock, so of course they would use negative images of Hydras if that was useful to them. Only why would it be useful to them? Erec remembered the race also made Cyclopes out to be terrible creatures, and Haenry certainly proved that wrong. And there was a ferocious dragon in it too. All lies. Of course, some of the things in the MONSTER race, like the giant mosquito, the minotaur, and the ginglehoffer, seemed fairly depicted.

He turned to Tina. "Before I left, there was a huge parade in Alypium with nasty pictures of Hydras, and even dragons. I knew something was wrong when they made the dragons look stupid and evil. I should have questioned the rest of it too." He looked in all of her eyes, one at a time. "I am so sorry, Tina. I had no idea."

Then something occurred to him. "Wait a minute. I thought you said in your letters that monsters were coming to attack you. Remember? I thought I was supposed to save you from them. What monsters would those be, then?"

Tina said quietly, "The mobs of people from Alypium that are coming to hurt us, Erec. That's what we call them here. They are the true monsters, Erec."

Erec called Jam into the room. "Jam, I'd like you to meet Tina."

"So pleased." He held up the scroll. "Did you hear this thing was the cause of young sir's unfortunate comments? Terribly sorry if you felt bad, modom."

"Jam," Erec said, "I just found out. Tina is a Hydra."

Erec watched as Jam's expression went from shock to fear to confusion to consternation to regret. "I am so sorry, modom." He shook his head, seemingly at a loss for words.

Erec was still trying to absorb this information. "But why would Baskania want people to think badly of Hydras? Wouldn't that be a waste of time for him?"

Jam shook his head. "No, Erec. It's the oldest political trick in the book. Unite people by fear. They'll all crowd behind the one who they think will save them. It could be about anything. Fear that certain people are nasty and out to get you, take your jobs, are smarter than you, stronger than you. Fear that the world is coming to an end, and only one person can save the day. Fear that another group is all wrong and will make mistakes to hurt you. Make people afraid enough and tell them you will save them, and you have instant power over them. Not the way decent people come to power, but unfortunately decent people are getting harder and harder to find."

Tina nodded. "Our family used to live in Alypium, and I had lots of friends like you there. But then, a few years after King Piter got hypnotized, Baskania started a big campaign against us and the Valkyries. He got President Inkle to pass law after law saying we weren't allowed to work at certain jobs, couldn't play in parks, took away our rights one at a time. Then we all had to move into a small area in the outskirts of Alypium. But even that wasn't enough, because soon after that we all got kicked out into Otherness. By that time most of us were glad to get out of there. We built a great city here, and we aren't missing anything.

"But Baskania didn't want to let it rest at that. He had to keep the people afraid, I guess, to keep his power over them."

"So," Erec said, "he's told them you are coming into Alypium to ravage them and hurt their children. It's silly. Anyone who talked to you would never think you would do anything like that."

"It's amazing how some people respond to fearmongering," Jam said.

"But there are some people who don't." Tina smiled. "I still have a few friends in Alypium who remember me for me, and they won't get into this whole vogum thing."

Erec tried to remember what that meant. "They're saying that the vogum are Hydras and Valkyries that grow more powerful together . . . something like that?"

Tina shook her head. "It's pathetic, really. Vogum is our word for family. It's our way of describing our close relationship to the Valkyries. We help each other, need each other, really. They help us cook and clean, teach us the ways of the stars. And we raise them from seeds, which isn't easy. The methods of growing and raising Valkyries have been passed down for generations in the Hydra families."

"What do they look like?" Erec was curious.

"You met Rowena, right? She's our Valkyrie. She's great. We love her."

Erec's eyes widened. "Rowena and the silver-haired girls on the streets are the Valkyries? How could anyone think they're evil monsters?"

Jam sighed. "I don't think most Alypians think about what Valkyries are truly like. After so many years of hearing hateful things one stops remembering the truth. Unfortunately, even I lost track. When people tell you somebody hates you, is stronger than you, out to get you, you slowly forget."

Erec thought about General Moreland and his troops that were coming along with the crowds of angry Alypians who were eager to "show the monsters what's what." Even the name "Monster Bash" now gave him the chills. Tina was right. He knew who the real monsters were.

CHAPTER TWENTY-ONE
The Archives of Alithea

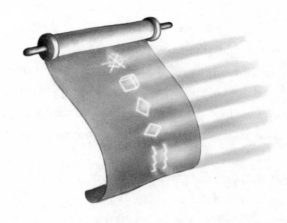

I BETTER FIND MY brother and sister," Erec told Tina. "If I
don't, tomorrow they'll be fed to the ..."

"The what?" Tina asked.

Erec stared at her, confused. "Someone told me that they
were going to be fed to the vogum. That would be you. I don't get
it. I heard the vogum were demanding two children to eat."

"More lies," Tina said. "It's ridiculous the things people will say
about us."

"So where are Danny and Sammy then? Rosco said the Hermit took them to Lerna. I better try to find them before the Monster Bash tomorrow. And don't worry, Tina. I'll do everything I can to protect you and Lerna."

Erec and Jam walked the streets of Lerna aimlessly. Erec felt frustrated. "I don't know how we're going to find them, Jam. If they are here they could be anywhere."

Jam agreed. "If anyone is hard to find, young sir, it would be the Hermit. He has ways of appearing and disappearing that amaze me."

"Why does he have the twins? Rosco Kroc said he was probably using them for political reasons to feed to the monsters and upset President Inkle."

Jam glared. "Mr. Kroc is full of all kinds of ideas, I think. Have you seen the Hermit doing anything wrong?"

Erec thought. "Rosco saw him with the twins, and I heard them with him once too. And he's sneaky. He pops up in the strangest places, and he says some weird things too. He's always laughing at me. Once, when I was upset about what the people in Alypium thought of me, he said maybe I did fix the scepter and the Lia Fail in the coronation ceremony so it would look like I should be king. And this is the guy that King Piter is using as a seer? He seems ridiculous."

"Yes, but does any of that mean he kidnapped the twins?"

"I don't know. But Rosco said he saw them all together."

They followed a small crowd into a hall and saw that a wedding was taking place between a creature with the heads of a goat, a lion, and a snake, and a small, squat green thing with a long bridal veil. The crowd consisted of the most unusual creatures Erec could imagine. He backed out, eyes wide.

Jam said, "I suppose Lerna welcomes anybody that needs a place to go."

Erec nodded. Lerna was different, but the people, odd as they were, seemed much more welcoming than the Alypians. But maybe the Alypians weren't at fault. They had been frightened for years by Baskania, and probably were not at their best anymore.

They turned a corner and slammed to a halt. Right before them stood the Hermit, gloating. He had a turban wrapped around his head that continued all the way down his body, which made him look like a mummy with his face sticking out. "Ahh. We found each other now. But had you any doubts? Silly Jam Crinklecut. Crazy Erec Rex. Nice white stripe in your hair. Seen something interesting? Changing your looks again?"

"Where are Danny and Sammy?" Erec's voice shook. "What did you do with them?"

"Hmm. What did I do with them?" The Hermit tilted his head in thought. "I found them, I suppose. Brought them to your mother for help."

"My mother has the twins now?" Erec realized his mother was probably worried, wondering where he was.

"Oh, no. She has no idea where they are." The Hermit laughed. "But I told her you were all right."

Erec felt angry. The Hermit was making as little sense as usual. "So did you give them to my mother or not?"

The Hermit seemed to sense Erec's anger, which threw him into fits of giggles. "Of course I did!"

"So she has them?"

"No, no, no." He tilted his head back and forth merrily.

"Well, where are they then?" Erec ground his teeth, ready to pounce on the Hermit. "I heard them with you in Alypium that day, behind the bush."

The Hermit laughed in delight. "I was tracking them down. I am an Imitung. That means I can reproduce voices." He put a hand on his hip and threw his other hand out dramatically, saying in a voice that was identical to Erec's, "Well, where are they then?" He giggled. "Silly, silly Erec Rex. I tested the air with sound waves; see if they had been nearby. Maybe you can find them now. I had a new pair of Seeing Eyeglasses made for you." The Hermit produced a pair of bright red plastic cat-eye glasses and handed them to Erec. "You like the style?"

Erec took them with suspicion. "You had these made for me?"

"I did!" The Hermit beamed with pride. "You and I were so close. The closest. I was the only one who believed you. And here you are, ten years later, and you have far less of a clue than you did when you were three!"

Erec squinted at him. The Hermit had yet to say a thing that made any sense at all. Erec was two then, anyway, not three. It didn't seem worth pressing him for any more details.

He thought about Danny and Sammy, then put the glasses on. Suddenly, he was in the ice rink in Alypium. The twins whizzed by him at breakneck speed, obviously well practiced from all their time having fun there. "Danny!" Erec shouted, but the music and talking were too loud there, and Danny didn't hear. He tried to shout for Sammy, but she didn't respond either.

Then Erec's eyes zoomed in on a figure across the room. Unmistakable in his black cloak, carved staff, and scarab amulet was Balthazar Ugry. He stood scowling, watching the twins as they glided by on the ice.

Then another figure caught Erec's eye. It was an odd-looking man with a green scaled head: Rosco Kroc. He crept closer and closer to Ugry. Erec's heart leapt. Rosco must have finally tracked the twins down. He found them with Ugry, and now he was going to rescue them!

Suddenly, the twins slid off the ice and walked to the snack bar. Erec's vision went along with them, so he lost sight of Ugry and

Rosco completely. He tried shouting to them, but they could not hear him over the music playing there. Then they vanished, suddenly made invisible, and there was no sight of anything but Alypians who had been ice-skating and munching on snacks. Because of the noise, Erec could not make out the twins' voices.

He watched for a long time, but nothing changed. A noise echoed around him. "Ohm." He took the glasses off. The Hermit stood on one foot before him, the other leg crossed in front in a semi-lotus position. His arms were crossed straight out in front of his chest, and his eyes were closed. "Oooohm," he chanted.

Jam shrugged. "He just started doing this, sir. Seemed to go into a trance. Are the twins okay?"

"Yeah, for the moment. I saw Ugry with them; he must have been the one to kidnap them. But Rosco found them. So hopefully he'll save them now."

The Hermit put his other foot down and opened his eyes. "I saw into the future. I know what will happen."

"What?" Erec and Jam leaned forward.

"Too sad," he clucked, shaking his head.

"Tell me." Erec felt his anger rising again. "What did you see?"

"Other than the egg sandwich I will eat for dinner tomorrow?"

Erec closed his eyes, breathing off steam. "So that was it, then?"

"Yes," the Hermit said, and nodded. "That, and that the twins will be saved. They'll be just fine, thanks to you, of course. But then you will come down with a terrible disease." He sniffed, faked crying, and then burst out laughing so hard that real tears did run down his face. He snatched the glasses out of Erec's hand. "That's enough of these now. You know the twins are okay."

The twins were all right for the moment, that was true. But Erec wanted to know what would happen next. It was reassuring that the Hermit said they would be fine, but Erec had no clue if he could believe him. "Can't I just look through them again?"

"No, no, no." The Hermit shook his head, elbows out and palms pressed together, obviously trying to look mystical. "If you had them you would never put them down, and that becomes spying. They will be fine. You know enough to relax about them. Now you need to concentrate on what you have to do for your second quest."

"My second quest?"

"That is why I am here. To watch over you during your quest."

Erec had not thought about it. "I'm sure I've been kicked out of doing the quests. Miss Ennui said if I missed more classes they wouldn't let me do them." What had his second quest been? Oh, yes. To stop the monsters in Lerna. How confusing was that? Did the Fates want him to attack the poor Hydras and Valkyries? Or did the Fates have a different idea of who the monsters were? Well, Erec had to do what he had to do—defend Lerna. Whether or not it had to do with a quest, he had no clue.

Erec and Jam walked slowly back to Tina's house, absorbing what the Hermit had said. As much as Erec was relieved that the twins were not about to be fed to fierce monsters, he was still worried about them, and his task at hand was beginning to seem much more real. There was nothing else to distract him, nothing else to think about. Tomorrow was the Monster Bash. General Moreland and the Alypian army would descend on the citizens of Lerna, along with the mobs of angry Alypians that had followed them into Otherness. And Erec was supposed to fight them all off himself. He remembered how excited Damon Stain had been about "bashing the monsters."

He looked at Jam. "What am I going to do?"

Jam must have been thinking the same thing. "I don't know, sir. If only King Piter were back he would help, I am sure. But you can count on me to stand by your side, sir."

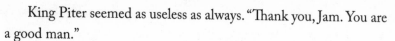

King Piter seemed as useless as always. "Thank you, Jam. You are a good man."

"I just do what I have to, young sir. We do what is right. We don't have a choice."

"No, Jam. We don't."

There was a massive gathering of Hydras and Valkyries on the lawn in front of Tina's house when they returned, far too many to fit inside. When they saw Erec approach there was an uproar and wild applause. Erec laughed. The applause had a wet clacking sound from the Hydras' tentacled hooks hitting each other.

"Three cheers for the conquering heroes!" Hydras grabbed Erec and Jam and threw them onto their shoulders. "Hip, hip, hooray!" Someone started singing a victory chant, and others joined in. It felt good, very good, to have people on his side, no matter what they looked like.

When they were finally put down, Jam made his way to Erec. "Young sir, I have to thank you. I have enjoyed my life serving at the palace; don't get me wrong. I would not have traded it. But I have never been called a hero before. Even if it is a misplaced title."

"No, Jam." Erec smiled. "It's not misplaced. Another man might choose to sit on the sidelines or go home. No matter what happens tomorrow, you are a hero."

Jam blushed. "Again. All thanks to you, young sir."

Tina appeared at Erec's side. "This is my father, Steve. He organized this gathering to discuss our plan for tomorrow. We have to be prepared."

Steve looked very much like Tina, but with short, dark hair nearly covering his horns and trendy wire-rimmed glasses. Erec thought he had a nice smile. He was getting used to the Hydras. The Valkyries didn't take much getting used to, but they seemed to have far less personality.

Steve smiled at Erec. "Thanks for helping us, kid. We have a lot of faith in you, seeing what you've done so far freeing King Piter and saving Patchouli's eggs in Nemea."

Erec couldn't resist adding, "I also found all of the baby dragons that have been missing. We hid them so that Baskania won't find them. After . . . tomorrow"—he avoided using the term "Monster Bash"—"I'm going to find their parents and return them safely."

If the crowd had been excited before, now it went wild. Erec and Jam were thrown into the air, Jam not looking too happy about it, and the cheering seemed like it would never stop. Not that Erec wanted it to. It had been a long time, way too long, since anyone had thought well of him. Except for his close friends and family, of course, but this seemed even sweeter. He could almost hear Bethany telling him not to care what people thought so much, but it really did matter to him. He knew that.

Steve patted Erec's back. "It was a miracle you were sent to us in our time of need. We have faith in you, Erec. Of course we have a plan, but if you have better ideas, we are ready to listen."

Erec had absolutely no plan at all. Suddenly he felt ashamed to accept so much applause and credit. He had no idea how to save them. Just because he did those other things in no way meant he would be able to defend Lerna from what was coming. He knew how frightening the angry Alypian mob had been, and he had been powerless to stop them. He was fooling himself. The only thing that could possibly save them was Aoquesth, and that would be the dragon's doing, not his.

Steve spread a map of Lerna onto the lawn. "There is an area to the north of Lerna called the Untier Bluffs that is surrounded on three sides by tall cliffs. We are going to gather there, prepared to fight, before the Alypians arrive. That will protect our backs, so troops can't sneak up behind us. They will have to come from the front and we will be ready. The area is on a hill, and they will come at us from lower ground, so we can see them well.

"We have brought all of our weapons here to sort through. You can look them over first and choose which one you wish to use. I have a suggestion for you, but it is your choice.

"I do not know how far they will push this with us. If they see we are prepared I think they will retreat and leave us alone. They are coming to kick us around, not get hurt themselves."

Erec relaxed. Steve had things well under control, and he was right. The Alypians, who were acting like bullies, would probably go back home if they saw a bunch of weapons pointed at them. "My friend Aoquesth, a dragon, is supposed to come help me tomorrow, so he is on our side too."

Steve grinned. "That's great, Erec. It's just one piece of good news after another with you."

In the house, rows of conventional weapons were lined up with strange things Erec had never seen before. He picked up something that looked like a huge metal lollipop. "What does this do?"

Steve pushed it back down onto the table and said, "It's a noise banger. If you aim it at someone it amplifies any sound they make and shoots it back loud enough to stun them." They wandered through piles of swords and spears. Most of the Hydras and Valkyries waited outside, but a few followed behind them. Erec looked at remote controls, wishing he knew more than how to move something from one place to another. He had his remote, and if he was desperate he could try to move a person or two, but he doubted he could. Steve showed him small whistle darts, spinning discs, and gongs that sent people into a stupor. "You need good earplugs for that one, and make sure you're not close to any of us."

The fly hunter from the outskirts of Lerna sidled up to Erec and opened his palm. "You might want to use one of these." He held three tiny slingshots in his hand. "I wouldn't give them to just anyone, you know."

Erec thanked him and said he would think about it. He picked up a stick with a long wire attached. "What is this?"

"That's an AMAW3, an antimagic, antiweaponry device. You hold the stick and wave the rope in a circle and it makes a force field that blocks out anything coming in. Try it." Erec whirled the rope in a circle and a blue haze formed within it. Steve tossed a metal ball into the force field Erec had made and the ball popped in a tiny explosion and vanished. Steve handed Erec a huge steel megaphone. "This is what I thought you could use. It controls sound waves. The person who speaks through it can be heard well, over everything else that is going on. When the Alypians are approaching, and even when we are fighting, you can be talking to them, telling them to go back home, and that we don't want any trouble."

"Believe me, they wouldn't listen to me. I think I'll use the AMAW3." Erec examined the stick, happy with his choice.

Tina, who had appeared beside him, took the megaphone to use for herself. "You didn't think I'd let you go without me, did you?"

Erec and Jam slept in spare rooms in Tina's house. Erec practiced all morning spinning the AMAW3 wire. The faster he spun it the bluer the force field that it made. Tina and Rowena threw balls and sticks at him, and he jumped in front of them, making them vanish in a shower of blue sparks. It seemed the right choice. He would be out in front, doing his best to protect everyone.

He could hear the Alypian bands playing, psyching up their crowds. At least he would know when they were coming. The Monster Bash was supposed to start at one o'clock. A loud roaring noise made him jump. He looked up and there was Haenry, and with him was a group of Cyclopes, long clubs in their hands.

"Haenry!" Erec ran over, so glad he came. "This is great. Now we're really going to be safe." He told Haenry about all that had happened.

"I wouldn't have missed it," Haenry said. "Anything for Erec Rex. Vaerna and I reunited with our daughter, Vaeronicae. We're so happy now, and it's all thanks to you." He wiped away a tear.

"I don't know if I had anything to do with that." Erec laughed.

They assembled at the Untier Bluffs before noon. Erec was in front, ready to stop any incoming weapons with his AMAW3. The Cyclopes stood beside him, looking fearsome and brandishing their clubs, and masses of Hydras and Valkyries were behind them, ready with their weapons. Erec hoped nobody would have to use them. He knew how impressive they must look. Maybe the Alypians would just turn around and run home.

He felt confident and ready. Aoquesth was not here yet, but even if he didn't show up, Erec thought they would do just fine. They were perched on a hill, protected by cliffs on all sides, with a great view of where the Alypians would come from.

Before long, faint music from the Alypian marching band wafted over the hill. Troops of soldiers in fatigues marched behind a short man covered in medals and ribbons—General Moreland. Another battalion of pale soldiers wearing scarves marched alongside, led by King Pluto. Behind and around them were masses of Alypians and Aorthians, some waving pitchforks and others carrying swords and bayonets. They drew closer, and Erec could hear the general's voice projected above the crowd with a large, metal megaphone like the one Steve had shown him.

"There are the traitors," General Moreland shouted. "Look at

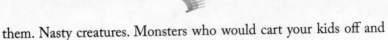

them. Nasty creatures. Monsters who would cart your kids off and terrorize your countries with their claws and fangs."

Oh, give it a rest, Erec thought. These poor folks just want to be left alone. Off to the side of the armies, Erida and a group of Harpies hovered over Balor and Damon Stain and Rock Ward. Well, this must be the second quest for them. Stopping the monsters in Lerna. The Harpies would think Erec was helping the monsters. On the record books, Balor, Damon, and Rock would be the winners of this one for sure. Erec wondered again what monsters were really supposed to be stopped.

"Don't anyone fire first," Steve said. "We can't spark things off. Wait and see what happens."

The armies drew so close that Erec could see the expressions on the faces of the Alypians and Aorthians, not that he wanted to. They looked drawn with rage and a kind of empty despair that told of their underlying fear. How could anyone get through to people like that?

He could hear General Moreland shouting again. "And there you see the infidel, Erec Rex, standing against us and with the monsters. You all knew he was a phony, out to serve himself. Now here's your proof. He will do anything to get power over you, even side against you with these brute beasts." The crowd shouted and waved their weapons.

Erec could see Thanatos Baskania striding past the army up to the general. His eyes met Erec's and twinkled.

Suddenly there was a shadow over the sun. Aoquesth swooped into view, so huge, sleek, and stunning that there was a collective gasp from both sides. He looked fiercer and more beautiful than Erec had ever seen him. His glittering black, jointed wings were spread wide in the sky, and his head was held high, glistening with red and purple-black scales. He lighted near Erec and surveyed the armies on both sides.

"Well, here we are," Aoquesth said.

Erec felt even better now with the dragon next to him. "I hope they just go away."

Aoquesth snorted. "Don't count on it."

Baskania's snide voice echoed above the noise of the crowds without a megaphone to help him. "Dear citizens of Alypium and Aorth, do not fear when you look at the terrible monsters that are before you, threatening you with their worst. I would not let you get hurt or trampled by such beasts. See that dragon? He would burn you to cinders with his fiery breath and feast on your remains. See those Cyclopes? They can't wait to pound you to shreds. But I won't let any of that happen.

"And look what else I see up there with them? Isn't that Erec Rex, the boy who supposedly wants power to rule over you? What do you think of him now? Hmm . . ." He tapped his chin. "I think I shall be kind and understanding. Always best to give people a second chance after they have disappointed you, see if they are ready to mend their ways. Right?"

The crowd responded with boos and hisses.

"I think I'll give this stupid boy a chance to survive, because I can't help having a big heart." Baskania put his hand over his chest. "Erec, I want you to see what your choices are. First, I am going to disarm that dreadful dragon next to you." He pointed his finger and a whoosh of black smoke rushed toward Aoquesth, who then choked and coughed.

"Are you okay?" Erec asked Aoquesth.

The dragon nodded. "It is true. He took my fire out."

"And now," Baskania said, waving both hands in the air, "I will disarm the creatures, melt their weapons like snow in the sun." Swords drooped like banana peels, clubs dripped to the ground like melting candle wax, spears crumbled into heaps of muck. The AMAW3 in Erec's hand turned to dust and blew away in the wind.

"Now, you see, Erec," Baskania continued, "you have a choice.

You may come to our side as a hero of Alypium and Aorth, show us you have mended your selfish ways, and lead us in the destruction of these monsters. Then you will be properly with me, on my side against all enemies, and I will fully appreciate you. I know you did not like when the citizens of Alypium were against you. Now is your chance to be their favorite. They will always remember this day when Erec Rex saw the light and returned to the path of good.

"Or . . ." He paused. "If you are not reformed, if you do not want to do what is right, you may remain with those monsters and take what comes your way."

If only he had the scepter. Erec craved it more than ever. The last time he had faced Baskania, Erec had been the more powerful one with a scepter in his hand. Now he was just a boy, alone on a hill with a bunch of unarmed victims.

"Well, Erec?" Baskania arched an eyebrow. "What will it be?"

A nagging thought deep inside told him that he had a choice of dying or being a hero in Alypium, something he had wanted from the start. He should go down there, throw up his arms . . .

But there was no way he could do it. He had to do what was right, no matter what happened to him, no matter what these people thought of him. He shook his head and put his hands on his hips. He shouted to the crowd, unsure if they could hear, "I'm not coming down. These are not the monsters. You are the monsters." Jam stood beside him and nodded bravely.

Baskania laughed and turned to his people. "Well, I guess some folks never change. At least I can say I tried, right?" He turned to General Moreland and growled, "Let's do it."

The general gave a command and the army and angry hordes rushed toward Erec and the citizens of Lerna. Erec stepped in front, looking around for something to fight with. Haenry and the other Cyclopes ran toward the armies, fists raised. Black arrows shot

THE MONSTERS OF OTHERNESS

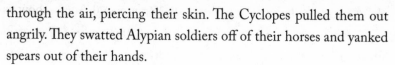

through the air, piercing their skin. The Cyclopes pulled them out angrily. They swatted Alypian soldiers off of their horses and yanked spears out of their hands.

"Stay near me," Aoquesth said to Erec.

Steve ran by with a stick he had broken off of a tree. "Erec, whatever happens, thank you." He charged toward the Aorthian army. The Hydras and Valkyries had nowhere to run. Some cowered near the cliffs behind them, but most fashioned weapons from branches, rocks, and plants around them and charged at their attackers.

Erec was amazed at the fighting skill of the Valkyries. Legs swinging in front of them and long silver hair flying behind, they flew at the invaders with deadly force. Silver shoes kicked weapons from hands with precision, then felled enemies in the field. They were fearless.

One of the Cyclopes fell, a saber sticking up from its chest. Others grabbed clubs from Alypians and swung through the battlefield, knocking foes down. Baskania watched, laughing, a gloating King Pluto at his side. Alypians, Aorthians, Valkyries, and Hydras lay bleeding in the grass. The armies against them seemed endless compared to the few from Lerna left standing. Erec tore the end of a stick into a point, and Aoquesth handed him something white and shining. "Take one of my teeth. It will fasten on to that branch with its sticky end and will make a good spear."

Erec ran toward the oncoming army, arrows whizzing by him. He could feel Baskania's eyes on him. Aoquesth was at his side, nudging him out of the way when something came too close. The black arrows bounced off of Aoquesth's scales, not bothering him at all. Erec saw Haenry lying flat on the grass. A soldier in armor raised a sword over him, about to strike. Erec charged toward him and flung his spear. It clanged against the soldier's armor, sending him flying off his horse. Haenry sat up, holding his side, green

blood trickling down. "Protect yourself, Erec. Get behind me."

A mass of angry citizens with pitchforks and pickaxes surrounded a Cyclops, swinging at him from all sides as he batted them away, howling in anger. They finally overcame him, and he fell, green blood spattering the grass in front of Erec. Haenry raced to them, arms over his head, with a deafening roar. The Alypians screamed and scattered. Tina appeared with the huge steel megaphone in her hand. "This wasn't melted with the weapons," she said. "Try it."

Erec put it to his lips. "Stop! Now! Stop!"

The battling armies tumbled to a stop, confused as to where the order had come. They looked around, surprised. Erec continued, megaphone at his mouth. "Do not attack us. We mean no harm. These folks up here look different, but they are really nice people inside. They just want to go home, take a hot shower, and forget all of this. They don't want to hurt you. Can any of you think of a time they hurt anyone?"

There was a confused rumbling in the crowd, as if some of them were actually listening.

"Ignore that fool," Baskania's voice thundered. "Crush him. He is against you all."

Erec raised the megaphone to his mouth, but this time it did not work. Baskania must have muted it. "Get them! Fight!" Baskania raged. The armies raised their swords and the battle raged again.

If only they could know the truth, Erec was sure they would lay down their arms. How could he let them know?

An Aorthian soldier galloped toward Erec and shot a black arrow. It whizzed through the air toward him. He froze, unable to move fast enough to dodge it. In a flash, it was a foot from his chest. Suddenly, red and purple light beamed from the Amulet of Virtues around his neck. The arrow curved away, bending like a noodle to the side, piercing Erec's arm.

He pulled the arrow out, blood dripping down his skin. Luckily, the wound was not deep. His amulet had protected him. He closed his eyes, wondering how he could stop this fighting.

It was then he realized what he had to do. The Archives of Alithea were in his pocket. If he unrolled the scroll, everyone that saw it would know the truth. It would only work once. There could be no better time than now.

Erec pulled the scroll from his pocket. Baskania's eyes instantly narrowed when he saw it. He pointed a finger at Erec and something shining flew from it.

It was as if time stood still. Each fraction of a second seemed to take an hour. Erec could see a shiny silver and black dagger shooting toward his heart. He was frozen by Baskania's magic, could do nothing but watch what he knew would be his instant death. The smoking blade shot forward, forward, closer. Erec knew he would never be able to open the scroll, stop the onslaught, save the Hydras.

It was too late.

When the dagger was just feet from Erec, Aoquesth dove in front of him. The blade shot into the neck of the dragon, piercing his scales. Black smoke rose from the handle, and purple blood dripped down his side. Steam fizzed from his nose as he collapsed at Erec's feet. "Stand on my head." Aoquesth's voice was faint.

In an instant, Erec stepped onto Aoquesth's head. He opened the Archives of Alithea, and Aoquesth stood, rising high for all to see. *Tell the truth about the Hydras, Cyclopes, and Valkyries,* Erec thought. Light blazed from the scroll like a torch in the night, bursting into thousands of white beams in all directions. The symbols printed on the scroll glowed like fire. Aoquesth staggered under Erec's feet, and Erec almost fell.

The soldiers and mobs stared, mouths open. They could see the shining scroll . . . and they knew.

Aoquesth stumbled, lowering his head. Erec jumped off right before the dragon collapsed thunderously onto the hillside.

Weapons dropped from hands. Tears fell from faces. People fell to the ground, dropped off their horses, hugging the Cyclopes, the Hydras, and the Valkyries. People apologized and shook hands.

Baskania gave Erec a look of pure hate, and then he vanished.

Jam said, "Baskania can't quite kill you now, with everyone knowing what's going on. He thought he had it all wrapped up—you come to his side or you die."

Haenry pulled himself off the ground and limped toward Erec. He tried to give a Valkyrie a friendly pat on the back, and she sailed twenty feet into the grass. King Pluto scowled and rounded up his army to head home, sending the wounded back with his scepter. The Alypians stayed longer, and General Moreland paced and shook his head. Steve brought Dr. Shandy to help those lying on the grass.

Erec sat down and stroked Aoquesth's face. His eyes were partly closed. "Are you okay? You saved my life."

"I know, Erec. Go find a jar . . . and hurry."

Erec called to Tina's family, who rushed back with a glass jar from a nearby house. He sat by the dragon. "Thank you, Aoquesth. The jar is here. What should I do with it?"

Aoquesth panted a little steam. He looked weak, sick. "I want to give you something before I die."

"Die?" Erec must not have been hearing right. "You'll be okay, won't you, Aoquesth?"

"No, Erec. The thing that Baskania shot at you was a death blade. He wasn't taking any chances. It is powerful, and even I am not able to resist it, especially as I have been weak lately." He took the jar from Erec. "I want you to have my other eye. I won't be needing it anymore, and I'd like to keep them both together anyway. Then you will be able to have the true sight of a dragon. I am sure you will

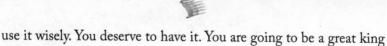

use it wisely. You deserve to have it. You are going to be a great king someday."

"King?" Erec had not for a minute thought about the second quest or becoming king. It seemed too late for that anyway. He looked at the Amulet of Virtues around his neck. A second of the twelve sections was now glowing a dusky purple-blue and had another black symbol on it.

Aoquesth looked at the amulet. "That symbol means 'justice,' doing what is right even if it's not easy. It's another trait of a great ruler. You showed that today." Before Erec could stop him, Aoquesth plunged a claw into his only eye and pulled it out. "Put the jar under my claws Erec. Is it there?" He dropped his eye into the glass.

Erec gulped, setting the jar on the grass next to him. He rested the back of Aoquesth's head in his lap. "You did that for me?"

"It's funny." Aoquesth chuckled, weakly. "I've pulled both my eyes out for you now. And I've never felt I've done a better thing."

Erec thought. "But you looked into the future. Why didn't you see that this would happen?"

Aoquesth's head rested more heavily into Erec's lap. "I did."

"And you came anyway to save me." Erec fought back tears, stroking Aoquesth's head. "Don't die, Aoquesth. Tell me how I can help you."

"Nobody can help me now, Erec. I'll be with my darling Nylyra soon. I chose it to be this way." His voice was quiet now, and Erec had to bend close to hear. "Take my eye to Heph Vulcan. He'll bind it to the back of your other one and you will have both in place then. Two dragon eyes are very powerful for a human, but I know you can handle them, Erec. Maybe you'll be able to do the dragon call someday. I've been too weak to do it myself lately."

Erec looked where the dragon's eyes had been, then looked away. "The dragon call?"

Aoquesth's voice was barely a whisper. "You can try. Call the dragons with your eyes, the same way you spoke to the Substance with your eyes to make it open."

Erec could not thank Aoquesth, or even ask how he felt; his voice was too shaky. All he could do was hold the dragon around his neck until his last steamy breath had flown into the sky.

CHAPTER TWENTY-TWO

The Other Eye

EREC AND JAM walked the streets of Lerna that night. Erec's arm had been bandaged by Dr. Shandy. He hoped that each step would bring him closer to knowing why Aoquesth had saved his life, had given him everything. But, in the end, he only felt further from understanding anything at all. He was exhausted, but the loss he felt kept him going, one step at a time, through the city, as if he was afraid to come back and face reality again.

He showed the Amulet of Virtues to Jam. "I guess this means I'm still in the running for king." He laughed. "I'm sure I'm officially kicked out according to the Labor Society, but it doesn't seem like it's under their control."

"Who knows whose control it really is under?" Jam said. "Sometimes I think the Substance itself is in charge here."

Erec nodded, remembering what he had seen of the Substance when he made a hole in it with Aoquesth. "Yes," he said. "You just may be right."

When they reached Tina's house there was a huge party going on. A pair of tentacles whisked Erec high into the air. "Here he is! Three cheers for Erec Rex! Three cheers for Jam Crinklecut!" As much as Jam looked flustered by being tossed about, Erec could tell he loved the attention. Hydras joined tentacles and sang songs, passing around jugs of cider and nectar. Erec wished he could join in the merriment, but he felt cold inside. Aoquesth was dead and it was his fault. If he had only been stronger, able to defend himself, then the dragon would be alive right now.

Steve put a tentacle around Erec's shoulder. "Kid, you did it. I don't know how to thank you. You risked your life for us. And you turned down fame and fortune, even when you thought you would die. You're something, I'll tell you that. If you ever run for king, you have my vote." He chuckled to himself. "Anyway, without you we would have been dog meat. So thanks."

Erec shrugged. "I didn't do anything, really. Just got lucky. I only wish Aoquesth was as lucky."

Steve sighed. "It's sad. But he chose to do what he did. Remember that. He had lived a long time, too."

Erec still held the glass jar with Aoquesth's eye in it, although he tried not to look at it. It was gruesome and made him sad, but he did not want to put it down.

Tina gave Erec a tentacled hug. "You are my hero, Erec. Can I still write to you after you go back to Alypium?"

"Sure." He smiled at her. "Send a picture next time too. I know a lot of guys who would think you look totally awesome." She turned reddish and grinned. Erec was glad the Archives of Alithea were used up now so that he didn't blurt out the rest of what they might think.

Erec turned around and there before him stood the Hermit. "Ahh, here he is, the hero du jour." The Hermit cackled. "Ready to get that eye put in?"

"Huh? Now?" Erec gripped the jar, not quite ready for anything. "I need to go find the twins. I think I know who has them."

The Hermit grinned. "A time for eyes and a place for twins. The eye needs to go in now. Heph Vulcan is waiting."

Erec found Jam and said good-bye to Tina, Steve, and the others at the party. The Hermit led them through a Port-O-Door, and they were instantly in King Piter's Castle. It felt strange to travel so far so quickly. But while they were still in the vestibule, the Hermit touched the map screen to bring them to the other side of Alypium. They walked out into a waiting room of a small office.

A coat rack very like the one Erec grew up with ran out to greet them, then strode away, disappointed that they did not have anything to hang on it. The rug at the door reached up around Jam's feet and polished his shoes, making Jam laugh. The chairs all bounced invitingly, and even the light waved a pull cord at them in greeting.

"Come in," a hearty voice called out. Heph Vulcan was a broad, stout man with a short dark beard and dark hair. He wore a sleeveless gray shirt, loose pants, and a gray cap. He looked like a lumberjack. His hoarse voice had a New York accent. "You must be Erec. Glad to finally meet you. I've heard a lot about you. You're using the eye I made for you ten years ago, I hear. Now you want the other one done?"

Erec nodded. He wasn't sure what having Aoquesth's other eye would do to him, or if it was something he really should have. But it was a part of Aoquesth. He had saved Erec's life, so it only seemed right. This is what Aoquesth wanted, his last request.

Erec thought about what having one dragon eye did to his cloudy thoughts. What would two do? Aoquesth said two dragon eyes would be very powerful for a human being, but he was sure Erec could handle it. Erec wished he was as sure. He wanted Aoquesth to be here to show him how to use it, like he had started to show him how to use the first eye.

Heph Vulcan led them through a shop filled with objects he had brought to life. Erec lay on a table that reached metal arms around him to hold him still. Vulcan waved a syringe over him. "This won't hurt a bit. You'll wake right up when it's over."

Erec gulped. "Do you know what having two dragon eyes will do for me?"

Vulcan shrugged. "You're the only human who has one at all. I would know; I'm the only one who can fuse dragon eyes to human ones. Of course Thanatos Baskania would not need me for that. He uses eyes in his own way. So I suppose he might have one."

Erec was not reassured to find out that no other human had ever experienced having two dragon eyes before, especially knowing how having just one affected him. He was glad Jam was in the room. Vulcan gave him a shot, and all went black.

Erec awoke suddenly, not sure how long he had been out. Jam looked green, like he might throw up at any minute. "Is young sir all right?"

"I'm fine. What's wrong, Jam?"

"Oh, nothing. It just was an . . . interesting procedure, that's all."

Erec did not feel different at all. He looked around. His eyes moved normally, and his vision was okay. It was a relief. Maybe he would never even notice he had the other dragon eye.

It felt good to come back through the Port-O-Door into the castle. After the wilds of Otherness and the strangeness of Lerna, Alypium actually seemed humdrum, something Erec never thought he would think. But there wasn't time to settle back into life there. He had to find Ugry and save the twins, if he still held them captive. He felt terrible about leaving the dragon hatchlings in the Nevervarld for another minute. Aoquesth had said they would only last a few days, and Erec knew that place was not pleasant. As soon as he rescued Danny and Sammy, he would head straight to get the hatchlings out.

"Jam," Erec said, "will you stick with me a bit longer? I'm going to find Ugry now."

Jam grinned. "Like glue, sir. Like glue."

Ugry was not in his private offices, so they wandered through the west wing. Erec looked in the dining hall as he walked by, realizing how hungry he was. Bethany, Jack, and Oscar were inside munching plates of deserts. They looked up in shock.

Bethany ran up and threw her arms around him. "Erec! You're back! The Hermit told us you were okay, but we were so worried! Did you do the second quest?"

Erec nodded. "Yeah, only I didn't even know I was doing it." He wolfed down some food, dessert first, and told them what had happened. Jam eyed the food as if he did not feel comfortable digging in, so Erec handed him a plate. "I'm going to find Ugry now. Do you guys want to come? Then I have to get the baby dragons out of the Nevervarld. I hoped you might come with us there, too. We could use your help."

Jam's back straightened as if he was glad Erec assumed he would be going with him. "Let's pack some food for the trip, sir."

Bethany looked at Jam. "Erec, aren't you going to introduce us?"

"This is Jam Crinklecut, the head butler of the west wing. Don't you remember him?"

She turned pink, staring at Jam. "Oh, sorry. I didn't recognize you."

After Jam made some packs of food for the road they asked a maid in the west wing if she had seen Ugry. She pointed toward the throne room. "He likes to go there and think."

They pulled open the heavy doors and walked into the large throne room. The last time he had been here King Piter's scepter flew through the air to him, saving his life. The massive room looked so empty now. From where they stood, the immense throne looked small. Huge chandeliers hung above them, and ornate tapestries and drapes covered the walls. After a long walk across the room, the fifteen-foot, gem-studded gold throne rose above them. An enormous round diamond was embedded in its high back.

Upon it, Balthazar Ugry sat deep in thought. At the base of the throne, his foot rested on the Lia Fail, the rough gray rock that had screamed during the coronation ceremony. He slowly raised an eyebrow and scowled. "And to what do I owe this pleasure?"

"Where are Danny and Sammy?" Erec demanded, hands on hips.

A smirk lit Ugry's lips. "Oh, this is rich. Are you accusing me of something, boy? As usual?"

"I happen to know you kidnapped the twins. Where are they?" Erec tried to look menacing but was aware that they had no way to make Ugry do anything at all, or even protect themselves from him. Maybe he should have found King Piter first.

Ugry put his fingers to his mouth and feigned shock. "You

happen to know this, do you? Then why, pray tell, did you not inform me sooner? If I had kidnapped the twins I would just as soon know." He glared angrily. "You're lucky I have a use for you, or you might not be here to annoy me now. Why don't you kids and your servant run away and play your little games somewhere else. I have some important matters to consider."

Erec gnashed his teeth. "But I saw you with them. And you're always carrying candy wrappers, and—"

"If you want to know, I have spent some of my time looking for your brother and sister in Alypium, since you and King Piter have been gone. I did not have luck, unfortunately. I could sometimes tell where they would be going, but not when. I never could find them."

"But I saw you at the ice rink when they were there. You were with them."

Ugry rolled his eyes and grimaced. "I was there looking for them. I thought I saw them, but somebody else saw me first. Before I knew it, I was spinning around the room in a whirlwind. By the time I got out of it they were gone."

Erec stared at him, not comprehending. Ugry leaned forward, an eyebrow up. "What is this? I'm sensing something on you, something with hints of an old power." He stepped off the throne and lifted the Archives of Alithea out of Erec's pocket. "And where did you get this?"

Erec tried to grab it, but Ugry whisked it away. "It's mine. Patchouli gave it to me after I saved her hatchlings. It's used up anyway."

Ugry looked it over. "So it is. But there is a tiny amount of magic left in it. Not enough to use the scroll again, but holding it might help me see where the twins are now." Ugry closed his eyes, the scroll tight in his fist. His face strained and tensed, then finally relaxed. "They're in Alypium. We will go there now." He lifted the side of his cape, and the six of them were suddenly standing in . . .

Rosco Kroc's house.

Sammy and Danny looked up in shock as Erec, Ugry, Jam, Jack, Oscar, and Bethany appeared in front of them. Rosco jumped to his feet, but in an instant was flattened to the wall with a blue force field gleaming around him. Ugry's eyes blazed. "So, crocodile face, this is what you've come to. Kidnapping, is it now? Sorry to see how such a sweet kid ends up."

Rosco threw spells at Ugry, but little blue sizzles from the force field stopped them. "That's right, old buzzard," Rosco said. "Why don't you take a stroll back through the valley of the shadow of death and bring young Erec with you!"

Everyone stared at Rosco. Sammy's face turned red. "Why did you say that?" She sprang to her feet and threw her arms around Erec. "There you are! We were so worried about you! How are the other kids? Is Mom out of the asylum yet?"

Danny walked over and gave Erec a hug. "Hey, kid. Glad you finally got here. You'll like it here." He looked at Rosco and Ugry. "I think there has been a misunderstanding. Rosco didn't kidnap us. He's helping us. Mom sent him to get us this summer when she was carted off to a mental asylum. I thought the other kids were being watched by someone else. Rosco said we'd see them soon, and Mom needed her rest."

Erec looked at Rosco in disbelief. "How could you?" He looked at the twins. "Mom is fine. She was kidnapped this summer and stuck in King Pluto's dungeons, not in a mental asylum. She's been back a long time and worried sick about you guys. We've been looking everywhere for you." Erec bit his tongue to keep tears from coming. His face felt hot.

So, he had been right when he originally thought Rosco had the twins. He never did look in the other room that day he had come here searching for them. Then again, he could barely move at that point. Erec looked at Rosco through the force field. "Why?"

Rosco sneered. "They were valuable. They are thirteen-year-old twins with the last name Rex. They might be important. It was a prestigious assignment from the Shadow Prince. I have no regrets." He looked at Oscar. "Remember that, Oscar. No regrets. I know what you think of me now, but someday you will understand."

Danny and Sammy were talking at once, confused. "Mom's okay? Rosco lied?" Tears streamed from Sammy's eyes. Danny threw a boot from the floor at Rosco, but it bounced off the force field.

Oscar came close to the blue light of the force field and looked blankly into Rosco's eyes. "I will never understand. You lied to me. You lied to Erec's brother and sister, kidnapped them from their family." He bit his lip and backed away, shaking his head.

Rosco shouted to him, "You'll see someday! You're like me, you know."

Oscar spun toward him, face red, and yelled, "I am not like you. I never will be. Just leave me alone."

Ugry looked down on Oscar with hatred. "As for you, because of your association with this criminal, I will make sure you are no longer allowed to participate in any quests with Erec."

Oscar looked up, lip trembling, hot tears streaming down his face. "But I didn't know. It's not fair."

"Nevertheless," Ugry hissed, "one cannot be too safe."

Rosco shouted, "Balthazar—don't you see? You're the cause of all the problems here."

Oscar walked up to the force field, hatred in his eyes. "I'll get you someday, Rosco. Just wait. I promise."

Rosco looked at him with affection. "I know you will, buddy. And thank you for it. Meanwhile, nobody holds old Rosca' hostage." Starting at his feet, his body twisted into a green whirlwind behind the force field, and then he vanished.

* * *

June O'Hara looked up in shock as Erec, Bethany, Danny, Sammy, Oscar, Jack, and Jam walked into her house through a Port-O-Door. "Oh, my." She looked around, hand over her heart. "Erec? Danny? Sammy? Oh . . ." She ran to them and threw her arms around them again and again. "The Hermit told me you would be okay, but I was so worried. There was nothing I could do."

They talked for an hour, telling one another what happened, and repeating the good parts a few extra times. June kept asking Erec what his new dragon eye was like, but it really felt no different than before he had it. She still had not managed to take her Seeing Eyeglasses off of the alarm clock. The twins wanted to hear about the trolls, and Bethany asked a few times for more details about what Tina looked like. Jam focused on Rosco's escape. But when Erec talked about Aoquesth, the room got quiet.

Jam spoke up. "He was a good friend. And we had better go finish our job there soon."

Jam was right. The dragon hatchlings had been in the Nevervarld for close to three days, which seemed like pure torture, and might well be near their limit. Erec hoped they were all right. "Jam and I should get them out now. We have to bring them home. Maybe we can sleep there with them, then start to walk with them into the dragon territories in the morning. It may take a long time."

"Or"—Jam winked at him—"we could go there with a Port-O-Door and bring them straight back into the castle for the night. I could fix them up there, and Ezzy Mumbai could tend to them if they need it. Then in the morning, straight through the Port-O-Door into dragon territory. No long walks where we could be spotted."

Erec grinned. "Great idea, Jam. Let's do it." June was grabbing the twins tight to her sides, and Erec gave all of them another hug. "I'll be back soon."

Erec, Jam, Bethany, Oscar, and Jack went through the

Port-O-Door back into the west wing of the castle. Erec said, "It's really late, guys. You don't all have to come. You can see the dragons at the castle in the morning."

Jack stretched. "All right. I'm tired anyway. I'll see you tomorrow."

Oscar's face was drawn. "I think I need to go kick something. Now I don't have a tutor anymore, and I can't do any of the quests. Rosco is going to die." He looked up at Erec. "I'm not coming. I'm too pissed off."

"I'll come with you!" Bethany grinned. "It's been pretty boring around here with you gone. Time to meet some dragons!"

CHAPTER TWENTY-THREE
The Dragon Hatchlings

EREC HANDED BETHANY the Archives of Alithea so he could get into the Nevervarld again. She put them in her pocket. Then Jam, Erec, and Bethany stepped from the vestibule of the Port-O-Door into the darkness of the Jotnar night, near Trollebotten Cave. The air was warm, and crickets hummed evening ballads in their boggy bars and puddle pubs. Somewhere nearby a sheep *baa*-ed, which seemed strange as there were no animals in sight.

It took a minute for Erec's eyes to adjust. Jam led the way to the cave entrance. The hole in the Substance was about thirty feet away, so they all counted footsteps, searching for the small fig tree that marked the spot. Bethany shouted, "I found it! It's the Nevervarld. I can tell, my hand is in it. It's not a feeling you can forget."

Erec and Jam ran to where she was kneeling. Erec put his hand in with hers. Cold dry sparks licked his skin. He was not looking forward to going back in, but at least he was not left in there for days like the poor dragons were. Well, soon they would be out and home safe with their parents, and he would be done too. He could not wait to get back to the castle, have a hot mug of cocoa, and climb into bed. But, first things first.

Bethany and Jam both wished that they could be the ones to go into the Nevervarld, since Erec had done enough. He took off his Sneakers and slid his feet through the hole he and Aoquesth had made in the Substance. As he lowered himself through the space his breath quickened. Quick in, quick out. He would not have to be in there long. Bethany sat nearby and stuck her hand through the hole so he could grab it when he was ready to come out. As Erec plunged himself into the Nevervarld, he heard another *baa*, which must have been from the same lost sheep.

Black and white specks of static sizzled and sparked around him, erasing everything that Erec knew was real. He gasped and grabbed his arms to feel something solid. As before in the Nevervarld, he could not tell if he was moving or holding still, but everything was in motion around him, spinning flecks of something he could not grasp. He closed his eyes, but the bits were still there, all around him and inside him. He heard the familiar voice in his mind. *Thank you. Yummm.*

Bethany's hand sparkled near the hole like a beacon of light. But where were the dragons? When he had left them here they were bright, glowing intense colors, and their thoughts were so noisy they were overwhelming. But now only the crushing white noise of static that Erec could not identify as sound or silence filled his ears. Panic coursed through him for a moment. How would he find them? What if they had died?

He tried moving farther out, away from Bethany's hand. Pinches of energy were sucked from his body into the emptiness, and he was already getting tired. Focus. Think. He tried to see into the motion, look for shapes or figures. Then it occurred to him that maybe there was a reason the dragons were not here. Maybe somebody else had gotten to them first. What if Baskania had them now, or had their eyes already? His heart sunk. But he could not turn back; he had to look further and make sure.

It seemed doubtful the dragons were here, because they glowed so brightly before that they had been hard to miss. His mind spun. Nothingness enveloped him, sucking him in, taking his energy away. Sharp sparks of pain flicked around his body, draining him. He began to get confused, but he remembered the dragons. He had to find them.

Swirls moved around and through him faster now. Where were the dragon thoughts? Where were his own thoughts? Was he swimming in the specks or were they swimming in him? Help! Please help. *Where are you?* he called out in his head. *Dragons! I am here to take you home!*

Nothing. But he was sure he had communicated with them here before. If they were here, their thoughts were gone. Maybe they had not made it. He heard the Nevervarld within him, *You are not dead. You are the human with the dragon part. But you don't have long. Leave now or give yourself to us.*

But he could not do that yet. Something had to help him here. Then he remembered the lion skin flowers. They came to him here twice before. Maybe they would help him now.

Flowers! Where are you? Help me find the baby dragons. Please.

Something nudged his hand, pulling him somewhere. His other hand, his face, everything was covered in soft petals. They were moving him deeper into the Nevervarld, far away, where he would never get out, never see the light of day.

It was confusing to even remember what daylight was like, what he was like. Where was he going? He was so tired. It was hard to remember.

Shapes moved in front of him. Or was he moving in front of them? Dull, dark images floated in the swirls of specks, quiet and lifeless. It took him a while to realize that these shapes were the dragons. Didn't they have color? Life? He was not sure why he or they were there. Maybe if he just went to sleep it would all be okay.

His eyes were closing. The thought fluttered through his mind that he might have been here longer than before. Maybe when he awoke everything would be clear. The flowers pushed him into the dragon heap, dumping his body with theirs. It was okay. They looked comfortable. It was dark now. The darkness was filling him, taking him away.

But then he startled, only slightly, just enough to wake him up, when he brushed against one of the dragon hatchlings. Its color was gone, but it still had something solid and real about it. It did not respond to his touch, but he felt more and there was a chain—the shadow of the metal chain holding the dragons together. He grasped it. This is what he'd come here for. The dragons. The chain. He pulled, but nothing happened. His mind was too weak, too tired. Concentrate. Erec focused, pulling harder. Nothing happened. What was wrong? He was trying with every ounce of his energy. Then he remembered. To move here he had to use his body as well as his mind. He wasn't sure which one he had forgotten, but he yanked one more time, and the chain moved.

Something swam with him, guiding him and the dragons somewhere far away. Where were they going? It was only the semisolid feel of the chain in his grip that kept him alive. A bright glimmer appeared and grew into a sparkling vision too bright to look at. It was a hand. Bethany's hand. If only he could reach it, he knew everything would be okay. It was coming closer now. Small soft movements around him were pushing him to safety.

Thank you, he thought. It was all he could manage.

And then her hand was in front of him, so bright he could not look at it. He reached, not sure if he could ever make it, grabbing the chain and stretching toward safety, toward life.

Her hand grasped his, and he gasped in shock. Warmth sizzled through him. He had not realized he was so cold. Bethany's hand was so full of life. He held on as she pulled him to safety, into warmth, knowing it was like a kind of rebirth and it would hurt at first, but he was ready. He hoped the dragons were ready too, and that they were still alive.

With a yank he was through. Violent colors and sounds assaulted him from all angles. Noises, shapes. In a rush, Erec identified the sizzling, flaming spheres in his eyes as stars. They burned into his head, stinging him. Someone was pulling the dragons through the hole. He was glad because he never would have been able to do it.

It hurt to look at things, but they slowly materialized before him. Grass. Sky. He realized he was gripping Bethany's hand tight, even though the feeling overwhelmed him with pain. He looked at her, ready to see her face even though it would be too much.

But it was not Bethany's face. It was somebody else's. The eyes of the person who held his hand seared into him, looking through him like he was a broken shard of glass.

So many eyes.

Baskania loosened his grip on Erec and laid him on the dirt. The last thing Erec heard before he passed out was a cackle of glee.

Erec shivered, the air freezing him to his bones as he huddled under the bush. His father appeared with his boss. They had found him and the boss was yelling at his father. Erec's dream misted over. But it wasn't his father. The dream had been tampered with, put in by the Memory Mogul. The man was familiar though. And the boss—even more familiar. His voice was the same as . . .

Baskania said, "They're coming to. It won't be long now, boys."

It was Baskania's voice. Baskania was the boss of the father from his nightmares, the father he always had thought was his own, but who was just an implanted memory. The knowledge of this gave Erec the chills. He lifted his head, which had been lolling at his side, and tried to move, but he was stuck. He fought against his bonds without luck.

Images formed before his eyes, and they did not hurt him now that he had slept. He could see Bethany and Jam near him, both tied upright to poles with the same magic rope that had bound Erec during the coronation ceremony and that was holding him now.

"Erec," Bethany whispered. "Are you awake? Baskania and the Stain boys were hiding behind some bushes. They surprised us after you went through the hole."

Baskania strode to Erec, hands on hips. His face had seven eyes showing. It was not as many as another time Erec had seen him; this time there was enough room for his mouth and nose. He wore a cloak of fine black pin-striped linen. It looked like a cross between a sorcerer's cloak and a stylish suit. Behind him stood Balor and Damon Stain, along with a boy with white fuzzy sheep's wool growing around his head and face and running down his neck. Long leaf-shaped ears stuck out of his head like a lamb's. His eyes, though, were the same steely blue as Balor and Damon's. When he looked at Erec, *"Baa-aa-aa"* popped out of his mouth, and his hand flew over his face in embarrassment.

"Don't stare at Dollick," Baskania said. "That's rude. I see you are awake, Oh, he-who-would-be-king. You have been trying your best to take the throne away from these nice Stain boys, now haven't you? Well, that has come to an end. You and your friends will not be around to plague Alypium anymore. Balor and Damon here will finish the quests with Rock Rayson, Rock will get suddenly ill and die, and he will hand over his kingdom to Dollick. These boys will give the scepters to me for safekeeping, and they will rule the world under me."

Baskania leered at Erec. "And it all starts now. You thought you had tricked me, boy? No one gets the better of me. I wanted to kill you in Lerna with all the crowds cheering me on, but I'll get to kill you now instead. I wanted to slaughter my dragons for their eyes when I was done there, but instead I'll do it in a few moments. And then I will go on from here to learn something that will make me invincible. Not only will I have all these dragon eyes at my command"—he swept a hand toward the pile of little sleeping dragons—"but I will also have the greatest secret of all at my disposal. The clues to the Final Magic."

He pulled a bundle of leaves from his cloak. "Creeping albatross. This will unlock the mystery, and it will happen tonight." He laughed. "Too bad you will not be here to see my triumph. But you may die knowing that I will be all-powerful before long."

One of the hatchlings snorted. Balor pointed. "They're waking up. Look."

Several of the dragons moved, eyes still shut. "Good, good." Baskania said. "In a few minutes they will be back in this world enough so their eyes will be fully functional. Then we may slay them."

Damon jumped up and down. "Oh, goody! Slay, slay, slay. Can I do it first?"

Dollick knocked Damon on the head with a hand that looked like a hoof. "I get to do it first. I don't ever get to have any fun. Why don't you guys let me do the quests with you?"

Balor sneered at Dollick. "Because you look like a sheep, retard. You think the people of Alypium are going to want you to be king? Wait till they don't have a choice, then you'll get your revenge on them."

"All in good time, boys." Baskania gloated. "For now, we'll have to choose which we want to kill first—the dragons or these nasty humans."

Erec closed his eyes. It was too late. He had tried so hard to stop this from happening, but he couldn't do it. The dragons would die. And Erec's life was over. Even worse, he had dragged Bethany into this . . . and Jam. Baskania would take all the dragons' power, learn the Final Magic, and destroy the world. Erec had let everyone down. Especially Aoquesth.

If only Aoquesth was here now. He would take care of things.

Erec's breath caught. Aoquesth.

There was something he could try. And just maybe, possibly, it could work.

Balor walked in front of Erec's face. "I think we should kill a few dragons, then this butler, and then some more dragons, and then Bethany. I think Erec should watch her die. Then we'll do him last." He grinned.

Think. How did Aoquesth describe it? Love. That's it. Love. Erec squeezed his eyes shut. It was hard to think about love when he was so filled with hate. But he had to do it. Just like when he was seeing the Substance, making a hole in it. He had to reach deep and feel . . .

Love.

Aoquesth rushed into his head. Those gleaming scales, fiery rage against his foes, wings of black slicing the sky. Then his mother, his family. Danny and Sammy were safe now. Trevor, Nell, Zoey. Bethany. He thought of the times they had shared together.

But Baskania's cackles sliced through his thoughts, inciting the hate in him.

Love. He reached out to the love he knew was there, stronger than his anger, stronger than his hate. He turned inward, feeling the love itself, freeing it inside him, calling to it. Why wasn't it working?

"It's ready! It's ready!" Damon jumped up and down. "This one's awake." Sure enough, the dragon hatchlings were tumbling over each other, making small roaring noises. "I go first." He brandished a gleaming dirk, its blade shining on a red hilt, then grabbed a dragon by the head.

"No, me!" Dollick tried to wrestle it out of his hands. Baskania looked on with amusement.

Love. He could hear Aoquesth's voice in the back of his mind.

Dollick grabbed the dirk and plunged it into a dragon. The tiny thing chirped and gagged, eyes wide in shock. He pulled the blade out, purple blood dripping onto the ground. The dragon baby's eyes met Erec's as it fell. A peep came from its throat, and then it was still.

Erec stared at the baby lying in a heap on the grass. He could hear Bethany crying. The thing almost looked like a little Aoquesth. His heart opened, and love filled him completely. He couldn't help it. Any anger that was in him was washed away by the sadness and fullness of his love for this baby beast, for Aoquesth, and for the world.

He squeezed his eyes shut. Hot tears streamed down his cheeks, stinging and burning like acid. When he opened his eyes, everything was dense, jungle green. Thick strands and clumps of white netting, the Substance, gleamed around him. Erec could see the hole in the Substance he had made with Aoquesth.

His dragon eyes were out.

Erec reached deeper. Love. He threw it into the heavens, reaching with it above all the madness. He gleamed it high with his dragon eyes. Aoquesth's eyes. He could remember what Aoquesth had said: "Call the dragons with your eyes . . . the same way you spoke to the Substance with your eyes to make it open."

He heard Bethany sniffling next to him and Jam's teeth chattering.

Dragons! His eyes projected his love into the skies. *Come save us. Your hatchlings are here. Baskania wants to kill them. Hurry! Please!*

The world looked beautiful. He could see the Substance living and breathing, much clearer than when he only had one dragon eye. But he was not going to try and change it like he'd done once. He would just wait and hope.

"Well, look at this," Baskania gazed at Erec. "It looks like someone has two dragon eyes now. Hmm, all the better for me, since they'll soon be mine."

Erec stared at the sky. Nothing appeared. Maybe it was hopeless. Aoquesth had not been sure Erec could do the dragon call. Even Aoquesth was not powerful enough to do it toward the end of his life.

"Hurry. Please."

Balor walked up to Jam, spinning a remote control in his hand. "I can't wait to kill one of these retards. This will be fun."

Damon grabbed the knife and plunged it into another dragon. It shuddered in his grasp, choking as Damon pulled out the dripping knife.

"Save its blood," Baskania said. "We'll need it later."

Grinning, Balor pointed his remote at Jam. "Say good-bye, loser."

The sky was empty. Erec looked at Jam in apology. Jam smiled back as if to say it had all been worth it.

Then a swoosh filled the sky. And another. And another. Balor looked up and tripped backward. Broad, stretched black wings cut through the air, scales glittered, and fire shot like lightning bursts from a stormy sky.

Erec looked up with his dragon eyes, and connected with dragon after dragon. They saw him, knew him through his eyes, and understood. A dragon wing brushed Balor into the bushes. Talons poured from the air, grabbing Dollick and Damon Stain, pulling hatchlings to safety, melting the chains that held them. Balor emerged and swung toward Erec, teeth gritted. He pointed his remote control, but a dragon knocked him down.

Baskania's eyes narrowed with hatred. His lips curved into a deep sneer, then he raised an arm. The two dead hatchlings that remained on the ground flew into his hand. Then he disappeared, the three Stain boys vanishing with him.

A dragon cut through Erec's, Bethany's, and Jam's bonds with her claws. They collapsed on the ground, panting in relief. The dragon sat with them on the grass. It was Patchouli. "I see you have both of Aoquesth's eyes now. He must have really believed in you." She looked around. "It looks like he was right."

Dragons were thanking Erec and flying home with their hatchlings, many with green tears falling and talking about the two hatchlings that had died. Patchouli stayed to make sure Erec and his friends were okay. It felt good to rest, to look up at the stars. This had been a long day.

Patchouli stretched a wing. "Thank you, Erec, once again. You saved my children, and now you have saved everyone else's. The dragons are forever at your service."

Erec's smile was tinged with sadness. "I had some help, you know. Jam and Bethany each did their part too. I just wish all the hatchlings had made it." He thought about the two that had died, unable to understand how Dollick and Damon Stain could have wanted to kill them.

"I know." Patchouli sighed steam. "I do too. But you saved all the others, Erec."

Jam handed Erec a wet towel. "You might want to wipe your face, sir. There are green stains under your eyes."

Erec was glad Jam was yet again prepared for everything. He cleaned his face, wondering if the stains were from dragon tears.

An odd giggle filled the air, and then the Hermit appeared, spinning through the air in a wild dervish dance. "Greetings, King Erec." He bowed low. "Or, then again, maybe not!" He fell on his head.

"What are you doing here?" Jam asked.

"Dancing. Laughing. Spinning. Much better than sitting on the ground like a lump."

Erec was too tired to pay much attention to the strange man. "I think I better get some sleep." Then, suddenly, the world in front of him swirled into a dense, overpowering green that was filled with the Substance. Each particle of it that hung on the webs of the Aitherplanes moved, swirled, and spun like its own little galaxy. He stared harder and could break down the particles into smaller ones with his eyes, and build them up again. Then his body exploded in a roar, an eruption that was so intense it stunned him. His hands prickled, claws popped from his fingers.

He knew it was a cloudy thought, or a premonition, but it was stronger than any he'd had with just one dragon eye. What was happening to him? Another roar racked his body, and then he got a vision, so much clearer and fuller than any before.

Explosion. Destruction. The entire world in ruin. Devastation. The planet shattered.

Things were moving fast, confusing, like a film running backward at top speed. Now he was watching something happening before the destruction, and something before that. He couldn't catch it all, didn't know if he was supposed to.

The image kept moving back in time until . . . today. Now. Something was happening right now that would lead the world into chaos. And he could see what it was.

Thanatos Baskania was leaning over a well, sprinkling a liquid into it and saying a spell. He was getting his grandmother out of the well.

The intense green was gone, his claws had disappeared, and Erec looked around the room.

Bethany and Jam stared at him, stunned. It was only the Hermit who hopped over to him and said, "Welcome to the future."

CHAPTER TWENTY-FOUR
Creeping Albatross

EREC FINALLY FOUND his voice. "I got a cloudy thought. Something bad is happening right now. I have to stop it, or . . ." He could not describe what chain of events would happen if he did not intervene. "Baskania is getting his grandmother out of a well. It has something to do with him getting the Final Magic, and it's going to ruin everything if I don't get there right away."

"Where is it?" Jam asked.

Erec's cloudy thought had been clear. "The well is in Cyprus, in Upper Earth. It's near the ruins of the ancient city of Salamis, near Famagusta. I know just where to go. The Port-O-Door will get me there. I have to hurry."

Jam said slowly, "Baskania's grandmother has been dead for a long time."

The Hermit nodded. "He is bringing her back." Everyone stared. Bringing her back from the dead? "She knows the Great Secret—where the Final Magic is hidden. She was a wise woman. Baskania must have finally found the creeping albatross to bring her back. It was supposed to be extinct. And he has the dragon blood now too."

Patchouli looked at him sadly. "I would go with you, Erec, but I cannot go into Upper Earth."

"I understand. Thank you."

Bethany crossed her arms. "Well, I'll go with you."

"Me too, sir," Jam said.

"No." Erec held his hands up. "Please. This is walking straight into danger. I may not come out again. And I would not be able to do it knowing either of you could be hurt. I have to go alone."

Erec's urge to go to the well in Cyprus was as strong as any cloudy thought; all the more so because he knew what was at stake. He stood up. "Time for me to do this."

Bethany threw her arms around him, tears rolling onto his shoulder. "Don't, Erec. Let's just tell King Piter and let him handle it."

"That's a laugh. King Piter has yet to handle anything. The cloudy thought came to me, and I have to follow it. I don't have a choice." He put a hand on her cheek. "Take care of Wolfboy for me again, if I don't come back right away." He hugged Patchouli, then he walked with Jam, Bethany, and the Hermit to the Port-O-Door vestibule and shut the door on the black Jotnar sky.

Erec easily found the ruins near Famagusta in Cyprus on the Port-O-Door map from the tiny green corner of the screen labeled "Upper Earth." He shook hands with Jam and gave Bethany another hug. "I'm sure I'll see you soon." He smiled. "Don't worry about me." The Hermit patted him on the head. Then he walked through the Port-O-Door alone.

It was nighttime in Cyprus, but Erec's eyes were used to the dark. He knew where to walk—around this corner, down a hill, then past rows of towering Ionian columns that shot into the dark sky. He saw somebody and froze . . . but it was just the headless statue of an ancient Cyprian woman.

Around another bend he saw the well. There was Baskania, three extra eyes open on his forehead, with Balor and Damon and Dollick Stain in tow. He was pouring things into a large glass vase. "Balm of Gilead, dittany of Crete, sandalwood, fresh dragon blood, and my prize." He pulled out a clump of frilly leaves with tiny blue flowers. "Creeping albatross, thought to be extinct. The missing ingredient I have so long sought." He stirred it into his concoction.

Baskania's voice thundered, "Abandon all hope, ye who enter here, for nigh is the colossus of the night, the towering strength I am giving to you." He shook a beaker and poured it into the well. "Oh, annus mirabilis . . . rise! Rise!"

It was too late. Baskania and the Stain boys reached into the well and pulled four people out, one after the other. In fact, the people showed no interest at all in coming out. They shouted and grunted, trying to push their rescuers away. A terrible smell of decay wafted from them. Two of them, a boy and a girl, jumped immediately back into the well. A young man stood shivering, grasping himself. He kept looking into the well with longing, as if he too wanted to jump in, but instead he crouched behind it, shaking violently, grasping his arms as if he was sick.

An old woman with tangled gray hair tried to tug herself free from the Stain triplets. "Let me go, you badly made imitations." Her gathered moss-green, ankle-length skirt swished around her feet as she struggled. Tight green sleeves with wide maroon flared cuffs and a white lace bodice surrounded with maroon fabric made her look like she had walked out of a museum. She glared at Baskania. "You oaf. Let me go back to my nice sleep. You have no right waking me up like this." She pulled harder without success, and her eyebrows lowered. "I knew Magda wasn't raising you right. That child had no sense. Look at you, Thaddy. You take after me. Use your powers to do some good. You could do so much for the world."

Baskania sneered at her. "Shut up, you old wretch. I saved your life for one reason. You know the prophecy, the Great Secret of where the Final Magic is hidden. Where is it?"

She yanked but could not pull herself away from the triplets. "Even if I remembered, I would never tell you. You would destroy the world with it. Look what's happened to you, Thaddy. Your mind is corrupted with powers that you should never have had, things you should not have learned. You cannot have this one. Now put me back and go."

"Stupid old woman." Baskania's eyes narrowed. "You can't fool me. In coming back from death you know everything you have ever known, and you can see into the future of your offspring as well. So tell me, where is the secret to the Final Magic? I knew that note of yours mentioned something about a miniature. Is it hidden in a toy?"

Erec noticed the young man behind the well had run off. Baskania's grandmother shook violently. "I cannot tell you. If you find out, it will be some other way. So let me go back to my death. This life you have put upon me hurts my bones. I need to get back."

Erec crept closer, not sure what to do. If he could just surprise the Stain boys, maybe she could break free and jump back to her death. Baskania's beaker had been emptied; hopefully he had no more to bring her back again.

Baskania tilted his head and said in a sickeningly sweet voice, "Grandmother Cassandra, I did not want to have to resort to this. I am afraid I will have to make you talk." He raised two fingers and pointed them at her.

Erec's body tightened, ready to pounce on the triplets. But before he could move, someone behind him ran and hurled himself against their feet, then took off running into the night. The Stain boys stumbled and fell, tumbling over themselves. Baskania's grandmother broke away, dusted off her dress, muttered a thank-you over her shoulder, and threw herself into the well.

"Who did that?" Balor stood and dusted himself off.

Baskania stared into the distance, fuming. "The butler did it. Erec Rex's friend."

Erec's heart pounded. Jam had snuck here behind him! In moments, Jam was kneeling at Baskania's feet, tied with magic rope. "Are you here alone?" Baskania fumed. "Where is Erec Rex?" He paused, chin in the air. "Aaahhh. Very interesting. I sense something close by, something that is just what I need." He smiled, kicking Jam over onto his side in the dirt.

"Erec," Baskania called in a singsong voice, "come here, boy. I have a treat for you."

Erec took a step back. He could sense Baskania probing in his mind.

"I think you have something I want, and I have something you want. Maybe we can make a little trade. You give me that worn out scroll in your pocket, the one that doesn't work anymore, and I'll give you your butler friend back. Sound fair?"

Erec stood frozen. Baskania must have read his mind enough to know he had the Archives of Alithea. Even though it was worn out, Ugry had used it to find out where Danny and Sammy were. There was no way Erec could give it to him.

"Don't be silly," Baskania replied to his thoughts. "Balthazar is a seer. The scroll just made clearer what he could already see. I am not a seer, unfortunately, and I have no dragon eyes yet to help me see the future. The scroll is useless to me. But I am a collector of old artifacts. It would be a good trade for me still. And I'll spare your friend here."

Erec wondered how he could get Jam free without giving Baskania the scroll. He obviously couldn't trust him. Then a vision appeared before Erec's eyes. It was a gleaming scepter, filled with magic, hope, and promise. It twinkled, calling out to him, radiating power. Erec reached for it, but it pulled back just beyond his touch.

Baskania's voice was soft. "This is your scepter, Erec. Yours to control. I promised it to you the first time we met, but you turned it down. I wanted you to be on my side, work with me. It's not too late, you know. I can help you, give you everything you always wanted. Come to me, stand at my side, and the world will be at our feet."

Erec hungered for the scepter, wanted it more than he ever did before. It had made him whole. He could feel the power it commanded rushing through his body. Its roots grew through his mind, deeply embedding themselves like a monstrous weed. If the scepter was his, he could get rid of Baskania for good, he was sure of that. He would fix the world, cure it of evil.

"That's right," Baskania's voice purred. "You could do anything.

I would let you. You'll learn to respect me, and I will respect you. You earned it. Now give me that used up trinket and save your friend's life."

Why was he even thinking about holding onto a worthless scroll when Jam's life was at stake? Erec could not remember. If he cooperated now, Baskania would be on his side. There was nothing wrong with that. He would get a scepter for sure, and now he knew that was what he needed the most.

Erec stepped out of the shadows, holding the Archives of Alithea before him. It flew out of his grasp into Baskania's hand. Magic ropes fastened around Erec.

Baskania turned the scroll over in his hands. "That's right, boy. Good work. Now with a little luck I'll get this gem in working order once again." All of the eyes on his face glowed as he stared at the scroll in concentration. A white haze formed around it, moving and changing the parchment until it looked like new. "That's better. Nothing a little Substance couldn't fix. Now let's see how it works."

Erec looked up with helpless rage. He had been tricked. Baskania was going to use the scroll to find out where the secret to the Final Magic was hidden. His eyes glowed with greed. "Now, I believe to work this I just need to open it up."

Erec looked for Jam, but he was gone. What happened to him? Did he escape somehow? Something tugged at his back, then the ropes around him loosened.

Baskania seemed oblivious, his eyes blazing as he stroked the scroll. He pointed at Erec. A black beam shot from his finger. Right before it reached Erec, it dove off-course and into the Amulet of Virtues. The two colored segments absorbed it. Baskania growled. "Not to worry. That thing isn't strong yet. I'll kill you after I enjoy my precious reward." He stroked the scroll.

Fingers loosened the ropes around Erec, but he held still, waiting for Baskania to focus on the scroll before he broke free. But should he run? Leave Baskania to get what he needed from the Archives of Alithea? Then again, what could he do to stop him?

Maybe . . . It seemed a long shot, but he had to try it.

Baskania held the Archives of Alithea up high. Erec backed slowly away, out of his loosened ropes. The young man who had been in the well winked at him.

"How did you get me out of there?" Erec asked quietly.

The man held up a knife. "Silver," he whispered. "Cuts through the magic. Lots of these in the houses around here. People know how to protect themselves."

The young man looked familiar, but Erec was sure they had never met. "I'm your great-great-grandfather," he whispered. "Nice to meet you, Erec. Now get out of here. It feels awful to be brought back to life after all this time. It's time for me to dive back in that well."

Erec found Jam backing slowly away from Baskania into the darkness. Baskania opened the Archives of Alithea. Erec could see the scroll from a distance. There was only one thing he could think of to do: Ask it a question. It was his only hope. Maybe if there were two conflicting truths the scroll would get messed up somehow. Or maybe it would answer his question and not Baskania's.

In a flash, the scroll was open. Erec concentrated and asked it a question. It was a stupid question, but it was the only thing that popped into his mind.

"How old am I?"

At the same moment, Baskania's voice thundered, "Tell me the secret of the Final Magic, and where it is hidden." The scroll burst into flames in his fingers. Two red beams of light shot from the scroll toward Baskania and Jam, and two white beams flashed toward Erec and Jam. Then blackness filled the air, and the scroll's ashes crumbled into the dirt.

Erec knew. And he ran. Footsteps and a figure sprinted close beside him. It was Jam. They ran past the columns and up the hill to the Port-O-Door, slammed it shut, and fell on the floor of the west wing.

Bethany was sitting vigil by the door with a pillow. She sprang to her feet and threw her arms around them. "You're back! You did it!"

"No." Erec shook his head. "He got the best of me. I gave him what he wanted—the Archives of Alithea—and he used it to learn where the Final Magic is."

Bethany was quiet. Jam said, "Sir, you did your best. He has ways of getting into your head. You could not help it. But I am not sure that Baskania got the information he was looking for."

Erec looked at him. "Did you see the scroll? Do you know the truth?"

Jam nodded. "Yes. I know two truths, from the two beams of light. The one I shared with you, that the secret of the Final Magic is hidden in the mind of the smallest child of the greatest seer of the first king of Alypium. That is what you and I know."

Bethany's jaw dropped. "That's me."

"And?" Erec said.

"And the secret I shared with Baskania. That you are thirteen years old."

CHAPTER TWENTY-FIVE

The Golden Ghost

EVEN THOUGH IT was the middle of the night and Erec had been through more than he could imagine, there was no way he could sleep. He wandered the halls with Jam and Bethany, stopping in the kitchens to get plates of pizza and brownies.

"I'm thirteen," Erec said to no one in particular. "The same age as King Piter's dead triplets."

Bethany shivered. "The same age as Danny and Sammy."

Jam added, "The same age as the Stain triplets."

He didn't want to think about it. He had found out too much recently. His only memory of his dad was not his real dad at all, and the guy's boss in his dreams had been Baskania. His own memory had been taken out and sold to someone else.

"You know," Bethany said, munching a chocolate peppermint cookie, "I looked into my family lineage. Right up the family tree. There was no Bea Cleary. I was bummed, thought I might be related to that great seer from back then."

Jam said, "We're definitely going to need to keep an eye on you, modom, in case Baskania finds out you hold the secret of the Final Magic."

"Do you know it?" Erec asked.

She shrugged. "I don't think so."

Erec hoped walking the wings of the castle would get the images out of his head. Baskania raising his grandmother from the dead. Aoquesth falling to the ground. Balor pointing his remote at Jam. He wondered if he would ever be able to sleep.

"Hey, here are the stairs to the catacombs below the castle," Bethany said. "As long as we're walking, let's go down. They were abandoned for ten years when the castle was on its side, since the basements were covered up. I've been curious to go there."

They wandered through a maze of twisty passages until they were well lost. Jam opened the door to a dusty old laundry room with washing machines that sat motionless, not running around trying to lap up clothing, as Erec had seen others doing before in the castle. He shut the door, disgusted. "They went too long without being fed," Jam said.

They were shooed away from the dungeon entrance by two silver ghosts dressed in glowing armor. Soon they spotted a door with a gold handle. Erec opened it and walked into a vast room. A golden, glowing figure rose and glided toward them. Erec could see features on his face, but also could see right through him.

Jam gasped. "It's a golden ghost. Do you know how rare—"

The ghost smiled. "Yes, we are rare. How can I help you?" A tall box stood behind the ghost. It looked like a thin coffin with solid gold sides and a pane of glass in front.

"What is that?" Erec asked.

The ghost smiled. "It's King Piter's most treasured possession. I am here to guard it."

"What is it?" Bethany asked.

The ghost pointed behind Erec. "Why don't you ask him?"

King Piter stood behind them. He laughed. "Thank you, Homer, for calling me. I should have known you would find your way here before long, especially with Bethany's inquisitive mind. Well, I suppose I can tell you what this is. It's well guarded, but even so, this is the reason I turned the castle on its side as I was falling under Hecate Jekyll's spell. So nobody could get to this.

"It's a Novikov Time Bender. It took many years to have it made. I do not know yet if it works. The time has not been right to test it. But I plan to use it one day, to right things that went wrong in the past. It is not to be used lightly." His eyes settled on Erec. "Let's go upstairs now. I think your mother would like to see you again, Erec."

Erec noticed the scepter in the king's hand and eyed it hungrily. He forced himself to think of other things.

"The dragons send their thanks," King Piter said. "You did more than I was able to do. In fact, when I consulted the Hermit, he told me that you had everything under control." He chuckled.

"I had help. Aoquesth . . ." Erec was at a loss for words.

Bethany put her arm around him. "Want a cloud cream sundae

before you go home? I know where they keep everything in the kitchens."

Jam put a hand up. "Please, modom. It would be my pleasure."

King Piter spoke quietly through tight lips, as if he was holding back a laugh. "If it is okay with you three, I'd like to fix your hair now."

It seemed an odd thing to say. But when Erec looked at Bethany and Jam his eyes widened. Their hair stood out like wooden blocks around their head, hardened into a solid mass. He reached up and felt his head, but his hand hit something that felt like a brick. "What happened to us?"

The king smiled. "I think you picked up an ailment that's common in Otherness. Probably never got vaccinated for helmet hair?" He pointed at the three of them, and their hair flopped down softly around their faces again. Bethany giggled.

"I'm going to stay home for a few weeks," Erec said, licking cloud cream off a spoon. "I could use some boredom after all this. And I'd like to hang out with Danny and Sammy for a while."

Bethany smiled. "I'll tell your tutors."

Erec's hand flew to his face. "Ugh. Could I please get new tutors when I come back?"

King Piter nodded. "I'll do what I can. Are you ready?" He walked with his hands on Erec and Bethany's heads to the Port-O-Door in the west wing. Jam shook Erec's hand, and Bethany gave him a squeeze.

Then Erec turned his back on the world of magic and entered the world where the only thing that's magical is in our hearts.

Ten Years Earlier

T HE GOLDEN GHOST had been clear. June O'Hara had to get these two three-year-old children and the baby to safety as fast as possible. And that meant Upper Earth. Obscurity. Well, after all this, that was fine with her.

Before she performed the spell on Erec, she pulled his face to hers. She would miss his wildly curly blond hair and rugged looks. He had always been big for his age. Well, best not to stand out now. She held her breath and pointed a finger at him.

His sister looked at him and let out a wail.

"Shh. Quiet." June patted her head. "It's still Erec, honey." She looked him over. Good. His hair was dark now, with a hint of red. She had tried to make it straight, and the front worked but the back was stubborn, holding on to its wild curl. Well, she could have done worse. His blue eye shone the same as always—that was a line she could not cross, would not want to ever change about him. Hopefully someday he would get his other eye back with the dragon's eye attached to it.

She hugged his sister, already missing her beautiful blond curls. With the point of a finger, the girl's beautiful features melted and transformed. Not bad, June thought. She could live with that. The baby boy began to cry, and June picked him up and bounced him in her arms, unsure how to comfort him. He probably missed his mother. Well, they would all have to adjust now.

She looked around the castle for what could be the last time. Her Seeing Eyeglasses were around her neck, so she would not be totally out of touch. In her pocket was her favorite alarm clock, and next to her stood a tall wooden coat rack that she had taken from Balthazar Ugry's chambers. He would not need it now. The coat rack skittered back and forth across the floor, dancing an occasional jig in a nervous fashion. It had been chummy with Balthazar's tuxedo jacket, so she had to have it with her. It was the closest thing she had to that coat. She choked back a sob.

May the coat and the coat rack someday reunite.

Meanwhile, the Memory Mogul awaited.

AND NOW TAKE A SNEAK PEEK INTO
EREC REX'S NEXT ADVENTURE:

The Search for Truth

CHAPTER ONE
The Substance Channel

I T MUST HAVE been a dream. That was the only explanation Erec Rex could think of for what had just happened. Yes, a nightmare. That's what it was.

Thirteen-year-old Erec blinked a few times, waiting for his bedroom to appear. It did not. In fact, his skin still looked disturbingly green. And his fingernails—were they shrinking before his eyes? They hadn't really been long claws a moment ago, had they?

After waiting another minute, Erec squeezed his eyes shut,

wishing he was anywhere else. The sad fact had sunk in—he was not in bed after all. He was lying on his back in Fork-Out Grocery. Heaps of sparkling pink notebooks and toppled stacks of diaper boxes were scattered all around him in a big mess on the floor.

At first he thought he was covered in snow. Then he saw the slashed boxes. Torn white fluff from shredded Lil' Dumpling diapers covered everything around him like a Christmas display. But who would have shredded the diapers all over like that? He ran his hand through his dark hair, which was straight in front and wildly curly in the back, shaking diaper fuzz from his head.

Then Erec noticed gray dust sprinkling down from a black, charred hole in the side of a nearby case of spaghetti boxes. It looked like someone had blasted it with a flamethrower. Who could have come in here and done this? Someone really ransacked this place.

Erec gulped as a realization dawned on him. If he truly was here, in the grocery store, and he had not been dreaming, then maybe . . .

Could *he* have done all this?

This was not good.

A little girl stood staring at him, her lip trembling. She tugged on her mother's skirt and pointed at Erec. The mother glanced at him with disgust, as if he was a delinquent who made a mess of store displays for fun.

Erec wished that were true. Because what really happened was far worse than a bout of bad behavior. What had just happened, in fact, should never have occurred here, in New Jersey, in plain sight of normal people.

Erec hid his eyes with a diaper fluff-covered hand. He had to face the facts. He had begun to turn into a dragon.

His adopted siblings had seen it too. All five of them had been swarming around the grocery store, dumping unhealthy sugared products into their adoptive mother June's cart faster than she could take them out. Danny and Sammy, thirteen-year-old twins with sandy brown hair, and Nell, eleven, had watched Erec grab hold of a shelf when his head began to spin. Nine-year-old, redheaded Trevor had popped around the corner just as Erec's vision faded out. And Zoey, just five, with wild blond curls and hazel eyes, was staring at him when he woke up on the ruined store display.

But it was what happened in between his vision fading and waking up among diapers that made Erec's heart race. He'd had a cloudy thought.

Cloudy thoughts were what Erec called the strange commands that took him over at times, forcing him to do whatever they said. His whole life he had to deal with being overcome, when he least expected it, with orders appearing in his head. Cloudy thoughts made him do things like run to the bottom of a staircase and hold his arms out. He would feel like an idiot crouching there, but then a little girl would tumble down the stairs into his arms. He would have saved her without even knowing she was coming. Cloudy thoughts had also saved his own life many times, giving him extra strength and telling him what he needed to know to survive.

But things changed. Erec inherited first one and then the other eye of his dragon friend, Aoquesth, who died saving Erec's life in a battle. The dragon eyes were now attached to the back of his own eyes, and carried special powers that he looked forward to discovering. The first one had made his cloudy thoughts more intense, with visions like premonitions. But now that he had two dragon eyes, his cloudy thoughts were different, more powerful than any he'd had before.

Erec took a breath. What *had* just happened to him in the grocery store? Right when he picked up a carton of his favorite cookies, Chocolate Springballs with cherry centers, everything had turned green. His eyes had swiveled around so that his dragon eyes were facing forward. His mind seemed to race through time so fast he couldn't make out what was happening. He remembered grabbing the metal shelf for support.

Then the vision in his head slowed down and showed him something terrible. His best friend, Bethany Cleary, was in danger.

Thick white ropes and webs hung in the air. Bethany was panting, long dark curls plastered against her sweaty face. She was backed against a wall, trapped. She had been running away from three boys, one with white, fuzzy hair covering his head and neck, another with an odd gray cap that stuck high over his head, and the third with black hair and an evil glint in his steely blue eyes. Now she was cornered.

Erec gasped. It was Dollick, Damon, and Balor Stain. They were the triplets working with evil Prince Baskania to overthrow the Kingdoms of the Keepers, the unseen magical realms connected to ours. Erec had been amazed when he found the strange place, and more shocked to learn he had been born there, in Alypium.

Balor Stain pointed what looked like a normal television remote control at Bethany. Her body stiffened as she was magically lifted from the ground.

A shadow appeared, morphing into a tall man with silver gray hair that grew into a sharp widow's peak. A cold blue eye peered from his face with a dark gap marking where his other eye should have been. Today his forehead was wider than the rest of his face. Across it gleamed seven more eyes, each from a different former owner.

It was Thanatos Argus Baskania. The Shadow Prince, as his followers called him. A smirk snaked across Baskania's face. "Ah, Bethany Cleary. Daughter of the great seer, Ruth Cleary. Too bad she had to go so young, too, eh?" His voice sounded like nails on a chalkboard, making Erec's bones shiver.

Bethany glared at him, unable to speak or move.

"But Ruth was in my way. Just like your friend Erec." Baskania cackled. "Soon he will join your mother and you, along with everyone else who is an obstacle to me."

Erec filled with rage as he watched the horrifying vision unfold. He clawed the air around him, vaguely aware that his skin was turning scaly and green, and claws were sprouting from his fingers.

Bethany looked furious. She struggled with her invisible bonds.

Baskania sucked in his breath. "Well. The Fates have smiled upon me at last. I was fascinated to hear the secret you just told your friend. So you hold the key I have been searching for." His voice lowered to a whisper. "Somehow, you will teach me how to use the Final Magic. Control over everything I desire, life and death. Amazing." He smiled, the corners of his mouth twitching. "If I can't find the answers I need from torturing you alive, I'm sure I will discover them when I remove your brain."

Erec roared in fury at the image in his head. He lost control, thrashing and clawing. Something hot came out of his mouth. It made him feel better for a moment, but not for long.

A rope spun out of Baskania's palm and wrapped tightly around Bethany. "Say good-bye to the world, Bethany Cleary. You'll be safe in my fortress for the remainder of your short life." He snapped his fingers. Baskania, Bethany, and the Stain triplets disappeared.

That's when Erec opened his eyes into the white diaper fluff, the would-be snow of Fork-Out Grocery.

Nell appeared at Erec's side with the help of her walker. "Erec, you . . . you . . ." She pointed at the charred hole. Black strands of spaghetti poked from the boxes around it. "Fire came out of your mouth."

Erec stared at the boxes. He had breathed fire?

But how? Erec shook his head. So this was what his dragon eyes were doing to him? Turning him into a dragon? He shouldn't be here, in Upper Earth. If people saw him shooting fire here, they'd lock him up.

He gulped, thinking about what he had just seen happen to Bethany. Had she already been captured? Did Baskania really find out her secret—that somehow she carried the key that he could use to learn the Final Magic?

Baskania not only wanted to rule the Kingdoms of the Keepers, but he also owned huge megacorporations all over the nonmagical world, and led a political movement trying to take over the United Nations. If Erec had not stopped him, Baskania would have taken over the Kingdoms already and destroyed them. That was reason enough for Baskania to want to kill Erec—but he also craved Erec's dragon eyes for himself.

What Baskania wanted most of all was to learn the Final Magic, magic so powerful that nobody could ever stop him. King Piter, ruler of Alypium, had told Erec that the Final Magic would make Baskania lose control and destroy the world.

Erec froze. His cloudy thought wasn't over yet. A message filtered into his mind that told him the rest of what he needed to know.

Bethany was not captured yet. Baskania had not found out her secret. But he would. Erec's vision would come true, and Bethany would die—if he didn't get to Alypium immediately and stop his friend Oscar Felix from ruining everything.

Panic seized him. How would he ever get there in time? He knew that in just three hours Bethany would tell Oscar the secret, one that nobody should ever know about her. And somehow because of this, only three minutes later, she would be captured by Baskania and would die.

"Mom," Erec snarled between gritted teeth, "we have to go *now*. Buy the food later." He took a breath. Maybe she didn't understand. "I'm telling you, Bethany is in danger. I have to get there fast. I don't think I'm going to make it in time."

June nodded, but kept putting groceries onto the conveyor. She glanced around to see if anyone was listening, then said, "Relax, Erec. I'll get you there as soon as we get home."

"But, Mom . . ." He wanted to yank her out the door. "It takes time to catch a train to New York. And to get to FES Station. Then I still have to take the artery there, and then find Bethany, wherever she is. We have to go now."

June tossed a box of Flying Count cereal onto the counter, her brown hair pulled into a ponytail. The cashier lazily scanned cracker boxes and put them in a bag. She seemed to be moving in slow motion. June said, "I understand, Erec. That's why I'm going to get you there immediately. As soon as we get home."

"How can I get there immediately?" Frustration filled him. She just didn't get it.

June looked around and then whispered, "I have a way to get you to Alypium straight from our house."

"But—" Erec's breath caught. He knew his mother was not supposed to perform magic in Upper Earth. If she did, the wrong people might find her again. Normally he would never want her to do that. But Bethany would die if he didn't get there right away.

She noticed the look on his face. "What's wrong? I thought you'd be happy that you don't have to go through FES Station."

Erec shrugged. "There's no choice. You're right. You'll have to send me there by magic. I just worry about you getting caught."

June smiled. "But I won't be doing magic. I got a new Vulcan product that will take you. They're not trackable."

Erec's mother had bought things before from a store called Vulcan, in the Kingdoms of the Keepers. Strange things, like an alarm clock and toothbrush that acted like they were alive. Well, Erec thought, whatever this new thing was that June had bought, it had better work, and fast.

After paying the cashier, they walked through the parking lot, zipping up their jackets against the chilly January air. A heavyset woman with dark hair, a very white face, and too much makeup bumped into Danny right as they were leaving. She turned her head away quickly before Erec could get a good look at her. Danny looked up and said, "Oh, excuse me," but she was gone.

In the car, Danny and Trevor played keep-away with an apple. Danny made Trevor list statistics of his favorite sport, springball, each time he caught it. That was easy for Trevor, until Zoey intercepted the apple and ate it.

Erec barely noticed what was going on around him. All he could see was a scene from the future where Baskania captured the best friend he ever had.

June pulled a small silver ring out of a box. "Amazing," she said. "Hard to believe this could actually work."

Erec raised an eyebrow. "It better." The little shining band did not inspire confidence.

"Don't worry," June said. "Vulcan products always do what they're supposed to. It'll be interesting to see what happens. This," she held out the ring, "makes a Substance Channel. The ring carves a wormhole into the Substance around us, and it can take you anywhere. You direct it as you go." She turned the ring over and frowned. "Well, you should be able to understand this better than anyone else. You can see the Substance when your dragon eyes are out."

Erec nodded. His dragon eyes let him see the nets and webs that carried channels of magic all over and through the earth.

June rubbed the ring in her hands until it began to glow. Then she pulled, stretching it until it was bright and thin, like a glittering hoop for a circus animal to jump through.

"Ouch!" June jerked her hands away from the ring. It hung in the air, glimmering. She rubbed her hands together. "That felt like an electric shock."

Erec pointed into it. "Am I supposed to climb through there?"

Suddenly, the ring began to spin. Soon it was whirling so fast that there was no way Erec could go near it. He was afraid it would slice into him if he touched it.

The faster the loop swirled in the air, the wavier it looked. Instead of a circle, it became ripply, glowing as it grew until it was Erec's size. Then it stopped suddenly and hung still. It was round again, but now it pulsed with greenish light. Erec carefully put a hand through the ring. An invisible force pulled his fingers, as if to guide him in.

"You're supposed to think of the place you want to go while you're in the Substance Channel," June said. "Focus on it. And let me know you got there okay."

"Sure," Erec said. "After I find Bethany, I'll e-mail you on the MagicNet."

"Okay. I can always check on you with my Seeing Eyeglasses." June had a pair of glasses that let her see whoever she missed the most, anywhere they were. For a while the glasses had been stuck on their alarm clock. June had to send the clock to a Vulcan store to get them removed.

Erec put his arms through the ring, then he slid his head through. Instead of coming out the other side into the room, he was surrounded by darkness. Before he knew it, he was sucked into space.

* * *

It was a strange feeling, floating on nothing in the blackness. He was hanging in stillness. And he didn't seem to be going anywhere. How much longer before he would arrive?

Then Erec realized he had not given the Substance Channel any directions. *Alypium*. He focused his mind on it. He had to get to Alypium, fast.

Suddenly he felt himself whizzing through space. It was as if a tunnel were being carved around him as he went. Relief surged through him. Good. He would get there soon and find Bethany. But where in Alypium was she? And how would he find her?

Then a thought occurred to him. Maybe the Substance Channel would take him straight to Bethany if he concentrated on her instead of a specific place.

He thought about Bethany, saying her name in his head. "Take me to Bethany Cleary." He thought about her tanned face, her dark, wavy hair. Then his head filled with the image he had seen of her in the future. Frozen against a wall. Ropes around her. Scared, helpless. About to die.

Please, he begged the Substance, *get me there fast.*

The memory of his cloudy thought haunted him. The man he hated more than anyone in the world was going to hurt Bethany. The one who had killed his dragon friend, Aoquesth. Erec pictured Baskania, seven eyes across his forehead, standing before Bethany, ready to torture and kill her because he thought she had the secret of the Final Magic.

Erec felt a jerk, as if he suddenly had shifted direction. He was yanked sideways, then thrown into the light on a hard floor. When he looked up, the ring hanging in the air above him vanished.

He dusted himself off, relieved. He was indoors. But this place did not look like the Castle Alypium. It wasn't a shop, either. The room he was in was large. The air was thick and hard to breathe, but then again he always felt this way when he first arrived in the Kingdoms of the Keepers. He had to get used to it.

A group of people stood nearby. They were all looking at him.

But only one of them stepped forward and smiled—the one with seven eyes across his forehead.